Singer-Songwriters

Singer-Songwriters

Volume 1:
David Cousins • Arlo Guthrie
Iain Matthews • Ralph McTell
Al Stewart • Richard Thompson

NICK AWDE

DESERT♥HEARTS

First published
in 2020 by
DESERT♥HEARTS
www.deserthearts.com
www.bennettandbloom.com

info@deserthearts.com

© Nick Awde 2020

Typeset and designed by Desert♥Hearts

Printed and bound in Great Britain by
Marston Book Services, Didcot

British Library Cataloguing in Publication Data
A catalogue record for this book is available from the British Library

ISBN 978-1-898948-99-5

*

For Knox,
who took the
singer-songwriter's
craft to punk

Contents

Special thanks

. . . to Peter Breuls for his many thoughts and opinions on the European perspective on singer-songwriters; Miharu Kanai for his thoughts on music in general; Thea Khitarishvili, Lydia Thomas, Nina Robbins and Laurence Chabert for their support during the early and later stages of assembly/editing; all the wonderful singer-songwriters who have shared their thoughts here and their equally wonderful families who made me so welcome, especially David Cousins and Iain Matthews for their particular support for my vision for this book; Robert Kirby, much missed and whose opinions are the real reason this book exists; and huge huge huge thanks to Knox, Fred James Hill, Dean Friedman, Roger Goode, Lach and Andy Thompson for their illuminating conversations over the years.

A touch of further reading
For an insight into how the launch of the British Invasion in 1964 meant that the UK was no longer the poor relation when it came to popular music, may I recommend Spencer Leigh's 'Strangers on the Shore', an article in Record Collector, subtitled 'The Beatles' generation were not the first British invaders of the US charts — but few noticed the bold pre-1964 vanguard. Why did so few Brit pop acts make it in the States before the Beatles?' It's at recordcollectormag.com/articles/strangers-shore.

Disclaimer by impoverished writer
Under ideal conditions it would have been logical and feasible to research and publish this book in six months or so, but the economic reality is that it took several years to piece together. Far more than planned. The odd section may therefore need updating or contexts may have changed. However, that's the nature of the beast and so I have left everything as I found it.

Introduction

A bit of social and historical background

Prelude . . .

This is a book about some of the musicians-slash-poets — five Brits and one American — who were key to creating the idea of the modern singer-songwriter. You'll find answers here from these contemporary voices to such questions as what makes a singer-songwriter, what defines their craft, what drives them . . .

However, rather than following a song-by-song chronology or analysis of technique, this book instead focuses on the nature of a singer-songwriter and the background they grew out of. Direct from the horse's mouth, it's also a manual of sorts that goes some way to explaining the balance between voice and instrument, the interrelationship between songs and audience, performance and creation, spirituality and society, interpretation and collaboration, the channelling of musical influences and the politics of the day — and how to pay the rent while staying on message, the simple act of being true to your roots. It also sheds light on the eternal question of which comes first: the words or the music.

The particular singer-songwriters who share their thoughts here are part of a creative wave who grew up in the melting-pot decades that followed World War Two and came of age during the cultural explosion of the late Sixties and early Seventies. Often defined as 'folk', they started in a post-Beatles, pre-Hendrix world where they gathered in London to forge a new form of singer-songwritership that took its reason to be from Ewan MacColl and Bert Jansch, its fire from Woody Guthrie, Lead Belly and Bob Dylan, its soul from Hank Marvin and the Beatles.

Admittedly, as you're about to discover, it wasn't exactly like that — there's really no singer-songwriter type set in stone, nor is there a single genre by the name of folk, and indeed none of the musicians in this book sound anything like each other. 'Singer-songwriter' however does sum up the common experience that links a musical generation, an experience that empowered them to address specifically British issues (through a mostly English lens) in their lyrics, yet freed them to absorb the old music and new vocabulary that was rapidly evolving on the other side of the Atlantic. Importantly, this generation emerged at a never-seen-before point in history, when the whole world had no choice but to redefine itself as it came to grips with new ideas and technologies — both exciting and terrifying — as the future flooded into a post-global conflict Pandora's Box that was now opening up to release control to the people of everything from culture to consumerism to civil rights.

The UK's emerging singer-songwriters caught that wave and rode it, documenting and sharing their journey in song as they crisscrossed the country's venues. Their voices continue to ring clear across these chapters which trace the course of how they still respond to the constantly changing landscape of music and society around them, along with coping with the vicissitudes of the music business that gives them a platform. There's a lot of biographical and cultural detail which many readers may already know, but there are many who won't. It is important for a book like this, produced at this point of the twenty-first century, that it should not assume prior knowledge but instead introduce these visionary lives to new generations and audiences.

For example, it's good to learn that notching up a chart hit or two early in your career doesn't necessarily limit you to the eight-year lifespan that popular music seems to build its industry model on, that you don't need to leave the stage after a 'commercial peak'. In fact, when the records sales dip and gigging takes over once more to pay the bills, these singer-songwriters at the drop of a hat can play any size venue or audience — be it their local pub or the Albert Hall — solo or with band, acoustic or electric. It's an adaptability that the rest of us can only envy.

What this introduction itself also takes a look is the wider picture of the changing world that opened the way for David Cousins, Arlo Guthrie (who holds up an American mirror to the UK's evolution), Iain Matthews, Ralph McTell, Al Stewart, Richard Thompson and their contemporaries. It's not an academic analysis of revival vs popular, progressive folk vs traditional, UK vs USA, but more a personal observation of how it all fits into the bigger picture, how music is shaped by and shapes society, how it leaves its mark. However, since the musicians here are commonly viewed as 'slash-folk', this intro, without imposing the genre on them, will examine aspects of the folk music revival and how the word 'folk' represents not just a musical style but a far deeper-rooted idea or indeed attitude common to us all. There's also a bit of added historical backdrop (which you can skip) to help show how the revival of folk and new folk is directly linked to the reinvention/rediscovery of British popular music that enabled it to stand on the global stage as if it had always been there (which it hadn't), and how much of the infrastructure of today's music, such as our world-leading festivals, is owed to folk.

I hope this will also help explain why society needs singer-songwriters, if only because their words and music have played such a powerful role in the human rights movement around the world, creating a universal voice, crossing barriers and promoting unity and equality. Of course that's not to say that every singer-songwriter should be filed under protest or activism — music after all has more than one way to move the people — but what you're guaranteed to find in every singer-songwriter is an *opinion*.

Defining a singer-songwriter

So to the question: what is a singer-songwriter? Well, she or he can be many things. One definition floating around the web is 'individual performers who remain largely acoustic, but who rely mostly on their own individual compositions'. Stating the obvious, this means you (more or less) sing, you write (some or all of) your songs and (ideally) play an (ideally acoustic) instrument (ideally guitar, often on your own). Then add to this an indefinable extra depth to the lyrics and arrangement, a spiritual Factor X (which can be in the interpretive *performance* of the songs) which sets it apart from most of popular music.

The singer-songwriters in this book are significant because of the contribution they have made and continue to make to creating and solidifying our contemporary definition of what they do. At the same time they prove that point that there are no set-in-stone rules — in the UK at least — opting rather to adapt styles and themes without compromising ideals. And more often than not, it takes an individual performer-writer to pull this off since band dynamics tend to deny deviation from the stylistic formula or lyrical order.

If they were still with us, John Martyn and Nick Drake would undoubtedly round out the field in this book, and the reader is urged to check out their lives and work if they aren't aware of them (for a summary of Martyn's life and career along with a brilliant note on the 'progressive' element, see 'www.loudersound.com/features/john-martyn-a-portrait-by-tommy-udo', a 2008 obituary by the brilliant late Tommy Udo for *Louder Than Sound*, subtitled "Folk? Rock? Blues? Jazz? John Martyn was a mixture of all four and certainly one of the most progressive artists of his generation . . ."). Folk arranger supremo Robert Kirby intended to share his impressions of Drake and the times they shared together, but sadly he passed away just as our conversation gathered momentum and this book is very much in his memory. Meanwhile, by way of apology, Roy Harper sent me a photo of himself standing at the bottom of a massive concrete hole contemplating a new project in a field in the heart of Ireland.

Unless otherwise stated, all quotes in this introduction are from the chapters in this book. And the chronology at the back may be useful for reference (or debate).

Bards & Co

A singer-songwriter is a bard. Also an ashug, griot, mawak'i, skald, troubadour, minstrel, and any of the other terms found all over the world. These are more than singers of songs, more indeed than poets. Whatever you call them, what they do is share stories through rhythm or music — indeed most of humanity's early poetry and literature, sacred and profane, was set to rhythm or melody not just to inspire but also to help preserve in the memory of those entrusted with transmitting it when there was no writing.

Bards were 'genealogists, astrologers, praise poets, historians, court minstrels, and artisans'. They would recite history and myths during festivals or rituals, praise the departed and spread the latest news, supporting rather than subverting the system — serving the people and the ruling elites with equal empathy. At times they were hailed as sacred vessels, at others condemned as subversive vehicles.

They're also performers of course, and central to this is their relationship with the audience, a defining feature of the contemporary singer-songwriter that links directly to traditional storytellers found all over the world and throughout history, be it the troubadours of France, griots and mawak'is of West Africa, ashugs of the Middle East or bluesmen of America. With their example before us, we can easily imagine how Homer's Iliad would have been performed, how the Sagas were recited, the Shahname intoned. And without going down an overly mystical path, there's often the added tangible shamanistic element that comes with the ability of the bard-storytellers to tap into the collective psyche and how they're trusted to reflect it back to society through song.

The idea of itinerant is important too. Like the bees, bards have always been key to pollinating traditional societies. In worlds lacking permanent art or writing and thus limited means of recording, the system of orally spreading news, transmitting ideas and keeping things in the human memory for future generations was key to preserving not only the collective culture but also the spirit, dreams and aspirations of a people — their identity and much more. Bards had licence to wander the villages where strangers were otherwise suspect. Taking and giving back from settlement to settlement, they stored, moulded and distributed the consensus of opinions, thoughts, dialects, customs, rituals and histories, hopefully filtering the highest common denominators into song (the oral form most conducive to memorising and transmission), sharing what was learned at the previous village with the next.

The music was important too. Poetry in traditional society was recited, chanted or sung to rhythms or melodies like rap today, and at certain points the accumulation of stories or histories would hit tipping point and take on a life of their own, a process that gave us the global epics, honed by centuries of oral transmission to be finally preserved for posterity when writing appeared on the scene. Take away their hallowed status of 'world classics' and these works become what they truly are: the living representation of a period of people's thoughts, deeds and aspirations, not echoes from a dead and fossilised past but the living voice of people who lived, loved, died and struggled just as we do. The voice of the bards gave a voice to the people.

Their nature changed radically, as everything was to change, with the advent of the Industrial Age, accelerated beyond the point of no return by the momentous upheavals and progress of the twentieth century. 'Traditional' values shifted, as did social relationships, and culture needed to change with them. The rationale for storytelling shifted, the nature of performance evolved. The new consumerism unleashed across the globe after World War Two fused the acceleration of technology indelibly with society, and the nature of tradition found itself flipped on its head: teenagers, little red houses, space race, the Bomb, computers, amplification, disposable packaging . . . the currency of urbanisation and globalisation where everything is up for grabs — if it moves, bottle it, package it, market it, and, if you can't, discard it.

How then could music and song respond to the new rules without getting lost?

Breaking the mould

The unparalleled access to music in the twentieth century wrought by the technology of recordings and the growing live concert circuit converged in an outcome that was conflictive. The commercialisation that allowed popular music to spread also had the effect of trying to kill its soul (just as it killed off the live circuit in the UK from the Eighties onwards) as creativity became more about fashion, sex, bling, anything that could add profit rather than value. And so by the end of the Seventies we saw profit take over as the main driver as the corporate structure of the music biz matured and dictated what we should and shouldn't listen to. It's a battle we're still confronting today, amplified by the deceptively limitless vistas of the digital age.

The generation represented in this book set the standard for what I suppose you'd call 'integrity' in song in modern popular music. As we'll see, these British nascent singer-songwriters showed that neither the protest of their American peers and inspirers nor the shock of the new need be a central factor, but rather the confidence to lay bare the nation's soul: folk music in the sense of the people's music. Meanwhile a very British element of provocation could not be denied since the popular music of the Fifties/Sixties was bubbling in the same pot as Peter Cook's satirical Establishment Club, the Lady Chatterley censorship trial, the Notting Hill race riots, the decriminalisation of homosexuality, the abolition of the death penalty — and the domino-like collapse of the British Empire.

As for motivation, it's tempting on the evidence of this book to come up with things like a pattern in family upbringing — fathers lost in the war, absent fathers, stepfathers, Celtic forebears — but the common thread is really the simple fact of growing up in the UK's postwar years, taking all hardships and opportunities as given. It's a period increasingly documented music-wise by studies such as Pete Frame's *The Restless Generation: How Rock Music Changed the Face of 1950s Britain* and my own *Mellotron: The Machine and the Musicians that Revolutionised Rock* (which, combined with this volume, begins an ongoing series on the social history of the UK through music) and now a growing list of biographies from the musicians themselves. These accounts help fix this particular generation as complementing rather than diverging from the pop-rock of the Beatles and Stones and the sophisticated rockers of the Seventies. This generation wrote songs driven by the social circumstances of their times, in most cases responding emotionally rather than politically to audiences old and new — as do their successors today. And no matter how music-biz resistant you happen to be, pop has always been a reference point since it was pop that drove the money (plus it has a bit more of a beat, which can help at times).

The new postwar singer-songwriters had to also respond to the evolving gig circuit and major label economy. London has always been the nation's main creative hub and it naturally offered a practical as well as cultural point of reference that brought the singer-songwriters in this book together to cohere as a generation that includes Nick Drake, John Martyn, Cat Stevens, Roy Harper and Ian Anderson (the latter pair [plus my school's geography teacher] intriguingly from the same Blackpool school, Anderson recalling that the only reason he left was because Harper did).

The city's cultural resonance with New York, a parallel hub, kicked in to mutual advantage. Despite the challenges of long-distance communication and cost of inter-continental travel in those pre-internet/ budget airline days, the Brits had unparalleled access to their USA counterparts in folk, blues, pop and rock in ways that their predecessors had never had. The American pioneers gathered from across their own continent to the Big Apple came over to London en masse and travelled the country: Alan Lomax, Bob Dylan, Paul Simon, Peggy Seeger, Pete Seeger, the American Folk-Blues Festivals . . .

Right time, right place in fact — and, luckily for us, right people. And although what this generation accomplished was not always commercially reciprocated in the USA, their impact has resonated there on many other levels. Indeed it's revealing that of this book's five British subjects three of them — Thompson, Stewart and Matthews — are or have been long-term residents of America.

More on America

The influences unleashed by the Second English Folk Revival, which took place between 1945 and 1969, spearheaded by Ewan MacColl & Co, pervades these singer-songwriters, as does the two-way influence of Lomax and Dylan as we'll see. But for the generation growing up in the Fifties and coming of age in the Sixties, there was simply far too much going on to feel any pressure to commit to any one school of music or thought. Pertinently this was unlikely to arise in the USA (save New York) because of the sheer vastness of the country which precluded truly national connecting hubs like London or Paris. And all over the UK you could access things like Delta and Chicago blues without prejudice, within a national psyche in a way very few Americans were physically or culturally able to tap into. Plus in Britain you'd have to try hard indeed to escape skiffle, *Peter and the Wolf*, 'Jerusalem', the Shadows, the Beatles, Flanders & Swann, Jake Thackray (who channelled Frenchman Georges Brassens and Belgian Jacques Brel) . . . the list goes on. Crucially, UK radio of the time was truly national and all-encompassing in its coverage of genres. Conversely in America the radio stations aligned themselves to the cultural ghettos of country, rock, pop, black music — a significant hurdle to any meaningful progression in the UK sense.

'Folk' is a handy label for certain fusions of music that carries value but it's a term that comes with its own baggage in the UK, particularly England. The unfairly maligned 'finger in ear' stuff of the First British Folk Revival, which ran from 1890-1920, is still taken by many in the UK to be what folk is, yet it represents just one strand of an explosion of styles, genres and cross-overs, united by the wider remit of reflecting society,

Folk revivals in the UK & USA

"It seems rather singular that England should not possess any printed collection of its national songs with the airs as they are sung at the present day; while almost every other European nation possesses several comprehensive works of this kind." So wrote in 1879 the musicologist Carl Engel, a German who had settled and worked in Britain.

The national movement that started around the same time was headed most visibly by musicologist Cecil Sharp, who promoted the revival of English folk music as a response to the view that English art music since the death of Henry Purcell in 1659 had relied heavily on European composers and styles and therefore was indistinguishable from foreign national forms. The folk revivals in the UK were closely linked to the English (=British) Musical Renaissance movement from the late nineteenth century to the Sixties of the twentieth century. The search for a distinctive English voice led composers like Ralph Vaughan Williams (from around 1906) to directly incorporate folk music in their works.

However, despite the efforts of the First British Folk Revival, as it came to be known, folk music and dance continued to decline. The new forms of media such as the phonograph and films with sound failed to spread folk. Instead, from the 1920s onwards, they had the effect of popularising American music throughout British culture (ironic since many of the American songwriters and composers were European in origin). The result was a further decline in traditional music. Exposure to the American Folk Music Revival directly sparked the successful and lasting Second British Folk Revival.

First British Folk Revival, 1890-1920

Key musicologists, musicians & composers: Francis Child, Cecil Sharp, Ralph Vaughn-Williams, Percy Grainger; *Scotland & Wales:* James Duncan and Gavin Greig; *Wales:* Nicholas Bennett
Key themes: Traditional, academic, re-creation, documenting & anthologising of folk songs, transcribing rather than recording, search for a non-foreign musical identity, emphasis on a classical music

response, dance & dance music, Board of Education in 1906 permits teaching of folk songs in schools, reappraisal of hymns, romanticisation of rural society, ignoring of urban songs and music hall.

Second British Folk Revival, 1945-69

Key musicologists & musicians: *England:* Ewan MacColl, A L Lloyd, Alan Lomax; *Scotland:* Hamish Henderson, Calum McLean; *Wales:* Dafydd Iwan. *National:* Martin Carthy, Shirley Collins, Hamish Imlach, John Renbourn, Peggy Seeger, the Copper Family, the Watersons, the Corries.
Key themes: Non-traditional, generating new contemporary folk music, left-wing outlook, awareness of Irish folk, urban songs, work music of the 19th century, sea shanties, industrial labour songs, bawdy songs, recording the Child Ballads, skiffle, Topic Records, Campaign for Nuclear Disarmament, BBC Radio programmes (*As I Roved Out* by Peter Kennedy and Seamus Ennis, 1952-58), record labels, folk circuit of coffeehouses, clubs and festivals.

American Folk Music Revival, 1940s-60s

Base: New York
Key musicologists & musicians: John Lomax, Alan Lomax, Lead Belly, the Weavers, Pete Seeger, Burl Ives, Woody Guthrie, Odetta, Harry Belafonte, Big Bill Broonzy, the Almanac Singers, Kingston Trio, Jan Baez, Bob Dylan, Peter Paul & Mary, Phil Ochs, Tom Paxton, Buffy Sainte-Marie, Judy Collins, Tom Rush, Ramblin' Jack Elliott.
Key themes: Square dancing, political, rural, protest songs, John Lomax recording for the Library of Congress from 1933 — later joined by his son Alan, Harry Smith's *Folkways Anthology of American Folk Music*, Newport Folk Festival, spirituals, blues (not a folk genre in UK), Caribbean (calypso), Hebrew, Spanish, sparked folk music boom in Ireland in the mid 60s, Vietnam War, 'We Shall Overcome', McCarthyism, bohemians, coffee houses, college campuses, ended by the British Invasion.
—Browse the Smithsonian Institute collection at https://music.si.edu/listen
(Also see the chronology at the back of this volume.)

enriching and even changing our lives as folk's mover and shaker MacColl always envisioned it, i.e. politically aware, earthy and *real*. Crucially too, folk in the UK today is ever-adapting, progressing, fusing and unfusing. Go to a gig by any of the musicians in this book and, bar the odd homage, you'll search in vain for museum galleries of hits, genres, periods or otherwise. Folk in the UK therefore is an *attitude*.

Interestingly, it's safe to say that the majority of today's Brits (more correctly English) would be hard pushed to come up with more than a handful of classic English folk pieces, bar 'Greensleeves' and the *Blue Peter* hornpipe theme, and yet they might unwittingly list a string of songs from American country, Appalachian folk or Delta blues. And within our wider folk canon of music hall, musical theatre and pop hits pre-Fifties, we're strangely lacking enduring English counterparts to classic American social commentaries like 'Brother, Can You Spare a Dime?' or 'The Gold Diggers' Song (We're in the Money)'. And certainly no 'Strange Fruit'.

That American presence in British music had dominated since the Twenties, and even when the Brits had taken their place on the world throne of popular music in the Sixties, the following micro-generation that emerged in the late Sixties-early Seventies utterly embraced and integrated America into British pop/rock. Elton John & Bernie Taupin's *Tumbleweed Connection* and Rod Stewart's *Gasoline Alley* encapsulate it all (both of which LPs, released in 1970, unashamedly and remarkably for the time refused to yield a hit single). Their rhythms and rhymes are pure blues and folk Americana . . . and yet could not be less American. It's worth noting here that elsewhere the European and Latin American developments of guitar-led folk were notable for transposing the romantic tropes of the troubadour to actively reflect politics — e.g. nova trova in Cuba and nueva canción in Chile/Argentina — and were equally notable for being blues-free (although rock and pop do get a look in).

Still, no longer king of the world, American music post-Beatles had to get in the queue along with everything else. Everyone everywhere was swimming in an ocean of influences, new sounds, new chords, new books, new thinking. New technology particularly was ramping up the ante in the Sixties, for example, as Arlo recalls, going "from no-mic venues to mics in fifteen years", along with amplification, two-track to 24-track, radio stations, charts and beyond.

A question of style
What the singer-songwriters of the Sixties did was break out of the folk mould — although that's not exactly correct. What in reality they did was to take the troubadour mantle to the next level, a paradigm shift from

traditional to contemporary mover. This was more than an upgrade: a realigning of the job, redefining the performer-audience relationship, adopting new languages without subverting the format, adapting the material to new audiences, the new ways of travelling to those audiences.

And with audiences ever expanding in reaction to the new genres, sub-genres, revivals and crossovers emerging all over the Sixties-Seventies, it was no surprise therefore that things converged in a period (mid-Seventies) where these new singer-songwriters rode their wave to the level of commercial success (i.e. chart hits), most notably McTell's 'Streets of London' (a re-release of his 1969 song) and Stewart's 'Year of the Cat' (originally a song about British comedian Tony Hancock who committed suicide).

Statistics for the music business are such that, given the length, breadth and depth of their output, singer-songwriters like these are bound to come up with a pop hit song or two, maybe even an album. Certainly star producers like Alan Parsons (Al Stewart, engineer on Pink Floyd's *Dark Side of the Moon*), Gus Dudgeon (Ralph McTell, Elton John) and Tony Visconti (David Cousins/Strawbs, David Bowie) could sprinkle their magic on an already great song to make it chartworthy in an intelligent way.

But that was just part of the journey. At least on the evidence they've given here, it was also no surprise that they rejected offers to repeat those successes. This wasn't a rejection of the ability to make a living, but a side effect of the basic need to keeping moving forward rather than repeating yourself. Sticking to the same formula imposed by the record companies wasn't an option.

So it was soul vs sales. Stewart's evident frustration at the pressure to turn out *Time Passages* as *'Year of the Cat 2'* is revealing: "We put the obligatory sax track on the record to get airplay but increasingly these were the songs that I didn't care about at all. It meant that we went through a period where we were trying to cater somewhat to American radio stations because that's what made it work in the first place. And instead of having them chase us, we were chasing whatever we thought they were playing. That didn't work at all and I ended up making a series of albums that I didn't really like, and which eventually that led me to throwing the rulebook out the window and going back to playing the songs I do like."

Talking to David Mead for musicradar.com, McTell sums up the predicament: "After 'Streets of London' was a hit in 1975 to 1976, there was too much pressure to repeat the success that came accidentally, and was not the course I would have chosen. I never went into music as a career. The career happened because of music."

Part of the puzzle for their record companies was that the music they'd signed up had always been a form of fusion — it couldn't help be anything else. It was never going to stand still. A 'hit' from a record label's point of view was doomed always to be 'accidental' as McTell puts it. Of course folk had been a solid cover-all in the early to mid Sixties but as experimentation took over and other world music forms were introduced, music in the UK stopped falling into the safe categories of pop | jazz | blues | folk | music hall | classical. It didn't help — indeed it's never helped — that the creative fusion that comes naturally to British culture in general moved too rapidly to establish a reliable pigeonhole system that could keep up. In fact the reintroduction of English folk itself was only made possible because it was an open-ended process of rediscovery. But that's a whole different book.

The British group Pentangle, formed by Bert Jansch and John Renbourn, personified the dilemma. Writing in 1969, *The Times* critic Henry Raynor debated their output of the time: "It is not a pop group, not a folk group and not a jazz group, but what it attempts is music which is a synthesis of all these and other styles as well as interesting experiments in each of them individually."

Further insight comes from Richard Thompson, talking to Robin Denselow in *The Guardian* about the fusion opened up by Fairport Convention: "We thought that if we're in the charts and it's taken seriously, it could change peoples' attitudes to British music and you might have people stopping using American accents when singing. It was totally revolutionary at the time. Rock music with an element of British traditional music in it was pretty much our innovation, and I'm very proud of that. And when people in other countries saw what we did, it was possible for them to contemporise their own cultures."

Folk, blues, R&B, rock'n'roll psychedelic, all synthesised, morphed and splintered into innumerable genres, yet were unified by creative curiosity and a socially-aware drive to grab your audience and communicate with them. In *Mellotron*, discussing how progressive rock is wrongly considered through the ossification of a mere half decade's worth of (British) albums, I point out that what prog rock really represents is an open-ended journey forward, the bluesman's way. The clue's in the name — 'progressive'. And so we'll touch on the nature of progressive folk further down.

A brief history of culture in the UK

But first a couple of questions: Were British audiences looking for singer-songwriters after the Beatles, Kinks, the Who and Rolling Stones had already changed the face of music forever? Or had Britain always had singer-songwriters? Here a look at the strange history of culture in our isles will prove illuminating.

Every country has a surprisingly different definition of what the word 'culture' means to them, but the UK especially stands out because of its complex, often disparaging view of culture, tightly connected to class conflict and what we ourselves would acknowledge as a healthy suspicion of the elitism that accompanies 'culture', historically a foreign import. And in fact our country does have a definable conflict with culture, its divisions apparent even today, that stretches back in an unbroken chain to the sixteenth century: the Kingdom of England and King Henry VIII's split with the Roman Catholic Church and Europe.

This seismic political/economic schism saw Henry break away from the mighty Catholic Church in Rome which provided the centralised mechanism that stabilised the fractious kingdoms and princedoms of Western Europe (Christendom), unified by the crossnational links provided by the common culture of the religion, language (Latin) and traditions that we all inherited via the old Western Roman Empire. Henry sought more control over his economy, but what was disguised as a religious row set into motion a self-imposed sequence of shifts in English (later British) society that, like the policy of Brexit, established isolation as the new national event horizon.

By establishing his own state Church of England with himself at its head, replacing the Pope and the Church of Rome (and robbing the clergy dry), Henry was effectively splitting with Europe on far more levels than resolving the dogmatic question of who was God's earthly representative. The resulting loss to England of the centrifugal force of Western Europe — unified as it was and still is not only by the Pope in Rome but also by Roman Law, the Holy Roman Empire and the Peace of Westphalia (all of which live on in today's European Union) — meant that stimuli such as the new blood of immigration, common markets and beliefs were excluded physically and mentally by the English Channel and North Sea. And so England was left to confront itself. After Henry's ill-gotten gains from plundering the church possessions of the kingdom ran out, his strategy and those of his successors turned from defending independence to preserving isolation. Belligerent nation but a backwater sums it up.

As is the wont of paranoid absolute rulers when the going gets tough, national programmes were established to root out and eliminate first the Enemy Within (English Roman Catholics) and then the Other (foreign [= Papist] influences). And when the perceived threat was considered to be held at bay by the times of Charles I, where much of the mutual suspicion both in and out the country had been laid to rest (ominously, by no means all), three curious things were well under way by the mid seventeenth century that had their beginnings in Henry's unilateral declaration of Schism from a century before.

Firstly, by encouraging anti-Catholicism in the nation's sentiments and then actually enshrining it in legislation, Henry, his daughter Queen Elizabeth I and their heirs legitimised a hostility that permitted an enabled English society to target an Otherness, whose definition they shifted according to contingency, thus laying the grounds for the later regional reactions to the centrifugal forces of London and the Church of England that constituted the breakaway regional non-conformists/dissenters such as the Methodists, Quakers and Levellers.

Secondly, this hostility put a throttlehold on the import of anything from French wine to high art to ideas. Although the years of Elizabeth's long reign were seen as a Golden Age of culture and exploration, along with the emergence of England as a world naval (and eventual trading) power, society was characterised by extremes of rich and poor, not helped by a rising population which triggered rising prices which led to further rising poverty. In addition, reduced demand in the early years for woollen cloth, England's main export at the time, can't have helped. With the Renaissance blooming all over Europe, 'Golden' is a somewhat relative description in its application to England.

However there was gradual benefit — if irony — in the fact that, bar the few decades during Tudor times when English Catholics were hunted down and executed as domestic terrorists along with a lot of sabre-rattling in the direction of France and Spain, the presence of Europeans on British soil built steadily as Protestant refugees from the Continent arrived in our safe haven of anti-Papism. And of course, smuggling was also a major import of things foreign.

Thirdly, the destruction of England's culture didn't stop with Henry's Dissolution of the Monasteries between 1536 and 1541. Iconoclastic movements were permitted to smash the heads off statues across the nation, a highly visible warning to the cultural sector to toe the party line. Of course, this being England, no one actually had a clue what that line was. What there was, was a controlled constriction on the development of culture along with the economy and society, spreading devastatingly to the Celtic areas of Wales and Cornwall, thence to Scotland and Ireland. The Renaissance would hardly have seen its genesis in England.

That underlying principle of isolation therefore persisted with all its possibilities, tested and enshrined in legislation. Which brings us to the ruthless policies aimed at eradicating folk culture within England and the rest of the British Isles and its replacement by officially approved forms, crystallising during Elizabeth I's time and which continued right up to the late twentieth century. Folk music, for example, is a particularly useful indicator not for what it is today but for what it represents, as a cradle of everything that is 'folk' about our islands and indicator of what we have lost, the collective soul cynically taken from us by our government and state church. This was a process also gaining motion in Europe where, as with the national Church of England, the major instrument of conformity-through-destruction was the Roman Catholic Church. But this was less effective since Europe could not be sealed off in the way the British Isles were by geography and ideology in near perfect laboratory conditions. It would be hard in Europe, for example, to replicate the events in the seventeenth century that led to the banning by Oliver Cromwell's republic of virtually everything that entailed expressing yourself (including Christmas, music, theatre and dancing) — all of which we would place in the category we now call folk.

Culturally this brought about a paucity in the isles centred around the English heartland from Tudor times to the nineteenth century, accompanied by the systematic century-on-century obliteration of the neighbouring Celtic cultures. The singular exception, of course, was our written tradition which thrived uninterrupted, despite censorship and disapproval from government and church, from Shakespeare to Dickens, as did oral literature in the Celtic lands, since oral traditions are not so easily destroyed. However, compared to the great cultural leaps made in Europe, our visual and performing arts suffered grievously, especially as foreign artisans were excluded. Strangled of meaningful interchange with others, music of course suffered the same fate.

It wasn't so long ago that you could witness this leached legacy. I vividly recall record shops in Eighties Europe where the pop racks were brimming with British acts to the detriment of local talent, but under 'England' in the classical music bins with grim invariability there'd be a tiny section with a couple of collections of Byrd and Purcell . . . and then nothing until Elgar. (Apposite then to note that a book of 31 essays by German novelist and playwright Oscar Schmitz was published in Germany in 1914 under the title of *Das Land ohne Musik: englische Gesellschaftsprobleme*, which translates bleakly as *The Country without Music: Problems of English Society*.)

High culture has always depended on patrons in high places, who in the UK finally started to import artists from Holland and Flanders (Holbein, Van Dyck), composers from Germany (Handel, Mendelssohn) as a means of kickstarting our own homegrown creatives. (Indeed the idea of German imports was later extended to sorting the troublesome genetic-politics of our royal family.) Architecture and crafts got a massive injection from the Grand Tours of Europe undertaken by the growing wealthy classes, refugees from Europe and of course there was the stimulus of the British Empire as it evolved.

As for homegrown music and theatre, however, they had intertwined fortunes and had to wait until the nineteenth century to be 'rediscovered' by the nation. And even then they were forced to follow a path driven by commercial demands to cater to the growing leisure and mass entertainment markets, most obviously seen in the boom in the tea gardens, resorts and music halls. Needless to say, neither music nor theatre with a local provenance received any wholehearted seal of approval from the ever suspicious authorities and elites — being viewed as less controllable, as is the prerogative of all live phenomena.

It is the well-documented history of British theatre that provides a chilling picture of the pressures that also befell our music. Theatre buildings were closed and performances banned across the country in 1649-1660 by Oliver Cromwell's Puritan-controlled Commonwealth, aka the English Republic, because they were deemed places of uncontrolled human gatherings, fuelled by the energy of live performance. Performers and audiences were a dangerous mix that were to be kept apart and discouraged in large measure.

The Restoration in 1660 saw the dictator-led republic discarded and the monarchy restored to the throne in the shape of Charles II. But Parliament chose not to restore theatres to their original status, instead it established the 'Patent Theatres' or 'Theatre Royals', i.e. a handful of officially licensed establishments bizarrely somehow intended to cater for the entire country. The idea was that any performance of 'serious' theatre without a royal patent (permission) would be deemed illegal. The performance of music was also affected because though while other theatres were permitted everywhere, they were restricted to genres like 'comedy, pantomime or melodrama', i.e. singing and dancing had to be combined on the same stage in order to prevent the whole becoming dramatic or subversively 'serious'. Again, this was as much about the audience as the performers. Gradually the government lost its monopoly as our thought police, but we should remember that it did keep its right to censor theatre right up to 1968.

Music being a more nebulous thing, more difficult to identify and physically contain, it had naturally found all manner of ways to thrive without needing to go underground. Its links with dance aside, much of the subversive thrust of music developed in blatant plain sight of the authorities with things like political street songs, which were not only sung on every corner but in fact contributed to the economy through sheet music sales as part of the burgeoning printed ballad trade from the 1590s onwards. The deceptively plain-speaking hymns of the Non-Conformists added a further sociopolitical dimension to the increasingly vocal voice of the people.

This highlighted the deeper, more problematic layers of the nation's isolationism, and our creators of music often found themselves having to appropriate their own culture in order to keep pace with the Renaissance and what followed in Europe. There not being much popular middle ground or aspirational higher ground save for humdrum church chorals and inaccessible foreign court imports, our indigenous folk music made a direct leap to the 'commercial' level at the same time as our society took its first steps towards modern consumerism, unfettered by the quality control of the new Europe that was emerging from its Renaissance-chrysalis. Tabloid-style, politics and high society (celebs), gossip and scandals fuelled the British public's uptake of the scurrilous street songs of Elizabethan times and beyond, the snippets that became our unique canon of highly politicised nursery rhymes, the broadsides (broadsheet ballads) of the sixteenth century, the 6,500 hymns set to the eighteenth-century words of Charles Wesley. We're still singing most of it today.

By the eighteenth century, as Great Britain became a world power and prosperous, words were assured a safe place in the people's domain as English literature developed around the novel, poetry, journalism and lashings of satire. Nowhere were music and words so wickedly fused as in John Gay's *The Beggar's Opera* of 1728 — a simply stunning 'anti-opera' that lampooned society through the fashionable European high art of the day over 45 scenes and 69 short songs set to broadsheet ballads, opera arias, church hymns and folk tunes.

All this was taking place during the Enlightenment in Europe, a period when people converted the Renaissance's opening up of society and the arts into ideals of social liberty that undermined the authority of the monarchy and the church and paved the way for the political revolutions of the eighteenth and nineteenth centuries. The Brits were finally taking their place along with the Europeans and were actually in the lead, opting though for civil society and the Industrial Revolution rather than the overthrowing of hierarchies and monarchies on the Continent (tellingly, one way of timing the Elightenment begins brightly with the publication of Isaac Newton's *Philosophiae Naturalis Principia Mathematica* [Latin for *Mathematical Principles of Natural Philosophy*] in 1687 and ends ominously with the French Revolution in 1789-99). We were finally connecting with the rest of the world, through our thinking and then our trade. However 'serious' music remained the preserve of the Europeans, especially the Germans, whose upper classes were busy funding and promoting composers like Bach, Haydn, Handel and Mozart. We weren't realistically going to get a look in . . .

And then arrived the imperial, industrialised nineteenth century (and

Beethoven and the popular/commercial French/Italian composers), when all culture came under the microscope, indeed every aspect of our lives, was studied, classified and assessed for future use/worth/profit. The same conditions that were creating the platform for our new self-expression were also responsible for the setting for the coup de grace to eradicate our traditional music. Mass-produced organs, for example, were replacing traditional means of creating music in the churches, just one step in the coordinated obliteration of popular culture in the name of (Christian/ imperial/colonialist/socialist) morality (for which read: industrialisation) designed to undermine and replace the folk culture that protected the country's still beating pagan heart. The folk singer-songwriter bards who had always been a part of this started to die out too.

The die had been already cast as early as 1559 when Elizabeth's contribution to the Reformation was to impose the Act of Uniformity which required everybody by law to attend Church of England services and use the Book of Common Prayer (printed in English not Latin, the common language of fusion with the cultures of Europe) — empowering yet isolating through imposed unity . . . And from Elizabethan times onwards there followed the relentless campaigns against Midsummer maypoles, New Year bacchanals, traditional healers (witches), local customs and traditions everywhere. Our dialects and indigenous languages (let us remember there are still four surviving in the British Isles) were intentionally weakened and allowed to wither away — and all their lore with them. And all the while our traditional connection with the land was eroded by the state's enabling of the aristocratic landowners, whose disproportionate landholdings remain a corrosive blight on these isles.

No surprise then that by the final decades of the nineteenth century most of our traditions were gone forever. Inspired as they undoubtedly were, the well-meaning cultural revivals since the eighteenth century have tended to be romantic in nature, such as the Gothic Revival, along with restorative reactions like the Arts and Crafts Movement. The reality was homogenisation by means of *Hymns Ancient and Modern*, high street fashion, railways, clocks, weights & measures, the workhouse.

By the 1880s the British nation therefore found itself aspiring to middle-classdom and so felt confident to look back and appreciate what it was losing in identity in terms of traditional culture, albeit coloured with the pervading romanticism and a desire for sanitised reinvention: Morris dancing, mummer plays, Dickens' Christmas, Santa Claus (one of the many American Euro-rehashed imports to come), Pugin's Houses of Parliament. Our home-grown music languished at second tier or lower in relation to the 'high culture' urban output of Europe, rated an impossible benchmark for our own work, just as American music would be in the next century. It is no surprise that the English folk revivalists of the late nineteenth-early twentieth centuries had to sail to the Americas to find what we had lost. And it is no small irony that it was emigration that was the instrument of preservation, since so much of our folk had been forced out in the hearts of those who made the Atlantic crossing in search of better lives.

Nevertheless, the groundwork was being laid for British music to take its rightful place in the world — although no one could yet work out how or in what form. As we approached the twentieth century and then tipped over into it, the classical side of things rode on the gentle revolution of Elgar, Vaughan Williams, Holst and Britten (the last being a pivotal symbol of Britishness even if his output was never up to the mark), who between them more than made up for the lost centuries. In the process of creating a distinct identity for British classical music they were also creating that of folk. Indeed, for these composers and their peers the rediscovery of English folk was a shaping force, emboldened by outspoken movements like the English Musical Renaissance, which sought to free British composers from foreign musical influences so they could write in a distinctively national idiom.

British popular music was also (somewhat) unleashed, giving us the chain that took us from Gilbert & Sullivan (*The Pirates of Penzance*, *HMS Pinafore*, *The Mikado*) to Ivor Novello ('Keep the Home Fires Burning', 'Rose of England', 'Some Day My Heart Will Awake') and Noel Coward 'Mad about the Boy', 'Mad Dogs and Englishmen', 'I'll See You Again'). Meanwhile, linked to the work of the classical composers above, roots folk music was ticking over in between the First and Second Revivals. Dance also saw a related folk revival.

At the same time, the *idea* of music worldwide underwent a seismic shift with the introduction of recorded music after Thomas Edison's phonograph, invented in 1877, and Guglielmo Marconi's radio transmitter/receiver in 1895, which opened up choice for people — or, rather, allowed music to respond to people's tastes. Mainstream music continued to be dominated by the latest craze from Europe or the USA. In fact by the Twenties it was New York rather than Paris, and increasingly black American: Charleston, tango, rag, jitterbug, boogie woogie, jive, rumba, samba.

By the end of World War Two, when society was readjusting and building new institutions for the new future based on the welfare state and preserving world peace, the majority of the United Kingdom was still looking overseas for a lot of the music that they took into their hearts: Mozart, Cole Porter, Schumann, Glenn Miller, Louis Armstrong, Ella, Rodgers & Hammerstein, Caruso and Callas . . . To be sure these and their

British counterparts had soul and appeal, an enduring universality, but the idea of music with a message that shared such qualities yet wasn't couched in doggerel or satire was missing from the landscape, even if perceived as being not actually needed. But with taboos falling like dominoes as freedom of expression grew on all sides, people were becoming ready for anyone with a message. And it was only a matter of time before those who knew how to write and sing in the right language would appear to step into the role that was taking form within society.

After the painstaking reclaiming of English folk and the reinstatement of Celtic folk through the various folk revivals, spurred on by the parallel efforts in the USA and the galvanisation of World War Two, folk music came to be seen as an art form genuinely representing the people rather than as an academic or niche exercise. This was part of a wider progression reflected in the wartime propaganda documentaries (Crown Film Unit) which led to postwar films such as 1949's *Whisky Galore!*, the official war artists working on the home front as well as in the conflict zones, the theatre of Joan Littlewood's Theatre Workshop (MacColl's *Uranium 235*) — it was all convincing (and entertaining) soapboxing that gave British culture and *ideas* to the people. And, once owned, the people were hardly going to give that back.

Luckily the decades and generations had rolled our national snowball of creativity over and over enough times that it had now grown mighty enough to hold its own. Our music's response was an open-ended one: to claim and create entirely new genres in response to British society's own evolution. As we've seen, new folk was one such response/genre, from which emerged an even more sophisticated service to society in the shape of the modern (folk-rock/folk-pop) singer-songwriter who filled the gap left by the century-long vanishing of our traditional bards and troubadours.

Step forward then London of the Fifties/Sixties (both of which decades were equally swinging). Gone was the national idealism, gone was the hard-edged soapboxing, now the nation's music was spinning in a magical world complete with tribes, languages and economy. In just a handful of Soho streets, folkies rubbed shoulders with popsters, rock'n'rollers, producers, pluggers and labels. Up the road was Denmark Street, the UK's Tin Pan Alley, with its publishers, agents and studios, while round the corner was Archer Street, where jobbing musicians gathered for pick-up gigs. Jimmy Page (Led Zeppelin) played guitar for Al Stewart, Rick Wakeman (Yes) played keyboards for Strawbs, Gus Dudgeon (Elton John) and Tony Visconti (David Bowie) stepped into the producer's seat for our singer-songwriters. Down the road were some of the capital's legendary music instrument shops like Macaris.

The folk clubs and coffeehouses, numbering more than 300 at their peak, proved pivotal in crosspollinating everything in a national network with London at its centre. In the USA the coffee cafes were the breeding grounds for the Counterculture movement as well as music, but in Britain where the brushstrokes are finer, they provided not only a platform for alternative creativity but also a filter for that American parallel experience.

It's worth pointing out that in the UK coffeehouses have served as forums for coming together and spreading ideas ever since the first coffee stall opened in London in 1652. From Samuel Johnson and the tulip bubble to the Pret a Mangers and co-working spaces of today, they were also a gig circuit in the Fifties and Sixties that provided income for performers who were able to launch out on the strength of this niche market. It has proved essnetial for creative survival to this present day, given the relentless destruction of the UK's live circuit by governments, local authorities, record companies and pub chains since the Eighties, which inadvertently created the modern festival circuit, based very much on the folk model.

When the Sixties came the Beatles, who revolutionised music — and our thinking — by revealing a new way to produce it. Helped in part by the DIY ethic of the folk (and theatre) circuit, the Fab Four with fifth Beatle George Martin in the producer booth proved you could write and play your own songs within a self-contained group. Incredible as it may seem to us today, this was a truly mind-blowing innovation. And once they had empowered countless would-be and actual musicians around the world to do it for themselves, there was no going back. English folk itself could no longer be seen in isolation and, like so much of popular music in general, would always be viewed at least in part through a Beatles filter.

There's the interesting argument that the Brits do groups best, like the Beatles, while the Americans do the solo artist in a group best, like Bruce Springsteen. As a variation on the theme, the British singer-songwriters who sprang from 1965's *Rubber Soul*, the album that opened the doors for so many other genres such as psychedelic and progressive rock, were *solo* practitioners of the Beatles' *ensemble* way of working. *Bed Sitter Images*, *Eight Frames a Second*, *Fairport Convention*, *Strawbs*, all were debuts that took music in quite an unexpected yet somehow familiar direction, all further complicated of course by the fact that the latter two albums were band efforts.

And so the Brits went from strength to strength until inevitably, bolstered by the USA's monolithic music business constructing itself around them, it was the North American singer-songwriters who overnight took over the limelight at the turn of the decade: Joni Mitchell, Neil Young, Carole King, James Taylor, Jackson Browne . . . This also heralded the point when the UK's singer-songwriter flame was shared in an unexpected but very British way after the Beatles imploded in 1970. Musical imaginations were suddenly released, free to fix their own horizons now that the top spot had been relinquished. Musicians were also able to resist the centrifugal force of London and instead went out to reclaim the rest of the country after centuries of cultural imbalance.

After an unsurpassed handful of years in the Seventies when the world revelled in glam, prog, punk, reggae and everything else under the sun, new generations of singer-songwriters started to turn up in groups, following in the Ray Davies/Kinks tradition: Elvis Costello & the Attractions, Paul Weller of the Jam, Robert Smith of the Cure. Solo-style exceptions still shone through such as Joan Armatrading and Billy Bragg. And Weller and Bragg sort of answer the question of where all the protest songs went (more of which later).

By the turn of the Eighties it was clear that we had finally won the battle against ourselves for the right to our own cultural expression. And, regardless of what was lost, regardless of the hostility to popular culture that still lingers in places high and low, never was there a more British statement than our new music.

Progressions in attitude

Back to prog . . . Progressive folk seems a worthy cover-all to explain the idea of singer-songwriters. To quote various definitions from across the web, it was 'originally a type of American folk music that pursued a progressive political agenda, but in the United Kingdom the term became attached to a musical subgenre that describes a substyle of contemporary folk that draws from post-Bob Dylan folk music and adds new layers of musical and lyrical complexity, often incorporating various ethnic influences.'

The tag 'progressive' is an after-the-fact justification really, but, as we've seen, there's no doubt that everything was always available on the British musical table. From the outset BBC Radio had crammed everything onto a single music station, i.e. the Light Programme, that broadcast to the entire nation, no matter their generation or tastes. When Radio 1 came along in the late Sixties, you'd start the day with poptastic Tony Blackburn on the Breakfast Show and end it with edgy John Peel at night. TV did the same — with *Old Grey Whistle Test* arriving as a thoughtful late-night complement to the more saccharine charts show *Top of the Pops* in 1971.

Like punk, *pace* the purists, progressive folk is an attitude. You know it when you hear it. In the Fifties and Sixties most musicians absorbed American techniques, while those brought up in a Celtic environment brought value added to that collective table. Guitar, acoustic or electric, kept the torch aflame and the British guitarists proved the timeless rewards of progressing their styles again and again. (The process of reclaiming our cultural heart finds a good summing up in the Beatles originating from Liverpool: a northern [not London] town, a British-Irish [Celtic] community, an international [USA] port.)

While influences in the UK ranged from Dylan to James Taylor via Lead Belly or Robert Johnson, what many of our singer-songwriters at the time were producing was more analogous to Joan Baez and Judy Collins in terms of style and trajectory. There's a melody in their guitar lines, the accents tellingly are only softly American, the lyrics are polished by the tunes, the timing less busy.

And here's the thing: unlike nearly all their American peers, there was no significant folk in the upbringing of the (English) Brits. Their first encounters with folk came via records and live with Jansch, Graham & Co only once they'd hit the circuit. The idea of fusion/progression was learned from the Beatles, Shadows et al, the structure from Guthrie/Dylan & Co, and traditional folk could only be reached by passing through those waves.

As McTell observes: "Of course some might argue that my sort of singer-songwriter emerges from the troubadour from centuries ago, but it's really from Woody and then Dylan, and then all the things that have happened post-Dylan, meaning it is a new art form in a way."

Talking to *Record Collector* in 2018, Roy Harper adds: "What I wanted to do was carry on a tradition of social commentary. All of those old blues songs were doing that, so that was a major impetus. Then it developed from that first urge. I don't think pop music was ever involved. It wasn't like I was ever going to write 'Please Please Me'."

Thompson takes it up: "When Dylan went electric, that kind of legitimised serious lyrics in popular music, so that was a big clarion call for us, and we definitely wanted to pursue that kind of area . . . We have to play music that's true to our roots, music that will mean something to the audience because it's true to their roots as well, it's where they come from. So somebody's going to come and invent a style of music that fits our time and place. And the time is the rock'n'roll era but the place is Britain. And we're English, Irish, Scottish, mixed, whatever, so this is what we have to do. So we've got to take these old ballads but blend them, fuse them, with rock'n'roll and create this music that will mean a lot to us and hopefully mean a lot to the audience."

Hence folk rock, another much-used cover-all. It's interesting to note that one of the sparks for Dylan going electric was 'The House of the

Rising Sun' by British blues-rock group the Animals. A traditional folk song that had ended up in the USA from Europe, sometimes known as 'Rising Sun Blues', it was picked up by the Lomaxes and subsequent recordings included versions by Lead Belly, Woody Guthrie and Dylan, on his eponymous debut 1962 album (for which he nicked fellow New York folkie Dave Van Ronk's arrangement).

The Animals' version was a transatlantic hit in 1964. As a traditional folk song recorded by an electric rock band, it has been described as the 'first folk rock hit' after which 'the face of modern music was changed forever', and was the first British Invasion No 1 in the States that wasn't by the Beatles. Dylan says that when he first heard the Animals' single on his car radio, he braked, jumped out of his car and banged on the bonnet, inspiring him to go electric.

Talking to *The LA Review of Books* online Thompson expands on the fusion possibilities that opened up to his generation and to his band Fairport Convention in particular: "When *Music from Big Pink* by the Band *[note: four-fifths Canadian]* came out, we had to take a serious look at ourselves. This was a perfect blending of American roots, and in our earlier incarnation, it was everything that we wanted to strive for — except that we totally lacked the cultural background to do that, coming as we did from suburban North London. So we had to say, 'Okay, now is the hour — now we have to, with some urgency, create a truly British form of rock'n'roll, so we can excel in something indigenous, as the Band had excelled.'

"So we went right back, to the sixteenth century in some cases, to find the old ballads and great old stories, and we found ways to update them and give them a contemporary urgency by adding electricity and a backbeat. When Sandy and Swarb *[fiddle player Dave Swarbrick]* came into the band, they brought a lot of knowledge of that music with them. The rest of us knew it to a degree, but also furnished the rock'n'roll element. I return to this music all the time. It is never far from the style I play. I think there was a Sixties way of doing it, but subsequent bands and musicians have found variations of interpretation."

A really important point is that for the UK, aside from the Celtic cultural regions, there exists no national default for musicians to return to after they've launched out into experimentation. In the USA even the grungiest rockers can revert to their folk, blues, gospel, country heritage in a blink, whereas for us it would, in the case of most musicians, just seem odd or contrived. In the UK you just have to keep moving. Again that idea of progressive. And this sums up the hard-to-replicate vitality of British music and the culture that surrounds it.

Message in a song

Music is a dangerous thing. For a start, along with dance, it taps into a collective primeval consciousness in a way that other art forms don't and usually can't. And music isn't just about gathering minds and souls in a room or a field. If you're alone, you can sing to yourself aloud or in your head, as you read a poem, novel or newspaper. Still, music, like theatre, is best when it's a social dialogue, a shared communication where people gather, their emotions brought together at the same moment, on the same beat. It's not something governments can easily control therefore, particularly when self-expression or resistance is channelled via the combined medium of music and dance (a modern UK example being raves). Music with words that have a message are especially hard to stamp out because they can be transmitted orally — you don't need recordings, just a good ear or just a good memory. You can eradicate the singer-songwriters but their songs will live on.

However it's always been something of a puzzle that in England (i.e. non-Celtic UK) there's no definable body of protest songs that have been taken up by the people in the way done in countries like the USA, Spain, Chile, Italy. So, to come back to that idea of protest and the question: does a song need to contain a message? Well if you can't dance to it, the answer is more likely to be yes. But it's a bit more complicated since the art of the true singer-songwriter is offering the audience the *choice* of what they hear. Protest is just part of the message.

And this leads to the question of context. The UK didn't face the huge challenges posed by the American rifts in society, reflected by songs such as Joan Baez's 'We Shall Overcome' (see below), or need to. Of course life isn't perfect here (a fact long documented in our traditional urban/industrial folk songs) but there has been a steady consensual commitment to the improvement of life in the UK driven by society and worked out by the government. The troops tend not to be sent in to quell protest — with the tragic sustained exception of Northern Ireland, which in fact did generate a wave of protest songs, in addition to its own homegrown canon, from elsewhere in the country such as Paul McCartney's 'Give Ireland Back to the Irish' (banned by the BBC, a master study in how *not* to write a protest song) to 10cc's 'Rubber Bullets' (almost banned by the BBC, in fact about an Attica State Prison riot). The conditions of society are therefore key to establishing the framework for protest and what levels it can explore. Anyway, the strength of the true singer-songwriter is to make songs that adapt to their times. As the Seegers, Guthries, Baezs and Dylans of this world have shown us, a song can be a pop song one moment, a weapon for change the next. And with boldly polarised songs like 'Imagine' and 'Working Class Hero' John Lennon showed how far the Brits can take it if so minded.

Indeed, if so minded, in addition to mood, the modern singer-songwriter sets out to create a change in attitude, summed up in *The People's Music* and *Revolution in the Head: The Beatles' Records and the Sixties*, Ian MacDonald's ahead-of-their-time studies about the impact of popular music on society. Songs now were allowed into the mainstream to tell their story on a higher/deeper level than the saccharine parlour songs, faux-romantic lieds, throwaway Broadway tunes and Tin Pan Alley verse-verse-choruses that had clogged up the twentieth century so far. Even the stories already being told were shifting: from 'This Land Is Your Land' to 'My Generation', from 'Little Boxes' to 'The Needle of Death', from 'The First Time Ever I Saw Your Face' to 'Eleanor Rigby'. Songs also created their own story: 'We Shall Overcome' for example called for change and so helped launch the folk-protest movement in the USA which supported the civil rights movement, struggling against racism and social justice across the nation.

The social and political stakes in the USA are as overwhelming and monumental as its vastness as a continent, and a geographically small country like Britain offers no room for that sort of full-on injustice and conflict. But even in America, it's hard today to find the indignation that broke down the doors to people's minds in the way of Seeger's 'I Ain't Scared of Your Jail', Dylan's 'Masters of War', the Staple Singers' 'Freedom Highway', Gil Scott-Heron's 'Johannesburg', Marvin Gaye's *What's Going On*, Aretha, Nina Simone, Curtis Mayfield, Grandmaster Flash & the Furious Five's 'The Message', N.W.A. At least we've always known that Dylan never had a monopoly on protest (nor on folk it seems, to quote 'Anti Blur' by Lach of the Anti-Folk movement: 'And either you know, or you don't / Because Dylan killed Folk / And we were dancing on its grave').

The strands in the UK did eventually converge, highlighting the political/cultural protest of the Scottish, Irish and Welsh, the Northern balladeers and the new folk-with-a-conscience of Billy Bragg, and songs like the Special AKA's 'Free Nelson Mandela', the Specials' 'Ghost Town' and Steel Pulse's 'Ku Klux Klan' (revealingly the first two are ska, the latter reggae). Yes, protest is to be found in every corner and nook of the country if you look, but a finely tuned sense of satire on a truly national level counters a lot of the negative zeitgeist and means that nothing need be overstated, things find room to breathe, there's no pressure to make a statement on behalf of the nation.

Iain Matthews sums it up: "The inspiration comes from an honest place. I wouldn't write a song just to write a song. I would only write a song if I really felt that I had something to say. And whether it be personal or worldly it's all coming from a good place. I don't set myself up as a prophet or anything, I try to be reasonable about what I say. I make observations more than statements."

Cousins brings another perspective: "The astonishing thing is that people identify with my songs. They don't necessarily know what the songs are about but they can identify with the words. They give a lot of people comfort, and — this is not being pretentious in any way — I cannot tell you the number of people that have come up to me in America and said, your song 'The Winter Long', the last part of 'Autumn', was our wedding song. 'Grace Darling' is another song that people have got married to. I've also had people write to me with highly personal things like, 'I was in hospital having electric shock treatment and the only comfort I got was from listening to your songs.' "

Talking to *Record Collector's* Larry Jaffee, Stewart says: "What I like about the singer-songwriter thing is that it's never in fashion, never out of fashion. It exists really totally outside the constraints of pop music . . . [I]n the folk scene, Richard Thompson makes a record, it might sell 50,000 copies or whatever, but he's never going away. He can do it when he's 100. He's never in fashion, never out of fashion. It's a little like the old blues singers. Same thing. You don't have many hits, but you have an everlasting career. I like that — but it's a pain in the butt that you can't get your records played on the radio. But c'est la vie. They'll play 'Year of the Cat' but they won't play 'Night Train to Munich'."

From Woody to grime

Which all brings us to Woody Guthrie . . . and folk activist and musicologist Pete Seeger. Woody's story after all is also very much Seeger's. Woody toured with the latter's newly formed folk-protest group the Almanac Singers in the Forties, while Seeger (who died in 2014) championed Woody's work after his incapacitation and death as a result of Huntington's Disease — Woody was hospitalised in 1956 until his death in 1967 — and went on to a long-time collaboration with Woody's son Arlo. Seeger was likewise a major influence in the UK, where he was a frequent visitor, and a permanent claim on our isles was made by his sister Peggy, who moved here in 1956, forging a lasting creative and activist partnership with MacColl, whom she subsequently married.

Seeger would have left his mark if only for his folk revival protest songs like 'Where Have All the Flowers Gone' (with Joe Hickerson), 'If I Had a Hammer (The Hammer Song)' (with Lee Hays of the Weavers), and 'Turn! Turn! Turn!'. The fact that these songs continue to be covered today is a testament to their accessibility to audiences far beyond the folk revival and civil rights movements.

Seeger was also one of the folk singers responsible for popularising the spiritual 'We Shall Overcome', which Joan Baez conveyed to a global audience with her own version, once again demonstrating how the vehicle of folk music can transcend activism to enter the mainstream, in this case with a traditional song that became the anthem of the civil rights movement in the USA. Such songs after all doubled as pop songs, which is precisely where all folk songs ultimately started (the ones that weren't originally sacred, that is). But our view of 'pop' took on a very different filter during the twentieth century worldwide, creating something of a schism with 'folk'. Aside from laying down the foundations of the electric era, introducing the idea of the group that wrote and performed their own songs like the Beatles, and the business that eagerly followed to market it all, the late Forties-Fifties also unleashed the modern avatar of the singer-songwriter, embodied for very good reasons in the persona of Woody Guthrie.

Woody was a different animal to the bluesmen, troubadours and saga singers who have stood on the stages of music since history began. For a start he wasn't a folk artist in the sense of being a son of the soil or scion of satanic mills although he did know a lot about being raised in deprivation.

He grew up in Oklahoma. His father was a businessman who ran into debt from failed real estate deals and eventually went to work in Texas as Woody's mother succumbed to the slow death of Huntington's disease — the genetic degenerative neurological condition which was to claim Woody's own life and those of two of his children. By way of musical upbringing, he learnt the old ballads available at the time and traditional English and Scottish songs along with a smattering of blues.

Woody had credentials therefore but this didn't mean that he had to be subject to the limits of class or region — or history. He came of age in the late Thirties (he was born in 1912) during the Great Depression (he lived on the periphery of the Dust Bowl) that affected the USA and Europe. Everything was changing — radically, rapidly, violently — *because it had to*. To the point that popular culture found itself empowered to tackle taboos with confidence, challenge the hierarchies of politics with a lessening fear of threat, criminal consequence or ostracisation. At the same time, and not uncoincidentally, popular music was gaining unprecedented outreach thanks to radio and recordings.

Woody ran magnificently with the times and showed the world how the modern singer-songwriter can go deeper and wider, taking advantage of the new tools of mass media, expanding sociopolitical boundaries, adapting to audiences and, as society changes, acting as a sounding board for the people. Songs like these, slices of storytelling, should also be a conversation: around the dinner table, at the pub, the workplace, in bed.

Politics, sure, but also poetry, love, history, family, traditions, the future. All the things that affect us. As Woody, who for a while was given the nickname of the 'Dust Bowl Troubadour', declared: "I am out to sing the songs that make you take pride in yourself and in your work." And that means respect for your life in his work as the man whose guitar bore the label *This machine kills fascists* openly let people understand that not everyone can or needs to be urged into taking to the barricades for world-changing action, but that everyday life can throw up overwhelming struggles on the tiniest levels for us all.

Though cut short by his illness, Woody's working life and example were jaw-droppingly productive. Songs like 'This Land is Your Land', '1913 Massacre', 'Deportee' and 'Pretty Boy Floyd' each represented collections of hundreds of other compositions that reflected changes in society and gave a voice to the people affected by those changes. The wartime government recognised the useful propaganda in this and gave him commissions to report on the war effort, resulting in epic reportages such as 'Grand Coulee Dam'.

Folk pioneers like Seeger and musicologist Alan Lomax also recognised his talents as did audiences the nation over, and yet Woody hasn't translated to a significant number of other countries, although the indirect momentum of his legacy has carried weight. So why is he so well-known today? Simple: he inspired Bob Dylan who channelled Woody to directly shape modern singer-songwriters the world over.

Woody's words and music inspired people, but his genius was also *how to do it*, which Dylan recognised. And so Woody, having recast the idea of the singer-songwriter as worker-activist through the experience of the Dust Bowl, became the defining influence on Dylan, who cast himself in Woody's mould (following Guthrie's own philosophy of 'steal it!').

Dylan for his part reworked this into an artist-activist role at the turn of the Sixties through the eyes of the established New York intellectual scene, which was always on the look out for the next wave of enfants terribles. Dylan had a similar mid-West provenance to Guthrie, coming as he did from Minnesota from a middle-class shopkeeper's family. Aged 19 he went straight to New York as a budding folk singer-songwriter where he made regular visits to Guthrie who was by now permanently in hospital. Incapacitated by his progressive disease, Guthrie was physically unable to come to the UK as part of the wave of North Americans like his colleague Seeger. He could be there in spirit however thanks to Dylan who was physically here and who transubstantiated Woody to the UK's musical community in as direct a transmission as you could wish for.

Having announced that he intended to become 'Guthrie's greatest disciple', in New York Dylan got to know Guthrie's protegé Ramblin' Jack Elliott, who similarly idolised Woody and had become the acknowledged practitioner of his repertoire. Elliott, a doctor's son from Brooklyn, is another key component of the chain of transmission that includes Seeger, Dylan and Arlo Guthrie. Dylan asked Elliott to teach him as much of Woody's style and technique, as Arlo was to also ask. In a 1984 *Esquire* magazine interview, Elliott recalls: "I was flattered. Dylan learned from me the same way I learned from Woody. Woody didn't teach me. He just said, 'If you want to learn something, just steal it — that's the way I learned from Lead Belly.' "

Ah, Lead Belly . . . This being America, of course behind it all there was a genius who was black. Born in Louisiana on a plantation in the late 1880s, Huddie Ledbetter moved with his family when young to Texas. He left school early and by the age of fourteen he was already a popular draw at juke joints as a blues/American folk player across the Jim Crow South. During this time he linked up with Blind Lemon Jefferson, a few years his senior, and developed his signature 12-string guitar style. When not playing, he made his living from labouring, and was reputedly legendary for his ability to pick a thousand pounds of cotton a day.

Lead Belly's popularity as a performer however had its drawbacks. As he later drily observed: "When I play, the women would come around to listen and their men would get angry." In 1918 he killed a relative in a fight over a woman, and was sent to prison in Huntsville, Texas, serving a twenty-year sentence for murder. He was allegedly let out early after singing for the state governor, who'd earlier vowed never to pardon felons.

Lead Belly ended up in prison again in 1930, this time for attempted murder after a fight at a party, and he was incarcerated in Louisiana's notorious Angola Farm prison plantation (he did time again for a stabbing in 1939 in New York). At Angola he was discovered by the musicologist father and son team of John and Alan Lomax, who were recording prison songs at the time. The relationship led to their sustained support for Lead Belly and his moving to New York after his release.

In Manhattan he failed to stir black Harlem audiences, but instead found a home with the white left-wing nascent folkies, ending up in the company of Woody and Seeger (who adopted Lead Belly's 12-string style). His work presaged Woody's, and their mutual exchange was tight enough for the Smithsonian Institute to release *Folkways: The Original Vision (Woody and Leadbelly)*. Like Woody, Lead Belly's influence continues to this day, hailed by Lonnie Donegan, the Beatles, Dylan, Kurt Cobain and many many more.

Lead Belly was also the first American country blues musician to find success in Europe, and his songs — both originals and definitive reworkings of traditionals — reflect Woody's enviable diversity. As the Lead Belly Foundation (leadbelly.org) says, "his songs could not be put into one category. He wrote children's songs, field songs, ballads, square dance songs, prison songs, folk songs, and blues." He left a catalogue of 500 originals and standards, and shortly after his death in 1949 the Weavers (with Seeger) had their first hit with his song 'Goodnight, Irene', a million-seller that went to No 1 in America. Tom Waits later covered the song, joining an august list of (prominently white) musicians attracted particularly to his reworkings of folk standards — the Beach Boys ('Cotton Fields [The Cotton Song]'), Creedance Clearwater Revival ('Midnight Hour'), Led Zeppelin ('The Gallows Pole'), Kurt Cobain/Nirvana ('Where Did You Sleep Last Night').

So steal it, as Guthrie said. Steal it, as has always been the prerogative of the bards, but shape it and make it your own. But it's less the words or lyrics, it's more the willing transmission and reception of a way of life and thinking. It's songwriting and performance with honesty, truth, where imitation is sincerely praise. An extreme example is the Orthodox Christian icon painters, whose art *demands* that they copy — any innovation is frowned upon. Bards are entrusted to pass on not only the skills but the material too, minor embellishments permitted. This is how the Sagas survived long before they were written down, how the English folk songs lasted long enough to be rescued from the Virginias. True innovation would not work, unless in the hands of someone who proves they know their stuff. And the post-Guthrie generations have certainly proved they know their stuff.

If anything summed up the response of Woody's own generation to the changing times, it wasn't going to be the melodies (which were often recycled) but the words, which took on a new urgency and potency. Guthrie rightly appropriated language as a vehicle to report on a modern world, where nothing is fixed any longer. With national epics like 'Grand Coulee Dam' or achingly personal ballads like 'Hard Ain't It Hard' he showed how words could take the imagery of poetry and the candor of newspaper print. If only by sheer force of his prodigious output, he showed how words could spread news, ideas, culture, entertainment, emotions, personal triumphs and losses in a way that mainstream pop music or literary poetry could not.

Weaving all that technically into the music was also a process in which Guthrie surpassed, where he transferred the simplicity of Lead Belly's vocals/guitar delivery to the catchy mass appeal of radio and records. It was a hard act to follow, especially as the paradigms were on the point of permanently changing.

As we've seen, Dylan followed Woody's act by using Ramblin' Jack Elliott as the bridge. Elliott himself is not a songwriter as such but an 'interpretive troubadour', a repository of Woody's technique who passed on that knowledge to Dylan, along with his nasal singing style (Dylan was sometimes referred to as the 'Son of Jack Elliott'). Elliott was also part of that First Wave of Americans who came over to the UK, mostly New York-based, who showed the UK's singer-songwriters how they had rediscovered folk in its widest sense and so solved that puzzle of how to harness it to pop culture.

In the sleeve notes to his 1985 compilation box set *Biograph*, Dylan summed up the puzzle: "The thing about rock'n'roll is that for me anyway it wasn't enough . . . There were great catch-phrases and driving pulse rhythms . . . but the songs weren't serious or didn't reflect life in a realistic way. I knew that when I got into folk music, it was more of a serious type of thing. The songs are filled with more despair, more sadness, more triumph, more faith in the supernatural, much deeper feelings."

So folk simply might mean anything that isn't rock'n'roll. Certainly it's music that demands to be performed. In fact this is music that goes in search of its audience. Even with recordings, radio, the internet to disseminate, the music still needs to keep moving, to place itself in front of real-life audiences everywhere. What singer-songwriters have in common is a light bulb, guitar/piano, own material/out of copyright material, ability to come up with a response instantly (they keep writing/performing till they drop), a voice judged foremost on its ability to convey words (which is why none of them seem to lose their voices as careers progress) — and possibly the ability to live out of a suitcase as a way of life if not a philosophy.

A response to the changin' times

All the arts in the twentieth century looked for a response to the momentous changes it ushered in — Picasso's 'Guernica', Joyce's *Ulysses*, Joan Littlewood's Theatre Workshop, Peter Cook's Establishment Club — and, as we've seen, Woody Guthrie's revelation was to take the traditions and plonk them into the mainstream. Like the mystique of the Wild West, he embodied that boxcar romanticism, the authority gained from travelling amongst the people while singing songs for the people in the age of consumerism. As an American he was able to re-politicise folk/blues in the way that the Beatles as Brits were able to politicise pop/rock'n'roll. Again, it needs to be emphasised that the genius on both sides lay in the understanding that (party) politics didn't have to come with the package, although a morality or appreciation of values did.

As Arlo Guthrie points out: "I think my father and his friends found themselves at a crossroads in history where the songs that people sang and had handed down had become political because the way of life was disappearing. So even a dance or fiddle tune, the playing of it, the passing it on, was political in the face of an encroaching culture that minimised not only that kind of music but was attempting to profit from it, which meant that it had to be dumbed down to reach a larger audience. It was inherently political although it was not politically charged."

There had been a pre-war revolution of sorts on both sides of the Atlantic via popular music with Cole Porter, Noel Coward and the show tunes (*Porgy and Bess*) or the doomed doggerel of Weimar cabaret, but something was lacking. Society wasn't ready yet, although for a good 150 years it had been testing its limits as one taboo after another fell to the liberation of art, literature and classical/popular music. But things like race, gender, sexuality, true social equality and economic empowerment were still barriers to how far you could take a song, even if it was jazz.

Location? That was already a fixed economic decision. You had to travel to London in the Fifties/Sixties/Seventies just as the North Americans needed to get to New York, San Francisco or LA (which created an often uncomfortable East Coast/West Coast divide). London monopolised the press, studios, record labels, agents, bookers, publishers (and lawyers). The concert venues, clubs and working men's clubs of the rest of the country mainlined into the capital to keep the home touring circuit burning. The capital was also the retail hub for music equipment and records (a time when a record pressing sold out in those days, that was it: there were no more copies), and the first pit stop for your American peers flying in (Heathrow airport). The national institutions of BBC Radio and TV were based there. There was nowhere else the budding singer-songwriter needed to be — and Al Stewart points to the year 1966 as the door that beckoned them through. The respect of London once earned, you had the seal of approval to go back to the rest of the country — even America.

And once through that door, the music business swept you up and pushed you into creating that hit whether you wanted it or not . . . Stewart sums up the dilemma that awaited when discussing his 1976 global hit *Year of the Cat* in *Q* magazine: "The record was so expensive to make, and because of all the promo tours we did, I think it personally cost me a quarter of a million dollars. You had to pay the record company back, you had to pay the producer. It worked out that during the period when I was having successful records, I basically broke even on the entire thing. Whereas years later, when I was just going out with an acoustic guitar and wasn't really making records anymore, I finally began to make money."

Bert . . .

An apologetically brief aside here on Bert Jansch (1943-2011), who was one of the pivotal figures of the UK's post-war folk pioneers and whose songs, guitar technique and sheer conviction continue to influence musicians today.

Jansch (pronounced 'Jansh' but often as 'Yansh') created a bridge between the folkies and the popsters in the Sixties, the middle ground he created showing the way forward for the new singer-songwriters. The measure of his influence can be seen in the similarly influential range of musicians who namecheck him: in the UK people the likes of Roy Harper, Donovan, Nick Drake, Pete Townshend, Jimmy Page, Johnny Marr and Bernard Butler; in North America the likes of Paul Simon, Neil Young, Thurston Moore (Sonic Youth) and Gordon Giltrap, who released an acoustic guitar tribute in the shape of the mini-album *Janschology* (2000).

Born in Glasgow and raised in Edinburgh, Jansch left school early to delve into the folk scene, and by 1960 he had launched off into the national circuit where he shared stages with the likes of Anne Briggs and Martin Carthy. He made the move to London in 1963, and spent spells busking around Europe like Ralph McTell. In the capital he was a mainstay of folk clubs like Bunjies, Les Cousins, the Troubadour and the Horseshoe, and worked with Davey Graham, Wizz Jones, Roy Harper, John Renbourn and Sandy Denny as well as the rest of the musicians in this book.

His first album *Bert Jansch*, released in 1965, is one of the milestones of popular music. Recorded at the Camden home of folk revival producer Bill Leader, the album was instantly hailed as a singer-songwriting bible. His protest song 'Do You Hear Me Now?' was covered the same year by singer Donovan, a fellow London-based Scot, on his *Universal Soldier* EP/single. Also on the album is 'Needle of Death', an enduring anti-drugs lament written after a folk-singer friend died from a heroin overdose. Poignantly ahead of its time, you can hear its echo in songs like Neil Young's 'The Needle and the Damage Done' (1971/72). Guitarist Jimmy Page's reaction to the album, quoted in Roy Harper's biography, is immensely revealing: "When I first heard that LP, I couldn't believe it. It was so far ahead of what everyone else was doing. No one in America could touch that."

Jasnch's partnership with Renbourn and the interplay between their two (acoustic) guitars resulted in the birth of 'folk baroque', captured on 1966's *Bert and John*. The pair went on to form the group Pentangle with singer Jacqui McShee, bassist Danny Thompson and drummer Terry Cox. With the odd break, Jansch recorded, collaborated and toured extensively right up to his final year.

It was in the early years of his career that he found himself hailed in some quarters as a British answer to Bob Dylan. However, in Colin Harper's *Dazzling Stranger: Bert Jansch and the British Folk and Blues Revival*, he cites his musical influences unequivocally: "The only three people that I've ever copied were *[American blues singer-songwriter]* Big Bill Broonzy, Davey Graham and *[Scottish folk singer-songwriter]* Archie Fisher."

Company for the road

The UK's musicians have never needed to take the lone road. The manual has always been open and accessible to all and can be added to by anyone with a bit of talent. The points of musical reference are out there for all to share. Like other countries, the UK's post-war social revolution reflected its circumstances and heritage, seen in our case through the lens of a once great nation weakened not only by its war experience but also by having traded its instruments of world leadership during World War Two in return for the support of the USA — who de facto occupied the UK and the rest of Europe after the war's conclusion by establishing military bases all over our countries and attempting to replace our industries and trade. (As a pertinent aside, post-war UK was massively in debt to the USA by being the *largest recipient* of the latter's European Recovery Programme, a.k.a. the Marshall Plan, with much of the reconstruction aid weighed down by loans and major concessions like Trident.)

The USA for its part was totally revitalised by its war experience and turned now from its pre-war isolationism (provoked by World War One and the Great Depression) to become the world superpower it had hankered after becoming. But back on the home front, the nation was rocked by the internal struggle for racial equality and civil rights, squeezed by national anti-democratic policies rendered immutable by the constitutional clash between the corporate-driven federal government and the states entrenched along Civil War lines over liberty and equality.

Britain, on the other hand, remained a place where all our issues sat visible on the table and were up for grabs (in a more or less considered way), a situation that created breathing space, consensus and the right to agree to disagree. Censorship, the death penalty, the Established Church, abortion, equality of gender, race and class, loss of empire, nuclear armaments, immigration, employment, education, the loss of 'Made in Britain' — all came to public debate, and the government, however reluctantly, eventually joined in. Even the right to party was being debated in Parliament by the late Sixties.

The catalysts had already been unleashed during World War Two, pre-accelerated by World War One and the Great Depression. The steps towards social empowerment despite the perilous unpredictability of the war years are simply extraordinary, well summed up by the writer JB Priestley, (most famous for his dystopian play *An Inspector Calls*. In 1940 he was commissioned by the war government to give a series of short propaganda BBC Radio talks under the title of *Postscripts*. The idea of the Sunday night broadcasts was to strengthen civilian morale during the Battle of Britain. However Priestley's left-wing beliefs instantly brought him into conflict with the authorities, who were aghast to learn that he was drawing peak audiences of 16 million, i.e. 40 per cent of the adult population was listening to the 'voice of Britain'. Only the country's wartime leader Winston Churchill was more popular with listeners, a fact noted by writer Graham Greene, who observed that Priestley "became in the months after Dunkirk a leader second only in importance to Mr Churchill. And he gave us what our other leaders have always failed to give us — an ideology."

I know this is an introduction to a book about music, but we've already delved into history so perhaps it justifies sharing this example of Priestley's plain speaking, his *attitude*, broadcast on July 21, 1940, eleven days after the start of the Battle of Britain: "We cannot go forward and build up this new world order — and this is our war aim — unless we begin to think differently," he told the nation. "One must stop thinking in terms of property and power and begin thinking in terms of community and creation. Take the change from property to community. Property is the old-fashioned way of thinking of a country as a thing, and a collection of things in that thing, all owned by certain people and constituting property; instead of thinking of a country as the home of a living society with the community itself as the first test.

"And I'll give you an instance of how this change should be working. Near where I live is a house with a large garden, that's not being used at all because the owner of it has gone to America. Now, according to the property view, this is all right, and we, who haven't gone to America, must fight to protect this absentee owner's property. But on the community view, this is all wrong. There are hundreds of working men not far from here who urgently need ground for allotments so that they can produce a bit more food. Also, we may soon need more houses for billeting. Therefore, I say, that house and garden ought to be used whether the owner, who's gone to America, likes it or not."

This ideology of a socialist future (and undisguised criticism of the government) eventually pushed the authorities to pulling the plug on Priestley's broadcasts — but not before he had laid the seeds across the nation for the birth of the welfare state and the post-war landslide Labour election victory that set it in motion. (Undeterred, he immediately published *Postscripts* in book form under the confident title of *Britain Speaks*.) Need it be pointed out that this was during Britain's Darkest Hour?

Back to to the evolution of the UK's music, which was everywhere in wartime Britain, especially dance music. The Mantovani Orchestra and Edmundo Ros' Latin-American dance band were already shaping the landscape for the post-war music scene. Over from America, Glenn Miller toured the country in the summer of 1944 (he was to die later that year over the English Channel) with his specially formed fifty-piece Army Air Force Band, giving an incredible 800 performances. Like Woody Guthrie, he also lent his music to the war machine in the form of propaganda and counter-propaganda broadcasts (many songs recorded were sung in German and Miller himself spoke in German about the war effort).

The post-war years immediately after the war's end were extraordinary in their own way too. Churchill, who led the War Coalition but sold the country out to the Americans as part of our war deal, was voted out in 1945 in an election that Labour won, a landslide victory that Priestley helped pave the way for. His fellow writer George Orwell then managed to better *Animal Farm*, published in 1945, with another masterpiece, *1984*, in 1949 (which was in fact about his own times).

The Edinburgh Festival Fringe was launched in 1947 as a political, near anarchist reaction to the Edinburgh International Festival, itself established to bolster peace in Europe through the unifying power of culture. Then came the Festival of Britain, a national exhibition and fair which brought a much needed blast of colour to the nation in 1950. A couple of years later Theatre Workshop took the Ewan MacColl-scripted show *Uranium 235* (about nuclear arms) to Butlins holiday camps, while the anti-nuclear movement took root as the Campaign for Nuclear Disarmament took off in 1957. Meanwhile the groundwork for the NHS and revamp of education system advanced, accompanied by reputedly the world's biggest building of social housing outside of the Soviet Union.

Although levels of society in the UK remained excluded and impoverished — a legacy that lingers to this day, particularly in the North of England and parts of the other three nations — there was always somewhere to go, somewhere to be heard, even if it turned out to be limelight-hogging London. Being at the centre of things didn't remove the challenges but it did spotlight the tools for empowerment and set the stage for it. And the UK's musicians responded magnificently. The exposure of media and the high street and the records and instruments imported from the USA was enough to give the new generations time to absorb and to come up with a Suitably British Response that stunned the world with the unexpected twin-pronged teamwork of the Shadows, whose eloquent instrumentals spread across the world market, followed by our one true voice in the shape of the Beatles.

Taking up the torch

Although British music had dwindled in stature since Tudor times because our rulers had cut us off from outside influence, people had never stopped creating music, no matter the standard. And, funnily enough, this lack of baggage proved to be a huge plus like no other when our national musicians were finally called upon to respond to the Brave New World we now find ourselves in.

The singer-songwriters in this book are representative of UK music — and our wider culture — in that a formula or genre is a suggested route rather than a rule book. A distinctive feature of British music is the way musicians are able to work within a definable genre while keeping their own sound and impact distinct. This can prove puzzling in a cultural environment like the USA where fusion and cross-over are genres in themselves, not an attitude.

An example perhaps is when, a few years back, I gave someone I knew in America a CD of Vashti Bunyan's *Just Another Day*. His response was to send back a collection of songs by a Maine *folk*-folk singer lauding rivers and lumberjacks. I was expecting David Byrne or Edie Brickell. I was disappointed at the failure of the exchange I'd initiated, but then realised that music, for all its universality, doesn't have to be all things to all people. What we hear — *and how we hear it* — is dictated by our cultural upbringing and, just as important, the reassurance of our cultural surroundings.

It's not always a given that non-Brits will get our singer-songwriter credentials. Britain being Britain, we've seen how it's logical that our singer-songwriters don't let genre limit them. We don't therefore really have a Newman, Springsteen, Young or Mitchell (the latter two being Canadians), but we do have Ian Hunter, Noddy Holder & Jim Lea (of Slade) and David Bowie. So the next step for the Sixties acoustic guitar format fused in folk clubs as documented in this book was taken in the Seventies and Eighties towards electric *rock/pop* bands formed around the likes of Siouxsie (and the Banshees), Elvis Costello (and the Attractions), Paul Weller (the Jam), Glenn Tilbrook & Chris Difford (Squeeze), then Robert Smith (the Cure), Morrissey (the Smiths) and leaping to the limitless array that followed — Florence Welch (& the Machine), Kano, Sleaford Mods.

The solo path wasn't abandoned, of course, and we rejoice in a continuous line that includes Ray Davies, Gerry Rafferty, Ian Dury, Joan Armatrading, Kate Bush (the UK's Joni Mitchell), PJ Harvey (ditto), Katie Melua and Stormzy. And then how do people like George Michael, Paul Weller, Ian Curtis, Gary Numan, Annie Lennox, Joe Jackson and the sublime Mark Hollis fit in? That bedsit introspection, socialist outlook, Pythonesque sense of the absurd, sympathy for the underdog has clearly gone from strength to strength. Punk, new wave, goth, britpop, grime, music still simmers in society, refusing to go into the museum.

Now, not all of it is everyone's cup of tea but even if the handed-on baton is not apparent, it is there, united by that same progressive spirit. Just as I've argued for prog rock in *Mellotron*, the art of the singer-songwriter, in the UK at least, isn't a style but will always be an attitude, a genre-fluid movement forward, forever seeking new voices and audiences.

A conclusion

Here's an ending that offers my own personal impressions . . .

Ralph McTell? I still feel the frustration at finding the sheet music for 'Streets of London' ripped out of every fake book by wannabe buskers in every library in North London during the Seventies and Eighties. And then his song 'England' pissed me off for so many reasons when it came out in 1982 that I actually wrote a folk-satirical yet heartfelt response 'England My England' (now on Nick Awde & Desert Hearts, *Blues for Blighty*, 2020). Much later, Ralph magically sent over signed copies of *Alphabet Zoo* to my kids who had gleeful punctuated our interviews. And though I never even attempted the ragtime bits, his acoustic playing was a major influence for me with its perfect balance of American and English.

Richard Thompson! Amid the Seventies rage of punk and icy prescience of Krautrock, it was still possible to be shocked by the daring simplicity exuded by the cover of Richard & Linda Thompson's 1975 album *Pour Down Like Silver*. I saw the beturbanned Rumi-like evocation as a cultural finger up to society that hit you right between the eyes. Then there was 1979's *Sunnyvista* with its cover of an expectant Butlins-style family plonked in Technicolor atop a grim grey view of the Brutalist Rowley Way Estate down the road and a title song, sung by Linda, that summed up the times like a caustic riposte to Woody Guthrie's 'This Land Is Your Land'. I've been a fan of the whole Thompson family ever since.

As for Iain Matthews . . . Hearing Joni Mitchell's original always gets me working out the musical journey that took Iain from Fairport Convention to his otherworldly version of 'Woodstock', a classic in its own right up there with Joe Cocker's version of Lennon & McCartney's 'With a Little Help from My Friends'. And Iain did this with a bunch of other UK musicians who had probably never set foot in the States at the time. Listening to his a cappella arrangement of the traditional 'Blood Red Roses' had exactly the same impact on me as hearing the Stranglers' 'Peaches' for the first time. And then the surprise of every album, satisfyingly not to everyone's taste. And being blown away by the discovery that he was in a band in Seattle with David Surkamp *and* Doug Rayburn of

Pavlov's Dog — another left-field journey. And the joy of being handed a bootleg tape out of the blue of their *Music for Mallards* after years of searching pre-internet for the real article.

Arlo . . . Arlo! My younger brother Fred James Hill, when we were teenagers, in between playing Iron Maiden, Deep Purple and Todd Rundgren on his Woolworth's guitar, painstakingly learning 'Alice's Restaurant' from a crackly Swiss Cottage Library LP as the entire household spent a summer listening to him taking apart the epic song — guitar-picking, lyrics, the film. Then later the insights into Arlo's worldview through understanding how he had been a carer for his father and, through my theatre side, when I realised that his mother was Marjorie Mazia, a key part of Martha Graham Dance Company and who taught dancer/ choreographer Merce Cunningham. And then the collaborations with Pete Seeger and the Guthrie Family — all the songs I'd avoided as a kid suddenly made sense!

David Cousins . . . what can I say? His generosity and hospitality over the years, his knowledge, his business tips. At a time when I suspect I preferred Hudson Ford to Strawbs, I somehow felt compelled to buy *Hero and Heroine*, just based on the album cover, in a small record shop in Ely with coins found by rummaging down the back of the family sofa. I had no idea what the album was about and struggled to reconcile its visionary folk-prog with the Strawbs of *From the Witchwood* and 'Part of the Union'. Fast forward to 2001 and I proudly merged my music and theatre halves by catching the first ever batch of Acoustic Strawbs gigs at the Edinburgh Festival Fringe. And then the sheer magic of David playing my MelloFest mini-festival with Robert Kirby accompanying on Mellotron.

And Al Stewart . . . Although I never truly lived in Britain's Bedsit Land, there was an unchallenged litany of albums shaped by its denizens, topped by the likes of *Tapestry*, *Astral Weeks* and at least one Nick Drake if not two. Amid the LPs piled up in the rooms of elder sisters and brothers, students and teachers, it was *Orange* and *Modern Times* that remain impressed in my memory with their winding lyrics. And then realising that Al's guitar skills, like those of Greg Lake, Rod Stewart and Tom Jones, perversely transcended his work on his recordings, thanks to the discovery that he came from the same guitar laboratory, i.e. Don Strike in Eastbourne, whose alumni included Robert Fripp, John Wetton, Lake and Andy Summers. I started to pay attention to his musical decisions as well as his lyrics. And then, just as all my mates got into Al through *Year of the Cat* and *Time Passages*, bang, he was gone from the commercial world. I was impressed how he simply turned his back on it and got on with the rest of his career. I still am.

Nick Awde

David Cousins • Arlo Guthrie
Iain Matthews • Ralph McTell
Al Stewart • Richard Thompson

David Cousins
(Photo by Michel Parent)

1

David Cousins

'So we started our own folk club...'

David Cousins was born in Camberwell, South London, on January 7, 1945. His birth surname was Hindon and he was raised in West London, where he co-founded the Strawberry Hill Boys in 1964 — he also completed a degree in statistics and maths at the University of Leicester. The bluegrass Strawberry Hill Boys evolved into the folk-rock Strawbs, which included Sandy Denny in its 1967 lineup. With band members sharing out songwriting duties — Cousins' input has been the constant and defining factor — the band released albums such as the acclaimed debut *Strawbs* [1969], folk rock epic *Grave New World* [1972], prog epics *Hero and Heroine* and *Ghosts* [both 1974], and *Blue Angel* [2003]. The band worked with producers such as Gus Dudgeon and Tony Visconti, and Nick Drake arranger Robert Kirby played with the band for a couple of years. Cousins has also produced occasional solo albums such as *Two Weeks Last Summer* [1972] and *The Boy in the Sailor Suit* [2007] as well as collaborations such as *Hummingbird* [2002] with keyboardist Rick Wakeman. After a hiatus during the Eighties, Cousins returned full time to the music business in the Nineties. Strawbs record and tour in two formats: Acoustic Strawbs and an electric version based around the *Hero and Heroine/Ghosts* line-up of the band from 1974. He has also had a parallel career in radio station management and consultancy, and founded Witchwood Records, a stable for Strawbs and Strawbs related releases. After dividing his time between London and Devon since the early Seventies, he is now based in Kent. He has published a collection of annotated lyrics *Secrets, Stories & Songs* (with bonus CD) [2010] and a book of memoirs *Exorcising Ghosts: Strawbs and Other Lives* [2014].

Let's start at the beginning: where you were born?

Me? I was born in Camberwell, in London.

But you weren't raised there, were you?

Not really, no. I moved around a lot when I was young — Bournemouth, Chiswick. Most of the time I was in West London. My father died. And my mother moved around a lot. She and her mother ran a guesthouse in Sussex Gardens, near Paddington in Central London, for a while. And then she became an insurance collector, and then she worked for the council. She wanted me to be a council worker too — "You'll get a pension!"

You must have gone to a few different schools.

I was settled in West London by then so my first junior school was in Chiswick. In fact as an adult I moved into a house where, until about ten years ago, I could look out of my bedroom window and see that first school I ever went to — so that was going round in circles.

What was the schooling like in the Fifties and early '60s? Was there pressure on you to achieve or were they giving you your own way as part of the New Society-style educational system that was introduced post-War? Either way, it must have been a stimulating rite of passage.

At the time I never realised that we were part of the new educational system. We were taught correct spelling, grammar, mental arithmetic. I even remember doing calculations like eight one and halves equalled twelve and we seemed to do everything in twelves, which was rather a bizarre way of doing things.

Do you remember things like furlongs and ells?

Yes, very much so. And I'm absolutely horrified now they cut out imperial measurement. They've allowed us to keep miles and pints but everything else has gone. I used to look at my grammar school playing field as being twenty acres so I can now visualise what ten acres is because it was divided into two fields. But now that would be four hectares which doesn't seem to register somehow.

Are your memories particularly vivid about your childhood? Of course you're too young for a wartime childhood but you must have memories of post-war austerity. Such as seeing your first banana or your first orange?

I do remember my uncle bringing me my first banana, which was quite a shock. I don't remember eating it so I'm not even sure whether I liked it although I do remember being given it. That was bizarre. As for growing up, my second dad was a school caretaker and so we grew up living both in and around schools. So it was a slightly strange upbringing being very closely associated with the school in both directions: living there and going there. That was quite curious. Dad was the caretaker but he was a brilliant caretaker as far as I was concerned because the school floors were always polished. He was an ex-Army man, a boxer who fought light heavyweight in the Army championships — a very well built and very handsome man.

So that was a good family relationship?

He was very, very hard on me. I used to get the belt across my backside because I wouldn't eat certain things. It was a very tough relationship. But when the time came that I really realised I loved him, it was when he was dying of leukaemia and he was helping me to modify my banjo. His hands were shaking so badly trying to operate a tiny drill that he couldn't do it. And I suddenly realised how ill he was and I realised how much I loved him. That was about when I was about sixteen.

That means you lost two fathers within a short period of time. Do you know much about your real father?

He was a sailor, in the Royal Navy. He died at the end of the war.

Did he die as a result of the war?

It was all been hushed up and I'd rather not talk about it. It was friendly fire. I only found out many years later from a senior admiral who told me what had really gone on.

So it seems there was a lot of security at home yet it was still somewhat different from many other families. Did that make you disruptive at school, or did you put your head down and get on with it because you knew your stepdad was part of the system?

I should imagine I was always very well behaved at junior school. But at senior school I became a sort of rebel against the system. I was bullied very badly in the first year at senior school, but then I was sort of very bright and did well in exams. But it was even years and odd years for some peculiar reason. Although I'd studied French and German, they didn't let me do Latin or

English Literature, therefore there was no way I could go to university and do English or Arts so I got stuck in the science stream. I was just as good at science anyway, although I didn't really work very hard. I've got a very good memory and about three weeks before the exams came round I used to sit and get the notebooks out, write out a page of it, read it and then write it out again and then it was committed to memory.

Since it was the Sixties, did you bother to turn up to your final exams and get your A-levels?

Oh yes. Applied maths and physics. I wanted to do A-level German but nobody guided me into that because the system was very much 'girls and boys'. The boys did sciences, the girls did art and things like that. And the science master said we've got a shortage of scientists, therefore all you boys are going to do science — which was totally inappropriate. Well not exactly inappropriate, but I did want to do German at university. They said I had to sit yet another exam for that, to which I said, "Sod that, I'm not doing it." So I signed up instead for mathematic statistics at Leicester University.

Did you finish the degree?

Yeah.

That makes you rare for your generation.

Growing up in a council house and going to university, I suppose so . . . It didn't occur to me at the time.

Yours — and the baby boomers before you — was a generation where so many people didn't even bother finishing their O-levels, they just dived in because there were so many opportunities around.

But my mother was typical of her own generation too: determined that I was going to go to university. So I did. I was one of three, and the eldest.

There was more pressure on you perhaps?

Possibly.

So where did the music start creeping in?

I played piano when I was a kid — when I was eleven years old I started taking lessons. Fortunately, or unfortunately, my piano teacher encouraged me to play what I wanted to play, which was the pop songs of the day rather than actually studying classical piano. The curious thing is I've often found that people who study classical piano find it hard to write songs as such. We've had some wonderful piano players with us in the band, but people like Rick Wakeman and Blue Weaver find writing songs difficult. They can write melodies but then writing words to go with them seems difficult, putting the two together.

At school I got on okay with the school music teacher, Mr Brookes, but the school music lesson was us sitting listening to 'Solveig's Song' *[from Peer Gynt by Edvard Grieg, 1875]* which I can remember to this day because he played it every term. We were maybe encouraged to come up with a melody and write the notes down, but the music lessons weren't encouraging. I had the idea I wanted to play clarinet but they were too expensive to buy. In the end I gave up my piano lessons because every time somebody came round the house my mother made me sit there and play for them — and I hated it, absolutely loathed it. So I stopped doing piano. And then Lonnie Donegan came along and that was it. I heard his music and wanted a guitar and so I started to play the guitar.

At school were loads of other kids picking up guitars and starting up bands?

No, it was really just *[guitarist & songwriter]* Tony Hooper and myself who formed a band. We bought guitars and sat in the common room playing them. We joined the school orchestra for one concert but it was awful. We were the two rebels. I always had this "I'll show you" streak in me somehow and it made me more determined.

So making a living out of music seemed logical given that music was one of the things that gave that rebelliousness an acceptable face in the Sixties.

Yes, but I didn't make my living out of music to start with. At college I was playing music as well as running the jazz and folk clubs. But when I left I had to get a job, so I went into advertising where, because I'd got the degree in maths and statistics, I became a media researcher. I then went to work for a company doing printing for local newspapers, and became a specialist in the local press. I can still tell you the title of every local newspaper left in the country, and probably its print dimensions and circulation too! After that I set up my own company doing marketing surveys. Remember I was very, very young and gradually playing more and more music at the same time as working at the company, so inevitably one had to give way to the other.

Music took over because it started appearing everywhere. I just couldn't carry on in business with my hair getting longer and longer despite the fact I was doing surveys for local newspaper groups, and they were being written up in *Marketing Week* and *The Financial Times* and so on. So I packed it up and went into playing music full-time, which coincided with us getting our first recording contract with Sonet Records in Denmark, and then there was no way I could carry on doing surveys. I did carry on in a way for a couple of years but that was incredibly difficult to do.

So, as I say, the music took over. But from the beginning I always brought a business element to running a band. I've still got the documented books of gigs all entered with receipts and accountancy fees and so on. And I still know people from those early days who gave us a bit of help. Colin Newman, the junior who did our first accounts when we were Strawberry Hill Boys, now runs Secret Films Records, for example. All those connections go back many years and I've maintained them.

What made everything unique for us was the fact that I was producing a radio programme for Danish radio. I first met Tom Brown — who was *[BBC radio DJ]* Alan Freeman's replacement on *Pick of the Pops* — in Denmark when I was doing one of my very few solo tours and we became good friends. Tom was doing a folk music programme for Danish radio because of his perfect English accent. When he came back to England, they didn't want to lose the programme on Danish radio so they asked him if he could do one once a month from London about the pop music and news that was happening there. Tom phoned me up and asked if I could help. I said yeah! And he said, "Well do you know any pop singers?" So I said, "I've got Pete Townshend's phone number." He went to interview Pete and then asked me if I'd be his producer. We produced that show from 1967 through to 1974.

We should have really been foreign correspondents based at *[former BBC World Service headquarters]* Bush House, but because we were doing a pop music programme we were put in Radio 1's brand new studios. So I got to know all of the DJs working there very well as well as the producers, like Johnny Dealing who was Head of Radio 1 at the time. John Peel we used to pass in the studio at night on Sundays when he was doing his programme and we were doing our ours. We were interviewing all sorts of people like Keith Emerson, Lonnie Donegan and Mary Hopkin, doing their Top 10s of all time. I've still got the recording of me interviewing David Bowie after his first American tour. I got to know them all — and that's how I learned an awful lot about the radio business which kept me in good stead for later.

So you're learning your craft and the business at the same time.

Exactly. Plus there was an enormous amount of pop records coming out —
Hendrix, the Stones, the Who — all those records passed through my hands
and I put them on the programme. So I was listening to all of this stuff at the
same time as I was actually playing music in the evenings. And then, when I
heard the Nick Drake album *[Five Leaves Left, 1969]* when it first came out, I
thought it was lovely and put it on the programme. Then when Strawbs
wanted to do string arrangements, I went to see Robert Kirby who did Nick's
arrangements, and we became his second ever client. It also meant I also got
to know the agents, like Black Heath Enterprises, and record label people like
Chris Blackwell. Because I was that close to it all and interviewing their
clients, they became interested because they could see me working as a
musician at the same time as running this radio show. All because I'd done the
radio show and I knew the records.

*So what does one do with all that on offer? Was there method in the way you
moved into the musical side of your life?*

No. All I ever wanted to do was to make a record. I'd already made a few as a
session musician — I played on an album by the Clancy Brothers & Tommy
Makem *[Sing of the Sea, 1968]* and people like Dave Travis who was a country
singer *[Pickin' on the Country Strings, 1968]*, playing banjo. When the band
played on a Steve Benbow album, that was the first time we ever had our name
on a record — Steve billed it as *Songs of Ireland by Steve Benbow with the
Strawberry Hill Boys*. Suddenly we had our name on a record even though it
wasn't ours. To be honest though, because we were a bluegrass band, and one
that wasn't writing many songs at the time, nobody in the UK was interested
in signing us up.

Then, as is well documented, I bumped into Sandy Denny in the
Troubadour in Earl's Court. I invited her to join the group, she said yes, we
went down and had one rehearsal, then we made some demos at Cecil Sharp
House which went over to Denmark to Karl Emil Knudsen — owner of *[record
label]* Sonet Denmark — who said they were the best thing he'd heard since
the Beatles (which was obviously very flattering!) and he signed us up. We
went to Denmark and made the record, and then it was my job to go and sell
it to a UK company, which is not the way things usually operate. Usually the
manager does it but because I knew the people in the business I was given the
job.

But as a musician, you can't actually go and sell your own product. You've
got to have this intermediary in between you, who can negotiate on your

behalf when things go wrong with the record company or just to get a better deal. Physically going out to sell your own record to a record company is incredibly difficult. But I managed it somehow and sold it to Phil Solomon at the record label Major Minor — Phil had a Top 40 hit with David McWilliams' 'The Days of Pearly Spencer' [*Solomon also managed acts such as the Bachelors, Van Morrison's Them and the Dubliners*]. And then, as soon as I got Phil interested, Sandy said, "I don't want to be a pop singer. I'm going to join Fairport Convention." It broke my heart at the time. I could see her point of view, but I could equally see our point of view. We sang well together — Tony, myself and her — and I thought the image was good, but she just didn't want to be Dusty Springfield, although frankly, she would have been equally as successful as Dusty in the jazz and mega pop vein. She had the voice for it. In fact she could sing anything.

Potentially there was a fruitful writing partnership between the three of you?

Not really. When we started out, I wrote most of the songs and then we decided that we were going to be like everyone else did at the time and be the new Lennon & McCartney. But I soon realised that I was writing most of the songs and giving away half of them. So that didn't last very long. Sandy did write 'Who Knows Where the Time Goes', which we were utterly mesmerised by. In fact Sandy sang and played it so well that I couldn't think of anything I could play on it that would add anything, so she did that track on her own, on *All Our Own Work [Sandy Denny and the Strawbs, 1967, unreleased until 1973]*. Although I saw Sandy many times in the years after that, we never ever thought of writing together. She covered one of my songs 'Two Weeks Last Summer', which I was thrilled with. She asked me to write another verse for it, which I did. But the reality of writing together never came about.

So what happened next, bandwise?

We were told about a guy called Gus Dudgeon who had just produced his first album — Ralph McTell's first album *Eight Frames a Second* [1968]. And so Tony said, "Well I'll have a word with Gus and see if he wants to be our producer." Gus did, and we went round to his flat, sang him the songs. He loved 'Oh How She Changed' and 'Oh Am I Dreaming', and he said, "Those are the two I want to record, and I think we need to orchestrate them." So he brought in the arranger he had worked with, Tony Visconti *[Eight Frames a Second was the first album Visconti arranged]*, and suddenly we had the two most successful producers of the Seventies working together on our first ever single.

Of course, the fact was that our record was made in the Sixties before anybody had actually heard of Gus Dudgeon and Tony Visconti. Still, there we were in 1968 recording our first single with those two, which was quite extraordinary. And off we went.

Strawbs went on from strength to strength, and gave you an unexpectedly versatile platform for your songwriting, which wasn't all introspected Tortured Starving Artist material, but highly visual mini-movies from you being out there in the Big Wide World, around and about in the Big Society.

They're all about that.

If you're a musician out on the road all the time and encountering a wide cross-section of humanity, you're catching a very different slant on life. It's that minstrel thing: you travel, you spread news and innovation to the populace. The annotations and observations in your book of lyrics Secrets, Stories & Songs *[2010] capture that spirit perfectly. What made you decide to do the book?*

I thought Bob Dylan's book was very good *[Lyrics: 1962-2001, 2004]* and I then started looking around at others. Obviously there's lots of lyric books for the Rodgers & Hammerstein sort of songwriters, but contemporary songwriters seemed to be somewhat under-represented by comparison. And then I got thinking that if I put out just a book of lyrics, people would still ask, "Well, what're the songs *about*?" So I figured I'd put a few little notes in. But as I jotted things down I started to realise that the songs meant an awful lot more than I'd ever thought they did. Of course I knew what each song was about — but after you add in all the details about them, they take on a life of their own.

'The Vision of the Lady in the Lake' *[Dragonfly, 1970]* is a good example. I was driving past the Hillfield Park Reservoir *[a nature reserve]* alongside the A41 in Barnet at seven o'clock in the morning. There was this lake shrouded in mist and it looked absolutely mysterious, and all of a sudden I dreamt up this whole legend-fantasy. The whole song came out of that one little experience. To add that type of background detail to the song makes it much more visual if you like. With 'Josephine, for Better or for Worse' *[Dragonfly]*, people might think "oh, he met some person called Josephine" but when you read the lyric of what it's about, what the song is about, it takes on a whole different characteristic — since it's really about the endurance of people.

As you're taking direct inspiration from tangible things, nothing is too oblique in terms of imagery.

Oh they're still oblique, because I don't necessarily give away all of the inspiration. That's for the next book!

Another duality, then, is that your songs are universal but also very, very British in feel even if there happen to be American or other influences — not only in content but also performance.

Interesting. In fact that never really occurred to me until recently when I read in the papers someone saying that it's much more natural for people nowadays to sing with an American accent. And I thought how bizarre, because I never have. That's something I've always tried to avoid. Even at a vocabulary level, there's probably only a couple of songs where I've had to use words like "ain't" and I've tried to avoid that one like the plague.

But that's British dialect too.

Not really.

Not even in songs?

I don't think so, no. Of course sometimes I need to abbreviate things because otherwise the language sounds unnatural. You do have to write in everyday speak but I try to avoid Americanisms. But then I am highly critical of myself — for example, on *Dragonfly*, I say "'til the sun comes shining through" gush, gush, gush! I must have seriously thought I was Robert Burns or one of the romantic poets, it really is so over the top.

But that's looking at words in the cold black and white of print. The lyrics take on a totally different life when they have the melody and arrangement behind them.

Absolutely. But the melody tends to detract from the lyrics and that was a convincing reason for putting a spoken-word CD of the lyrics in the back of the book.

So how did they look to you once you'd disassociated the melodies?

The storylines are incredibly strong. 'The Vision of the Lady in the Lake' as a spoken word piece is a pure story. I've had people round who are not in the slightly bit interested in Strawb music or anything like that, but who can listen to its story and are mesmerised by it, and say "put on more!" The lyrics take on a whole different context when you listen to them as spoken word.

I wanted to do a collection of lyrics because I have so many of them. There's nearly 250 songs there, and I've put in stuff that hasn't been found before. A lot of it is frankly not brilliant, but the interests of being complete also made me think it was important to show people how writing works. I started writing *not* things like "I love you babe" but instead starting with a feeling and then seeing how it all gradually shuffles into a pattern. In the book you can see how that has evolved.

I also realised that putting the songs together this way is essentially autobiographical. Not only is this a song, it's also part of a life, although it's not so spelled out. Putting the songs in chapters gives me the framework for that autobiography but I'm not going to make it just go from beginning to end. We jump around and that's where the interesting parts come in. What's especially interesting is the hiatus of when I worked in the radio business — don't forget I stopped for twenty years. If you look at the index, you can see that I list all the dates, from 1967 to '77 all the way through, and then suddenly the songs stop in 1978 and they only start again in 2001.

With the songwriting hiccup of a musical in 1990.

Some songwriting yes, but it doesn't really start again in any significant way. That's a consistent twenty-year gap and of the two albums from that period, *Don't Say Goodbye [1987]* and *Ringing Down the Years [1991]*, there's in reality only eight new songs.

That's all you wrote in those twenty years?

That was it.

Impressive to think how you picked it all up again as if the fallow years had never happened. When you're young, you're thinking you've got keep churning it out because if you stop, the muse will abandon you, your mojo will wilt, the well of inspiration will dry and you'll never get any of it back again.

It was different for me. I had to keep going in the Seventies writing songs, because we had to keep making records. We were making one every nine months and the pressure was immense to keep coming up with stuff. It became increasingly difficult. And then when I stopped playing, after I went into the radio business, I realised that all of those eight songs from that twenty-year period were written on a piano. Not one guitar song there. In fact I hardly ever touched the guitar then, for the simple reason that I wasn't travelling. I didn't have the inspiration, plus because I was working in a totally different environment there wasn't the need to write songs.

Basically you weren't sitting in the back of a tour bus strumming as the world passed by your window.

Exactly. There was no need to write and there was no drive, no pressure on me to write the constant flow of songs needed to make an album. I only did it because particular songs needed to be written. So that was the time when I wrote — I needed to write — the Sandy Denny song 'Ringing Down the Years'.

What about the musical? We're cheating on the song count here!

Uncle Tom Cobley & All was on for a week at the Drum Theatre in Plymouth. There was a friend of mine, Chris Smith, who used to be a lighting designer on the road, and he came round one day and said, "Look there's this competition for a new musical in Plymouth, do you fancy writing something?" And I said, "Well I haven't really got time." But he said, "Well I've got the idea for a musical about Uncle Tom Cobley *[a character from the Devon folk song 'Widecombe Fair']*. It's for children." So I said, "I'll tell you what, come round tonight and I'll see what I can do."

Chris had some of the words and I started strumming along, and in that one evening I wrote all the melodies for the songs we had then. I still have no idea how that happened. Then Chris suddenly said, "Oh we need a song in here to link it along." So I strummed the guitar again and out came completely new words too which we used. That particular song was sung by Tom Cobley and the Gypsy Queen: "It was back along a summer of forty years / I'll tell you a story to bring you tears / The likes of a romance so few hears / I long for my long lost love. / She had startling eyes of sapphire blue / She lived in a house where camellias grew / But where she came from no one knew / I long for my long lost love. / He stood as tall as the mighty oak / And smelled as keen as the forest smoke / Russet cheeks and chestnut hair. / I know that voice somewhere. / I loved a man who burst with pride / Rooted deep in the countryside."

All that came out in five minutes — because I needed to do it. The need to write a song was there simply because I had to come up with something. I instinctively went straight into songwriting mode, and out it came. That line "She had startling eyes of sapphire blue, lived in a house where camellias grew", I still don't know where it came from, it was just there.

You once told me that you met Lionel Bart around the same time — a wonderful coincidence. So what happened to Uncle Tom Cobley?

The only thing that exists is a handheld video of the whole stage show. It lasted about an hour. Nobody may ever hear it again but I can sing the whole show to you now: "You've got to help yourself / Get along in this world / Pick a pocket / Skin a rabbit /Help yourself. / Help yourself / Get along in this world / I don't give a toss / It's not my loss / Help yourself. / . . . No one gives you nothing / In this mean old world / Don't take it all for granted / Help yourself!"

Chris sent it to *[musicals producer]* Cameron Macintosh, who wrote back: "Unfortunately the storyline is too parochial, it's too West Country and it won't transfer to somewhere like the West End." But he loved the melodies and loved the tunes. And that was it.

So, when I need to, I can write incredibly quickly, but at other times I can take a lot of time going through, poring through the words of a song and crossing things out. The point here is that some of songs write themselves.

For example, one time we went up to Scotland to Fort William for the New Year. That's at the head of Loch Shiel, and we tried to get up Ben Nevis but couldn't because the mist was down. In fact I never ever did see the whole of Ben Nevis. When I got back to the hotel that day, I wrote down these notes: "Crossing the wire bridge / To the cottage in the glen / Wading through the waterfalls / Water gushing down the rocks / In a joyous torrent."

Later on, I sat with *[Strawbs bassist]* Chas Cronk in my cottage in Devon and said I'd got an idea for some words, but I didn't have the notes from Scotland with me. So as Chas played the chords, I scrawled down completely new words in as much time as it takes to write them: "The watchers on the hillside stand in silence / As the dawn appears / Then they gather to their horses in an instant / As a sun-shaft sears / Through the morning mist which hangs low in the valleys / Like a serpent's tail / Both poisonous to enemies and heroes / In the soldier's tail." Chas stopped and asked, "Where did that come from?" Once again I had to admit, "I've no idea." But later as I was going through my papers to put the lyrics book together, the notes suddenly turned up. So these are the first impressions that gave rise to the later song, in this case 'The Soldier's Tale' *[Deep Cuts, 1976]*.

So none of it was lost, it was all in there.

It was all buried deep in the subconscious. In fact, the next day on that Scottish trip we drove out ahead of Loch Shiel to the Glenfinnan Monument *[marks the beginning of the Jacobite Rising in the 1745 when Bonnie Prince Charlie raised his standard on the shores of the loch]*, and I started to think about Bonnie Prince Charlie. So that impression of the Young Pretender in 'The Soldier's Tale' would be a total mystery to anybody. But now in the book, with the inclusion of those notes in the explanation of the song, people can see where I got that idea from. I hope it'll encourage other people to do what I do, to make notes about what you're seeing around you, jot them down.

Again, a whole load of notes gave us the song 'A Glimpse of Heaven' on the very early album *From the Witchwood [1971]*: "The side of the hill was a patchwork quilt / Neatly stitched with gorse hedges and old stone walls / The trees were bare just waiting for spring / To whisper its magic words / Before they conjured up strings of bright green handkerchiefs / The imprint of the tractor wheels could clearly be seen / In the mud on the road."

That's more than displaying the mechanical craft. That's revealing the underlying, physical focus of the thought processes at work.

That's exactly what I wanted to explain. Suddenly I thought this is really interesting for the reader. It makes the song more interesting because you can see the thought process. When I started on the lyrics book, I did wonder am I giving too much away? But I thought long and hard about it, and concluded no, tell people where it came from. If there's a bit I don't want to explain then I won't explain it and it'll stay mysterious.

In the book you've only put in what you felt was necessary, on the other hand the volume itself is pretty full-on physically.

We're lucky because of Tony Hamilton, who I've known for donkey's years. Our first job together was when we published a radio advertisers' guide back in 1980 when I went into the radio business. He now runs his own marketing company. Since he also writes books, he was the one who said I ought to do one too. He put me on to the idea of digital printing and that didn't work, so I'm glad we went full colour offset.

That's the sort of go-it-alone get-up-and-go that you've been doing for a while.

Definitely. We started as a little record company in 2004. We did the Edinburgh Festival Fringe as Acoustic Strawbs and we thought we'd better make a record so we made a record *[Full Bloom, 2004]* and release it ourselves. To date that's now sold almost 10,000 and so it trickles on. From a small start, we've now got thirty-odd albums in the catalogue.

How did you manage to grab back your previous albums from the Machine?

It's taken time. I've only managed to get one back from Universal and that was my own solo album *Two Weeks Last Summer [1972].* To do that I had to go through John Kennedy, who was head at Universal UK, and told him that I was having terrible trouble. He wrote a letter and the next thing I know the head of business affairs had said, "Come in and see me when you're in Los Angeles. I'm going to write this contract myself but don't ever tell anybody!"

I can't get the rest of the Universal ones back, but almost everything else from before that we've grabbed back. The later Polydor albums were also due to us, and now the only one I haven't got back yet from that period is the Arista album *Deadlines [1977]* — and I think if the contract was anything like the Polydor contract then we'll be able to get that as well. I've also bought all my songs back from the liquidator, so I own them all now.

So you own the publishing to all your songs now?

About 90 per cent of them.

That must have required a huge amount of detective work. Or is it more like fishing where you sit and wait for the right opportunity to pop up?

No. We were pushing at the door, and our management suddenly realised that if they weren't careful something was going to happen. I was using *[accountancy group]* KPMG as a battering ram. But that was when I was in the radio business where I was surrounded by people like Sir Ian Amory, the chairman of DevonAir Radio, which all had a degree of considerable weight about it. Then I got a note saying they would sell the songs. So I bought them back. Best thing I ever did in my life.

A lot of songwriters can but envy you.

My publishing is all under one umbrella. But I did make one dreadful mistake and people should take note of this. My publishing is under a trading name, Old School Songs, but it's not Old School Songs *Limited.* If it was 'Old School Songs Ltd', I could sell that company and I could apply taper relief over seven years and so the tax on it would be virtually nil. But because it belongs to me as an individual, I have to pay capital gains tax on it.

It's a sole trader name.

It's David Cousins' trading name. So people should take advice on when they set up their own company. Take legal or accountancy advice. Not that I want to sell my catalogue, but it is an asset, it's there should I ever need to sell it. Of course you will pay regular tax on it, but if you ever want to sell it as an asset then that's when you hit capital gains tax.

The variants are interesting. Somebody said they wanted to acquire my catalogue the other day. I replied, "I don't want to sell 100 per cent of it." But the offer was, "Oh no, we only buy fifty per cent of your catalogue. We buy the publisher's share, you keep your writer's share." They were prepared to buy just the publisher's share, because that way they control the catalogue.

We could look at Paul McCartney who's kept missing out on the rights to his own catalogue of songs. With all the weight of his position and money and it's still posed a huge challenge for him, although now with the 1978 copyright clause in the USA, parts of that catalogue may start to creep back into his hands.

In fact, in the early days when they made *[Beatles publisher]* Northern Songs public *[1965]* I was going to buy shares in it. The worse thing I didn't do. But at least we were one of the very first groups to ever set up our own publishing company. We had Strawberry Music from day one. I recently found a contract stating that we actually owned 'Who Knows Where the Time Goes' at the time, all under the umbrella of Strawberry Music. I also found the first inquiry from Judy Collins when she covered the song, asking for a release of our release of that title. It didn't mean anything at the time. Who was Judy Collins? I didn't know. I do now. But that wasn't a problem because we owned those songs. I then absorbed some of them into another catalogue — unfortunately that company got wound up in 1978. But in the end, I bought them all back again in 1986/87.

So basically in 1978 the publishing company liquidated in order to—

—take the money out! It was a quarter of a million dollars. The publishers got their advance and I didn't see one penny of it. So that money just went to the ether. So in terms of songwriting, this book ought to be at least partly on legal affairs!

I'm still meeting songwriters who are paying off tied deals, even recent high-profile casualties like Alannah Myles.

You always have to tell yourself to keep tabs on it all. When we were touring in the States, all those years ago, we were signed to A&M and our management kept getting tour advances from A&M to help pay for everything. When you're touring round you think, "Oh good, we're getting seventy quid a week." Since we didn't earn directly from the band, we were quite happy to be able that way to afford staying in nice hotels and so on. But then you suddenly realise that there are no royalties coming to you. It was only ten years or so ago that we found out that we'd broken all of those advances, that we'd sold enough records and earned the advances back. We had started earning royalties and still do to this day. So even the old Universal catalogue which we haven't got back yet, at least we're earning money on that.

What was the bigger financial picture when you toured places like North America in the Seventies? If the management and labels were separating you from your rightful income, did they also hammer you with tax bills when you came back, which you wouldn't have been able to account for?

They tried to. The management wound up Strawbs Ltd and said that any tax due was down to the band. And fortunately *[keyboardist]* Andy Richards, who was one of the last to join the band, actually had a contract which stipulated that his tax was paid for out of the money which he earned. It was post-tax. So when we went to a tax tribunal we were able to show that contract and ask why should he be any different to us. And so the management got the tax bill back . . . and their response was to wind up the company. So again, you have to be incredibly careful.

If we can return to doing your own publishing. What led you to that, since when you started off it was very rare for songwriters to dare to challenge the system by setting up on their own? Was it simply the general innocence at the time of having the freedom to do whatever you set out to do?

No. I just wanted to have a company that owned my own songs, but at the time I didn't know anybody else that did it. Don't forget that this was 1967/68.

Interestingly, that was the same period when Quincy Jones did likewise in America, when he was just setting out as a recording artist and found himself confronted with his first contract.

People forget, but a copyright exists the minute you put pen to paper and you write a few words. I'm not a hoarder but every bit of paper I get I tend to stick in a drawer and shove in a box. So I've got all of the correspondence in a huge file like that in a garage from the Seventies with all of it documented. I've got all of our old BBC contracts. And most of my diaries. Even rough scraps of paper with little notes about songs are all shoved in a file. That's your copyright, you own it. It's only when you assign that copyright to somebody else or sign it away for good that you lose it. But that's what people used to do, and some of mine are still signed away for life. I still get the odd royalties on them but not very much.

The people I know who have got hold of their own catalogue or who are building up new songs, they tend now to do two-year-style contracts. They go to a publishing company, get an advance on the songs which they don't have to pay back at the end of two years. Personally, I won't ask for an advance because I think I'll get a better royalty rate. If I'd asked Sony for an advance when I moved my publishing to them, they would have said, "Yeah we'll give it to you, but we want 20 per cent for collecting." Because I didn't want an advance, they only charged 15 per cent. So it's another way of looking at it. You see, if you get an advance then the automatic thing is go out and spend it.

Better to harvest than to store.

That should be rule number one, exactly. No advances. Unless you know they're not going to sell anything, in which case take the money and run. But then that would be downgrading your own product. In reality, many song publishers don't do much but just wait for the money to come in, and the songwriter doesn't get a penny until they've earned fifty quid. And they'll need to wait a long time if some songs only earn a couple of quid a year. So in a hundred years' time you might get something. Some of the boys in the band signed exclusive songwriting agreements, but then the songs got sold to another company and now they don't even get their writer's share of it, they don't get nothing because they signed away that copyright, the full copyright.

So as long as they're in a contractual relationship with that first publisher they do get income . . .

They would get 50 per cent of it, but as soon as that company sells the copyright, if you've already sold all your rights then they can sell all those rights to another company and you lose all connection with those rights. As a lawyer once very clearly told me, it's an absolute disgrace in copyright terms but there's nothing you can do about it.

A slightly longer-term challenge is all the copyright on recordings coming up. After pressure rom people like Cliff Richard, the Beatles and the still mighty record companies, the European Union extended this from fifty years to seventy years. It benefits Cliff & Co but it further delays the chance of a musician controlling their recordings and so uniformly screws most other recording artists.

It's disgraceful, totally wrong. And this at the time when musicians and their families most need it. It's not the Cliffs and the Beatles — they're all pretty well loaded and well-heeled for their retirement — but it's the smaller artists that will suffer, those who need income at the later stage of their career. The odd fifty quid here or a hundred quid there from any type of royalties makes a heck of a difference.

Since we started our own company, we go through MCPS *[UK copyright collection society Mechanical-Copyright Protection Society, part of PRS for Music]* and we pay royalties on all our own records that we press. Eight per cent of the dealer price of the record goes to MCPS, who charge their 10 per cent, then it gets sent to Sony who collect it and administer it for me, or for me and the other writers on the album. Sony take their 15 per cent then send it back to us. So the more records we're generating, the more publishing revenue we're generating for ourselves. So it's a circular process that it has provided essentially a pension fund that was not expected. It's self-perpetuating in a way: the more records we put out, the more interviews you do on the radio, the more they play the music, you get more royalties.

It's turned out to be a significant revenue stream.

Yes. But that's only because we own our own publishing. If we were giving 50 per cent of that money away then it wouldn't be so good. It is an asset, so I would advise every songwriter to keep their own copyrights if they possibly can. Don't give them away and let somebody administer them for you, do a deal instead whereby you pay a bit extra if they get a cover version for you then, instead of charging 10-15 per cent for administering the copyright and collecting the money, you pay them 25 per cent if they get a cover. That's the way the business should be. It just takes time to organise it right.

Does that only come from experience, or can a young songwriter listen to your advice and start doing something about it immediately?

I think they would understand what I'm saying, but of course your own experience is important. Personally, I picked up all sorts of fascinating information over the years. Like when they very first made records — on cylinders — and somebody had said, "Well hang on what about the person who wrote the song? Should they get something?" "Hmm, give them 5 per cent." So the songwriter got 5 per cent. Then double-sided records came out, and they said, "Hang on there's a songwriter on each side. We've got the A-side, and that gets 5 per cent. What about the person who wrote the song on the B-side?" "Well, give them a quarter of the 5 per cent." So that was 1.25 per cent so the total royalty payable became 6.25 per cent. But it was divided equally between the A and the B side. And that was where the industry standard rate 6.25 percent came from. It was only a few years ago when it was renegotiated and it went up to 8 per cent, but that traditional calculation goes back to the very beginning of making records.

In a way, the digital world has gone full circle back to that first single side.

True, but in America they viewed things differently. They paid ten cents a track on the record for mechanical royalties. But because I wrote something like 'The Antique Suite' *[Just a Collection of Antiques and Curios, 1970]* at twelve minutes-plus long, I had to ask myself, hang on, that's on one side and it's something like 6 to 8 per cent divided by 2 to 3 per cent. In America if I've got one song that lasts twelve minutes and there's just two others on side one of the record that last three minutes, I'm not making much at all for my time. So I divided that one into four sections and called it a suite. That made four separate songs within the one song. Even though that was 1970, you still had to think. That's why an awful lot of my songs are done like that. Now you know, you can see why.

'Ghosts' has four bits in it.

'The Life Auction' is in two bits, 'Blue Angel' three.

I can see a trend here.

You had to be ahead of the game.

So a device that was lambasted for being pretentious in fact was a hardnosed "let's take on the American accounting system" system.

Of course. And I did get slagged off for it being seen as pretentious. But it's like being a grocer isn't it, a corner shop: nickels and dimes, pennies and farthings. That grocer's attitude has come in handy in so many other areas, such as when we did our boxed set *[A Taste of Strawbs, 2006, compiled with Dick Greener]*. We spent a lot of time on the design and there was a cash investment of 35,000 quid on that. By planning for pre-sales we got that money back.

Was that £35,000 a factor that you deliberately budgeted for?

I budgeted exactly what it was going to cost. We sweated a bit!
Did you include marketing in the budget for the Secrets, Stories & Songs book?

I built in a bit of a budget for promotion. There were other costs to take into consideration like wanting heavyweight quality paper to print on, which took a huge chunk but so be it. Just so long as I break even on the first orders. Once I've done that, anything else that comes in is put back into the company.

As a marketing tool in itself, the lyrics book has the potential to hit the parts that other marketing tools can't.

It has. And people pick that up. They read through it, find something interesting and they may well then just want the album. Some of those albums aren't ours, as I've explained, but hopefully they'll want the later Witchwood albums. A good example is our next-door neighbour, a part-time Frank Sinatra impersonator who sings in the pub to backing tracks. He doesn't really know anything about our music but when he heard the spoken-word stuff from the book after we'd had a few drinks late at night, he was riveted.

That makes sense to me, because you write vignettes and stories that absolutely need to be framed within a more complex level of language than that found in your average pop or rock song. It's no surprise to find that they work equally well in the setting of a spoken word recording as well as their original musical arrangements.

It gives you a whole different interpretation. For the CD accompanying the book, I came up with seventeen sets of lyrics to give the best idea of it.

Secrets, Stories & Songs highlights in many ways what being a singer-songwriter is all about: an individual who does songs from the heart, with a personal vision yet they're not soppy love songs—

Well, they *can* be soppy love songs.

—as opposed to the revolutionary types who write songs about politics, injustice and not about themselves. Although they can do that from the heart too.

I have written about politics but I don't think half the time people realise it — wider issues too — and I still am, even more so than ever. 'Revenge (Can Be

So Sweet)' *[Dancing to the Devil's Beat, 2009]* is about how throughout history we've seen the rise and fall of civilisations, so it's "A confluence of rivers / Once flowed out to the sea / Where forests grew abundant / And nature's gifts were free / Man built his mighty temples / And prayed at his own feet / But the desert sands were shifting / Revenge can be so sweet." So that's how we're destroying the world.

It works in other ways too. 'Copenhagen' *[Dancing to the Devil's Beat]* was written about Sandy Denny. So "Several years ago / A day in early spring / In a Copenhagen bar / I heard a skylark sing" sounds very simplistic, but then "In a slow-speed silent movie / There's a snow-kissed winter scene / Your pretty face / Is glistening with tears", then "In that half-remembered moment / Silent and serene / The town hall bells / Are chiming down the years." And this is all about her drawing the picture of us on the pavement: "A simple pack of crayons / A pavement master class / On a city centre street / Our fortunes came to pass. / They washed away your cartoons / In the Copenhagen rain / You were drifting in the mull of broken dreams. / A thin veneer of laughter / Hid the tantrums and the pain / A photograph / Is seldom what it seems." Because that was her. She did have tantrums and she did have a lot of angst in her life, and I know why.

If I hadn't had that picture of Sandy in my mind I wouldn't have been able to write those words. We were in Copenhagen and Chas was playing this tune, and I suddenly thought it would work with the story of being in Copenhagen with Sandy forty years before. We went round to Tivoli Gardens and had a look at where we'd played then and it brought back all these memories. The words just came out of the ether somehow and it was lovely to put them down in a song like that.

And they're still relevant too.

Yes. And then there's 'Beneath the Angry Sky' *[Dancing to the Devil's Beat]*: "War planes fly in terror waves / Orders are withdrawn / Horses rear with nostrils flared / A child is stillborn. / All afternoon, as hell pours down / Families stand like rock / Holding hands in fear and rage / Reeling with the shock." Not everyone would get the background unless I wrote in the lyrics book that in early 2000 I met up with *[Strawbs keyboard player]* Blue Weaver in Madrid and we decided to visit the Prado Museum where Picasso's painting 'Guernica' is one of the main attractions. That helps explain "Nothing moves, the town lies still / Behind its ruined face / A single oak defiant / In the silent marketplace." The oak tree is a symbol of Catalonia, although people might think Dave was just ranting about war.

Every song's got something else in it. Look at 'Wish You Were Here' *[The Boy in the Sailor Suit, 2007]*: "A view along the promenade, tinted pastel shades

/ Pictures of Madonna in her many masquerades / The young girl in her wedding dress / The vicar with a beer / A postcard from a long lost friend / Wish you were here." In the Ship pub where I live in Deal there are some tinted pastel postcards and I thought oh I'll write a song about those. And then the vicar is a friend of ours — well he's not a vicar any more but he was a vicar — so he appears in the song too. He doesn't know he appears in the song, but he does appear.

He knows now.

No he doesn't. He probably wouldn't get it unless I told him. And there's a song on the same album about my mum, 'The Smile You Left Behind': "At Mr Sainsbury's counter / She looked cute / The dairy maid / Met the boy in the sailor suit." My mum and dad — and *[pointing at family photo on wall]* there's my dad.

He looks so young — the boy in the sailor suit.

Yes. I have to write from a starting point, it doesn't have to be purely autobiographical but I do have to have *something* to write about, I can't just conjure up words out of the blue that mean nothing. Of course I have done that sort of thing before, but those songs are the ones that aren't successful.

I suppose that's what they call artistic 'truth'. People in theatre and art certainly talk about the truth in their own works. In a luvvie context it doesn't always ring true and seems a little over-egging things, but ultimately there has to be a 'truth' in a creative work because you're talking to an audience, with an awareness of that audience. It has to come from yourself and yet you're not just doing it for yourself, are you?

No. In fact, the astonishing thing is that people identify with my songs. They don't necessarily know what the songs are about but they can identify with the words. They give a lot of people comfort, and — this is not being pretentious in any way — I cannot tell you the number of people that have come up to me in America and said, "Your song 'The Winter Long', the last part of 'Autumn' *[Hero and Heroine, 1974]*, was our wedding song, the song that we walked down the aisle to. You know, 'Hold on to me I'll hold on to you'!" 'Grace Darling' *[Ghosts, 1975]* is another song that people have got married to. I've also had people write to me with highly personal things like: "I was in hospital having electric shock treatment and the only comfort I got was from listening to your songs."

That shows a degree of spirituality about the songs. I'm not a devoutly religious person but I do get moved by spiritual matters. Like going to Midnight Mass in the high-church Church of England church opposite the pub, very convenient. The smell of the incense and the archaic feel of the hymns is incredibly atmospheric, so I can write a song like 'Bringing in the Harvest' *[The Boy in the Sailor Suit]* which is pretty much a hymn as much as any hymn you'll ever hear, written about bringing in the harvest on the Kent coast. "Bringing in the harvest / We are gathering the grain / Weathered by the sun / And gently swollen by the rain / Golden days of summer gladness / Blood-red poppies tinged with sadness / Wheatfields gently waving / From a wartime aerodrome / Here's to those who work the fields / To bring the harvest home." I'd love to have somebody cover it as an actual hymn.

It hearkens back to 'We Plough the Fields and Scatter'.

A hymn! Something I can only write by driving around to look at old buildings and to go into old churches. "Bringing in the harvest / All the bounties of the deep / Rising from the seabed sands / Where shipwrecked sailors sleep." Living round here in Kent we've got the Goodwin Sands just off the coast. "Twisting currents test the stranger / Gathering storms bring hidden danger / A shift of wind can snap the teeth / Of any mermaid's comb / Here's to those who risk their lives / To bring the harvest home."

You almost can hear the pump organ behind that, can't you?

It's got one on the record. But these songs, as I say, are autobiographical, I like them for what I feel. And the pleasure I've got out of that over the years is the number of people who've been touched. But it doesn't happen anywhere near so much in Britain as it does in America. It doesn't matter if you don't sell millions of records, it's more important to have people who say they've gained some spiritual comfort from the songs.

In a way, that geographical factor makes sense, i.e. in America your songs will be less unfettered in hitting the heart since there's more of a folk (i.e. common cultural experience) element in everything Americans do around their music. So if you're labelled a 'folkie', in the UK that pigeonholes you into a genre while in America it more usefully indicates the universal grassroots appeal in your writing which leaves a door open in each song, no matter how electric it gets, thanks to the words. Which is why, when you refer to going acoustic as a band or doing spoken word, the noise comes down and the words naturally—

—the words go up. The words become more apparent. And in the book I explain all that, not what the words are about but a little introduction to the songs, and people feel that they're part of it.

You've always also done that live, haven't you?

I've always done it, even when I played with the electric band.

Most groups tend not to do that until they're way past their prime. But that's the art of the raconteur, which is hardly the same thing.

Exactly. You see, in the early days we did get carried away with being part of the 'hit culture'. It was exciting to have hit records and attract big audiences. But we always maintained that carrying on with talking to people. The only trouble was that an element of comedy crept into it, which I really didn't want to do any more because, live, Strawbs became more like a comedy show with musical interludes. It was ghastly. And when I wanted to stop, the band didn't want to, because the people were loving the shows. Now you look back and listen to recordings, and it really was a bit crass. As they say in the reviews, embarrassing. But now we can be serious, we can be humorous, equally.

I still crack jokes onstage but that doesn't matter since the songs are still intense songs. A good example is 'Grave New World' *[Grave New World, 1971]*, which was written about Bloody Sunday, something that I never specifically spelled out — although I have done precisely that in the lyrics book. People probably just heard me screaming "May you rot in your grave!" without realising that was what it was, which was a bit of a shame. And 'The Hangman and the Papist' *[From the Witchwood]* was written about the escalating violence the year before Bloody Sunday in Northern Ireland. And there we were, doing a song like that on *Top of the Pops [1971]*. Extraordinary.

Then a year later Paul McCartney hardly made it easy for himself with Wings' debut single 'Give Ireland Back to the Irish'. He overstated it, didn't he? And there was no Top of the Pops appearance since that particular song earned him membership of the Banned by the BBC Club on the evidence of its title alone! Pertinently, that's something that rarely happened to later British singer-songwriters, since the guys and gals who followed with similar attitude-to-be-reckoned-with tended to operate out of fully fledged electric bands like the Cure and the Smiths. You were very much a harbinger of it all, evidently. But that shift into bands for singer-songwriters meant that subsequent generations have found it hard to form any creative nucleus or movement with each other.

The 'classic' singer-songwriter that did emerge from it all and came next was Billy Bragg. The first time I saw him I thought he was brilliant. I thought Christ who is this bloke? Then I saw him in Canada, doing the same sort of show but this time I felt he was overpoliticising everything. Still, he has made a very good living out of doing that. I also think some of Elvis Costello's melodies are great. They say he writes vindictive lyrics but there's a lot more in there.

I'd say that Bragg and Costello were enabled to their respective thrones via the Highlander Syndrome peculiar to the UK, i.e. there can only be one. In Bragg's case particularly it seems the thinking was, "If we're going to unleash English (i.e. not Celtic) folk outside of the Cecil Sharp circuit, then let it be political, and if it be so, then we shall permit no one else to hog the podium." That's not in line with your particular legacy and yet you do seem to have been placed too in a league of your own, which must create certain obstacles in reaching out to the new generations.

Absolutely. My songs aren't mainstream songs. I've had a couple of hits like 'Lay Down' and 'Shine on Silver Sun' but they're not mainstream, although there are an awful lot of people out there who identify with the likes of 'Grave New World' or 'The Hangman and the Papist'. Imagine going onstage and singing 'Hangman' and it still gets the biggest cheer of the night for us. It's unbelievable. And it's not an easy song. It's not user-friendly. It's violent, aggressive.

And that's the sort of hi-definition contrast that defines your music . . .

The whole way through! Even when our first album *Strawbs [1969]* came out it wasn't our first one. If Sandy Denny and the Strawbs *[All Our Own Work, recorded 1967, released 1973]* had come out as our first record my whole life might have gone off on a totally different path. Because I do believe that on the Sandy Denny and the Strawbs album there were a couple of songs that would have been hit singles in that era. 'On My Way' and 'All I Need Is You' were good pop songs, they sounded fresh, original and listening to them now I think they were really good. But when the album came out six years later, it sounded dated because we'd all moved on.

So our first record was actually our second album, by which time we'd learnt a bit more about recording in a studio. We had Gus Dudgeon producing — remember that he had only just done his first album with Ralph McTell as producer and we were his second. We also had Tony Visconti doing arrangements, which is unbelievable. And then Gus said, "I don't like the sound of your voice, I'm mixing you down. People don't want that, let them read the words on the sleeve." To which I replied, "You know what you can do, son." So anyway we parted company and Tony took over the production and he was much more sympathetic and understanding.

Yes I don't have a great voice but I've got an individual voice. Well, in America I'm an individual, here I *grate*. Again it's very different the reaction in the UK to America. Bizarre. It's always been the same.

So even that second-but-first album wasn't as it seemed?

No it wasn't. The first version had already been turned down by A&M because we had all the ballads that we'd done with Sandy recorded with a 32-piece string section. The label thought the songs sounded gushing and said, "We didn't sign you for this, we signed you for 'Oh How She Changed' and 'Or Am I Dreaming' " — which were much more medieval because I'd moved on from those types of songs. I thought we were doing the pop songs but they said, "No we don't want these, go and record some more of what we do want." So I recorded songs like 'The Man Who Called Himself Jesus', and when *Strawbs* came out, all of the pop songs had gone and in its place came things like 'The Battle' which were much more up to date and much more advanced in terms of writing than anything I'd done before.

And darker as well. Well, more of that light and shade . . .

Oh and dark too! And that first album did create a huge stir in terms of record sales. Suddenly it sold 25,000 copies when the likes of Bert Jansch, John Martyn and so on were selling 5,000. But we weren't on the folk circuit, we were 'underground' suddenly, on the same circuit with the Edgar Broughton Band and so on, much more into that sort of era, doing *[BBC radio music show] Top Gear* and not the folk programme.

Admittedly that album was shocking in a way. To give you an idea, 'The Man Who Called Himself Jesus' was put out as our second single but the BBC banned it from daytime airplay. *[Comedy giant and former Goon]* Spike Milligan heard it and phoned up our office and asked "Can I have a copy of it?" and we straightaway replied "Yes, just so long as we can meet the great man!" So we were invited to a party, took our single with us, and there we were with *[Milligan's fellow comedy giants]* Eric Sykes and Hattie Jacques and all that lot. And Spike was very, very sweet. And he loved the album.

Immediately afterwards, a fellow called Denis Mitchell, who was a great documentary maker at the time, phoned up and asked, "Can Dave Cousins come along and meet somebody in Soho who I want to make a documentary about?" So I went along and it was *[gay writer & raconteur]* Quentin Crisp. We spent the whole day walking around Soho with Quentin discussing the idea that I was going to write songs for the documentary. Nothing came of it because the plans fell through.

Definitely, because of its lyrics, *Strawbs* created a bit of a stir in its very early days. We did 'The Battle' on *Top Gear* and the reaction was surreal. Love Sculpture's 'Sabre Dance' was on the same programme and we had equally as many requests for a repeat of it as Love Sculpture did. The album went into the Top Ten and A&M were going to release 'The Battle' as a single. But they didn't in the end because they got cold feet and said that at six and a half minutes long it wouldn't get airplay. It probably would have done.

Our production techniques and our recording were more sophisticated by then because we had that much more experience under our belts, therefore *Strawbs* was a much better produced and sophisticated record than our first one would have been. So with Sandy we might have gone on a whole different tangent and become the New Seekers or the Seekers with her, but she . . . well, she would have lasted five minutes. But we did what we did and we came out with these dark lyric songs that people loved and which suited the mood.

But then the second album *Dragonfly [1970]* went back much more to dulcimer and so on. On the third album *Just a Collection of Antiques and Curios* we had Rick Wakeman in the band, so suddenly that was a whole different effect. But the lyrical content still continued to be as dark, such as 'The Antique Suite' which really comes out that way if you listen to it now on the spoken word CD from the lyrics book: "The reaper stood before him in the room . . ." And then there's songs like 'Joey and Me': "Joey and me were out on the freeway / Leaving the city race . . ." The rhythm's already there isn't it, because it's not "dee dee dee dee daa, baby, baby, baby I love you". There's some lovely little bits and pieces in there that just make you sit back and really listen. So the albums as we developed had all these dark, thoughtful lyrics on them but we were always looking for that hit single. And that was the dilemma all the time, that's what made it very difficult.

What about periods such as the early Seventies where you had very different songwriting camps co-existing within the band, was that a determining factor towards that dilemma?

No. I always encouraged it because I couldn't keep churning out ten songs an album. So I got the other guys to write and they said, "Yeah well, thanks!" I thought everybody should share it. As long as I had the major feel of the album to keep the continuity going, it was all right. But then once we had the hit with 'Part of the Union' *[written by drummer Richard Hudson and bassist John Ford on*

Bursting at the Seams, 1973], that was it, because they said they wanted to do songs like that. And I said, "Well that ain't the Strawbs, that's not how it's going to work."

Richard Hudson and John Ford came up with 'Burn Baby Burn' *[a hit for Hudson Ford in 1974]*, which would have been the next single and I just didn't want to do it. I said, "No I can't do those songs. Lyrically it's not what I want to say." So that's when the whole split with Hudson Ford came about. It was quite apparent that I wanted to go my way and they wanted to go theirs, it was just a question of who kept the name. So then me and the new line-up went and made the album *Hero and Heroine [1974]* which was much, much darker than anything we'd ever done. And that's much the best album we ever did! In America it sold in bucketloads.

Intriguingly, there are all manner of Strawbs elements which are not on that album, or if they are then you have to look hard to find them. You're certainly harder-hitting and more cohesive on Hero and Heroine than on other Strawbs albums. You can see everyone for once falling into place throughout — musically, songwriting-wise, mood.

Cohesively, the second side of the album was the best thing we ever did, it flowed. We started doing the album from beginning to end on our current electric tours, and admittedly there's a couple of songs where I think "what *have* I done?!" but we do it anyway because that's what they want to hear.

Band members like Richard Hudson and John Ford were still incredibly inspirational for you in many ways. When you first started off, were people like Tony Visconti also inspirational, or at least influential?

Tony was very helpful in terms of my songwriting. One day he said, "I think you ought to read this book" and he gave me *The Tibetan Book of the Dead*. And I asked, "What's that all about then?" He said, "Oh, you know, just read it." So I read all that and gradually absorbed all this mythology and bits crept into the songs. Then I read *The Egyptian Book of the Dead* . . . God knows how I managed to stagger through all that, but again it's the language of the thing, blinking hard work but fascinating to do.

And then Tony said, "Oh Marc Bolan is inventing new words." I said, "Like what?" He said, "Oh he's inventing different words." So I said, "Oh all right, well I'll do that too." So I invented words like 'sparklebright', in 'A Glimpse of Heaven' *[From the Witchwood]*: "A string of diamonds formed a stream / That tumbled down the daunting cliff / To sparklebright on the beach." Obviously it could have been two words, but I don't think it was pretentious, just, you know, something that Tony told me was happening.

He was very encouraging in that sort of way. However, what he couldn't understand was how, in order to get myself into the mood for a song, I would put the guitar in a different tuning. There's lots of musicians that do this, but a lot of them don't want to give it away! So if people want to play those songs, they probably can't unless they know the tuning. If I get my guitar I'll show you what I mean. — *[takes guitar and strums]* — There's your normal tuning. But to get a melancholy mood I would go — *[tunes guitar]* — and put it in a modal tuning, which gives an incredibly aggressive but sadness to it. *[strums stridently]* So I can take it here — *[tunes guitar]* — which is more reflective. *[strums]* But then — *[tunes]* — I've totally buggered myself up now . . . *[tunes again]* So that is a much more powerful tuning, an open C. *[strums]* But if you put an F in the top . . . and sometimes I do change around these tunings to suit the mood of some of the words I've got . . . *[plays blistering sequence of chords]* You see you get that. But then in something like 'The Antique Suite' I started *[tunes]* with that tuning there. C minor for 'The Reaper'. And then the next part of the song. For 'We Must Cross the River' and 'Antiques and Curios' we were in C modal . . . *[fingerpicks]*

Those tunings instantly suggest new fingering patterns, don't they? They instantly push you on to something quite different.

Yeah, so the next two parts of the song are in that tuning, and then we come back to C minor for the final part 'Hey, It's Been a Long Time'. So each had its own different characteristic because of the guitar tuning. Somebody, I think it was *[BBC TV/radio music presenter]* Bob Harris, once said to me on a BBC interview, "Okay, you say you can put a tune to anything instantly." I said, "Yes!" So he pulled out *The Oxford Book of English Verse*, opened it at a page and said, "There you are. I've opened it at random, write a song round that." So I got the guitar out, had it in normal tuning. Then I said, "Right this is an Elizabethan sound, so let's put it into a tuning", tuned the guitar and within a couple of minutes there was a song. So I actively use the tunings on my guitar to create moods.

Is that a bit of a cop-out or . . .

No.

. . . is it utilising the instrument the way it should?

It gives a different feel and a characteristic. I was demonstrating it to a classical musician recently, they said, "Crikey that guitar sounds a different instrument whichever tuning it's in." *[strums guitar]* That's the open C.

You've gone from dulcimer to lute to bluegrass in two and a half tunings.

[strums guitar] So now you've got an open G which is a glimpse of heaven.

That's a classic open tuning though.

Yes. *[strums guitar]* But it's a happier sound. So I use those. It's not a cop-out but a way of creating different atmospheres and creating different melodies.

An old chestnut of a question then: do the melodies or the words come first?

Never know. Sometimes I'll come up with a little melodic pattern or a tune in my head. Probably only ever twice have I come in from the car with a tune in my head, dashed to a recorder put it on and sung it, and then the next day listened and said, "Oh I like that tune" and done something with it. The serious rule that I use, and always have done, is that if I can't remember the tune the next day, how can I expect anybody else to? So if the tune's not good enough for me to remember the next day . . .

Given that there's also a strong musicologist side to you, do you ever find the time to listen to other music in depth?

I don't really keep up with what's going on. I've usually followed Bob Dylan but I lost interest in him by the mid Eighties. *Under a Red Sky [1990]* and albums like that came out and I thought they were really poor. But then when he started to come back again later in the early Noughties I thought that was interesting, the melodies had become really good again. Except he nicks tunes and always has done. In the early days he nicked a lot of folk tunes. Dominic Behan was one particular case, where his 'The Patriot Game' became Dylan's 'With God on Our Side' but Dominic didn't have enough money to sue him. Although Dylan claimed, "Oh no it was a traditional song" that wasn't the case since Dominic had already done his own unique version of it. Later, in Dylan's *Modern Times [2006]*, there's 'Beyond the Horizon' — *[sings a couple of verses]* — the melody's so obvious I'm astonished that he hasn't been done for plagiarism of Jimmy Kennedy & Hugh Williams' 'Red Sails in the Sunset' *[1935]*. He's got more money than they ever had, I suppose.

Well, at least we get an idea of his listening habits.

I've done it myself. In the lyrics book I refer to one song 'On a Night Like This', but there's two other songs in it. Dylan did a song 'On a Night Like This' *[Planet Waves, 1974]*, not that it was anything like his tune. Then my wife Geraldine told me, "That tune, that's an old song." I said, "No it isn't." But it turns out that it was my mum — as I say in the lyrics book — who used to sing me "girls were made to love and kiss, and who am I to interfere with this" *[from the Thirties/Forties hit 'Girls Were Made to Love and Kiss', sung by tenor Richard Tauber, written by Franz Lehar in 1925]* so that melody slipped in — it was a subconscious thing.

Mind you, subconscious, i.e. acceptable, plagiarism is sort of allowed when they call it 'cryptomnesia'.

George Harrison didn't get away with it.

That was hardly subconscious was it? [Harrison was found by a US court in 1976 to have 'subconsciously' plagiarised Ronnie Mack's song 'He's So Fine', a hit for the Chiffons in 1963] Plus, where there's a hit there's a writ, though not in Dylan's case. But that distracts from the genuine 'music-of-the-people' inspiration that was a feature of those earlier days. After all, you started off in a period that saw a remarkable fusion of Brits and Americans getting together and actively working out their common heritage in a distinctly non-rock way . . . 'All That Folk' from the Dylans, Janschs, Renbourns, Seegers and Simons.

My inspiration came much more from listening to American folk music than English folk music. There was a musician called Suzie Shahn, the daughter of Ben Shahn, the left-wing social realist American painter. Suzie played a banjo, an instrument that fascinated me. She worked in the cloakroom at Eel Pie Island and I used to help her out every now and then. Not that I knew what it was at the time, but she introduced me to the music from the Harry Smith collection *[Anthology of American Folk Music, 1952]*. So I was listening to songs by *[folk-vaudeville banjo player and songwriter]* Uncle Dave Macon and all those people. But playing the banjo was all in the tuning and I ended up with all these banjo tunings, then wondered what they'd sound like on guitar. So I put them on the guitar and suddenly I had a whole new armoury for my guitar playing.

So the banjo starts pretty early as well.

The banjo was the forerunner of my guitar tunings, and that's where they came from. I'm still using modal tuning on the banjo. I looked through a list from *Guitarist Magazine* of tunings when I was putting my list together for the lyrics book. And one of the guitar tunings I use I couldn't see there or anywhere else because it's a banjo tuning.

That would break a few strings.

I've put in the book that if you break a string and poke yourself in the eye I accept no liability! So my influences were much more from American folk tradition than from the British folk tradition. I admired people like *[a cappella folk singers]* the Young Tradition, but now if I listen to harmonies like that I find them almost a historical document rather than a living, breathing organism, but I first started to write my own songs within that sort of feel, if you like. At one stage I had this daft idea that I wanted to write traditional English folk songs which nobody would know had actually come from me. Well that rapidly went out the window when I learned about royalties. Later, I found myself moving on to the early records by Jackson Browne — it's the melancholia of his music that I love, all the sadness. Absolutely beautiful.

There's echoes of that in his later work, but it certainly fills those first albums. He was only 16 when his songs started circulating, wasn't he?

He was incredibly young. They're lovely songs, many written long before the record. I also listened to Tom Rush. Obviously Sandy Denny, and then Judy Collins and Joni Mitchell. I did a TV show with Joni Mitchell where I was allegedly in a band playing guitar for her. But in fact I was like a spare prick at a wedding, I was totally unnecessary. She showed me a tuning that she'd worked out with David Crosby, and I straightaway went off afterwards and wrote a song around that. That's the sort of thing that explains how you can't play Joni's songs any other way. Her guitar tunings give you the whole essence, and you suddenly understand how she did it. Since David Crosby was also into guitar tunings, you can understand where some of that Crosby, Stills & Nash stuff comes from. Again there are lots of tunings within their music, especially from Stephen Stills.

Which must affect their vocal harmonies.

Absolutely. And so I've got all these curious influences. A lot from the American tradition and the banjo playing, some of it from old traditional modal harmonies, so now when we sing the reaction is "Christ, those harmonies are great!" but people don't always realise that they're sort of

English church harmonies. So when we played at the High Voltage rock festival it was bizarre because there we were in the tent with all these heavy metallers wandering around, and we're singing traditional-sounding Benedictus harmonies.

Did it go down well?

Yes!

Was that acoustic or electric?

Acoustic. When we tour with the electric band we're also putting in some of those old songs. So in the middle of all this prog rock stuff we'll suddenly go back to doing old harmonies again.

That's sort of prog isn't it?

Who knows what prog is? Nowadays I find that we do get slagged off as being old proggers — you know, "past it now they've done it all". We get slagged off today for stuff we did in 1972, and I agree, some of it can sound awful or perhaps embarrassing. But they don't read my sleevenotes when I say "This. Is. Embarrassing." *Mojo* for example did a dreadful review of one of our reissues, apparently saying it sounds, funnily enough, "embarrassing". Well I agree. I didn't want Universal to put stuff like that out but I can't stop them because they own that catalogue.

The curious thing is that none of this detracts from the body of work — even taking into account the gap where I more or less stopped for twenty years before starting again. Being able to come up with all the songs I've done in the last few years means it's all still inherently *there*!

Hardly surprising given that you're a different animal from most of your peers: you finished university, started later, didn't go busking overseas or anything like that.

No.

You've also consistently shared songwriting duties with others, and you manage to keep your own individual voice without overshadowing Strawbs or vice-versa. How do you do that?

By being determined, I suppose.

But why wouldn't it just be the 'David Cousins Show' all the way through?

Because I've never really had enough confidence in myself and I don't really like playing on my own. I'm an adequate guitar player and do all these tunings, but I feel much more comfortable playing with other people. Ralph McTell is someone who has always been a solo artist. When he did have a band for a while, it didn't work, it didn't suit his way of being. And yet he gets desperately nervous before he goes onstage — he's really shaky, very, very, very nervy. I'm not. I just go on and play and it doesn't really worry me at all.

You're literally 'just one of the band'.

Yes, but I'm the one that does all the talking upfront, who organises everything. I'm the one who does all the royalties, who organises the band. I get the agents and organise the tours and travel arrangements. If I give it to anybody else to do I never feel it's been done 100 per cent and I'm never 100 per cent confident of it, so I might as well do it myself.

When our distributor Pinnacle went bust on us in 2008, they owed us thousands of pounds. I thought what the hell do we do now? Probably the best thing to do is to make another album quick to get some cashflow coming in. So I immediately organised making another album and we went and did that. Spend money to generate money — other than say oh God, and then have to sell the house and pay off the debts, and the bank. No, just keep it going and go out and do something else. The book for example was done (a) because I wanted to do a book, but (b) I also needed something to generate more cashflow for the business. We sold a book upfront, people paid their money, we kept the company going, now we've got to pay the bill for the print. Doesn't matter, we're putting another album out now!

Trying to work out how to slot the songwriting in between all of that would baffle a lot of people.

As I've already described, I can work very quickly when I've got the incentive. With the most recent album I didn't really have many words at all. But I went to stay with my daughter in Majorca, sat in her back garden, and suddenly all these words came out. It's all down to making notes, writing stuff down.

Obviously the practicalities of a creative life don't always come that easy for singer-songwriters. That makes me think particularly of British female singer-songwriters like Sandy Denny who seem to have had far more of an uphill struggle and a lot less recognition than their male counterparts. Britain clearly had the potential yet somehow never produced a Joni Mitchell, Joan Baez or Judy Collins who survived from that generation.

I don't know why that is. Joni Mitchell's certainly an extraordinary songwriter. But there are others. I recently caught up with Claire Hamill at a festival — she was one of those who was a star burning brightly very young and then she sort of faded away.

A few of that late Sixties-early Seventies generation have started to record again, Judy Dyble for example. Even if they don't always write, they do have that singer-songwriter's ethos and craft in selecting their material and, where possible, actively working with the songwriters.

And that's how it should have always been, really. That's like a return to the Joe Boyd influence of that era where everything he touches is absolutely wonderful. Although Joe Boyd can exaggerate one hell of a lot.

Which makes me think of the whole thing: I think I can say that Strawbs were by far the most successful British folk group that came out of the folk movement, by far the most successful group, well above Fairport Convention and Steeleye Span and Pentangle in terms of volumes of records sold. But, as we all know, we never got the credibility for it over here. In America obviously it was a different kettle of fish.

The person who I do look at who deserves all the recognition has to be Richard Thompson. And in America in the *All Music Guide [allmusic.com]* they say that Richard and myself are the "shining alumni", as they put it, of the British folk rock movement. Over here people just ask, "What's Dave Cousins doing in the same league as Richard Thompson?"

Do you think that goes back to you usually being in a strictly band context?

Probably, yes. The other interesting one I can think of is Ray Davies.

He's ploughed his own furrow, band and solo.

And he's written books too. I once bumped into Ray coming off a plane and I asked him, "How are you getting on with your solo live shows?" He said, "When I started them I was absolutely terrified. I still am very nervous. But I stand up there, stamp my foot now and then and that takes it away." But he can't always do it on his own, he likes to have a guitar player with him.

But I never really got to know any of those singer-songwriters from those days. It was a mistake in a way to have moved down to the country to Witchwood, my cottage in Devon, and so to have moved away from the mainstream of the music business. Remember this was very early on, 1972/73.

A critical moment to have stepped out of the epicentre of London.

True. I was producing records at the time and suddenly all that disappeared too because I wasn't around. But again the move had its benefits in that I could write songs about the countryside which I wouldn't have written if I'd been in London.

It also removed you from the fall-out in the late Seventies when the music business imploded. But then again Ralph McTell moved out even earlier from London to Cornwall. When you were still around in the capital in the late Sixties, how did you see the role of the clubs? Within a stone's throw of each other you had all of these unique venues and also all the studios encircling them. There was nowhere else in the rest of the country that could compare.

Exactly. So we started our own folk club! I thought, "I want somewhere to play regularly." And there was a pub about 100 yards from my house, if that: The White Bear, Kingsley Road, Hounslow.

Clubs like yours made the periphery of London just as vibrant, but you also had to play Soho and the parts of the centre . . .

I played in *[Soho folk and blues club]* Les Cousins, even did an all-nighter on my own once there. That was hard work. Sort of midnight until six in the morning. *[Fellow Strawbs guitarist]* Tony Hooper refused to do it so I ended up doing it on my own. People dropped in and joined in, but God that was a slog.

Did you get paid for it?

Nothing I don't think. But I played a lot at the Troubadour in Earl's Court. We were fairly popular in the London Bridge clubs on the folk scene — but mainly because I was the 'fastest banjo player in the West'. Not that it had any merit and I started to find banjo very mechanical. It was only when I started to see some of the American players coming over that I realised the way they played the banjo was so much different to the way I played it. I think the way I play now is interesting because it's very melodic and gentle. When I was first playing bluegrass, yes I was fast, but when I saw the Americans' technique I thought, "I can't keep up with that." But anyway those were strange days.

Do you miss all that energy then or is it still around for you now?

It was good. I like playing acoustically again now, I enjoy it much more than the electric shows. Everybody wants to see the electric band but I think the acoustics are a much more attractive proposition because people can actually hear the words, and the words are the essential thing of what I do as a songwriter. Yes I write tunes as well but I think the words are what people come to hear. I'm more of a lyricist than anything else.

Do you think it's that poetic ability that makes a true singer-songwriter? Otherwise you're simply a composer putting tunes to words?

If you haven't got any words . . . When I read the words in some of the songs around, it's like "what *is* this crap?" Not that I try and set out to write words that are different, but everything essentially that I write is autobiographical. I'm sure Bruce Springsteen does that, I'm sure Bob Dylan does that a lot. When you find songs that have something to say, that's when they've got something within them that is saying something. Telling that story.

*

Arlo Guthrie
(Photo by Eric Brown)

2
Arlo Guthrie

'Music is the one language everybody understands'

Arlo Guthrie was born in New York on July 10, 1947 and grew up in Brooklyn. He followed in his father Woody's footsteps to become a singer-songwriter of songs of protest as well wider social commentary. Ramblin' Jack Elliott had absorbed Woody's style perhaps better than anyone and also lived for a while in the Guthrie household, and Guthrie credits Elliott for helping pass on his father's legacy, going on to perform regularly with long-time Woody collaborator Pete Seeger. Guthrie's first album was *Alice's Restaurant*, released in 1967 and featured the song 'Alice's Restaurant Massacree', notable not only for its satirical, first-person account of Sixties counterculture but also for its 18:34 length. A few years later, in 1972, Guthrie had another hit with 'City of New Orleans', pitched to him in a bar by writer Steve Goodman on the condition that Guthrie would only listen for as long as it took him to drink a beer. Usually a solo performer, he also had a band Shenandoah from the mid Seventies to early Nineties. He has also played with a wide roster of top musicians including David Bromberg, Cyril Neville, Emmylou Harris, Willie Nelson, Judy Collins, John Prine, Wesley Gray, Josh Ritter and Bonnie Raitt. He has also worked as an actor and made TV appearances, most notably in his 1969 film *Alice's Restaurant*, based on the song and co-written and directed by Arthur Penn of *Bonnie and Clyde* and *Little Big Man* fame. He played Woodstock 1969 and is featured in Michael Wadleigh's documentary from the following year, singing 'Coming into Los Angeles', slotted between Country Joe & the Fish and Crosby, Stills & Nash.

Famously you're the son of Woody Guthrie but you're also the son of Marjorie Mazia Guthrie, who was in Martha Graham's groundbreaking dance troupe and then founded her own dance school in New York. That must have been a doubly unusual upbringing because you've not just got the music going in but also the performing arts, and then all that filtered through New York when it was the centre of most things creative. Where exactly were you brought up in the middle of all this?

In Brooklyn, Coney Island.

Which in turn must have been an incredibly multi-ethnic/cultural place to be, added to which people came from all over to hang out there, so you had everything going on, didn't you?

Yeah, sure! My father had come from Oklahoma in the early Forties, met up with my mum . . . there's a book actually out edited by my sister which chronicles my father's time in New York *[Woody Guthrie's Wardy Forty: Greystone Park State Hospital Revisited, 2013]*. It's like every day, where he wrote what song, what apartment, who was there, what were they doing, what were they eating for lunch . . . It's incredible, it's like a Guide to Woody Guthrie's New York and thank God we have it because he chronicled everything. He was an extensive notetaker, who would write just consistently all day, all night, like a machine that didn't stop and he wrote whatever he saw and whatever he heard and whatever he read, and so we have this incredible record. But he was also the most disorganized human being ever to inhabit the earth.

That I've heard tell of.

On the other hand my mother was *the* most organised person in the history of the world, and so they were constantly at odds with each other, like polar opposites of a magnet that can't let go. So we had this wonderful life growing up with two people who were always at odds and yet always attracted to each other for the very reason they were at odds.

She organised him. Women do that sometimes, what we call back home 'fixer-uppers', you know, no words. Most of the time there's a male perspective of the world, that sees it for what it is or tries to assess it for what it is. I think women don't actually do that, they see what it could be, and you need both viewpoints to actually do anything in this world. So she saw in him something that could be, and he was looking at her as something that was attractive to begin with, and they approached their art like that and they approached our upbringing like that.

On my fifth birthday I got my first guitar. My father had decided he was going to get me one and the neighbour heard about it and said, "It's my daughter's birthday, would you get a guitar for her too?" And so my father went down into the city and bought two seventy-dollar guitars. Now even today I wouldn't get a five-year-old kid something worth seventy bucks of anything, so you can imagine what this was like fifty/sixty-something years ago. We were broke and my mother . . . well, shit hit the fan, as we'd say. She went berserk, she said, "How can you buy a kid a *guitar*?!" She had in mind some plastic instrument, you know, something like a toy.

And the neighbour also went berserk and said, "I can't pay for this, you can't do this to me!" And my dad said, "Look, if you get a kid a toy, he'll play with it for two weeks, and that'll be the end of it. If you get him a real instrument, they learn how to play it, it'll be a friend for life."

I still have the guitar, and a few years ago the Gibson company that had originally made this little three-quarter-size instrument asked me if they could reproduce it. They wanted the history of it and so forth, and I said sure, so I called my sister and I said, "They want to make this little guitar again and they want to like have a little Arlo signature guitar and they're gonna do a Woody Guthrie signature guitar too." So then I said to her, "What was the neighbour kid's name that got one?" And she said. "Oh, it's so funny you ask, she just called last week."

I had not seen this person since I was five years old, so I called her up and I said, "Do you still have the guitar my father got you?" She said, "Not only do I still have it, I still play it and now my grandchildren are playing it!" And I thought, "My freakin' father was right. He was right! We both have these instruments still. After fifty years we're still playing them, the kids are playing them, the grandkids are playing them." And I have loved that he was right and that my mum would have to agree.

What then was your mother's input into the performing side of you?

My mum, being a dancer with the Martha Graham Company, danced to the original music of Aaron Copland that was written for the Graham Company's performances — and so we grew up in both worlds. We had one foot in the backyard picking world where you just play what you feel and you learn your chops and your chords and you can play with anybody and do anything. On the other hand, we would drive down the road and my mum would have the classical music station on and we had to know who the composer was, what period of music it was and, if we were *really* good, who the conductor was and what version of this particular piece it was.

So we had a classical background *and* we all took music lessons, my brother and my sister and myself, so we could all read music by the time we were eight, nine or ten, somewhere in there . . . I've let most of it go over the years although I have had occasion to use it more recently when I did some recording with a symphony orchestra. Thank God I had that background, so I knew what the 'words' were.

I became a musician so I didn't have to dance! Well, that was the alternative, but my sister was laughing at me the other day because I still know the Martha Graham routine — you know, how to put your feet together, move your body. I remember as a kid we had to do it all the time. My mother would crack the weapon with all the first position, second position, all this stuff, but it doesn't really come in handy since it's sort of like algebra. You're just learning it, but as a musician you're not going to use it very often and that's what I thought of the dance and that's what I thought of the classical music. But it did come in handy later on.

It's all discipline, isn't it?

It's all . . . You know what it really is? Discipline isn't the knowledge of things, it's the ability to know how to learn something. And if you know how to learn something, there's nothing you can't learn, there's nothing you can't do. It could be language, it could be dance, it could be painting, it could be photography, it could be anything.

It becomes almost mystical then, doesn't it?

Yeah, break it down into the ability to absorb in a way that you can internalise it and then put it back out.

How did that affect you at school? Did you do well at school or did you bum out?

Oh yeah, I was a terrible student..

And the rest of your siblings?

Uh . . . I don't really know, I think they were probably better.

You were the eldest?

I wasn't the eldest, I had an elder sister, who passed away right before I was born, and my father had a previous wife and three children there. So I had elder half-brothers and sisters, but I am the surviving eldest.

So you weren't so interested in school, which is sort of understandable.

Not only did I have no interest, I had complete and utter disdain, and still do for that kind of education. It's totally morally and practically obscene.

You probably had the right to take that stance even as a child because it sounds like you had two highly moral parents who took pride in imparting the highest standards and they believed in you.

I know how I have learned how to learn things of interest to me, and it's really easy, it's not that hard. If you want to know something from somebody, you don't sit in front of them in a row of chairs. You wash their dishes, play on their floor, make sure they got something to, learn how to take care of them. If you do that, you will learn more than anyone else can possibly learn, because you will learn how to serve someone in a way that allows them to teach you without being a teacher, without being an instructor. You will learn as a friend or as a companion and there's no other way to really learn.

What was the religious side of it? Because Woody was brought up as . . . what exactly was someone from Oklahoma being brought up as?

He grew up in a typically non-religious Christian home. Then at twenty-one he married Mary Jennings, who was a Catholic girl, so he had roots when he was very young. Mary is still around by the way. She is the survivor of that generation and she is the matriarch and I can easily see why my father absolutely adored her. We were sitting at a big conference, one of those stuffy things, a few years ago, and she looked at me and she said, "Arlo, let's get the fuck outta here and have a Scotch and a smoke!" And I thought to myself. "For a ninety-something-year-old woman, she's hot!"

She was just not into bullshit. She saw things as they were, I think that's what my father loved about her, and she's still that way. All of her children have passed away, her long-term husband after my father passed away, and we all visited her — me, all of my kids and all of the grandkids inundated her and she was just with it. It's funny, in life it's not so much the biological stuff that counts. You really have an affinity towards people, it's almost comical, but it's not biological, it doesn't depend on who's who, it depends on what you're left with.

Chemistry being thicker than water. Since your mum was Jewish, were you brought up Jewish?

Yeah, we were raised typical New York Jewish, which means we didn't go to the synagogue so much, but we had to learn Hebrew and stuff.

So it was again cultural.

It was cultural, yeah. It was sort of left-wing Jewish, whatever, you know. Which also meant that the rabbi, just by coincidence, happened to be a right-wing guy named Meir Kahane. That name may not ring a bell everywhere, but he was the one that went on to found the *[FBI-listed terrorist group]* Jewish Defense League and he was the one that was murdered in New York *[in 1990]* because he was such an extremely sort of rabidly anti-Palestinian guy and he went berserk. And that was the guy that was teaching me. In fact the joke is that I was such a bad student that he started bombing things.

My father was a deeply spiritual man, not in the sort of traditional religious sense, but he read books on Eastern mysticism, he was really familiar with the sort of mystics, Eastern and Western. It doesn't really make sense to look at his life from any other way. I mean, here's a guy who decides purposely to give up attachments to the most fundamental of things in life: friends, family, money, fame, fortune, security. He volunteered to give them up. And why would somebody do that?

It's easy to say he was just a sick person, but then every other sick person with the same disease would do the same thing, but they don't, so that doesn't make any sense. I think that this is a person who has a sense of spirituality on a level that's really, really high, because that's what it takes to be somebody. If you wanted to emulate any of the great saints, whether they're Eastern or Western, whether they're Christian or Jewish or Muslim or Hindu or whatever they are, you have to be able to not become chained to anything, you have to be free. That freedom was his big embrace in life. That's what he decided to do and so he was able to go down to the store for a pack of cigarettes and then show up three months later on another coast with no feeling sorry for anybody.

In other words, if you were mad at him or if you were angry with him for being him, then that was your problem. He had no obligation to make you feel good about yourself — that's your job and I learned so freakin' much from that.

We're talking about serious spirituality then.

That's what I'm talking about, yeah, exactly! But that spirituality isn't religious, it can happen in any religion or it can happen in no religion.

Which is interesting, because from the outside point of view that isn't so apparent in one's first view of Woody. But all that immense respect and influence he commanded has to come from something, something that was more than merely Woody the Songsmith.

It's one of these things that's so plainly visible no one sees it.

There's also a spiritual element in what you've done yourself throughout your career. You said that you learned a lot, but obviously a lot of it must have naturally been passed down through to you. Are you aware of that or is it something you have to work on?

I have the kind of respect for my father that comes from stuff that is not easy to swallow, to have somebody who needs to be free when instead you want him to play with you or be there or bring you things or whatever. That's not easy to grow up with. But if you see it from the way I view it, it gives you an opportunity to deal with these things young and if you can get the B.S. out of the way when you're young, it gives you some time when you get older to actually enjoy it and admire it.

It's good to get the doubts and the fears. I've had all kinds of people writing all kinds of stuff about my father, but none of them were there although all of them have an opinion. That's fine, that's the way the world is. But the fact is that he was ill *[with progressive genetic neurological disorder Huntington's disease]* and I ended up being the one that had to take care of him in the ways that other people could not, even though I wasn't really old enough. For example we would bring him home from the hospital and he'd be walking as if he were drunk, like falling over, and I was the one that had to take him to the men's room. I was the one he was leaning on, my mum couldn't do that, she was a very small woman, and when you deal with this that young, it either consumes you or you consume it.

And that's the great lesson for me, that some people choose to become the people they are. I didn't really choose to be me. I mean, I may have, in some high-class spiritual way, but in a very practical sense I didn't choose to be me but I'm so glad that I did have those challenges. To deal with how people were looking at us, to deal with how people were thinking of us, to deal with him not being reliable in a way, it means I had to fend for myself, which I learned to do as a young man. Yeah, that's all tough stuff. It's not easy stuff.

There are plenty of people that would've said, "Well, the guy's not reliable." But they wouldn't see it from the perspective as I see it now, as admirable. I mean, what kind of person would take on himself the idea to show people how valuable they are as individuals. It's in every song he writes. It's in everything he does, over and over again repeatedly, it's you have a value, it's unique to be you, there's no one else in the world that has it, you have the opportunity to do something with the life you're given. In other words: nobody should be wasted, there's no such thing as a throwaway human being, no matter what their economic status is, no matter what their education, their colour, their size, their whatever. These are the things he teaches in every one of his songs. These are not religious teachings, they're not cultural teachings, they're beyond all of that, these are spiritual teachings. There's no other way to see it and it makes sense that way.

How old were you when you started becoming a carer for your father?

Eleven, twelve, thirteen . . .

That must have also affected your schoolwork.

I had no interest in that anyway and I wasn't very good at it. You know, if I was good at it, it might have been more exciting, but I just wasn't interested in it.

Did you flunk out of school or did you finish it? What was the minimum legal school-leaving age at the time?

We have two courses of mandatory school: one brings you through till you're about twelve or thirteen, and one then takes you through to about when you're eighteen. Somewhere in there is high school and before that it's elementary school. I got through all of that. I even went to college briefly, I wanted to be a forest ranger, that's what my chosen profession was.

I didn't like being around large crowds of people, I wanted to be off in the mountains, which I loved. When I found myself there, I had an affinity toward something natural, wilderness of things and still do, and when I was old enough and wealthy enough I just bought myself some wilderness and moved in, and I'm still there. So, I managed to accomplish it, but it took me a very roundabout road and I never intended to be an entertainer. I was always going to play music, but mostly I was just going to play with friends. That's what folk music was. Folk music was not a profession.

Because of your family especially, it's your inherited culture. It seems very American too, everyone sitting on their stoops, picking . . .

Well, that's what the idea was. But I don't think it's very American, because people do it all over. It's a very old tradition of Scotland and Ireland and other places where you sit around and play the traditional tunes and people dance. That's what folk singers did.

Very Jewish as well, certainly in the way that Eastern European culture was filtered via New York.

Right, and that's a very charismatic thing, where the singers come, they play the music, nobody really wants to pay them, but you can't have a Jewish wedding without them, you can't have a celebration without them and you keep an eye on your daughters when they're in town. Rock'n'roll was not a new thing, it's just a different word for a very old school.

So how did you end up as a professional singer-songwriter? Was there a key moment or did you just fall gradually into playing music for a living?

I was going to play music anyway with my friends and discovered as a young man that it could pay for pizza, and not only that, it was the best way to meet good-looking women. You just couldn't beat it. And so for me this was like, okay, pizza and women, what else do you need? I mean, how much more do you want? So, it satisfied the need of an eighteen-year-old guy — food and girls — and that was it.

You didn't become a singing waiter, though.

I was playing on the streets at first. I came over actually to Europe in 1965 when I was eighteen, just out of high school, just before college. I was playing in little places, I ended up on the Walking Street *[Strøget]* in Copenhagen and made enough money to do very well and I loved it. I would do it tomorrow. I have no qualms about it at all. I generally support the buskers I see, because that's me.

So how did it develop? Did you start off with your own songs or were you doing standards, or some of your dad's songs? Or whatever it was that people wanted to hear? The hit parade was evolving at light speed around you, and a lot of those songs could be easily reduced to effective performances on street corners.

When I was growing up the stuff on the hit parade was really the social world. We used to have school dances, which I don't think they have any more in the same way. These were sort of guarded events where the women would be on one side and the guys would be on the other side and everybody would be too shy to do actually anything and there'd be teachers there to make sure you didn't do anything.

But the music that they were playing was part of our lives. My first heroes, the first record I ever bought, was the Everly Brothers. I loved them and I finally got to meet them years later and do their TV show and I told them, "You know, you guys were it!" All of their hits were important to me. They had a sense of 'real' that someone like Elvis didn't quite have. The Everly Brothers were authentic.

When I grew up they definitely made an impression on me. It was like they came from Mars, but in a good way.

Well, Elvis was good for other things, he was more theatrical. What the Everly Brothers did was take the sort of traditional mountain music and wield it in a way that made it popular, but they were still genuinely them. Elvis was genuinely him, but that didn't come from anywhere, that came from the brain of Elvis as opposed to a tradition. I don't mean that in a negative way. Elvis assimilated a lot of stuff that didn't come from a tradition, that was uniquely him, he assimilated a lot of the Memphis tradition, a lot of the black tradition and things that the Everlys never did. But it's just different styles. I appreciated the Everlys and I knew all of their songs, and it wasn't that much of a stretch then to fall in love with guys like Bill Monroe, or the Dillards when they came out at first — I thought and still to this day that they would have been huge had they just waited twenty years.

But that was very symptomatic of the times you grew up in, because there was just so much happening. And it wasn't happening in sequence because the industry hadn't got in there to work out a sequence yet.

What actually happened was that somewhere in the Twenties and Thirties the Lomaxes had gone around — father and son John and Alan — and started recording these field songs and other rural sounds they discovered, like Lead Belly. And at some point at that time, for political and social reasons, my father and guys like Pete Seeger and others realised that they had been born in a time before electricity, when popular music didn't exist in the same sense that it does today. Nobody had record players or radios, instead there was a mass of publishing of music, so you would go to the store and buy some sheet music and you'd bring it home to play it on your piano maybe. Songs got around that way, or through the live shows that people performed.

So my father and others grew up in an era before popular music was popular. The songs they were singing were the songs that they'd been handed down generationally. At some point when popular music began to make its way through the electronic medium, people realised that this new music had to appeal to so many people that it didn't actually appeal to anyone, and so it lost a lot of its oomph. There was no history of anybody in it, there was none of the sadness, there weren't the murder ballads. The history of people was being lost. Yes there were the chain-gang songs, the gospel songs, the spirituals, the cowboy songs, the working man songs and all the factory songs, but the new songs weren't any of them. The new popular music avoided all of that, and my father and the other guys realised that if they didn't do something it was all going to be lost, that history was going to be lost, and so they started putting it in books.

Well, along come the Fifties, twenty years later, when some college students in sweaters discover some of these books and start pulling out the songs and they became huge. Guys like the Kingston Trio changed the course of music and for everything that came after that. And then, within the next five or six years, a young Minnesota kid shows up and says "whoah!" and now he's also using the same text, he's going back to the songs that these other guys had preserved in the books. So all of a sudden popular music became the music that had been saved. The style of it had re-emerged and became popular. But that was only a glitch. It didn't last long, it lasted for a few years, and then all of a sudden there were mega bands, like the Rolling Stones and the Beatles.

Which was the explosion of the first teenager generation.

I don't see it that way. I don't see it by age. It's really a matter of what kind of music was available for them to experience, and all of a sudden it creates an interest where anybody can be interested in music. And they are able to access that first history of music. So people find the blues, they find the old writers, they find the jazz, they find all the stuff, they listen to it, it makes an impact, it changes what they're playing, and they create something new.

Those songwriters needed to be musicologists, as we would call them now.

But we all do that. That's a feature of the human musical experience where we find these things, we internalise them and then they come out in ways that, say, Paul McCartney is still doing. What he is creating is not English music, this is music on a global scale that is popular. Okay, not as popular as it was in the early Sixties, whatever, but who cares?

It's the idea that the young musicians these days now have access to another forty years of music, the first forty years that I had access to. We have only had the recording industry itself really since the invention of something that could reproduce the sound, it's barely a century old *[e.g. probably the first commercial broadcasting station was PCGG in The Hague, the Netherlands, which started broadcasting on November 6, 1919, while electrically recorded records and record-*

players hit the mass market in 1925]. Recorded music more or less starts around the turn of the twentieth century, and we don't have a real history before that. Instead you have to go to Ireland or Scotland to some little tiny town where people still learn exactly what their family has been doing for the last four hundred years. And you *can* do that, but these guys are also lucky to have access to a hundred years of recorded music, even though much of that is still in its infancy.

> *Tradition has been fractured by the modern world. Of course these is the benefit of healthcare, washing machines, personal devices and stuff like that, so there is a pay-off, but family and society structures across the world have been broken up — and with that comes a break in direct transmission of art forms and culture. But you're saying that people can still go along and grab it for themselves.*

Not only that, I can guarantee you what the future will be within the next twenty to thirty years. We will be hearing more different kinds of Eastern scales in the music because of the wars in the Middle East. We will be hearing more and more of that in popular music. You know, the old saying is "if you lie down with dogs, you'll get up with fleas", and that's the way it goes. We're going to hear more melodies and ideas from, say, China. It's going to enter into the music.

It already has, but we're not that sensitive to it, but I guarantee you that that's where the music will go, there's no other way. We will hear it, we will say "what's that?", we will internalise it, and it will become distilled in our collective organs as it were. We will put it out in some way that the original guys may not recognise, although they'll recognise some kind of contribution, but we hardly won't even know it. It will float to the surface and only a real musicologist is going to be able to say, "This is from here, this is from there, this is from here . . ."

> *And that won't be so important in any case.*

It doesn't matter. Because what it will do is open the doors. Imagine if you had access now to the history of music, from China, from the Middle East or India or other places where we know the musicians who first thought about this or that. We don't have much access to that. First of all we don't speak the languages, second of all a lot of musical heritage there is not well documented for political as well as economic reasons. But all of that will come, and we will be able to have everything translated for us and we'll know the names and work of some of the great musicians who have appeared over the last five thousand years in all of these places all over the world. We'll also have more of the Native American stuff. The more stuff you lose, the more valuable is what's left, and so now you have people who are delving into it, saving what they can.

It's like what happened in Hawaii back years ago: the language was just about gone, speaking it was actively suppressed. Now every kid is taught it, they all know the songs, they're all writing songs in the same traditional way. Some of them have become very popular. There are radio stations now in Hawaii that just play Hawaiian music in Hawaii. How does that happen? There's no industry, there's no Warner Bros, there's no Columbia, there's no Google or anybody trying to save languages. That's not what they do. There's no money in it, but people will do it, because it has a value to the human spirit that can't be bought or sold so easily. There's a want, there's a need in there. It becomes another tool for a musician to know.

That process needs people for sure, but you can't do it on a reservation. You need the critical mass of a city, and when you have a city, you need newspapers, you need a radio station and if there's enough of a population there who want that radio station in that language, then the language gets saved. Hawaii clearly ticks all the boxes. If you don't have that urban conglomeration you're stuck.

Not quite true! There's a little radio station in Southern Colorado, for example, up in the middle of nowhere where Native American guys own the station *[KSUT, run by the Ute people]*, they're broadcasting in their own language, their people are now writing songs in it. There's no big city within a few hundred miles, so the possibility does exist. Cities may be the primary way and easier to find, but they are not the only way.

Words are important, aren't they? In your own songwriting, ideally you want to write something that does become universal, such as we're talking about here.

It depends what your motive is. There are professional writers, let's put it that way, and I'm not one. I'm not writing songs for people to like, I write songs for me and if people like 'em that's great and if they don't, that's fine. I do appreciate that people like some of my stuff, both the music and the words, and that's fortunate. That's a very fortunate circumstance for me to find myself in.

I've found that people actually do like the stuff that I've written. They're probably not as many today as they were thirty or forty years ago, but I made the decision years ago that the stuff that was popular, stuff that people still want to hear, was not going to be endlessly repeated. I wasn't going to do a concert of popular material and stick to that. Over the decades you end up spending the same couple of hours every day of your life repeating yourself endlessly. Who the hell needs that? That's Ricky Nelson Syndrome, you know. Ricky was a friend, and I know what he went through when people wanted to hear the hits and they didn't care about anything he was interested in. So I said to myself years ago, "I won't play for somebody else, I am playing for me."

I enjoy the music and I play with anybody that enjoys picking with me. I don't get a chance to play with a whole lot of other people, but I consider myself that kind of player, like a musician's musician. I wanna sit in with guys I've never played with before, just figure out what the hell they're doing and contribute to it on the spot. If I can do that, that's success for me. I don't really have an interest in being a professional writer in the sense that . . . I mean, I think it would be fun, it's something that I could probably do, if I really wanted to, but I have no interest in it.

That's the Bluesman Way, where the distinction gets blurred between the work you do out there, your own personal mission statement, your family and the music. It all just sort of comes together in one. You're born to do it, you end up doing it, and they'll bury you doing it. You have your highs, you have your lows, but you always know it's going go that way, so the idea is not to fight it but go with the flow and accept all the interaction with other people — audience, other musicians — that it involves.

I do want to make a distinction between being a professional writer and an entertainer. I consider myself a professional entertainer in that if I'm going to sit in front of a whole lot of people who are going to pay money to hear me, I'm going to do the best I can to entertain them. It doesn't mean I'm going to write trash to throw it at them. I think I have an obligation as a human being, whether I'm an entertainer or not, whether I'm a singer-songwriter or not, I've got an obligation as a human being to continue what I learned from those, who came before me, including my dad. Which is that everybody counts, there's no throw-away-people.

There are ways through the mire and the muck of time and space and you can successfully get through it. You need a sense of humour, you need some discipline. And if you're willing to indulge in the discipline a little bit, it'll take you further than you ever thought. Now that means kindness, a little bit of generosity, some kind of walking, or imagining you're walking in somebody else's shoes, those kind of things. It means limiting the amount of greed you allow yourself to the point where you don't want to be starved and on the backs of other people to get it, you don't want to be stealing from people or hurting anybody. That's my personal sort of code that I operate by. That's the way I was brought up, that's the way I brought my kids up. That's not unique to me.

So I have an obligation as an entertainer to do all of those things within the context of an evening. After a couple of hours people ought to feel better than when they walked in. If they don't, I didn't do my job, I didn't earn my money that night. And the truth is, most musicians will tell you, you can't pay them to play anyway. You're paying for all the other crap: you pay them to get there and you pay them to put up with people and you pay them for all kinds of other stuff. But when you're playing music there's no amount of money that can make you play better or worse, or be more inspirational or less inspirational. That's the free part, that's what you get for nothing because it can't be bought. But it's all the pain-in-the-butt stuff you have to do to get there that's what's worth a working man's wage.

So if you never wrote another song again, if you never sang another song, would you be content just hanging out guitar-picking with other people?

Oh yeah!

I don't think there's any further explanation that's needed here.

You know, my dad was right: the guitar has become the best friend I ever had. All you have to do is change the strings every once in a while and I've got a renewed friendship. I will be in towns on some nights or for days at a time where I don't know anybody and I don't want to know anybody and I don't want to go to the museum, I don't want to take to touristry, I don't want to go shopping — I got everything I need — I don't want to go to the beach, I don't want to play tennis. I don't want to do any of that stuff, I just want to sit there on a curb somewhere where the weather's nice and play my guitar and see what it's playing at.

I constantly learn stuff from that. There's a new way to do something — "I hadn't thought of that progression before!" — and it doesn't come to you unless you have those moments to do it. They don't come onstage so easily, the stuff you do onstage is basically already figured out. You might take a chance sometime, discover something by accident, but nobody I know goes on to the stage to discover stuff. You go there to play the stuff you already discovered, but there has to be a place to discover it then. There has to be a place where you don't know it when you begin, or how else do you learn it? You're just sitting there listening to somebody else or you sit there listening to the wind.

You've talked about language. Well music is the one language that everybody understands. You don't have to know any words. I've played with people I couldn't say a word to talking different languages, but you can sit down and you play and you can read it in their smile and in their body language and gesture, and it comes through the music. And if it doesn't come through quite right, it makes for some funny stuff, so you start laughing together. That's the best thing. Music is the greatest thing.

Politics is less unifying I suppose. For example, you're the generation that faced the draft for the war in Vietnam, an experience that no one in Europe had to face. Did going through that epoch shape you? Or do you think you had already hit the ground as a well formed political animal?

You could spend a year talking about that. I grew up with parents who were both not only aware but they were political animals, and socially political. And everything that they knew or believed became part of my very early life, to the teachers we had, to the schools that we went to, to the groups of people that I was introduced to, to the music that we heard, which actually predates the singer-songwriter era. It went back to a time when my classically trained mother and my self-taught father both shared a love of the tradition of music and specifically music that affected people's lives. And so the kind of music that I was introduced to involved the kind of singers who used their music politically, socially, spiritually, all of the different ways that music communicates the different parts of humanity. I learned to love it, as well as the individuals who were there from my very earliest memories – Lead Belly as well as others who were not as socially or politically active, guys like Ramblin' Jack Elliott and Cisco Houston.

I think my father and his friends found themselves at a crossroads in history where the songs that people sang and had handed down had become political because the way of life was disappearing. So even a dance or fiddle tune, the playing of it, the passing it on, was political in the face of an encroaching culture that minimised not only that kind of music but was attempting to profit from it, which meant that it had to be dumbed down to reach a larger audience.

We saw that happening all the time. Original songs that for example came from black, African-American culture, songs that were recorded and gained a small following were re-recorded by white entertainers, changed to be a little more acceptable and became big hits. And that went on throughout my very early life, through the Fifties. And so I grew up understanding that the nature of songs and the nature of the folk tradition was inherently political, even if the songs themselves were not.

Just the playing of them, just the passing them down created this culture that went all the way into the Sixties when the pivotal moment was Bob Dylan and Pete Seeger arguing at Newport *[July 25, 1965]* over whether people had sold out. Anyone my age would know what that means, but I don't think younger people know.

> *There's the leap to today, where it's hard for a young person to find such light and shade. Even the passing of the creative torch might be problematic because many would be asking, "What's my motivation in this please, Arlo?"*

Well if you look back and look at the early recordings of my father and Lead Belly, Sonny *[Terry]* and Brownie *[McGhee]*, Cisco *[Houston]* and all of those guys, they were making recordings of songs that everybody in rural America already knew. What was new was recording itself, so they were recording the music not only because it was fun, but because they considered it important. They considered the local traditions of the Appalachians, of southern hillbillies if you will, of the cowboys, of the labourers, of the miners. All of those songs come from all over the United States and in many ways Europe and Africa, and all of those traditions were important because they were concerned that the people would lose their identity. And I think they learned that from people like the Lomaxes *[father and son John & Alan]* and others who went around collecting the songs before they disappeared.

> *So it didn't come from nowhere, this desire, this appreciation?*

That's what I'm saying. It was inherently political although it was not politically charged. No one was framing it in a political framework but it was an attempt to galvanise or introduce to young people their own history and it wasn't geared towards any one statement of young people, it was geared toward everybody. So at a Pete Seeger show you would hear songs from Africa, you would hear songs from the Soviet Union back in those days, you would hear songs from South America and even, in Pete's case, Maine. There would be songs from everywhere so that somebody in the audience who had a relationship to any one of those places could find something in the songs that related to them.

And Pete did that until his dying day and he traduced songs that became big hits. I mean songs like 'Wimoweh' *[written and recorded by Solomon Linda in Zulu as 'Mbube' in South Africa, 1939, then released in the USA in 1951 by The Weavers, of which Pete Seeger was a member, as 'Wimoweh', then in 1961 with English lyrics by George David Weiss it turned into 'The Lion Sleeps Tonight' by The Tokens]* or other songs that were in some cases songs like 'Kumbaya' *[Southern USA spiritual first recorded in 1926]* which was an American song, had gone back to Africa, changed into an African song and discovered by guys like Pete who brought it back. So 'Kumbaya' was an American song called 'Come By Here Lord' and, well, only a guy like Pete would even think of not just loving the song enough to learn it and then bring it back and play it for an audience, but then go back and try to figure out where it came from. So people like that had an academic view and a political view and a social view, and that's what gave them or created for them the culture that I grew out of.

So as the generation following on, how do you reconcile all those strands? You're presented with something that is revolutionary but, as you said, it's not "let's use this music to bring down the state", it's "let's use this revolution for good work however one wants to interpret that". But this came about as a result of society changing, and so everyone was evolving in any case.

It seems to me the exact same way as the Beatles and the Rolling Stones started doing their stuff. I mean they knew the sources and they went with them, they listened to them, they absorbed them and they recreated them and it looked like a totally new thing to anybody who was not familiar with the sources to begin with.

And so out of that came the singer-songwriters who, as you've said, didn't actually exist when you were born but then in your formative years suddenly not only existed but were all around you, physically in your case. Then again there are rules that have been passed down from before, such as the idea of not being a permanent member of a band. In the long term you're always a solo performer in principle, even if you're working with other musicians around you. Obviously you're writing your own songs but if you're interpreting other people's songs that presumably is a choice that's just as significant?

Sure, of course.

How does that come into it? Are you applying a Pete Seeger logic to it or are you doing a more Americana approach, or is it just the Arlo Massachusetts roadshow concept?

One of the formative times of my life was the mid-Sixties, when I first went to England and I met some of the most incredible people who were singing in the sort of English tradition, guys like Alex Campbell and Peter Bellamy. But they were not writers, they were the links in a very long chain of people who were in one way, like in Alex Campbell's way, it was just a way of life: you drink and you sing. Peter Bellamy was an incredible scholar, and I remember meeting guys like Ewan MacColl who were furious at some of the contemporaries of mine for in a sense commercialising traditional music. And of course we all laughed, like when Roberta Flack recorded one of Ewan's songs and became a gazillion dollar hit, 'The First Time Ever I Saw Your Face' *[1972, much covered since MacColl wrote it in 1957]*. And so here he was, in spite of his opinions (and you could say his sense of humour there), with his music moving on in an odd way. And the time when Bob Dylan showed up in the early Sixties when the Beatles and others like the Rolling Stones and Donovan were emerging, there's a whole lot of the early singer-songwriters you might say, and they came from all these different traditions. But what was the same about them was that they were able to not only make a living but create an interest in the source material for those willing to go look for it.

A crucial point.

Sure, because it opened up a huge wave of interest in the blues, in the other kinds of odd eccentric material which at that time was only available in a recorded format. I mean, by the Sixties there were only something like fifty years of recorded music. Previous to that there was no recording. So a kid that grew up at that time like me had essentially five decades of recorded music to listen to. A kid these days has over a hundred years of recorded music to listen to.

It's a vast difference. It's exponentially so much more different, but anyone who's serious about music, or finds themselves in love with it, can go back and now have access to all of what I would call the source material, the early stuff. And they'll change it and do something else with it and it may not sound like anything that I do, but there's nobody I know of who doesn't know that it's there. Just take a guy like Bruce Springsteen, who's a scholar in his own way and has paid some kind of tribute to those that came before.

At this point, I'm living long enough to see that happen to me in funny ways, you know. There's nothing to say about it, it's just odd and funny and I take it with a grain of salt, but all of my kids play music, all of my grandkids play music, and it becomes like a language that you can speak with certain people. Most of the fun of music in the early days for me – when you mention whether you're by yourself or with the band – most of the fun wasn't in the performance, it was in the playing of it that was fun. It wasn't that you formed a group in order to perform, you formed a group because it was fun to play music with other people. And if it worked well and they like you, then you would think about maybe performing.

Music is totally a language because you create a dialogue, you're communicating.

And you're not only communicating with people who want to learn it or who are moved by it, you're also able to communicate with people who don't even speak the same . . .

. . . verbal language.

It doesn't matter whether it's English, French, German or Russian or whatever, music is music and it does transcend the spoken language. It's always done that.

> *You known for your songs with a message, but you're also known for your guitar playing. How does that work? Obviously you can create music without words but how does music make a singer-songwriter who they are? Is it the words or is it an understanding of the power of music which transcends the words?*

Well, there are plenty of people I know who are songwriters. A lot of them will get together, share songs with each other. The music is almost incidental to some of them, to others it's more important, and to some it's extremely important. For me personally I've always loved the idea that music, when I was playing on the guitar or the keyboard or some other instrument, should in some way reflect the idea of the words. So that if you heard something you would get an idea of what it is about, even if you didn't understand the verbal language.

> *You're presenting a structure and you're saying trust me, I'm a musician, I know what I'm doing, here's the song.*

The problem is that not everybody is a good instrumentalist. There arc probably a lot of people who got into songwriting either through poetry or through prose or who came from the spoken language. There are others who came from the musical language. It's a sort of polyglot of people. When you group them all together and say singer-songwriters, you have to know that that's a melting pot of a lot of different people who came from different places. Some of them are enamoured with the spoken word and some are enamoured with the music, and one becomes subservient to the other.

At some point in time it seems to me, anyway, that 'singer-songwriter' began to mean a sense of "What I have to say is more important than what you have to say because my feelings are worth you paying for." Now that doesn't really bother me. I would hope that I am distanced from that because that kind of self-expression, the need to express oneself, even though it may have been there in the earliest forms, even though it may be true for Lead Belly, that was not the major force of Lead Belly, he wasn't trying to express himself, he was expressing the history of who he and others like him were. So he became symbolic of something rather than the epitome of it.

And I think my father was the same way. He was not a good guitar player, I mean in the sense of musician. I thought he was a wonderful songsmith, because his words were so well constructed because he loved them and he knew them and he knew the effect on people when they were sung or spoken. And he played with that like an artist, which I mean in that sense of a painter, somebody who knows colour and knows structure, and it can have an effect, there's an impact.

I think my father knew what his impact was, he appreciated people who had it. I think I know what the impact of my songs are on people, otherwise I wouldn't be doing it. I wouldn't be doing it *successfully*, I should say. There are plenty of people who send in songs still to this day: "Sing my song, here's a recording, would you put it out, would you do this, would you do that?" It's partially wanting to believe that what you have to say and how you're saying it is worth doing. I never sort of felt that mine was worth doing, and that took me by surprise. So I didn't become a singer-songwriter in order to be somebody, I became a singer-songwriter accidently.

What was the breakthrough? No, that's the wrong word . . . what was the tipping point for you? Did that happen suddenly or gradually, or was it something like 'Alice's Restaurant'?

Purely overnight.

Oh, okay. Are you prepared to share that?

Oh I mean yes, I went to the Newport Folk Festival in 1966 or '67, and I didn't go as a performer, I went like as a 'normal person'. In those days normal people also carried instruments so that they could sit around and play music, so I went like that. They had what they called a 'free stage' which was like a milk carton, a wooden box out in a field and that was the free stage.

You get what you pay for.

I was standing on a box with a microphone, one microphone, and I played 'Alice's Restaurant' and the people there, maybe 150-200 people, went fairly berserk, and they said, "You have to play this again!" So later that afternoon I played it to a larger free stage and one of the big promoters for the Newport Folk Festival, a guy named Oscar Brand, who's still with us, heard it and said,

"Oh my God, you have to play this on the main stage." And I said, "Really? Oh okay!" You know, I was a kid!

And so they had me close the Newport Folk Festival that year. They were afraid that the crowd would scare me to a point where I was unable to perform, and so they had all of these singers come out and sing the last part with me. So one person did it first, well then somebody else came out like Judy Collins or Joan Baez, and with two people doing it, two more of them came out, and by the end of the evening there were fifty people all onstage singing 'Alice's Restaurant' with me. The next day it was in the *New York Times* and from that day on I was a singer-songwriter. It was literally overnight.

And what a backing band.

Yeah right, when you think of it! But I can't even remember it. I know the story because I've heard other people tell it, but I have no memory of it except for standing out on the box that day early in the mid-morning and having to do it three times in one day when I was seventeen or eighteen years old, whatever I was. For me that was incredible.

Well you can say that, but it's not everyone who'll go to stand on a milk crate in the middle of a field in front of a free audience and pull a song like 'Alice's Restaurant' out of their bag. That must have come from somewhere.

Well you can speculate, I mean *I* do at times! I don't think about those times very often, but I'd obviously written it at that point and so maybe this was 1965 or '66, I'm not even sure, although I think it was '66 and I'd been performing it in little coffee shops, little clubs around, and so I'd had some history of working before an audience, otherwise it would have just terrified me. And so I was pretty sure of myself, at least enough to get through it. I had been playing and singing for some years before that, mostly old songs, mostly my father's, you know, other songs that were important to me. But up until that point I was just a folk singer like a million other people who loved playing guitar. I had my heroes, I had people I loved to learn from, to watch, and mostly I just loved to hear it. I liked playing it with my friends but mostly what we did was go to hear other people.

And after that I pretty much had to stop doing that. I mean, it ended my ability to walk down a street and go into a club because at that point I had become 'somebody' as it were, much to my own chagrin, and then of course there was a record that was made and then the following year the movie came out. I mean it just got crazy, and of course I've been doing it ever since. Not that song, but I had become a singer-songwriter at a time when I think it was important socially, it was important politically, it was important in the tradition of it, and I still think that way.

To look again at your definition of singer-songwriter as it evolved then and as it logically became for new generations up to today and beyond, in that idea of bringing in the traditions of people, bringing in the thoughts of people and then channelling it all, do you think there's something shamanistic in there? This seems to be more than the trade of a troubadour, there is actually a need for people to have a true singer-songwriter around, or is that making something too spiritual out of it?

Well I think it's true, but I would go further and I would say that the same thing that that person is able to communicate to an audience must be communicated to that person themselves. So if it's something coming through you to go to somebody else, then you have to acknowledge that the end of that logic is that it's a very long chain and that everyone becomes just a link in it.

It didn't start with me, it didn't start with my father, it doesn't end with me or my kids or my grandkids or other people who like it. It's just if there's a message in the medium itself then there are certain things that I would say tend to take into account other people. It's not always true: there are singer-songwriters for every political party, for every religious belief, and some are more popular than others, that's because the ideas are more popular than others.

And then every once in a while you have someone who evolves through it. Take a guy like Merle Haggard. A great songwriter, nobody would question it, who started off politically in one sort of region of the world and ended up in another. Now how much of that was those messages coming through him or going to other people? I think at some point it becomes offensive to singer-songwriters in general to become pigeonholed as it were by their audience. You don't want to be locked into how people perceive you because you want to evolve yourself.

It happened to Rick Nelson, for example, who I knew and loved. He was a wonderful guy, a very sweet man, and did not want to be Ricky Nelson as other people had come to know him, he wanted to sing Bob Dylan songs and he wanted to express what he was thinking at the time and not what he was known for. And I think that happened to Merle Haggard – I'm not sure, I never talked to the man about it. I think it happened to Johnny Cash, Willie Nelson, it certainly has happened to me. Bob Dylan is probably the best example of it and I think there are some people who are willing to sacrifice their fame or fortune in order to keep evolving as a human being and to keep writing and there are others who will not.

But the reality of the business is so difficult, isn't it? Touring gets more expensive every year as income decreases from song sales, and of course those huge tax and alimony bills that seem to have inspired so many American songs.

Well aside from the regular day-to-day business of having a life, there are internal struggles that everyone has, and you come to view yourself sometimes when you're looking at yourself and take into account how other people see you. I mean that's what you have to do.

Otherwise you just become insane. So you take into account your surroundings, how people perceive you, their reactions to you, and what you say, what you do. Some people are more immune to that than others, but most of the people who I have admired – not just their talents, but their struggle and to keep creating, to keep exploring – those people have all had to struggle with this... Anybody who has become very well-known has become well-known in a place and time in relation to a reality, and when that changes it's difficult.

That's what happened to what we were saying earlier: to guys like Peter Bellamy and the Young Tradition and the groups that I played with like Pentangle back in those days, and others. You are known for a time and a place and a relationship to it, and you want to move on, you want to devour more, you want to learn more, you want to get better at it, you know, you want to be more familiar with it because you love it. And when the audience or when the crowds, or when the public I should say, says we don't care about who you are now, it's the old guy that we like *[laughs]*, some people, like say Joni Mitchell, will say, "I'm just going to stay home."

Which has to be crushing for some people, absolutely crushing.

It can be. And then you've got guys like Bob Dylan who said, "Well I never gave a damn, so I'm not going to give one now." And he's still out playing and he's still out writing and he will not be held to a time and place.

I suppose you can look at Bob Dylan and say well he can afford it, but it doesn't necessarily work that way does it? It's not always a question of money, it's a question of have you got . . .

It's a question of one's soul, and some people are willing to sell it and others are not. "My soul's for sale *[laughs]* but no one's buying!"

But then again, we could look at someone like you: from what we know of you, raised in a loving and caring family where everyone's looking out for everyone else, which you've passed onto your own family, you'd simply take the cheque and give it to everyone else in the family – at least that's what I'd do!

Well yeah, who knows? It's possibilities, until you're confronted with stuff, it's just speculation. And it's fun to speculate from time to time, but you don't want to get lost in that because there's no end to it. I know a lot of people who got lost in time. Guys like Phil Ochs who I greatly admired, a great craftsman, good enough guitar player, good musician, wonderful songwriter but who had lost himself to a time. He was so anti-war that he had invested everything in it, and when the war was over there was nothing left to fill. And so at some point you have to reserve enough for you. You can't go through it like being frugal to a point where you're not willing to invest anything in the time that you're in, but you don't want to invest so much of it that when the time changes there's nothing left of you. And it's a delicate balancing act, and every artist makes those judgements whether they're musicians or dancers or painters or poets, whether they're writers, everybody has to make that investment into a time in order to be important.

I mean there are guys that I knew when I grew up who sang the old ballads. They were the ballad singers, and they didn't have to deal with that, they weren't doing contemporary songs, the songs that were a hundred years and older was fine. And there was no real communication from the stage, it wasn't a performance, they were just there as sort of documentarians of these particular songs. They were important, they were part of history and I can think of like Ed McCurdy or some others or whatshisname . . . ? I can't even remember some of the names, but they were . . . Richard Dyer-Bennet. He was a guy that when I was a kid I would see all the time and he would sing all these Child Ballads *[305 traditional ballads from England and Scotland, and their American variants, collected by Francis James Child, late 19th century]* or whatever and they were interesting, they were nice, they taught you a little bit about humanity, that it hasn't changed all that much, whereas some of the songs that I absolutely loved because they were these great songs, highway robbers and thugs of all kinds, loose women. Whatever the songs were about, nothing's really changed as far as humanity goes, it was just hearing it from a language that was a little old, you might say, and that was fun.

And the tunes were wonderful, I mean tunes like 'Greensleeves' *[first registered as a broadside ballad in 1580]* are still popular, I hear it on the radio today, New Age versions of it and styles like that. So there's a lot to say for those folks for the reason why we have got those tunes, why we have those words and we have that humanity, but the ones that I saw were not necessarily performers, they were entertainers in the sense that people would go see them and they could sing or carry a tune and maybe even play an instrument.

But I think at some point that wasn't enough, it wasn't enough for the public and those songs were relegated to become almost academia. And so the real performers were the ones that were connecting with the audience about the times, who in the circumstances had something to say about it, you know. Some with humour and others with anger, and I knew a lot of them, I still do. And I was just finding myself and, between all of these different potentials, I realised at some point that there's an audience for everyone. My father said if you can stand on the street corner and have a crowd gather round you, then you're an entertainer. Well, almost anybody can do that. To get to play in the big hall behind you is a different story. That's a different kind of entertaining, but it's the same basic talent at work. And then some people are more . . . what's the word . . . *engaging*. If you can engage enough people on the street corner, you can stand in the big hall lobby, and if you get enough people to get the lobby filled, they might put you on the stage in the back. It just works like that.

From the free stage to the main stage. But is it the same way of engaging whether you're playing Carnegie Hall or on the corner outside on 7th Avenue?

Same, it's basically the same. It's knowing what the limitations are, obviously I remember I grew up at a time before microphones, I grew up at a time before monitors, we didn't have that stuff. Some people made the transition to those things easier than others, I still found it . . . You know, it was interesting because when I was a kid in school I remember being in the drama department of the school I was going to and the teacher telling us, "If I cannot hear you from the back of the room you are not projecting!" Well, projection was an idea that ended with the microphone, it ended not just in singer-songwriters or singers, it ended in movie stars.

And theatre actors, tell me about it.

Exactly. So when they make that transition from theatre to movie it's the same talent but it's a different ability, you have to know how to succeed in both. You may know one better than the other – I was a lousy actor as far as movies went because I grew up when you were projecting, I could not *not* project! I always spoke loud enough so that the last person in the room could hear me clearly. It was not good for movies.

You could have a Back to Basics tour – 'Arlo Guthrie: Literally Unplugged'.

[laughs] Well I don't even know if my voice could do it these days!

People possibly wouldn't understand that sort of thing, they literally wouldn't hear it.

Because I've been doing the microphone bit now for fifty years and I'm kind of used to it, there are techniques to that also. There were different kinds of microphones fifty years ago than there are today. And now I think there's a lot of young actors and singers who have to trust the ability of another person, which is the guy that mixes it in the back. The guy sitting in the back of the theatre in the booth is the one that you have to trust. Well, now you can allow your voice to be in whatever form it's in, whether it's a whisper or something like that, whereas in the old days the guy who made that possible didn't exist.

And the wider balance, from the singer-songwriter's viewpoint, usually involves a voice and an instrument or two, occasionally a piano, a banjo or zither, but usually it's an acoustic guitar. And that person at the back of the hall is changing the balance between the two — and the audience as that important other partner in the performance — creating all sorts of other nuances because of that intimacy. It's not just your voice?

Right. They're changing the quality of it, they're changing the volume of it, they're changing the relationship of the volume between the instrument and your voice, and unless you've got somebody you can trust it's out of your control.

If you've got strong material idoes it always matter how the delivery in a live performance gets across?

Oh, I've been working with the same sound man for over thirty years and there's a reason for that. It's not just because I like him, it's because I have learned how . . . I know what he's doing and I can tell, not just because of what I think is happening but from the reaction of the audience. And when the audience is very quiet and not giving me a whole lot back, I know that he's mixing it too low. I mean I know the guy, he's not listening to me, he's not going by my instinct, he's going by his own. But I trust him . . . at least, once I know what his modus operandi is, once I know what he likes, I can adjust mine to outsmart him as it were!

How do you respond to the audiences themselves? Can you change the songs in the set instantlt to meet or change a mood/reaction, or do you start on a journey with the gig because you know you're going to get the audience there? Do you go with the audience or even let them push you around?

Well there's different ways to do it, of course. I grew up at a time when nobody really communicated with the audience except for the songs themselves. Nobody actually said anything, or if they did say anything it was "And here's my next song . . ." and that was about it. And that was saying a lot! And I decided at some point that the saying or the talking between songs should be as entertaining as the songs themselves, so I started down that path and eventually I realised that I could create an evening, that I wasn't looking for the impact of one song or one story or one something in between that was off the cuff, I was looking to create a show that was a whole evening because I had also gone to see theatre.

When you go to see theatre or you go to see a symphonic orchestra, they don't say, "Let's leave this passage out tonight, the audience is this way, or let's leave that scene out, we don't need that tonight, let's take this scene from another..." — you don't do that. People come to hear the show, they come to see the show, and most shows, especially in the classical world, are advertised well in advance so you know what you're going to hear.

And that was also part of the tradition that I grew up in because my mother was classically trained. So I decided at some point many decades ago that I was going to create a show and not just a series of songs, and I still do that to this day. We give the tours, as it were, a name, there's not much swapping of songs or interchanging depending on the audience. What I do is create the show initially with an audience because one thing will work and something else won't, and once that show's together we call it a tour and we do that show for the tour. Next tour we'll start from scratch.

And it will actually be a different show.

And it will be a different show, right. But the days are gone when I'm going to sit around and just pull songs out of the hat and say, "Oh well I think I'll do this one", except if I can do them in very small intimate clubs which I love, because there's something wonderful about that too. But I have to generally sneak off to Europe or Scandinavia or somewhere where I can get away with that, because I can't get away with that here.

So what is the difference there? It comes again to being on the street corner in New York, getting a crowd around you but then playing the big hall up the road — the audience can only be different.

No, you know what it is? It has to do with the business and the politics of music, rather than the music itself. If I stand on the street corner in New York City and play some music which might be really fun for me and it might be fun for the crowd and then I six months later call up Carnegie Hall and say, "I'd like to do a show," they're going to say, "Well you're a street singer, you have no business being here." And I have a history of knowing what I'm talking about with this. I remember back about twenty years ago there were some clubs around the North East of the US that were still in the business model of paying performers, in other words they would guarantee you something, generally a couple of hundred bucks or something like that, and so people could do that.

Meanwhile the rest of the country had gravitated to a pay-to-play system, new clubs generally, even some of the old ones like the old Troubadour in Los Angeles that I was very fond of. Back in the old days they'd say okay, play a week and we'll give you so much money, these days they basically sell the tickets to the band and the band has to sell the tickets. That's a whole different way for clubs to make money and for musicians to starve, like they don't have enough ways to starve.

And so there were some clubs twenty years ago that still actually paid performers no matter who came and I thought I would go and help them out and do some benefits for all of these small clubs. And I said, "I'm coming, there's no money involved, I'll just show up." And I went and did them all. The next year I went back to the same places but to the theatres that I had been playing previously there and they said, "Oh no, you're a club artist." I said, "I did that because that's something I believe in." They said, "Well you know, we don't care, that was ten miles from here and you played that club, you can't play this theatre." So what's different is the business model, the politics of music, not the art of it. And if somebody is savvy in the business of it you make decisions at least with that knowledge. It doesn't mean you have to abide by it, it just means that you have to take it into account.

Wise . . .

Well that's just history, I mean I've been through this *[laughs]*. You know, I've played huge stadiums, I have played tiny clubs and played everything in between over the years. It's like a sine wave, it goes up and it goes down and it goes up and it goes down, and I'm fine with that because I love the music and I love playing so I'm going to do it anyway, I'm going to do it whether anybody comes or a lot of people come or nobody comes, I don't care.

That's what we want to hear.

Well that's just the truth of it. And so when I want to get to be able to play and not perform as it were, I'll go up to Norway or something like that, and

I'll sit there with a drink in my hand like the old guys, and somebody will say, "Sing this one!" — "Okay, sure, buy me a drink!" And you do it and it's fun, that's part of it, I love doing that. But I can't do that in the United States and continue a career with the tour buses and the bandmates and all the stuff. We save those moments for other places.

*

Iain Matthews

3

Iain Matthews

'It's just that for me it *is* about the lyrics'

Iain Matthews was born in Barton-upon-Humber, Lincolnshire, on June 16, 1946. He was raised in Barton-upon-Humber and nearby Scunthorpe. After leaving school early he worked as an apprentice signwriter before moving to London. There he became a founder member of Fairport Convention from 1967 to 1969, appearing on their first albums *Fairport Convention* [1967] and *What We Did on Our Holidays* [1969], leaving during the recording of *Unhalfbricking* [1969]. He changed his birth surname MacDonald to Matthews (his mother's maiden name) in 1968 to avoid confusion with King Crimson's Ian McDonald, and later in 1989 changed his first name's spelling to Iain. After leaving Fairport, he formed Matthews Southern Comfort to support his first solo album *Matthews' Southern Comfort* [1969], scoring a UK No 1 with a cover of Joni Mitchell's 'Woodstock' [1970], which unexpectedly started life as a filler track for a BBC Radio session. He left the band to record his second solo album *If You Saw Thro' My Eyes* [1971]. Forming the band Plainsong in 1972 he established a pattern that has shaped his work to the present day of alternating solo work with bands and collaborations, writing originals and interpreting the songs of others. He moved to the USA (notably Los Angeles, Seattle and Austin), where bands included Hi-Fi and More Than a Song. Losing his musical direction in the Eighties led to A&R work for Island Records and Windham Hill. After appearing at the Copredy 1986 Fairport Convention reunion, he returned with *Walking a Changing Line* [1988]. By 2000 he had relocated to the Netherlands, where he teamed up with Egbert Derix & the Searing Quartet, resulting in *Joy Mining* [2008] and a lasting partnership with Derix. In 2018 he published his autobiography *Thro' My Eyes: A Memoir*.

You've never been one for doing more than one project at a time.

No, not really. Possibly because I didn't start out as a player, just a singer, I think it's less likely that you do more than one project at a time. And I wasn't really a songwriter at that time either. So when you're only a singer you're less likely to do other things.

How did things unfold from that simple beginning? Was it you just concentrating on the next thing as it came along and things just followed on from each other right up to where we are at the moment? Or were there major events and influences that guided your career?

I've never pursued a career — it has just happened. It just built and built and before I knew it I had a career, and even then it was okay I have a career, let's see what happens next. I became a songwriter and I became a player, then of course the sideshow begins to happen and there have been distractions along the way, but still I've been quite choosy about what I've taken on and what I've rejected. I've taken on some quite unlikely things and I've rejected some very attractive things simply because they didn't feel as though they belonged to me but to someone else.

Can you define that sense of belonging? After all, you still have no fear of doing a cover version.

That's different because I do that on my own terms. At one point, when I lived in Los Angeles, I was invited to join the Flying Burrito Brothers — it wasn't an early version, it was probably the third generation Burritos — and I just thought well they want a songwriter, they want a singer, but where will this take me? It would have taken me into a third generation band that has a big name, and it just wasn't something I wanted to do. I really wanted to make another solo album and see what I could manage on my own. So that's one example.

You did decide to join Fairport Convention though, which must have been an amazing kickstart.

The fact that I've worked with Richard Thompson and Sandy Denny set me up in a huge part of my career.

And that must have been interesting for you all at the time because it was a learning period for everyone in the band.

Absolutely, but they were streets ahead of me. I learnt so much from that two-and-a-half-year situation.

It was a good place to cut your teeth since the band gigged extensively.

All the time! And then we were called in to record by Joe Boyd — "I think it's time for another album . . ." But it was only until after I left and Fairport did *Liege & Lief [December 1969]* that there was any serious direction. Of course everyone was becoming a songwriter at that time and you would see more and more original material appearing on the albums. Some bands come out of the gate showing you what they're really going to be, like Jethro Tull, but we didn't really have any of that. Well, maybe there was a hint of it on *Unhalfbricking [July 1969]* when Dave Swarbrick was guesting on the album. But I do think until *Liege & Lief* there was no serious direction for Fairport — there were ideas of course but it all kind of bottlenecked at that stage.

Do you think it needed you to leave to get them to focus?

Absolutely. And leaving wasn't all of my doing. Leaving was an 'agreement'!

So there was a sense that they were cohering, and you were the odd one out even though it was clear that you were also evolving.

I felt it, and I felt it very strongly. But I would have had to talk myself back into the idea of doing traditional material, which the band was really shifting towards at that time.

What was your objection to that?

I just didn't want to sing that folk stuff. When we began, the band were turning me on to all these contemporary American songwriters, singer-songwriters like Tim Hardin, Leonard Cohen, Joni, Dylan, Tom Rush, Tim Buckley, Phil Ochs. Yeah, you name it, David Ackles, Richard Fariña . . . I'm sure there are a lot more, probably a lot more than that.

You've already recited the litany . . . well, a significant part of it.

Oh, they were all American, the ones I was listening to. And then having brought all that in, the band then suddenly took a U-turn: "Right, here *you* go. Now *we're* going over here." And I thought okay, but I want *this*, I love *this*. I don't really see a future in *that*.

So after the Fairports you went straight into your first solo album.

Well it ended up not necessarily being a solo album. It ended up being called *Matthews' Southern Comfort [1969]*. But it was engineered to be a solo album. I took on management. I didn't know what to do at that time, so I went to several friends, just to get ideas. And *[BBC Radio 1 DJ]* John Peel of all people said, "You know, this might be coming completely from left field, but . . ."

Apparently Peter Frampton, who was in the Herd at that time, was a friend of Peel's, and Peter had these two managers who were songwriters, Ken Howard and Alan Blaikley. And John said, "I don't know why, but it just might be something that could work out for you if you were to talk to these people." He spoke to them initially on my behalf and explained where I was coming from and that I wanted to make a solo album. I think they saw me as an opportunity to feature their songs, so we met and talked, and that's exactly what they wanted, me to make an album of Howard and Blaikley songs.

I was interested but I wasn't interested enough to do exactly that. So we made a bargain, a deal — because they were really thought of as teenybop hit songwriters for acts like Dave Dee, Dozy, Beaky, Mick & Tich and the Honeycombs. The concept of them in music circles was that they wrote silly songs, when in fact they actually had some good strong songs. So I said, "Yes, if you write under a different name and if we do some co-writing together, plus I want at least two of my own songs on the album." They thought about it and said, "Okay, let's do it!"

I actually did get two of my own songs on the album, and I wrote lyrics for a couple of theirs, and the rest was all their material — Ken and Alan wrote under the collective name of Steve Barlby. A complete bastard really, forcing them to do that but they must have seen something there. And been very happy to do it.

They got me a deal with MCA — on Uni, a label that was just starting. The only tools they had were their songs and me coming out of Fairport, but it just seemed to click with Uni, and they got me a deal very quickly. And then at the last minute I pulled in some of the old Fairport people. In fact almost everyone I brought in to make the album were from that alumni: Gerry Conway, who's now with Fairport, but at that time he was the drummer with Cat Stevens, Richard Thompson came in, and *[bassist]* Ashley Hutchings as well. In fact Richard was brought in to produce the album, though he'd said, "I'll do it but I don't want my name on it." After doing a few songs, he told us, "Look, it's really easy, you can produce this yourselves." So we did just end up doing it ourselves.

Which was quite unusual at the time, for musicians to self-produce.

It was. And for them to go for a musician like Richard doing it in the first place was pretty amazing.

So there were no bridges burnt despite the former situation with Fairport Convention over musical direction. Nothing wasted!

No — and all those influences began to appear in what I was then doing, so they gave me that too. So that was *Matthews' Southern Comfort*, which was supposed to be an Ia(i)n Matthews solo album and at the eleventh hour I just decided, "I'm not ready for this, I don't know if I can be a solo artist." When the album was finished, Alan Blaikley said, "Well, let's give it a name, let's give the impression that it's a band and go from there and see what happens." I'd been listening to an Ian & Sylvia album, *Nashville [1968]*, and they had a song on there called 'Southern Comfort' that I really liked a lot. And somehow the album/band's name just sort of came up.

I remember being very young and thinking that's an unusual name. "Southern Comfort", it wasn't just the drink, it was more than that, and so it seemed strange.

We were more part of that sort of thing. We were more part of the hippy movement at that time than we were the Establishment. But we were also on *Top of the Pops* in 1970!

You've also maintained that evolving folk element, the fact that you can take completely American elements and make them your own. Which is also . . . well, to jump ahead, you've maintained that folk element as a vocalist too, you've got that wonderfully soft English voice, there's no gravel in it.

That must be my Transatlantic accent!

Well, Americans don't do what you do, that's the point. That first Southern Comfort album sums it up perfectly.

The first Southern Comfort album? I didn't really know what to make of that. I think most of the real direction for Southern Comfort came after that album was made. I'd put the band together by that time, and one of the musicians brought in for the first album was Gordon Huntley, the steel player. He was really the focal point in Matthews Southern Comfort because of his playing, because of the instrument and because of his age — he was a lot older than the rest of us.

Once we had that sound, having developed it for a live show, I then began to think things like that James Taylor song ('Something in the Way She Moves') or that Joni Mitchell song ('Woodstock') would work really well. So we started pulling outside material into that sound, developing songs and tailoring them for our sound. Once I began to see what we could achieve with that process, I then started writing my own material for that sound too. By the time we did the second album *[Second Spring, 1969]* we really had something going on, we were quite unique. No one else was doing it.

Again, as just a kid picking up on them, I remember the first three albums and thinking I don't understand any of this but it's great. As a kid you can do that.

But as you get older, you lose a lot of that naivety and you become more judgemental about stuff.

Which applies equally to audience and performer.

I think it's always there to a degree.

Which has to be a key part of the creative, moulding process, finding new things to challenge. That's why you do it.

Yeah. That's why I do it. I wouldn't say that's why everyone else does it but, yeah, I do it for the experience.

A bit of a therapist's question then, but are you compelled to write songs?

Not really. I don't push my songwriting very much. I go through stages of writing that are usually inspired by something, something happening, or the place that I live. I went through a period of pretty heavy writing when I moved to Los Angeles for the first time. And then again when I moved to Seattle I went through a big writing period. When I moved to Texas I went through probably the biggest one ever — it lasted for seven or eight years, just churning songs out because you're surrounded by songwriters. There's this give and take all the time in Texas.

What happened in the UK then as Southern Comfort began to unravel? Were you were unhappy with what was happening?

I just wanted to do more. I wanted more than what I thought that band was capable of offering.

Which was? A vision in your head?

A sound also. I quickly became tired of the sound we had. That band was what it was and that was the sound it made and I just wanted to go somewhere else and do something else. The next step was Plainsong after Southern Comfort. I met Andy Roberts and that was a revelation because he came from a completely different place — a real guitar player and one of those guys that would smoke pot and tune down his guitar to an open E and just play. He would get me high and I would listen. And I thought I have to work with this guy, it's revolutionary!

Was that easy to do? Could you get your management to sort everything and set up the deal, or was there a lot of resistance?

The management wanted me to be what they wanted me to be, and I wanted something other than that. It did prove to be a bit of a tussle. At the end, they just relented and thought, "This guy is going to do this Plainsong thing no matter what we say." So they just gave in and went along with it. Obviously we didn't want people who just went along with it, we wanted people who felt emotional about it. But we did have Sandy Roberton producing us — he was so focused and so gung-ho about the Plainsong music so we just paid off the management.

Literally?

We had to pay them off. But I didn't go straight from Southern Comfort to Plainsong, I did make two solo albums in between. In fact I made my 'classic' album right after Southern Comfort — *If You Saw Thro' My Eyes [1971]* — which in retrospect is probably one of the best things I've ever done, naive as it may be, simply because I didn't know what the hell I was doing.

I had great players, I had Andy Roberts there with me, and I got to sign to another new label, Vertigo. They'd just started off with Status Quo and Rod Stewart so they were up and running, and now they wanted a couple of singer-songwriters. You cannot buy that kind of publicity. They gave me what at that time was a huge budget to self-produce. Well not actually to self-produce since we had Paul Samwell-Smith lined up to produce the album because I loved what he'd been doing with Cat Stevens.

Paul agreed to make the album and then for some reason, maybe a couple of weeks into recording the album, he began to have problems and was away for a day when there was a session. He told me, "You do the session, it'll be okay, you've got a good engineer." We did the session and then he came back for a couple of days, then he was gone for two days, and eventually he just didn't come in at all. Before I knew it, I was producing the album myself.

So a special album in every respect.

Particularly once it hit the streets and the press got ahold of it. They embraced it and called it a masterpiece and so on. There were twelve songs on the album. Eight were mine and the remaining three were covers: two Richard Fariña songs, and one song by an American duo called Jake & the Family Jewels *[Jerry Burnham & Allan Jacobs]*. They made a couple of albums that you really had to dig deep to find *[Jake & the Family Jewels, 1970, and (as Jake with the Family Jewels) The Big Moose Calls His Baby Sweet Lorraine, 1971]*. I remember owning them at one point. Extremely clipped style.

And then your second solo album Tigers Will Survive [1972] came right on the back of that? Did people do two, three album deals in those days?

Three album deals. On the back of all the press, *If You Saw Thro' My Eyes* came out in America, it got fantastic reviews everywhere, particularly in *Rolling Stone*, so I went over and did an American tour, taking Andy Roberts and Richard Thompson with me.

Your first time in America.

Yes. It was a blast. We started out in Los Angeles, played at the Troubadour in Los Angeles for four nights. Well, we were supposed to play four nights, stayed at the Tropicana Motel off Sunset Boulevard, and we were on a double bill with Donny Hathaway. And we lasted one night. But to be fair, Doug Weston, who owned the Troubadour, liked us enough to say, "At the end of your tour, come back and we'll put you on with somebody more . . .", what's the word?

"Unusual"? "Complementary"?

". . . complementary." And he gave us Randy Newman! So we got to do the tour, went around America, became a good trio, and went back and played there, with Randy Newman, for four nights. And then you get back and the record company says, "Let's do another album."

Did experiencing America like that make you hungry for more in the same way that your time with the Fairports had got you stepping beyond their boundaries?

I certainly wanted to move to LA. I wanted to be part of that scene. I met some people (a) who liked what I was doing and (b) who said, "If you were here we'd love to play with you."

So the LA thing wasn't happenstance, it was something that went clearly into the master plan even though you say you didn't have one.

It definitely went in there. And then, within a year of Plainsong, Jac Holzman, who was running and owned our label Elektra Records, met with me one day in 1973 and said, "Instead of making another Plainsong album, what I'd really like you to do is to come out to Los Angeles and I want you to meet somebody and think about making a solo album for me." So he took me out to Los Angeles and I met with Michael Nesmith.

Who was busy co-creating country rock while moonlighting on the other side of the music business . . .

He was actually working within that Elektra umbrella. The Monkees were already a few years behind him, and Michael had made solo albums by then. He'd also become a producer and a studio owner, and Jac had given him his own label, Countryside. Jac put the two of us together although I wasn't quite sure why we were meeting. I thought does he want me to be partners with this guy? Does he want us to make music together? And then it became clear that he wanted Michael to produce an album for me, to be the facilitator. So I felt I wanted to leave Plainsong and move to California and pursue my solo career.

And you did.

I did. It was difficult. It wasn't very well received and I didn't do a very good job of it and . . . All those bridges have been mended since, but at the time it was very difficult, very emotional.

America must have seemed a long way away.

Sure.

But there you found a more receptive environment to craft your own

*songwriting, something that you hadn't really concentrated on before — as well
as finding other songwriters who matched your voice. That 'folkie' label made
more sense in the State where they've always had a broader interpretation.
Mind you, you're not helping people define you when you're on record as saying
that you listen to jazz.*

I think people expect me to listen to folk music. They definitely expect me to
listen to singer-songwriters and I just don't do that very much. I mean, I do
— I stay aware of who's doing what, but jazz is a real passion for me. Ever
since I discovered Miles Davis.

I was sharing a flat in London during the mid-Sixties. The building was one
of those old Victorian houses that were four storeys high and lined all those
big wide streets in Lancaster Gate — although I know the one I lived in has
gone completely. Every floor had something like three flats on it and
everybody knew everybody else and there were always parties going on. At one
of these parties somebody put on an album, by *[jazz drummer]* Chico
Hamilton, *Passin' Thru [by The New Amazing Chico Hamilton Quintet, 1962]*,
and I just had never heard anything like it in my life. It just blew me away. And
that was my first experience with jazz. And the guy said, "You like this? Listen
to this." And he played me *Kind of Blue [by Miles Davis, 1959]*. And that was it
for me, that was the beginning of my passion for jazz.

*That's really how people first discovered music, wasn't it? There were very few
record shops, plus albums were rarely played on the radio or television.*

Not much jazz certainly, no. And at that time I wouldn't have known where
to go to find it. Jazz wasn't on *[national BBC]* Radio 1, I know that. Most of the
music that I've discovered and liked has come from common word-of-mouth.
There are not many times I've gone into a record shop and picked up an
album and thought "hmm, this looks interesting . . ."

*Perhaps jazz from the likes of Davis appeals because although there are no words
it's all deeply lyrical.*

I don't know if that's it. I love words. I love good words strung together. I
think jazz just reaches me on a different level. It reaches me on an emotional
level sometimes, particularly with Miles Davis. I'm not a tutored musician —
I don't read music, I don't really understand music, I just feel music. And I
sense music. So jazz doesn't reach me on any kind of intellectual level, I'm just
open to it, and it comes in.

Obviously a song has to have good lyrics because they have to fit the melody or mood — and terrible lyrics can sink even the most appealing of melodies. But for me there also has to be personality behind those words, a great voice would be nice but it definitely needs soul. I think soul can be more important than the words.

Well you're not the only one that's not necessarily interested in lyrics. God, you can look at the songs that have been hits in the last fifty years and probably count on both hands how many of them have good lyrics. So it's not necessarily about the lyrics, it's just that for me it *is* about the lyrics.

That makes you a singer-songwriter. Which means exactly what to you?

It just means, I think, that people have to put a label on something. If it's not 'folk music' then it's probably 'singer-songwriter'.

And you think that's a very British attitude?

No, I think it's universal. It's a very American attitude, if anything. To come back to the question of lyrics, there are instances where, if the lyrics are half decent, I think a strong melody can sell the song.

But not necessarily?

But not necessarily. Not in general. It's more the lyrics, because people have made lyrics their own, they relate lyrics to their own circumstances and embrace those lyrics because of that, and so that becomes their favourite song.

Does this make you a modern poet?

Well, why not? In a loose way I suppose it does.

There is a difference, though, between the appreciation, or attitude, towards singer-songwriters in the UK and America, isn't there? In Britain people can be a bit suspicious whereas in America they're more accepting.

I think it's because 'singer-songwriter' for me is an American concept, and that's probably why the Brits are a bit stand-offish about it, because they don't really want to get too close to anything that's too American. I could be way off, but . . .

Hardly! The Brits and Americans have evolved similar slots in music traditions, haven't they? But of course things are going to turn out different in the mix. That rift in attitudes to singer-songwriter is particularly defined by the parallel evolutionary explosion in popular music on both sides of the Atlantic during the Sixties and Seventies. What we might hear as folk, Americans might hear as indie or rock, and vice-versa. Willie Dixon's 'You Need Love' becomes Led Zeppelin's 'Whole Lotta Love', Jethro Tull's 'We Used to Know' becomes the Eagles' 'Hotel California'.

Did the Eagles ever listen to Jethro Tull?

Sure. And to Matthews Southern Comfort.

Yeah. Because I was big pals with those guys when I first moved to LA, and I know they listened to *my* stuff!

But there's also the magic of seeing the confluences of all these influences.

In the beginning it either came from Ireland/Scotland or Africa. And then it sort of went backwards and forwards.

And they meet up in London, LA or Liverpool. Or even Scunthorpe, which is where you were raised.

True. In fact my mother was from Lincolnshire. She was from a small town called Barton-upon-Humber. And my father . . . I never knew my father, I grew up with my *(step)*dad, but I never knew my father, he was from Tottenham apparently. An anaesthetist. My mum was in the Army when they met. By the time I was born in 1946 they were separated and I grew up with this guy who I never felt was my father.

Was that problematic within the family home?

Only in later years, yeah, when I became a teenager. Then it became problematic.

You had siblings, but did you have much other family in Scunthorpe?

In that area we did. My grandma lived in Barton-upon-Humber. In fact most of my relatives lived there. We lived there too while my dad worked at the steelworks in Scunthorpe. And for the longest time, until I was about nine or ten years old, he was bussed to and from work. There were a lot of people in all the surrounding towns and villages who went to work at those steelworks. Because there were three steelworks, there was lots and lots of employment. Then the bussing just became too much and my dad decided we were going to move to Scunthorpe itself. They built a huge new housing development and we moved into one of these new houses.

So that made you very much part of that post-war generation. Brand-new housing estates, steel was still king and Britain was still sort of holding on in there. But it was also a time of austerity — and the steelworks could still be viewed by many as Satan's Mills — so was there any deprivation that you were particularly aware of?

Not really. As a child, everyone seemed to be well fed.

So you don't have memories of things like people celebrating the end of war rationing?

I remember rationing a little bit. I can remember going to the shop with my mum and she had these books and she would tear coupons out of the books and you'd get a bit of that and a bit of that, some sugar and, ridiculous, a couple of eggs. But in retrospect we were very working-class and we probably lived right on the breadline.

Whether there'd been a war or not . . .

Exactly. We didn't have a television until I was nine years old. And we had one of those houses where the fireplace was in what was sort of like a kitchen/dining room all in one.

Was the bath under the kitchen unit?

No it was upstairs! We had a *real* bathroom. And we had an outside toilet and a coalhouse and a bicycle shed. Actually it wasn't a bicycle shed, it was a laundry room — you know, they built these little brick bunkers with every house they made, a little brick bunker that had a toilet, a coalhouse and a laundry room. We had an inside loo as well.

That's right posh then.

Yes! So that's why I say we were *on* the breadline, rather than below it. I don't remember ever wanting much as a child. Although I didn't have a bike or anything like that, I don't remember ever wanting something like that. Nor did the friends I played with. We'd just go off and play in the park. So I didn't feel that I led a deprived childhood.

What was school like? Because again this was when the government set out to boost the system across the board and give the post-war generations a proper start in life.

I hated my school days. With a passion. I just didn't feel that I was well equipped for school. Maybe it was the teaching methods they had in those days, in the Fifties and Sixties. Well it wasn't even really the Sixties since I left school in 1961. I was fifteen.

So you left at the legal minimum of the time.

I was going to stay on and do a couple more years but then I was advised not to. I had one strong subject and that was English, and the rest of it I tolerated and they tolerated me.

If you left school at fifteen you had to be indentured in a trade, didn't you?

I left and became an apprentice. I was actually working as an apprentice signwriter, but the company I worked for was a painting and decorating company. So on paper it would have said "apprentice painter and decorator", but I was in the signwriting department.

Was that arranged by the school or by your parents or . . . ?

Our houses used to back up onto the next street, back garden/back garden. The man that backed up to our garden was a foreman or something at one of these places and he and my dad sorted it all out. I had no idea what I was going to do. I thought I was going to stay on at school. Then right before the summer holidays I found out that I wasn't going to. So I had to get a job in the summer so at the end of the holidays I could start work.

That must have been . . .

. . . quite traumatic. Fairly grim, to be just chucked out. Someone I know from my year, he actually did go back, but it was the school that said they didn't want him. He went back to school the next term and got frogmarched out by the headmaster.

I think that the Eleven-Plus exam they used to have was one of those first examples of either making you feel like a success or failure *[introduced in 1944 to test primary pupils at age eleven for admission to academic, technical or functional secondary schools]*. Eleven years old and you take an exam that basically determines the rest of your life. You either pass or you fail. You either go to grammar school or secondary modern. And instantly you're separated from friendships that you've made.

At the age of fifteen, if you'd just left school you could have kept on with your mates, because they still would have been living up the road. But if you've got to go to work it takes you into a wholly different world, and you will lose your mates in any case and instead end up in the company of a whole lot of . . .

. . . frustrated old men probably. But in retrospect, they always say that something good comes out of something bad. Working in that signwriting shop where they had the radio on all day long, blasting music out, was my saviour. Within a year of doing that, I was working at getting into a local band.

What was your first musical revelation? Had it happened earlier at school? Did they hit you with masses of classical music?

No. I don't really remember much. But my mum played piano. She was quite a good pianist. She wasn't a classical pianist or anything like that, but she liked Fats Waller and boogie. She'd buy sheet music of current music — she liked people like Jim Reeves and Val Doonican, so she'd play that as well. But she was also into buying albums of stuff that she liked, so she opened up that world for me. She bought a little Dansette *[record-player]* and LPs, which in turn I started to do too.

What religion was your family?

Presbyterians I think. Or nothing really . . . Church of England, but they weren't churchgoers or anything. They sent me to Salvation Army when I was a kid. I think mostly because the Salvation Army came knocking on the door — you know, "give us your kids!" Well they used to do that in the Fifties and Sixties, soliciting for churchgoers, selling their religion. My mum thought, "What a great way to have a peaceful Sunday." I didn't get much from the scriptures and stuff, they just wanted bodies. It got to a place where you had a little stamp book, and at the end of the year, depending on how many times you'd been to Salvation Army, you got a prize at the end of the year. Everybody got a gift every Christmas — a book — at the Christmas party. Depending on how much attendance you'd had determined what kind of book you got.

You must have picked up on all that Salvation Army music, the brass band arrangements and the hymns.

What I did learn in the Salvation Army was harmony. I used to get myself as close to the band as I could — they all took up the front two benches and then it was the rest of us behind them. I used to sit behind this kid, Melvin Thurlby — he was in the band, he played the trumpet and he sang. And when he sang it was strange because he was singing the same words and the same song, but he was singing a different melody. I was fascinated by what he was doing. I must have been, oh, eight or nine years old. Melvin explained to me that it was called harmony. But I also love brass band stuff! I have a real connection with that.

Was the Scunthorpe area full of brass bands?

Not really, that was more Yorkshire, more the collieries . . .

That's all the sort of experience that you can't learn. You have to live it.

Exactly, and that sort of stuff doesn't exist any more. Personally I feel I was in the right place at the right time. Everything converged just right.

After your first orange and banana, when did you see your first guitar?

Oh, that was much later than my first orange and banana! When I saw my first guitar was when I lived in Scunthorpe — it was in a pawnshop. I was leering through the window, they were electric guitars and I had no idea you needed an amplifier to play them. At some point I bought one. I don't remember whether it was any good or not. I do remember taking it home and looking at it, and not doing much with it. I don't know what happened to that guitar but it was a great thing to just kind of hold. You know, watch TV and hold your guitar.

But when you went to work, you'd got the radio on, you'd got slightly older people, you realise there's another world out there and you're getting older as well. And you're hitting fifteen, sixteen, which is when your body's telling you to break away, and your family would just about let you do that. Within a year of hitting that point, I realised that the town held nothing for me, there was absolutely no point in staying there.

I had friends around the corner who, every couple of weeks, would go down to London and buy clothes and come back and show everybody what they'd got, and they'd see bands and got to clubs. I started doing that with them and before I knew it I'd made a couple of friends down there in London and they said "Look, come, stay with us till you find something and just come" — which is what I ended up doing by the time I was seventeen.

Was there much resistance from the family?

Not really. In fact there was no resistance at all. I think my mum kind of saw the writing on the wall and she was happy for me to get out of there, because it wasn't a very healthy atmosphere at that point. And my dad just didn't care.

Was the music beginning to click in your head by then, or did this come slightly later?

I'd already been in a couple of local bands, singing Chuck Berry, 'Rockin' Robin', all the stuff that was flying around in the early Sixties. And I seemed to be somewhat in demand. I was headhunted from one band to another, so that made me feel good. It made me feel that I had something to offer.

I went down to London where my friends met me at the station and I just hung out for a couple of days. But I knew I had to get a job so I decided to work in Carnaby Street. I walked into shops and asked, "Do you need somebody?" And then I thought no, I need to be more picky about this. So I stood and looked around and thought, "Right, I want to sell shoes." So I went into the shoe shops. And the second shoe shop that I went into I met this kid that was my age and there was just a connection there right away. I didn't get the job, but he said, "Go next door, they're looking for somebody. And whatever they ask, just say yes. If they ask you if you've done it before say yes and I'll show you how to do it." So I went next door and I got the job and I made a friend. That was a Friday and I started on the Monday — I met my new friend at the weekend and he ran me through what I was supposed to do.

That was your entry pass into the environment you described where you then picked up on things like jazz. Which is something that surfaces unexpectedly in Joy Mining [Iain Matthews & Searing Quartet, 2009].

In my naivety I thought that to make an album like that, I had to be a jazz singer. I didn't feel capable. It took meeting *[pianist]* Egbert Derix and working with him to convince me that you don't have to be a jazz singer, just do what you do, do it as well as you can and do your best, and it will be perceived as a jazz album. And that's exactly what's happened.

You're doing fusion there.

Well it is fusion, I'm sure!

But that's a word a lot of people don't like.

They think of Kenny G.

Which has its place.

Does it?

Yes.

Yes? Far, far away from here . . .

But then you never took the king's shilling from the music business. Is that pure bloody-mindedness or because of the way you moved from project to project, reinventing and discovering?

Doing this must be the same as being a writer. You write one book and somebody comes along and publishes it and you think I've done it, I've written a book. So you've made an album, and you try another one, and you make another one and before you know it you've done five. And you think, well here's a body of work, I could die a happy man today. But then it just keeps going on and then you think, well it's gone on this long, so who's to say it's not going to go on even longer. Maybe I'll try something that I wouldn't normally do, I might not get another chance to do it. Maybe I'll try working with these people or working with these people, or writing with this person, what have I got to lose?

My career has gone precisely like that, jumping from one stone to the next and not really having a career plan but just wanting to experience things. Sometimes I've stayed pretty much in the same place and that's helped me make a series of solo albums. But even with those works, I feel that my writing has been influenced by different people and different events and so goes to different places.

But I've always felt that what we're doing is such a privileged existence, in the sense that we get to create, and we make it available for other people to experience. How arrogant is that?! In a way it's like letting people read our diaries except we deliberately sculpt their contents to make them attractive. Being a songwriter is like sharing your life with your own built-in therapist. Except instead of talking to someone about it, you get to put it down on paper, set those experiences or thoughts to music, and then hand it over to other people to listen to.

Well that's the job, isn't it? The challenge is to take care not to only write the good stuff when your life's in the shit, but finding the discipline to keep you above all that.

I agree, and I don't have to function on that level because I don't write about myself all the time. I try and spread it as thinly as I can. I write about topical stuff and I write about people that I admire, so it's not a case of writing when I feel like shit. But there's not a day goes by where I don't feel at some point in the day I feel that it's a privilege to be doing this. For more than forty years I've been allowed to do this.

You're looking good on it. You're sounding good on it.

How good can it get?! Having that attitude also really keeps your feet on the ground. I've never done it for the glamour, I've never done it for the women, I've certainly never done it for the drugs. I've done it for the music, the music is my drug, the music is my women, the music is the thing!

The collaborations too along the way, the people you meet, the people who inspire you?

All that comes because of the way in which you approach what you do. That's a by-product of the way you go about your business. If I was doing it for other reasons I would attract different kinds of people.

Then there is a consistency then that has informed your creative life? You started comparatively very young, precociously young some might say, and from the start seemed to exhibit a remarkable clarity and focus, even if you didn't know exactly where it was leading you. Does that come from the times in which you grew up or from your personality, your upbringing or the creative locations you found yourself?

I've no idea. *I* feel that from the very beginning, from the very first album I bought that my taste was already right there — The Impressions' first album *[The Impressions, 1963]* with all those fantastic Curtis Mayfield songs like 'Gypsy Woman' and the ones that followed like 'People Get Ready' *[People Get Ready, 1965]*. I wouldn't have got that from buying a Billy Fury album. Maybe an album of songs written by PF Sloan *[songwriter, Wrecking Crew session guitarist and subject of Jimmy Webb song 'PF Sloan']*, but nobody, no one other than Sloan at that time. And I just went on from there.

By the time that journey got you to LA, you made Valley Hi [1973] with Michael Nesmith, which was well received?

It was incredibly well received.

And then you also entered the cycle of album-tour, album-tour.

In hindsight it's not the way I would do it now.

It ignores your body of work for a start.

Yes it does. I look at people like Richard Thompson, who I feel did it the right way. Because he's such an accomplished player he was able to go out by himself and play his music and build on it that way, rather than make an album and go out touring then come home to sit and make another one. He was out there all the time. I didn't really start like that until the very late Eighties, which was the first time I ever went out with just myself and my guitar. If I had to do it again I would have tried to build a following that way.

But I was busy making albums in any case. I made a second album in Los Angeles, *Some Days You Eat the Bear . . . And Some Days the Bear Eats You [1974]*, which I thought was better than the first one, but by that time Jac had sold Elektra, David Geffin had come in, it was now Elektra/Asylum and there were twice as many artists. Well you just looked at the Asylum catalogue, the writing was on the wall, and I didn't get to make a third album.

So that explosion of opportunities had now become consolidation and rejection as the corporatisation of music by the labels started to set in.

But I was in the right place once again. Los Angeles was still a good place to be at that time because there were a lot of songwriters around — a lot of them not actively working — while there were also a lot of people looking for songs, which is how I got into my next situation. I still had a publisher still pumping me for songs and that was very important. So even though I wasn't recording I was writing. I wasn't on a retainer but I must have had money put by. I don't remember how I existed at that time, but I certainly had money. And then my publisher told me that the producer for the Flying Burrito Brothers was looking for a song. I had three new songs just done so I went down.

Now I'd already made friends with singer-songwriter Emitt Rhodes. He was in Los Angeles down near the airport. Early in his career he was in a group called The Merry-Go-Round and he made some solo albums, one of those first guys to play everything and produce it himself, sort of like the American Paul McCartney.

His solo albums are great.

They're definitely great. And it was through the record company that I met Emitt again and I went down to his studio. I demoed those three songs at Emitt's and handed them over to the Burritos producer Norbert Putnam. He chose 'For the Lonely Hunter' and played it for the band. The band rejected it but Norbert liked it so much that he said that just based on that one song we should make an album. So between him and my publisher they got me a deal with Columbia. Emitt was with ABC Dunhill.

I made that first album, *Go for Broke [1975]*, for Columbia and they promoted the hell out of it. They put me on the road and I had a great band. We toured a lot and I made another album, *Hit and Run [1976]* with the same road band, and that album I thought was just streets ahead of the previous one. It had sort of a jazzy edge to it because I had a saxophone player in the band and I wrote together with the guitar player in the band, Jay Lacy, who also had a jazz background. It was produced by Nick Venet, who's done some wonderful stuff in the past — he produced Don McLean and the very first Beach Boys album when he was a staff producer.

Nick was a producer that I'd admired from afar and when Columbia gave me a list of producers for the second album, I saw his name and picked it. There were some great songs, a lot of pace to the album and it just had this wonderful movement and we all loved it, Nick loved it. But the label wanted more poppy material, and so that was it with Columbia.

And that's when you ended up in Seattle . . .

That was when I ended up in Seattle. I was touring on the second album and met someone there. She came down to Los Angeles to stay with me for about six months, then Columbia let me go, so we moved up north.

How did you come to hook up with [Pavlov's Dog singer and songwriter] David Surkamp?

David had moved to Seattle around the same time. He didn't want to be in St Louis anymore, he just wanted to go somewhere nice plus he had a good friend in Seattle who was helping with his career. We ended up with the same management company and that was how we were introduced.

The two of you started the band Hi-Fi, which must have been interesting to compare with your Fairport and Plainsong experiences.

David and I talked for a few months before we did it because we were both doing other things at the time. The more we talked, the more it became apparent that neither of us had really paid our dues. You know, we'd gone straight into really nice situations and we'd never had to scramble and play in smoky bars, play four sets a night for people that didn't give a damn. We decided that we wanted to put a band together and try that and see what it was like. So that was the premise behind that. It was a three-guitar, bass and drum band. The first other three musicians were all from Seattle.

We were quite busy and we attracted some attention at one point, from Asylum of all places, who came up, looked at us and decided it wasn't for them. We put both of our albums out ourselves [*Demonstration Record, and Moods for Mallards, both 1982*] through a small production company called First American. We didn't do the whole legwork ourselves but we didn't put them out on a 'real' label. There's now a DVD of a half-hour TV special that we made, a documentary of that time, and you can see that our focus was being a live band. We got to the point where we could play three to four nights in the same room in Seattle and you'd get a good crowd there, three sets a night after nine o'clock.

That's certainly paying your dues.

It was fantastic. We were a dance band. Well, I mean that in the broadest of terms we were a dance band. For people we gave them their night out. They'd just come and dance the night away.

That must have given you unlimited scope to pile in the cover versions.

Oh yes! All sorts of things. I would bring in Buffalo Springfield's 'Mr Soul' or for an instrumental something like Fleetwood Mac's 'Albatross', and David would bring in the Yardbirds' 'Over Under Sideways Down' or T. Rex's 'Bang a Gong (Get It On)'. That made it a very eclectic kind of thing we were doing, but it worked because it was us doing it, simple as that.

There was even a Prince cover.

'When You Were Mine', yeah.

Who brought that one in?

I think I did!

And then presumably all that came to a close.

It just sort of did. David became difficult to work with, but not so difficult that it couldn't have been overcome. But at that time we made the mistake of not wanting to overcome it.

Well you also had other circumstances working against you, what with your network in Seattle of studio and record company going out of business?

No. It was really letting go of David that was the beginning of the end, it really was. *[Pavlov's Dog bassist/keyboardist]* Doug Rayburn then came in. We made *Moods for Mallards* when they were still both in the band. That made it a different band and after David left it was just as good but it wasn't the same. Well you didn't have David up front. He and I really balanced each other out because David was a wild man onstage but with one glance I could calm him down, and vice-versa. I was the quiet man on stage, but with one look from David I could get more animated. So it was a really fine balance onstage and it worked well. Even with the three guitars it was never overpowering, it was always just right, so it was a great band. When David left, that interplay was gone and it was just me fronting the band.

Which isn't what you'd want.

No. And then if that's going to come to an end you have to think about maybe moving on again. And at the same time my personal relationship was collapsing and I decided that I was going to leave the Northwest so I went back to Los Angeles — "Here I am!" So none of it was a mistake. I loved the

Northwest but I just wanted to get as far away from that failing relationship as I could and I had a lot of really good friends in Los Angeles. Between the end of Hi-Fi and leaving Los Angeles, 1980-81, I had a phone call from Sandy Roberton in the UK who had asked me about working on an album. We'd worked together on my albums before.

He certainly had that golden touch.

And still has. Sandy moved to Los Angeles and he runs the world's biggest producer management company, World's End Producer Management, and he seems to manage anyone and everyone in production on his roster. All the big ones.

So a call from him in 1980 meant to go and work where?

Still in London, although it was me who was still in LA. Sandy was still producing at that time, which he doesn't do anymore. He wanted me to make another solo album. So I made a solo album, *Spot of Interference [1980]*. We actually recorded it on a farm in Wales using the Maison Rouge Mobile studio. It's not one of my favourites.

Why wasn't it a good album?

Oh it was really just a flavour-of-the-month thing. It was very electronic and I wasn't writing very much at that time. I did a lot of cover songs and I just didn't think it was very good. We actually made a live video at the Marquee *[in London]* which is interesting. It's a great band, very tight, but it still wasn't one of my favourite albums.

The more covers you do, the less money you make off your albums so it must be brave to keep on doing the covers financially speaking.

Well I don't do it for the money, I do it for the music. I don't think in those terms. A good song is a good song, period.

But clearly you were happy to promote the album before going back to Los Angeles.

We made a concept video of the album, and I then took stock of what was going on and decided that maybe it was time to call it quits. That was my plan at least but I did want to stay in music. A friend in Los Angeles who was my publisher for Island Music said the LA office was looking to expand and develop an A&R department and he asked if I'd be interested in doing that. So of course I jumped at the offer. It was a way to stay in music, a way to make a living and a different way to be creative. So I started working for Island. It's funny because within two or three months I became closer to the guy who was head of Island's A&R in London and ended up doing a lot more work there than I did in Los Angeles. It was quite ironic.

One band I got signed in Los Angeles was Bourgeois Tagg *[later produced by Todd Rundgren]*, from Sacramento. They were kind of a progressive/funk rock band. Bands I worked with who got signed to the English label included the Rain Parade and the Prime Movers. And I also produced an Irish band called In Tua Nua. The fiddle player Steve Wickham ended up with the Waterboys.

Then I moved on to another A&R job with Windham Hill. They were starting up a vocal label and were looking for someone to A&R that. They were based in northern California, in Palo Alto, so initially I moved up there for while. Eventually when I established myself I came back down to work out of Los Angeles. But shortly after joining Windham Hill they decided they were not going to build a vocal label. They made two albums for it and then abandoned the idea, so I ended up working for Windham Hill looking for instrumental acts which was really not my forte. At the time I didn't particularly care for it, although in retrospect I did discover some really nice things that I've held on to that I like to listen to.

Looking at your more recent work, some of it's not that far away from that early Windham Hill ethic before it all got New Agey.

I suppose so. They did venture into more of a jazzy direction at one point. So the A&R work lasted for a couple of years, and then I started slowly getting the bug to write again another album. I went to the UK to play Fairport's Copredy Convention in 1986, the same year that Robert Plant did it for the first time. Robert took me aside and told me in no uncertain terms, "You should be making music. You shouldn't be doing what you're doing. You should be making music yourself, you owe it everybody." Then he said, "I want to hear another Iain Matthews album." I thought, "Okay, well that's good enough for me." So I began plans to go back and make another album.

Walking a Changing Line [1988] was basically a concept album which I wanted to be acoustic based, one hundred per cent the material of another songwriter, and to have a sort of New Age element to it, but incorporating as many keyboard players as I could, people whose playing I really like. Whether it was a piano or synthesiser or whatever it was, I just wanted these people on it. I made the album, some of the people I got, some I didn't. And then I took on management, they shot the album, and who picked it up?

Windham Hill?

Yeah! So I was welcomed back into the Windham Hill family.

So they did do vocal stuff.

They had an a cappella group at that time, The Nylons, and singer-songwriter Jane Siberry on the label. *Walking a Changing Line* was accepted very well. It was a huge surprise for a lot of people because it's not what they'd come to expect from me. I did the songs of Jules Shear, who's a great songwriter, a great lyricist, mostly known for other people doing his songs. He had a big hit that the Bangles did called 'If She Knew What She Wants' *[1986]*, Cyndi Lauper did another big hit called 'All Through the Night' *[1984]*. He co-wrote an entire Band album after Robbie Robertson left, *Tombstone [1991, unreleased and known as the 'lost Band album']*.

I knew Jules and his music from Los Angeles, when he first started in a band called the Funky Kings, and I liked his writing then. He was so helpful through the whole project, just feeding me demos and demos and demos, all of which which I still have. He must have given me a hundred songs to choose from. Once I told him, "I really want an a cappella song but I can't find anything in your catalogue that I can adapt", and he said, "I'll write something." So he wrote me 'On Squirrel Hill'. Really helpful!

Why him from the thousands of songwriters you could have chosen?

Championing the underdog. Here was someone I deeply admired and someone who was not on the tip of everyone's tongue. I wanted to expose him to listeners.

So essentially you're doing the Jules Shear Songbook.

Except most of them are songs that no one had ever heard because they were coming via new demos. So Jules was basically a new songwriter that I was exposing.

Is that something you would do again?

Oh, I don't know. Maybe! When making *Walking a Changing Line*, I had become really good friends with Mark Hallman, the guy who produced it for me. I was tired of Los Angeles. I wanted a new challenge, and Mark and I had talked about carrying on working together. He was living in Austin, Texas and so I ended up moving there for the next ten years. It's a good town. But that's the only attraction in Texas, the rest is a hellhole. But Austin has all these different groups of people. The University of Texas alone has 70,000 students, it's massive. They used to say when I was living there that the population decreases fifty per cent in the holidays.

Mark had a great background. He was very much into acoustic music and had worked with and produced Carole King, plus he was a writer himself and a really good guitar player. So we just bonded, I moved to Austin and, using that as my new base, we worked quite a bit on *Pure and Crooked [1990]*, gigged quite a bit, and did duos or even trios sometimes.

There was money in the gigs?

Yes. And Mark was my inspiration to ultimately go out by myself and play solo.

You've said that you wished you could have done that earlier. It seems an obvious move now, but why wasn't it so obvious then? Was it more a question of getting your guitar chops up to scratch?

Yeah exactly, I just wasn't capable. But Mark really made sure that I became a guitar player. He was relentless, he just wouldn't let it go. He made me into one. When I told him that I'd been offered a tour opening for Johnny Clegg & Savuka, but I wasn't going to do it because I felt I wasn't good enough on guitar. Mark just told me, "You're going to do this tour!" I replied, "But I can't do anything. I only know how to do one thing on the guitar." And he said, "One thing is good enough, but I'll make you into a fingerpicker as well. For this tour you'll be fingerpicking. We'll work on this stuff." And though I never actually made the tour, he did it!

That sort of step would be like getting up onstage to do stand-up comedy for the first time. Standing there with just one voice, one guitar. That first gig must have a been pretty nerve-wracking.

I remember doing a couple of warm-up dates. I went to Little Rock, Arkansas, where an English guy had a club called the Little Rock Folk Club and he'd been asking me for months to go play for him. I thought, "Little Rock, Arkansas? Miles away! That'll be a great place to go to do my first solo dates . . ." I thought it was just going to be some little out of the way club, but when I got there I found people waiting to see me play. That was my first ever show by myself. Well, I didn't say anything until the very end, and the moment I got through it I announced that it was the first time I'd ever played solo.

When you perform solo do you find that the repertoire is very different to what you would do if you had a band? Does that singer-songwriter ethos kick in?

It does, and I tend to pick from that Texas period. Of course I also do some older stuff as well as from my middle period, my LA period. I usually end up doing something like an a cappella version of those. Anything will work a cappella if you work at it.

If the songs are good they'll cut through anything won't they?

Exactly.

Do you tend to theme songs onstage in terms of the lyrics?

Not really. I talk quite a bit onstage to set songs up. I really like to make contact with an audience and talk about stuff. It doesn't even have to be the songs I talk about, I just like to make contact and to get some kind of ease with the audience.

The songs you were doing in Austin, were they quite American in concept?

No that's only on the new album *[Joy Mining]*.

Which makes it interesting that that crops up at this later stage, all that personal stuff.

I don't know. I think I've always written thematically, while I've also always tried to be as diverse as I can. I don't get much out of songwriters that just write about themselves and their lives all the time. I try to steer away from that whenever I can.

Do you still learn from other songwriters?

I think so. Particularly when you listen to as many songwriters as I have in the past I think you learn a lot more subconsciously than you do actively. But yeah, I learn by listening and watching, learn little tricks.

The craft is still . . .

. . . developing, absolutely! And even by *not* playing. For example, I don't play guitar with the Searing Quartet, I just stand up and sing. But even just by standing up and singing and working with them and listening to them I think I'm learning to be a better singer as well, because you sing in a different way when you're not accompanying yourself. You're freer to express yourself, you don't have to think about doing anything else.

So did your Austin period actively end in order to continue the progression of your work, or were things just starting to feel a little stale?

It had reached a peak and started to go down the other side — and at the same time my marriage was just not working out. The last five or six years I had been living outside Austin where I'd built a house, and it just wasn't working. I didn't care for the weather, I certainly didn't like the politics, and I began to think of leaving the USA because I could see myself in the future being there forever. So I made myself leave.

Did you have work to go to?

I had a *place* to go at least. I had a friend in Amsterdam who rented me a big room which was above his flat and that's where I started.

You didn't go back home?

No. I didn't have the opportunity to go back to England. The opportunity came from my friend in Amsterdam and that was what I did. But after I got back I did a big tour and made a new album *[A Tiniest Wham, 2000]. A*nd every town we drove into I was consciously thinking, "I wonder if this is the place, might this be where I want to be?" But it didn't happen. So we drove the length and breadth of the UK several times over and I just never felt any kind of affinity for any place that we went to. So I resigned myself to living in Amsterdam until I came to play Horst, in the south of the Netherlands, and stayed.

You picked a good time to move to Europe, what with all the energy buzzing about as people face up to the challenges of breaking down borders and laying the ghosts of the old orders.

The Netherlands is certainly a great country to live in.

People would love you there.

Then they'd hate me for not speaking the language!

So nowhere in Britain resonated for you?

No. I'm not much of a city person. I've done my city time. The problem about living in London was trying to find somewhere outside of London to move to. I couldn't even find a suburb, it just didn't work. So actually coming to Horst as the country town down the road from the big city was the best way.

I worked more in the first couple of years since I got here than I did when I lived in Texas those ten years. I suppose that's because I haven't been that available in the past. Historically I've also sold records in the Netherlands, 'Woodstock' was a hit here, Plainsong played here a lot in 1987. And they were just ready for me.

What is it that attracts Netherlands audiences at the moment to your work when you have to fight for that recognition in a country like Britain or, to a lesser extent, the States?

I have no idea. People here in the Netherlands are open to my music, they're not demanding of anything in particular, they just want to hear me play. I do go back to the UK and I play there a couple of times a year. Germany I play a lot. France I play a little bit. Belgium and Holland a little bit. That's all I need really. Don't really need much more. I go to Italy occasionally and Spain. Festivals, clubs, everything.

Did you turn your back on the States or did the States turn its back on you?

I think it's more the case of the latter. I tried going back to the States about four years ago to do a little tour and it was a total disaster. No one came and I got paid peanuts. So if somebody comes to me and says, "Can I set up a tour for you?", I'll say, "Sure go ahead and do it. But I don't have the time to convert anyone. I don't have the energy or the patience. If the doors are open, then of course I'll go and do it, but I'm not going to try and beat those doors down."

In terms of audience, then, are you limiting yourself to preaching/reaching out to the converted?

Whoever wants to listen to me, basically. I've just played a show in

Maastricht in what's usually a jazz club, and two hundred people came out. Egbert played with me so we did songs from the *Joy Mining* album and mixed it with some of my old material. But the audience didn't care what I played, it was fantastic.

Do you have a thousand and one songs in your head to pluck out a set from for a show?

No. At any given time I probably have about fifty or sixty. Some I remember the chords for and not the words, and vice-versa. I know there are musicians who are songwriters that can keep limitless songs. Richard Thompson's one of those guys, he just pulls anything out of his hat. I can't do that.

With the rare exception of individuals like Thompson, having a hat like that might make it more difficult to settle on a personal songwriting style.

I wonder. I wonder . . . When you can play anything, then of course you will play anything.

Back in Los Angeles did you set out to meet every singer-songwriter in town?

I met all the ones that I wanted to. There was a little clique of songwriters that when I first moved there that hung around the Troubadour: Jackson Browne, Tom Waits, David Blue, Henry Fry, this guy Ned Doheny who for a while was going to be next big thing. He started off with Jackson at the same time but Jackson was the one that made it and Nick was the one that didn't. Then there was JP Souther.

Who of course went into the Eagles.

Souther originally wrote for them. And Jackson was part of that, also writing for the Eagles. Don Henley and Glenn Frey of course went into the Eagles too. I was fortunate enough to find my way into all that gathering at that time — people talk about you, you talk about them, you get together and watch Richard Briars videos and play some music and do a few drugs!

We need to be reminded that this is what people do in Los Angeles. It's not all playing together and talking songcraft, instead you do a lot of hanging out.

You hang out, you go and eat, you go to Maria's and eat Mexican food. That was a good time. Joni Mitchell was still there at that time but our paths didn't cross although I had met her before when 'Woodstock' was a hit and she came to our show at the Palladium in London.

So what was her reaction to your cover of her song?

She never reacted to it. She never acknowledged it, at least not to me.

Including the Crosby, Stills, Nash & Young cover, it's extremely interesting to compare all three mega-versions.

I've seen what I've made from that song, so I shudder to think what Joni's made. Mine is mainly sales — having it initially sell and then having it on Best Of's and hit compilations. Joni gets a part of my sales too of course.

Nowadays the best way to get a hit like that is to tag a song at the end of a Hollywood blockbuster. It doesn't even have to go on the soundtrack.

Yeah right, the closing credits! None of my own songs have done that as yet, although I did have a performance of a Terence Boylan song, 'Shake It', that went into a movie at one point, on with the opening of the movie *Little Darling [1980]*. They took it from the album *Stealin' Home* [1978], with Tatum O'Neal.

Was that your publisher pushing it for you?

It was my label *[Mushroom Records]* because Terence had a different publisher. It was sort of a mid-size hit in the States. And it also appeared in the 2005 video game based on the movie *The Warriors [1979]*.

So, turning back to Europe. It's a natural home for you because it's a place which has always appreciated the song. Whereas America . . .

You forget, you lose track of what it is to be European living in the States — at least I did. I do assimilate whatever's going on around me and so I became very American. Whenever I came back to the UK and Europe I would notice it more and more each time how American I was becoming and how less European, and I didn't like it. I really wanted to be European again.

But not necessarily British.

Not necessarily British.

So there was a little bit inside of you that was fighting assimilation, because you came back not wanting to become a Brit again.

I was open to moving to the UK. It just had to be the right place. I didn't want to move somewhere in England just to move back there. I was quite content in Amsterdam, it's a good city to be in. It's a big place but it's a small town.

Turning then to the music business in general, you've obviously experienced hugely different facets of it. You've seen it from the hotbed that was London, and then the hotbed that was LA. While Austin I presume has always been a hotbed of musical creativity?

Yes, plus I've seen it from the other side of the desk also, doing A&R.

Then going up to Seattle and paying your dues mid-career.

It had to be done.

But you don't strike me as someone who has a high horse to climb onto so that they can go on about how awful the music business is, because music is genuinely every inch of your life.

Look at all the music that I have done. And I do listen as much as I create.

But on the other hand you must have some feelings about the music business because its general highs and lows have affected your own career, and still do . . . or are you totally out of all that?

It's funny, because when I was playing a gig the other day I introduced a song that was one of my anti-music business songs and I suddenly started explaining to the audience that I have several more like it. That got me thinking that I easily have an album full of songs that are anti-music business.

But a life in music offers quite a different road now.

It's changed so much. It changes every ten years or so, but even looking at those forty years it has changed so drastically. I don't envy anyone trying to break into the music business these days. Although, having said that, the good thing is that you can now record a great album at home. And you can have it heard. That's the upside of it. The downside of it is if you really want to get it into the hands of people, you have to be with either a decent label or a decent distribution company, and both are very rare nowadays.

Why has that changed? In the Sixties and Seventies you had brazenly mercenary record companies run by men who didn't have a clue, but they still managed to sign up good musicians — and back many of them all the way.

But the volume of music has changed so incredibly, there's so much around. So these people have become more picky about what they'll take and a lot of the time they miss the boat, overlook something that could be a masterpiece. My son-in-law Nemo Jones is a songwriter; he's made this album, he did it all himself, played all the instruments learnt to play trumpets so he could have horn parts on it, and great songwriter and great voice sort of a kind of Marvin Gaye kind of voice. He was the guitar player with Faithless for three years, so he does have the credibility to be with a good band. And he can't get arrested. He's got this great, great album sitting there and he doesn't know what to do with it. It's brilliant stuff that nobody will listen to because of, I guess, the sheer volume of things. And it *is* good. I've tried to get people to listen to it and it's like banging your head against the wall — they don't have time. It didn't come via a lawyer, it didn't come via a manager, you know . . .

Do you think it breaks that vital element of continuity?

I think it puts serious dents in it. It hinders it, like . . . I was going to liken it to a spit ball. You know what a spit ball is in baseball?

No idea.

It's a real hit-and-miss kind of pitch. You never know where the ball's going to go. And simply because of that a lot of the time it misses its target. That's kind of my Americanism side.

It's a good one.

Not as good as 'eating your own young', though.

I suppose there's a price to be paid for freedom. Today's up-and-coming artist doesn't have to go down the coal mines. If they want to be creative they can just do it at the drop of a hat or tap of a keyboard.

And they put it on the internet.

And five people look at it.

Or five million.

At least it's witnessed, which is important for anyone creative.

On YouTube I saw a fourteen-year-old Japanese rock guitar player who adapted one of the classic classical pieces, but this kid was doing it in his bedroom. He had something like three and a half million hits when I caught it. It's mindboggling. People usually put one of their tracks up there and are happy if they get a couple of thousand.

There's that pressure on you when you're young, you've got to pull off something big and huge. But when you're older, not many people in the business want to know even if you know how to hit your peak. But people with talent keep going regardless, don't they? That's what I call the Bluesman Approach: it doesn't matter what you do, you just do it because you do it, and one year it may be feast, the next famine, but you just keep on. Very Zen. Because you know it's right.

And you do it because you love it.

And you do it until you drop. Because that's all you know.

It is kind of like a virus. At least this music thing is. You try to get rid of it but it won't go away because there's no known cure. And it will lie dormant for a while and you think it's gone, but then it just rears its head and it's back again.

Like after you exchanged your guitar, well, voice in fact for an A&R desk?

Exactly. I also tried retiring a couple of years ago and then I met Egbert and it started all over again.

How long did you last on your self-designated shelf?

Nine months maybe. Enough time for my wife to up her workload and for me to dump a lot of mine. So there was a lot of confusion in the household for a while. Now we're slowly reversing it again. I'm picking up mine and she's letting go her side! But we're finding we're spending time together.

It's true what they say, you'll never get those family years back if you don't watch out.

That's right. And you know, I missed it with my first child. From my first marriage I have another daughter who has three children of her own now. I missed her growing up because we moved to Los Angeles when she was two and then within eight or nine months she and her mother had moved back to the UK. I missed her almost all of her childhood and I so, so regret it. It's there in the relationship — even though it's unspoken.

It goes with the industry doesn't it? If you've got to go out on the road it's what you have to do.

It's career or family.

The music business doesn't give you much in return on that level.

No it's difficult to take the family on the road.

If you're Paul McCartney, you can afford to.

True. And I had a friend in California, the songwriter Jesse Colin Young, who bought a mobile home and took his family with him on tour. He drove separate from the band and stayed with his family all the time. I think they had home schooling too, and a nanny with them all the time. So that was school on the road. But travel has never really been one of my big favourites. Fortunately, being a reader, if you travel with other people and share the driving, you can actually get a lot of reading done and stuff, but . . .

Perhaps we know how to cope with life on the road better now, but it doesn't help people twenty or thirty years back.

And tours don't happen that way any more.

How do you manage keeping your head above it all, to keep on making music and, as you said all the way back at the beginning of this conversation, to stay feeling privileged at do what you do, what you you enjoy doing?

Well that's precisely why. I'm doing it for the right reasons because I'm doing it for the music. The music has given so much to me, I just want to give back in whatever way I can. So I haven't been in it to either make it or not make it. So the stuff that could have become bitterness has become simply "so what?" In other words, it doesn't matter at all. I'm doing what I want to do on whatever level I'm doing it on. I'm still doing what I want to do, so it doesn't matter.

You also very clearly do the music for the listener as well and not just for yourself. What do you want listeners to get out of what you produce?

I want them to enjoy the music. I work very hard as a lyricist so I'd like them to relate to my lyrics. I'd like to feel that the lyrics are accessible and that they do apply to most people hearing them. In the end I would like people to embrace what I do for all the right reasons. Having said that, if they don't, then I'm not about to stop, I'll still keep doing it. This album in particular, *Joy Mining*, I've had so many people talk to me about a couple of the songs on it. The songs that people are relating to, the main one is 'God's Eye View' which is a song I wrote for my father.

I wrote it for my father who I'd never met . . . No, his surname was not Matthews, his surname was Pratt. I never met him, no. And it's a prayer really, it's . . . I regret never having met him and the closest I ever got to him was a photograph that my mother gave me that was taken on their wedding day that had been torn in half and the only half she had was the half with him on it. And you could just see her arm through his. And I never got a clear explanation about that photo, although, you know, you sense when people know why it is what it is. And that song just seems to touch so many people.

We did it recently on a Sunday morning TV show — it's primary jazz and classical music. We got invited to play so we did that song and we did the other song that I was going to mention, 'Waves', and within three days we'd sold twelve hundred CDs over the internet. On the strength of two songs. We did 'God's Eye View' first and when Egbert looked on his sales site he says that before he'd finished the piano intro to 'God's Eye View' there were over thirty sales before he'd finished the piano.

It's so reassuring that what you're doing is touching people. So that song has already more than validated doing what I'm doing right now just because I wrote the words, Egbert took those words and he put exactly the right music to them, exactly the right music to them. And that was the very first song we wrote.

Have you put your words to other people's melodies before?

I've taken other people's melodies and put my words to them a couple of times, not with any consistency. I don't think I've ever had somebody else actively take my words and put them to their music. This is the very first time.

So that's an interesting confluence of things for you, which also proves that you never get too far down the line for the inspiration to dry up.

That's right. A lot of the songs on that album are songs written about something solid. 'Waves' is one that really works.

Although for me the whole thing just works.

For me too. I really got my stories together for this album, they really worked out well. That's inspired us to take songs from different points in my career and give them to Egbert who adapts them to the Searing Quartet set-up. We do this theatre show where I talk about the songs and the experiences and we do jazzy versions of all these songs. Make an album to go with it and we're going to call it *'Sticktoitiveness'*.

We've talked about the concept of what makes a singer-songwriter. It's a label that declares you're not a rock guitar god or heavy metal singer, yet clearly there is a bit more to it than just writing songs and singing them. Do you go along with a definition like this, or do you feel it's something that's been imposed on you, that you're just doing what you do and avoiding the limitations of labels?

I came into this as a singer of course, singing acoustic music and listening to acoustic writers, and I think becoming a writer is really just an extension of your beginnings. You become influenced by other writers. I didn't play an instrument in the beginning so it was difficult to do anything but write lyrics. So I began by writing lyrics and having someone else put the music to them, and then I realised that to learn to play the guitar would be an asset and it would help my writing. So it's just something that evolves. Hearing great songs come out of people inspires you to be part of that and slowly, slowly, slowly you learn your craft and, hey presto, thirty years later you're actually a singer-songwriter.

Of the acoustic songwriters you've mentioned, were there any who were or are absolutely crucial in opening up those avenues for you?

They were all American: Joni, Leonard Cohen, James Taylor, Tim Buckley, American Sixties singer-songwriters basically. That was the beginning. And then of course the more you get, the more you want, and I just saturated myself with songwriters. I couldn't get enough of it.

You've never stopped covering other people's songs, and you've never been afraid to do a whole album of someone else's songs. Does that dilute you as a singer-songwriter or does it keep you fresh? Few singer-songwriters seem to extend themselves like that.

I've been in it for the music from the very beginning, whether it's my material or someone else's. A good song is a good song. I know some songwriters have a policy of only performing their own material but I don't feel that way. It's more making music rather than making a name as a songwriter. Like I said, being a songwriter is not a be-all/end-all for me, it's just part of the process. It was very organic to become a songwriter and it served me well, but it's not my motive for doing what I do. The music is my motive for doing what I do, and if I hear a good song, and particularly if it comes from a writer that people may not know about, then I do my best to expose that song.

Is there a message to what you do in the way that someone like Neil Young does it, where there's an issue behind every song. Or is it, as you said, an organic thing, if you have a message there is a message, at other times it's just doing what you do within music?

Exactly that. The inspiration comes from an honest place. I wouldn't write a song just to write a song. I would only write a song if I really felt that I had something to say. And whether it be personal or worldly it's all coming from a good place. I don't set myself up as a prophet or anything, I try to be reasonable about what I say. I make observations more than statements.

Then do you have any preferred areas of inspiration, themes that you return to, or is it again simply an organic thing where you adapt to where you find yourself going?

I've started to go back on my past, but I write about anything if it catches my imagination. I've been working on a song right now called 'Be Small' *[Iain Matthews & Egbert Derix, In the Now, 2011]* and it's about something that my wife Molly told me about how the Dutch kids of her generation were brought up, being advised by their parents to try and not stand out above the crowd, to fit in and be small. I was fascinated with that and so I started to put it into song form. It's just stuff that tweaks my imagination really.

Do you have a working method or is that again something that evolves from year to year?

I haven't really had a working method. I find myself more and more waiting for the moment to arrive, and it's usually lyrical. When you write lyrics you tend to have a cadence that goes with it and I tend to write the lyric and then I can look for the melodic part of it.

From the outset you've emphasised the lyric, which I suppose if you were a pre-war Broadway or Tin Pan Alley songwriter from the old days, the lyric would have been king and people would be humming the lyrics long before they heard the melody. The irony — at least from my perspective — is that none of them had to have any meaning and it was pushing it if they did contain a message. Without wanting to romanticise it, does the need to transmit a message or, better, vision put you in the direct tradition of the poets and bards of old? On the surface, all they needed was a catchy melody with a bit of a story to it and they'd get work everywhere they went, yet there's a mystique to their work since they come, spiritually as well as geographically, from somewhere else, which sort of makes it universal.

That's a nice idea. I hadn't really thought about it that deeply. It does work that way. If you have a guitar and you have songs and you have something more to say than "me, me, me" then you really can travel the globe and get people to listen to what you have to say.

Is there a difference in interpretation of that craft between the United States and the rest of us? Because you've said that you listened to the American songwriters when you started to develop your craft — but on the other hand, you're British.

I've never really listened much to British songwriters. Yes, the John Martyns and the Nick Drakes and the Richard Thompsons, but not really much more.

You were lucky because they were songwriters who were doing it around you so you couldn't really get away from them whether you liked it or not.

Exactly.

But then you didn't reach further afield in the UK but went straight to people from across the Atlantic like Joni Mitchell, songwriters that had a certain international element that America's sometimes good at doing and sometimes not so good at doing in reaching out to other audiences.

I don't find that. I don't really have to think about whether it will be good for an American audience or whether it would be good for a European audience. I just stick it out there and whatever catches catches, I don't really have time to consider that stuff. I think it's probably more difficult for an American songwriter coming over here and peddling his or her wares, because for those growing up in America the culture is just so much different. But I think I had the advantage of growing up over here in Europe and then living in America and then coming back here, so I understand what works and what doesn't. And I think my songwriting fills a lot of that middle ground.

Good point. Taking a couple of steps back to what you said about going out there armed with just your voice and a guitar: it's interesting that there aren't so many who do what you do who do it on a piano. Obviously the Sixties built on the mystique of the acoustic guitar, which on a practical level comes from the emancipation of being able to strum three chords and instantly get a singalong going wherever you happen to be (plus the fact that even an electric piano is a pain to lug around). But is there something else there, where channeling your voice via an acoustic guitar means that people can relate more to you, you can move about a bit more, you can project, communicate better than being seated behind a keyboard, even if it's while recording in studio?

It depends on a whole host of things. Your upbringing for a start. Look at Randy Newman: his father and his uncle both wrote show tunes and movie music so a keyboard was a natural thing. It depends who your influences are. If you grow up being influenced by piano music then of course you're going to turn to a piano. I think it's an unconscious thing — and by the time you realise that you can't take a grand piano on a train, you're already screwed!

Then do you see yourself fitting into any tradition as such? Do you have any sense of coming from like a Class of '68 or something similar?

As we've said, stylistically I've followed American songwriters more than British songwriters. There is a certain style to British songwriters of my era, all the Al Stewarts and the Bert Janschs. There's all the ones that grew up in the UK and stayed in the UK. John Martyn, for example, caught on to jazz very early on and his writing is influenced by that. And then the ones that became transatlantic are obvious — again, Richard Thompson is a prime example of that. And I sort of fill a lot of that middle ground. I'm kind of a 'curio' in a way because I'm neither British or American, and I'm influenced in my songwriting by both sides of the Atlantic. Maybe that's a reason why I've stuck around for so long because people possibly get a little bit more from me than they would from a straight American songwriter or a straight British songwriter.

> *There's certainly something that comes across in the way your voice and songs go together. You can listen to them from different directions at different times and always get something different out of it. And with your body of work you can't look at any one album and think, oh well that belongs to that period. Most of it doesn't date, which is always handy, and I would be loath to pigeonhole you into periods even geographically speaking.*

I think a lot of that is also because I realise my limitations, both as a player and as a writer — and simply my knowledge of music. I realise my limitations and I acknowledge my limitations, and consequently I don't think my writing has changed very much through the last thirty years. Of course every time you learn a new chord it changes a little bit, but in general I don't think my writing has changed that much. People more or less know what to expect from me unless we're talking about a more recent album like *Joy Mining* but then that's a whole other kettle of fish.

> *But on the other hand Joy Mining is still recognisably you.*

From a certain view, yes.

> *If you've had songs stored away in the back of your mind for twenty years which you're waiting for the right time to use, there has to be something quite special about them.*

It's really having a song make a connection with you. A song has to make a connection on an emotional level for me to go back and listen to it again, unless it's a very very clever song, and then that has the same effect. But in general it's a song that makes an emotional impact and keeps making that same impact over and over. For me, that's what keeps a song fresh.

> *People nowadays tend to shoehorn any old songs onto an album and that's one of the malaises of music over the past twenty years or so: a couple of hits jostling along with fillers or great songs that don't fit in. Even with download selectivity, you still want the choice of being able to listen to an entire album all the way through, confident that it's been designed that way by its creator. Songs on an album don't have to be themed, they just need to be songs unified as a collection by a common spark. If you're lucky, you might find something different every time you go back. Maybe that's part of what defines a singer-songwriter — or*

interpreter — that they can make every song count. Where it's done right, it can
be hard or even pointless to pick out a stand-out track.

Again, because I'm also an interpreter I have somewhat of an advantage over
pure songwriters because I'm not just limited to my own material. I can look
somewhere else for material, and stand more of a chance of coming up with
a solid album rather than an album with a couple of good songs on it and the
rest being just stuff that I knocked out. I think a lot of songwriters tend to
take whatever it is they've written in that period of time and put in on an
album regardless, without censoring it or without considering whether it is
album-worthy or not. It seems to be that, if it's a song they've written, then
it should be on the album, and I don't necessarily agree with that. I think we
all write average stuff sometimes and that's the kind of stuff that needs setting
aside and reworking. But that doesn't seem to get done an awful lot these
days. Songwriters just use what they have and then wait for the next batch to
arrive.

That's an important point to make: the need to put things in the bottom drawer
for a couple of months — or years.

Just using what you've got really limits careers too. That's why you see
songwriters come and go so much, simply because of that kind of approach. If
you don't edit what you do, of course you're going to end up with quite a bit
of average material, and by the time you realise what's going on, it's usually
too late.

You've heralded more than a few songwriters, but do you have a favourite great
undiscovered songwriter whose work you know but is less known to the rest of the
world?

My favourite songwriters these days, I can usually count on one hand. Elliott
Smith, who of course may not necessarily be much bigger than he already is
simply because he's not alive anymore *[he died in 2003 aged 34]*. There's an
American songwriter, Krista Detor, who I really like a lot. And this guy Nemo
Jones who is an English songwriter! I think he's probably one of the best
around but hardly anyone knows about him.

And of those you've already interpreted, who did you feel you really, really, really
latched onto something there?

Interpreted? Oh my God, it's so hard to think. John Martyn . . . I probably recorded four or five of his songs in the past. John's writing is undeniable. In more recent years maybe Richard Stekol — again an American songwriter on the West Coast. And Jules Shear remains a brilliant songwriter who still people are not aware of in general. In addition to the *Walking a Changing Line* album, I've done some of his other songs singularly too. I'm sure if I sat down and really put my mind to it I could come up with a whole host of them . . . Bruce Cockburn, Canadian, he's another one. On every level he is as good as a lot of the big-name songwriters but for some reason he just didn't make it internationally in quite the same way. I think it's how the stars align for all of us. They either do or they don't.

*

Ralph McTell

4
Ralph McTell
'Make sure it's got a great tune'

Ralph McTell was born in Farnborough, Kent, on December 3, 1944. He was raised in Croydon and named after Ralph Vaughan Williams (his father Frank had worked as the composer's gardener before the war). His birth surname is May, his stage name comes from the American blues/ragtime singer/guitarist Blind Willie McTell. McTell left school early and spent six months in the Army before going to technical college where he started playing guitar. His first album was *Eight Frames a Second*, followed by *Spiral Staircase* [both 1968], which included the first recording of 'Streets of London', recorded in one take. In 1974 he re-recorded the song which became a worldwide million-seller, winning an Ivor Novello Award. After this he experimented with touring with a full band to promote the accompanying album *Streets...* [1975], but dropped the concept. (Despite his unease with playing with bands live, McTell, Dave Pegg, Dave Mattacks and Richard Thompson formed an impromptu group in 1981 called The GP's.) Granada Television commissioned *Alphabet Zoo* [1983], a children's series built around songs written and performed by McTell. Reluctant to take on the project, he was convinced by the fact that Woody Guthrie wrote songs for children. He fronted another children's TV programme built around his songs, *Tickle on the Tum* [1984]. In 1992, the BBC commissioned and broadcast *The Boy with a Note*, 'an evocation of the life of Dylan Thomas in words and music'. He has published *Time's Poems: The Song Lyrics of Ralph McTell* [2005] and two volumes of memoirs: *Angel Laughter* [2000] and *Summer Lightning* [2002], combined as *As Far as I Can Tell: A Post-war Childhood in South London* [2008].

A read through your lyrics book Time's Poems reveals a remarkably consistent body of work. I'm presuming there's a lot more to come because that was done in 2005 and you're still writing songs, still performing.

I am! At the time of putting the book together I started thinking about the whole songwriting thing, how as you get older you realise how much more there is that you could be doing or offering to the art — if that's what it is. And I do think it is art of some sort, where it's up to the viewer/listener to decide how much of it is art. In its present form, songwriting really begins around the time of Woody Guthrie, and I've dedicated the book to Woody because it contains the very first songs I wrote that had substance, you know, the "I love my baby" sort of thing. Of course some might argue that my sort of singer-songwriter emerges from the troubadour from centuries ago, but it's really from Woody and then Dylan, and then all the things that have happend post-Dylan, meaning it is a new art form in a way. And as you get older you realise how much there is involved or could be involved in that writing process.

That question of art links into you being a poet too as opposed to just a bluesman or a troubadour. How did McTell the poet evolve? What spark came from Woody to light the torch you hold and which, presumably, successive generations of singer-songwriters will continue to hold?

If I'm absolutely honest, in the beginning I was just attracted to the sound of the acoustic guitar as played by one of Woody's sidekicks, a guy called Ramblin' Jack Elliott. He was not the real thing but sounded much more like the real thing than the real thing! I think he wanted to be a cowboy, and to play all the cowboy music he would have been aware of that was going on in America — which I didn't really hear at all, maybe a bit at the Saturday morning pictures or something. But it was all that cowboy music and the cowboy lifestyle and the freewheeling sort of lifestyle of the bum-on-the-road with his guitar, which Ramblin' Jack did a better, more attractive version of than possibly Woody did.

But then when I actually heard Woody, there was something about the integrity of his voice and his message, the simplicity of the guitar still twanging away there, and I gradually fell in love with the message. Here were the two things that had come together: my love of the sounds of the acoustic guitar, and then a meaningful lyricist who wrote in a simple direct way and a way to change the world and to echo my own beginnings — political awareness if you like. So they were the original stimulus, although perhaps that's a little bit too much of a rosy picture, as one tends to see it like that but there were probably a lot of other diversions as well.

But I have to say that I was obsessed with the guitar. It was in my hands all the time, I just couldn't put the thing down. And luckily for me there's only been just a brief period where I didn't play it for a few weeks. I play guitar every day and still love it and still get excited by the sound and effect it makes.

The writing side developed in a slightly different way. Whilst I was in love with Woody's essential message and his politics and his rather basic guitar playing, he indirectly led me to people like Blind Boy Fuller who was an intricate ragtime blues picker whose message was much simpler. A little raunchier and sort of more sexy, if you like, but the guitar playing was stunning. And then I heard Big Bill Broonzy who was darker and sexier and bluesier. And then I went on again to people like Blind Arty Blake and Reverend Gary Davis, who remain my guitar inspirations.

But because I'm an English boy from Croydon, I can't talk about sharecropping and I was never arrogant enough or pushy enough to pose like a rock'n'roller. My message is a much quieter one. But I could still use the techniques of the guitar player and when I started to write my own melodies they were essentially English, or at least the messages. The songs were English but the style was white and conventional but heavily influenced by the blues guitar players. So music was unwrapped for me through the guitar and through these guys but maybe a little bit more sophisticated than just simple three chords and improvisation around them — of which I will never tire — but I felt it was disingenuous for me to try and mimic that. Of course I have tried! I've got things on record where I've sort of had a go at it, but only in the sense that perhaps that Paul Simon or Bob Dylan might have nodded in that direction. Because we're not black, we don't have that sensitivity and we do have a different take on things because we're working-class or middle-class white boys or whatever we are, and our range of music is broader and huger and goes from Woody Guthrie to Hoagy Carmichael to the Beatles to classical music to European music and everything that kind of soaked in. I just can't single out the blues as the one single driving force in my music because it's not.

Do you think that with the people who turned you on, such as the guitarists you've mentioned, it wasn't their 'bluesness' as such but the fact that they were doing in parallel what you yourself did, that very punk thing of picking up a guitar and just doing it because that's the elemental tool that outs into reality what you want to do. You don't need amplification, you don't need to lug a whole piano around with you on your back, and you don't need a band.

Sure, but at the same time the great players would have loved to have been piano players. Of course the portability is a purely practical thing because if you listen to Arthur Blake, or Blind Blake as he's called, or Reverend Gary Davis, they sound like piano players. They play bass things as a left hand and they've got strings in the right hand. It's pianistic and polyphonic, and it has moving basslines and rhythmic approaches and inversions on the chords of which you can never tire. It can only just be something you aspire to get better and better at. And within that, of course, you need harmony, syncopation, counterpoint and all those things that make music so rich and attractive and wonderful. I still would like to play the piano, and I do use the piano at times, but I can't play it well enough to satisfy myself so I stick with the guitar.

> *Is is because you picked up the self-containedness offered by the guitar that you became a solo performer, at least live. In the sense that when you go on stage it's a complete sound as opposed to just some guy jangling away on a guitar.*

I like to think so, that's what I aim at. Often people have said, well they like the songs but they don't mean as much to someone who doesn't play guitar. If you play guitar and copy what I do and put the vocal line on it, it should sound pretty full. When I've been in the studio the bass player might turn to me and say, "Well what do you want me to do?" And I say, "Well play the bass." He says, "But you're doing that!" "What do you mean?" "What you're doing is bass is what you're doing, and harmony is what you're doing!" I'm quite convinced the guitar's six notes cover it pretty much.

For example, I've been working on a particular song now for three months: I got the idea and I've got the lyrics written down and I've got the tune but I'm now moving around on what I do in the bottom four strings when I play the chords, and having great fun doing it, and it's beginning to sound like a little band. That's what I want it to do. So my songs are guitar-and-voice songs, that's how they come. They don't come with just the melody line and the words, they come with a guitar part already written and that's all part of the whole thing.

> *That makes me think about not peaking at twenty or twenty-one but being able to let the well of creativity continue to flow. You always seem to come up with new takes on songs in terms of format and content, guitar and voice. If it's the guitar that's always keeping you going, it must be a good place to be.*

It is! It's funny, when people asked me when I was a kid what I was doing or what I was trying to do, I couldn't answer them. I can much easier talk about what I've done or what it was that I *was* doing because I now can look back and see what it was. This is an open-ended, never-ending learning curve, it's like jogging. If you start jogging as you get older it never gets any easier because you're working against the diminishing returns of the body's capabilities, so it's always hard. With guitar and with songwriting it's the same. You might get the ideas but there are always more elements to bring in to make it tougher and harder — and more worthwhile to do.

In other words, I haven't rejected everything and gone back to the simplicty of punk because the guitar and the songs and the ideas are still opening up. In my lyrics book, I tried to draw in the foreword my own take on the difference between lyric writing and songwriting and poetry — which is an art form which I absolutely love and don't fully understand and don't try to. I try to be poetic but that's not the same as writing poetry. But when you add that poetry and succinctness to an idea and your guitar, you're working within extra confines.

Look at lot of the young writers today. I was with a guy who was playing his stuff off of YouTube to me and I said, "Well these are lovely songs and I can hear the words but they don't rhyme." And he asked, "Does that matter?" The answer is yes it does it matter. The whole point of the exercise is to work within these confines to make something beautiful and aesthetically pleasing and *still* get your point across. This is what the succinctness of poetry and a proper song should be about to me, and I can't change that.

If I do, it's for effect. I have written songs that don't rhyme when the rhyme is so obvious that it's part of the spikiness of the tune and done deliberately. But I do try to achieve scansion and rhyme à la poetry while at the same time confine it further with a melody of structure and a brevity. I'm not very good at the brevity bit, actually, but I am trying! It's like the five principles of short story writing, where I think it was someone like Steinbeck who said: Number one, make sure you really want to say what you're about to say. Number two, given there's nothing totally new under the sun, bring some originality to the topic. Three, make sure you do this poetically if you can. Four, make sure it's got a great tune (this is my bit). And five, do it in the shortest possible way. And if you can stick to those principles I think you really have something.

Sounds good for achieving anything, really.

It is. I think it was ascribed to short story writing but it seems to work particularly with songs and it's something that I keep in the back of my mind always.

Bar the brevity obviously.

Bar the brevity. I'm still working on that one. And I do think that's why I love the poetry of the blues so much. I know it came to be almost a single track, where it's always about women and it's always about feeling a bit low or whatever, but there was some lovely poetry within the blues and working within that economy which can be something that's very impressive.

You wear your songs on your sleeve, you make it quite obvious where a lot of your inspiration comes from, and the ones perhaps that are a little obscure, well that's your business probably. Over the years have you always drawn inspiration from the same places you feel comfortable with or is that something that's always changing? Or have you done it batch by batch?

Very good question. I have to go back to my childhood . . . I felt it very keenly in the beginning, my father leaving the home. It happens to lots of people, I know, but for some reason it seemed to affect me very deeply. And although I didn't miss him because I didn't really know him, I was always aware that my life would be different, and the fact that my mum was one of them old-school women that went out to work and kept our little family together and all the rest of it.

But I was very kind of, can I say spiritual? I wasn't a Catholic or anything like that, but I was quite fervent religiously as a little boy. It took me a long time to work through all that and to realise that I now more subscribe to the *[chemist & thinker]* Peter Atkins sort of ideas on humanism and all that. I worked this out myself and I came to these conclusions at around about twelve or thirteen, which was catastrophic for me because my father died around the same time in an accident. I've always sought to believe that people can raise themselves up and that's why Woody Guthrie touched me. I had a belief in humanity which is tested on a daily basis because of the dreadful things that still go on in the world. Rather than reflect that in songs, if there's a chink of light, try and focus on that, draw people's attention to it and to a commonality of a spiritual need without believing in a religious ethic — because that's where I am. I think that humanity must pull together, must try, and I think music should help to lift people. It doesn't matter if it's a sad subject. There's even the kind of sentimental sad songs that I've written which are there to lift people up through my own experience.

So I think there's always been a need for a spiritual sort of recognition. And when it was taken away by my growing maturity and realisation that there probably wasn't a God then I felt that music fills that void for me — it's probably man's highest art. And, you know, you can be more specific about it if you add words, so you can actually *paint*. The music tends to be five or so points: it's happy, it's sad, it's mournful, it's delightful, it's danceable. But music isn't specific, so by adding words to tunes you can create something that fills a spiritual void. More than even painting — although they say that's probably the universal — I think music is the most important.

Music is probably the most universal art simply because it's something you can experience anywhere. You can walk in the street and hear it, you can be on top of a mountain you can still hear it, whether there's just one of you or millions. Whereas with a painting, you've got to lug it around and not everyone can experience it at the same time unless you've got a massive photocopy or put it up on the web, which removes a certain human element in any case. And books . . . well you do talk about them, don't you, but the actual reading bit tends to be a necessarily solitary experience, while film is a universal one. But it's music at the end that you can genuinely take with you anywhere, which is probably why we've ended up in the iPhone world. You can't put the Mona Lisa on an iPod, well you can . . . but music is subversive, it stays in your head.

You *can* put the Mona Lisa on an iPhone but it wouldn't be the same. Pictures do move me, photographs move me terribly, sad things . . . but music does something to me that nothing else does, it touches my emotions in a way nothing else does.

You evidently have had a clear sense of purpose from the age of twelve onwards of musical discovery, almost a duty, that reflects your own, deeply felt evolution through life. Does actually going and doing this in public . . . debase it is the wrong word because that's a terrible moral word isn't it? Does it reveal too much of what is privately going on inside you, making it over-familiar by projecting it night after night to a bunch of strangers?

No. I think you get another thing here. I don't speak to convert the world to my thinking. Some artists do. But that doesn't bother me at all. When we come together, when an audience and I come together, we work together for an evening, because an audience helps, an audience is part of it. I don't want to have everyone get up and dance. Somebody else can do that. But when we all sit down together — or I stand now but I used to sit to play — and the audience sit there, it's a two-way street. They're the receptors and I'm delivering the thing.

I'm simply trying to find the resonance in the audience and so, now don't get me wrong here, but it does feel like a celebration when it goes right. It's not hands-in-the-air-waving-and-I-feel-joyful, but it's a quiet thing that people take away with them afterwards. I know that from the letters that I get where people talk about getting their yearly shot of my concerts. I'm so happy that I get those letters, because you've never seen me push forward in the crowd to play my guitar or take a turn on sessions, I always leave it to other people. But when I go out on stage that's my performance limits, that's my celebration area, and it works.

It doesn't debase it, but of course it does mean that you have all the striving to create something that will make that make that resonance. You put it to the test, otherwise you just make records and not give a tuppenny toss what people fell when they're listening to it live.

You famously abandoned London very early on and found a home in Cornwall, moving down bit by bit and you've been based there ever since. We can talk about the happiness that that's brought you and how that fits in with your worldview but the bigger topic might be why you didn't go to America.

I would have liked to at one point. In fact I was just thinking about the musical side of things, about the fusion of music that was taking place in the mid-Seventies and the birth of country rock in the United States was somewhere in there. Perhaps through the Ry Cooder style of playing I could have made a contribution in that direction and maybe have found a way of broadening out the music. But that's what I mean, when I look back I can explain it better because it actually wasn't really what I was doing. That sort of music was a flirtation although it is something that I still love, and I still listen to bands that play that stuff well.

I actually did go out for a while to work with a guy called Danny Lane who was the drummer with Michael Nesmith's band. Danny had high hopes that I could make it, but it was no more than a flirtation with that musical idea of country rock. Essentially I'm English and what I do is English, and my past is there. I couldn't really have adapted and been totally happy with it. I have to do what I do.

Danny had been in my band when we were touring right after 'Streets of London' was a massive hit *[1974]*. The audience were shouting for the band to leave the stage and to get me back on my own. It was a terrible, terrible time for me. So I went over to America for a bit and I thought I could sort myself out and maybe make more of a go of it, but that was actually totally the wrong move. I came back to England and announced my retirement and then was persuaded to just wait and see.

My audience hadn't gone away, they were just a little bit confused! Since then, a lot of them have actually grown old with me, they've been incredibly loyal. And so I started working again and though we've done one other little minor flirtation with a couple of backing musicians, I've been solo ever since. I do prefer to work on my own, I think. You can pose with a cigarette in the corner of your mouth and a bottle of bourbon on the table, but if you're really honest about what you are, your music comes through and it will deny the sort of self-image that you might want to provoke. I am who I am, and I was better off coming back to the UK and staying solo.

Do you miss that spark of collaboration or do you find it in other ways?

I find it in other ways. I've co-written a couple of times and whilst both co-writes have been successful in their own rights, I'm not very good at co-writing. One was a song called 'Girl on a Bicycle' *[My Side of Your Window, 1969]*, written with *[American guitarist]* Gary Petersen and which picked up about half a dozen cover versions, which is not normally the way it is for me. And one was called 'I Love the Ground She Walked Upon', which I wrote with Phil Coulter, the Irish songwriter and producer. He's amazingly versatile — he's everywhere, he writes everything from 'The Town I Loved So Well' to 'Puppet on a String' with the Bay City Rollers in between, that's how he broad he is.

But in fact I'll despair when I'm writing a song even by myself because there's so many elements I'm trying to put in. If I'm patient they do come together. One of the songs on *Red Sky [2000]* was begun twenty years previously, but the idea had to be allowed to metamorphosise into something. That's one of the things I've learnt from Dylan Thomas. I can't say I learnt very much from his poetry in general, but sometimes you need a rhyme, and the rhyme that Thomas would use would lead him into a different area to what the original poem was going to be about — and sometimes you have to allow songs to do that a little bit. I'm always delighted when during my slow process I end up with a resolution at the end, something has resolved that wasn't going to and that you've come up with a really good punchline to finish with that your brain must have been working towards all the time without you knowing it.

When you started off, you rubbed shoulders with absolutely everyone as they were all making their first moves as singer-songwriters. Did you actively set out to collaborate with many of them, people in town during the Sixties as diverse as Cat Stevens, David Cousins, Paul Simon?

I was with all of those. I wasn't really influenced by any of them although I admired so many of them with their strength and their courage. I remember seeing Roy Harper for the first time when a lot of our contempories, I won't name them, thought he was an arrogant little whatever, an upstart. Which he was, but he was brilliant at being that. He was strong and confident and he played with conviction and passion, scary solos. There was me with my little timid voice and just hoping the guitar would ease me through, while he was a great big lanky skinny kid at the time with all that confident energy. While I'm cautious about making big sweeping statements, Roy relished them! And then I'd look at the poetry and the beauty of what Bert Jansch was doing — I've remained a lifelong fan of Bert's music and his guitar playing. And listening to the delicacy of John Renbourn and the intricacy of his guitar playing. And look at John Martyn, this curly-headed blond angel with all this bravado and

Scottish oikiness, and yet there's tenderness about him. And I even have a funny story about Paul Simon!

But you see, my whole thing was different in another way. Music is sexy when you're young and it has an appeal and people find you attractive through your performance on stage. However, I was married and had a little boy by then — and I'm still married to the same lady — so the peripheral sort of hanging out and all that didn't happen. Although Al Stewart swears that I was round at his place and all that, I never was! I was back home in my council flat, saving up to hopefully get a house some day and working every bloody day God sent. So although I didn't actually collaborate or seek to collaborate with anybody, I was full of admiration for what I call, or what Billy Connolly calls, the First Wave — because I think I was part of the Second Wave, I wasn't the Bert Jansch, Hamish Imlach, Martin Carthy, Davey Graham, Wizz Jones . . .

It's a sign of when you were born, something you can't really fake.

Exactly. Just a couple of years could make it that much different. The extraordinary thing was, I think, that Bert has helped me move to play with other people more. I always felt that there's certain artists whose strength and impact is diluted by precisely the number of people they choose to play with. Bert on his own onstage was always one of the most charismatic things, but certainly at that time he looked like he'd stepped out of a Laurence Harvey film. No pandering to fashion, maybe a pair of Levi's, and he looked like he'd come out of a factory or out of the building site or something. He just looked ordinary, he wasn't dressed like a beatnik or anything like that. But he had so much power, he had great guitar technique, he was a poet, he lived that free and easy lifestyle, it was quite enviable. He was the most genuine person where there were an awful lot of posers around. None of them seemed eager to collaborate until Bert found John Renbourn and they made *Bert and John [1966]* which led to Pentangle, but I still preferred Bert on his own. But we are talking soloists and there's a lot of them aren't there now? John Martyn did form a band later on down, but his reputation was really fixed as a soloist and they're all pretty much that way.

That's what you all had in common then at the time. Plus you all got labelled as folkies. That was a double-edged sword.

It was really. The reason for that is that although some of us were aware of folk music, mainly folk clubs were the only places we could play. The clubs were generous enough to allow the young socialist writers in, who then became *social* writers. Bob Dylan still writes folk songs in folk song format rather than rock'n'roll. He's never been able to break away from that and we love him for it.

But certainly my first gigs were in folk clubs, with exceptions like the Cousins in Greek Street *[Soho, London]*, which was almost exclusively contemporary singer-songwriters on a small stage. So it was folk clubs that supported us. I'm astonished that it's the only period in my life when I seem to have a complete blank. I didn't drink but I can't remember all the places I played, and I think the confusion is partly because by then I was that young man with a family, driving up to Liverpool and back in a night and things like that. I found some date sheets the other day which you just would not believe: Norwich to Liverpool, Liverpool to wherever, all over the country, every night of the week, trying to keep all that together!

If someone hasn't already done it, we need a map of the clubs of the time, which would help people get an idea of the mad scale of it all.

Oh, it was just amazing. Sometimes I go to places and say, "Well it's really nice to be in Burnley, I don't think I've ever been here before." And then at the end of the evening half a dozen people will come up and say, "You were at the Fox & Grapes in 1967. I saw you ages ago!" And I think, "The Fox & Grapes . . . ?" I haven't any memory of these places at all, but I've done my road time, put it that way.

It must have been an incredible time too, since your generation was part of that wave in Britain that was beginning to attract the Americans over, so the favour was being returned. American music was coming to you since you'd built on their efforts and legacy in a way that they couldn't and a lot of very curious Americans were now playing with you in the folk clubs.

That's right. People like Paul Simon were attracted, I suppose, to the folk thing, the folk ethic thing that also attracted Bob. And Bob Dylan and Martin Carthy are still friends. They will talk to each other on occasion, and Paul must have been attracted by the same sort of thing. I've only seen him a couple of times and not seen him perform because actually we were following each other around the circuit. When he was here, I was briefly in a bluegrass band called, for my sins, the Hickory Nuts. We quite a popular young outfit that were travelling around and I knew Paul was playing because we were playing the same sort of gigs as Paul in these folk clubs and so on.

I remember doing a solo gig, I can't remember what year but it's probably documented where Paul and I played at the Bexhill Folk & Blues Festival to which probably fifty old-age pensioners had turned up thinking they were going to get something else and fell asleep in their deckchairs to the Panama Junk Band who were on it — and me and Paul. At the end the promoter came out and he said, "Ralph I've got no money." And I said, "Well I'm not surprised." And this is my little story about me and Paul. He said, "I'd like to give you something but unfortunately Paul has insisted on his money." I said, "How much did he get then?" And Paul was on £20. He was on £20 and my fee was £7! Then the promoter said, "But I want you to have something!" And I said, "Well I don't want anything, Dave, I don't want anything, it's fine." And he said, "Look I'm going to give you this, I've got this from America and it's my most treasured possession . . ."

And now it's become one of mine. It was the Robert Johnson *King of the Delta Blues Singers* album *[1961]* on Columbia. I'd never heard this guy before but I took it, reluctantly, under pressure. I took it home and I still have it. It was one of those great moments in my musical life that I got this. I'd have spent the seven quid within a couple of weeks but here I am with an album that's lasted me from that time onwards and which still gives me enormous pleasure. Well I don't play the LP, I play the CD now. But that was all thanks to Paul Simon.

What happened to music after that period? Because it started to become split up into genres and the pingpong between America and Britain continued rather than it all fusing into one wonderful pool of transatlantic creativity.

It became an industry. I think it actually grew up in just two years. People started doing deals and buying records and promoting artists and accepting that the underground culture was just as important as the pop culture and you could create underground heroes. One thing was 'Eve of Destruction' *[1965, written by PF Sloan in 1964]* by Barry whatever his name was *[McGuire]*, let's write a protest song and do a pop promotion on it and it was a dreadful record but it was a huge hit wasn't it? And Donovan was plucked out of the folk clubs circuit and put up in the spotlight. He's a dear boy, don't get me wrong, I'm very fond of Mr Donovan, but with things like that I thought it was a betrayal of something rather beautiful when we were being told, or not being told, that it was being promoted as the music of 'the kids in the street'. It wasn't at all. We already had our heroes like Bert Jansch and still do, and he would never probably have been commercial. But an industry developed and that was it, that's what it was.

Well, there's the question then of how do you keep 'on message'?

You just have to. You look at what you've been doing, I think that's what it is.

It's not my job to take on the great groundswell of popular culture that determines what people want to listen to. It's like they're subjected to being compelled what they hear, what club they want to go to, do they want to wear those kind of trousers, that jacket? The things that keep you on this journey are never-ending . . . it can never end, you just get more degrees to excite and interest you and probably slow you down as well.

I think it's trying to be true to myself and knowing that time is finite for us humans and our time to contribute is limited. And, you know, I've always been self-driven that way. I've flirted and tried to make it more commercial and radio friendly and stuff like that, and it's been a *total* waste of time, because it's not helped, it's actually hindered. And sometimes you only realise, with experience and the passing of time, that if you just stayed on and stayed what you were doing, you'd be a much happier bloke than pushing yourself to run the 500 yards when you're only a sprinter or vice-versa. *[laughs]* You've got to pick your own . . . I have enough competition with myself, no need to worry about pleasing anybody else.

But you must have had huge pressure from the music business, especially after the explosion of 'Streets of London'. Were there any particularly horrible moments or potentially quite positive moments?

There were more disappointments than anything else, because by the very nature of the song, 'Streets of London' is perceived as a song of compassion for homeless people but it was actually written on a slightly different subject. That doesn't matter because the effect was the thing. But people were hoping for a follow-up or another song like it because the public response to it was enormous and they tended forget that the song had promotion for about five years, first in 1969 and so on, and I sort of regarded it as a step back.

But this was when I was signed to two major record labels at the time and they were continually hopeful. They were sort of sad that I didn't have the physical hot rock'n'roll pressure to do what they wanted. They liked me, especially at Warner Brothers where there was still an area within the label that nurtured people who they didn't really think would ever have major success, but gave the label some sort of credibility. I like to think that I was perhaps a little part of that. I was thinking particularly of Randy Newman and Ry Cooder, who were on Reprise, and others like that. They would have loved all this British contemporary stuff, and Warner/Reprise would have loved me to have had more success, but there was no real pressure.

Although I must say that I couldn't simply go, "Oh no, this is my way. I'm doing it my way!" I did try to please, as I've always done, even when they would ask things like, "Could you wear a different shirt?" or "Do you want to stand up to play that one?" or "Do you want to have some strings on this?" You know, things like that which I wouldn't say was really pressure. But I just knew what I wanted to write about and it wasn't particularly programmable or commercial. Without the radio and TV support you were kind of doomed.

Well you did something which for your particular generation was an extraordinary move. At the very begining of the Eighties you started up Mays Records, your own record label. As did Frank Zappa!

Well my brother, bless him, it was his idea when we realised that probably we weren't going to continue to get the support from the major labels. Bruce, my *[manager & younger]* brother, decided, "Why don't we do it ourselves?" We knew we had some sort of market and I just let him make the decisions and we went along with it.

The punk/new wave and indie groups had proved that this was a good way to go, but the people who preceded punk/new wave/indie didn't really cotton on to doing it that way until ten/fifteen years later.

You're right. It's not something that ever occurred to me. I had great respect for my brother's business acumen and just went ahead and did it. I think that's something you'll have to talk to him about more! But I think principally the label was mostly only for my stuff as I recall. I don't remember what else went out on it.

That would have made immense sense. Despite the fact that you trusted your brother with the move, did you feel that it was because you were down in the dregs or did you see it as a positive step forward?

No, I didn't think it was a step forward, no. I felt it was . . . I certainly wasn't depressed over it but it was an acknowledgement that having given it a shot in the commercial sense, it was the final proof that we would have to do it our way if we were going to continue to do it. And we could, you know, because if you sold probably a quarter as many albums yourself, you're in the same position financially. What we didn't know, of course, and we had to learn the hard way, is that a lot of success with records is about distribution and product awareness in the shops and assistance and the massive amount of money you need to promote. So we'd fast become a little cottage industry from that point on, and I think even though I didn't know the full implications, I accepted it quite quickly actually and just got on with it.

Aside from things like downloads and streaming, the business model now seems to be virtually no traditional distribution anymore and people have gone back to pre-Seventies sales and the best place to sell is at your gigs now.

That's true. It's things like point of sale, isn't it? If you've had a nice evening you take something home. And luckily for me, I've managed to acquire most of my back catalogue — not all of it, the first three records I can't get back, the ones that were on Transatlantic, I'd like to, if only to stop them interfering so much with our own efforts. Those are in every bloody petrol station in the country for a pound each or whatever they are, because of the first recording of 'Streets of London' on one of those *[Spiral Staircase, 1969]*. Funnily enough that's helped in a way because it has helped songs of forty years ago to stay alive and active publishing-wise, so a little bit of money does trickle in from that every year. It's amazing how often I'm asked for songs that I'd written forty years ago because people are aware of them from those records. But yeah, what can I say, that's the way it is!

So to start at the very beginning. You were born in Hammersmith, no . . . Croydon?

Neither! I was born in Farnborough, in Kent, apparently. My mum said to me that all the hospitals were full of mums having babies. I was born at the end of 1944, December the 3rd. My dad was a Desert Rat in the Eighth Army, and he'd been out in Ethiopia for some years before war broke out. When I was delivered I think he was around. I'm not sure, but he was due to go off to the war again and I know he did a runner at that point. He'd just had enough after seven years and had had a real tough time as a soldier, and it may have contributed to what happened afterwards.

So I was born in Farnborough in Kent, a town to which I have never returned, strangely, for some reason! And then we moved to, as far as I know, West Wickham which is just outside of Croydon, and from thence into Croydon when my dad come out of prison. I think he got a job there. Unforgiveably he was banged up in Colchester Military Prison for going absent without leave or whatever. Anyway, they set up home in a basement in Croydon, in an area which had some very fine old Victorian houses but which were very, very damp and wet. After the war, housing was at a premium, as it is now, so we were living in pretty awful conditions I have to say. But I grew up in this wonderful little street full of people who were quite okay and people who were deeply impoverished, and we all sort of had a wonderful time really. There was no TV, but certainly we had the pictures. I've written about it quite extensively in my book *As Far As I Can Tell [subtitled A Post-War Childhood in South London, 2008]*.

Croydon was heavily bombed, so it must have been like living in one big bomb site.

Definitely. We played everywhere like they were adventure playgrounds, areas that were being cleared and asphalted over for safety's sake. *[Concert venue]* Fairfield Halls was a bomb site before becoming a massive development, but I remember the space as it was, where we roller-skated. We went miles on our own — you know, we were lots of skinny little kids running around, you after the war, lots of fun, lots of outdoors, lots and lots of that.

When you were at school were there a lot of kids who had lost parents as a result of the war? And not necessarily because of fatalities, but as in your case where your father was a casualty of war in other ways and your family also suffered a form of loss.

That's absolutely true. The funny thing was that it didn't seem to me to be strange that there was only one parent in the family household because everybody went to everybody else's house and so there seemed to be more mums and dads. Amongst the working people there didn't seem to be many demarcation lines. If you were at Johnny's house then his mum would give you a bit of bread and dripping or whatever and a cup of tea and whatever. And because my mum was seldom home before seven o'clock at night because she was working, we were out on the streets.

So there were some children in the class that only had mum, but I never thought anything about it. I'm sure we were all just kids amongst millions in the same boat. A lot of marriages failed because people married on the hurry-up after the war obviously, and things didn't work out for lots of them. And remember that people stayed together and rubbed along a bit more than they do today, so I think there were some very unhappy marriages. But we had the streets and freedom of outdoors, that's why I feel my brother and I were incredibly liberated. You went in to eat and sleep and as soon as that was done you were out and about again. I don't remember spending much time indoors at all.

How did that fit in with school? There'd been all that destruction but then out of that came this incredible surge of physical construction like, as you said, Fairfield Halls, and also the construction of an entirely new educational system, health system and welfare as well. Did you feel that you were riding on that wave or again was it just what you did?

It's what you did. If it hadn't have been for the National Health I wouldn't be talking to you now because when I was five it was antibiotics that saved my life. I used to have to have lots of shots every night when I was in hospital, it saved my leg from an accident I had in Croydon when a lorry mounted the pavement and pushed me through a shop window, I think the driver was a bit pissed.

I survived that, although I would say I was traumatised. I seem to have been quite a sensitive little boy to whatever was going on and I was quite a nervous little kid. So I got great comfort from stories and from reading and having people read to me and my imagination was always very active. I also tended to be the gang leader, I must be honest, organising other kids. Not much good in a fight, so I avoided fights and stuff.

I didn't have many scraps but my brother Bruce said in an interview that he could always remember that I was very seldom alone because I just generated lots of kids around me. You got organised, whether it was running races round the block or quite elaborate games which you made up as you went along. But I think I felt lonely quite often and several times thought I'd had religious experiences with someone looking at me when I was on my own, like perhaps God was talking to me or something. I heard voices and I've written about this, like lots of voices all at once. I wasn't daft or anything like that, but my mum was pretty matter-of-fact and she wouldn't have been someone I could have talked to easily about it, although I do remember mentioning it to her. But you had to get on with things just like she did. She was on her own, she had to get on with it and I'm afraid we all had to get on with it.

Where was your mother from?

Winifred was born in Hammersmith but she was raised in Northamptonshire. She was born halfway through World War One. She grew up in the country in a town called Brackley which she doesn't have very fond memories of. Her mother and father met in service and when she was fifteen they pushed her out into service — all the family were away from home by the time they were fifteen. My uncle was twelve when he was shipped off to the Navy.

So it was that fairly brutal country life. There doesn't seem to be a lot of tenderness in the family, although my mum remembers her father with great affection. I think he was a bit of a mouse but he fought in World War One and I remember him quite well. He was a real Victorian country working-class bloke, who'd been a gentleman's gentleman, that was his claim to fame. He'd worked for a rich Dutchman and learnt some posh bits — you know, clean collar and cuffs and polished his shoes. Although they were all working class, they were what I would call upper working class, do you know what I mean? They weren't sink estate-type people. They cut the hedges and they were clean and tidy as best they could. My mum's dad was a postman and a bill poster, very ordinary occupations. On my father's side, I think my grandfather was an engine driver.

My dad was a bit of a naughty boy, got involved apparently in scraps and everything. He did a bit of bird *[time in prison]* after the war as well, we found out. And he met a very sad end, he was killed in an accident where he was trying to mend a defrosting unit in a butcher's shop. He'd become a butcher and he slipped and grabbed a live wire and was electrocuted instantly, which is a pretty awful way to go. And that was another great moment in my life where I can trace back a lot of the changes in my life — you had the beginnings of teenagehood at about twelve or thirteen when this happened, and I'd gone from quite high up at grammar school to very near the bottom. In fact within two years I was out and had joined the Army.

If we could step back then: so your father in fact left your mother when you were very little.

I was two and a half.

But he was around in the area?

He used to come back from time to time and pick up something and go again. We found out he'd had an affair with a woman in Croydon and they were living in Brighton, and then they moved out to a place called Loughton in Sussex, I think, which is where he got killed. But after I was six years old, I told him to fuck off basically. I don't know what happened, I didn't actually say that to him but words to that effect, I just had an outburst. We never heard heard from him again, he never sent a card or anything. I never ever had another birthday card or anything from him after that, none of us did. We never heard anything until 1959 when somebody read in the *News of the World* that a man with the same name had been killed in an accident, and one thing led to another and we found out that he had died.

Did your mother remarry or anything like that?

No boyfriend, nothing, no. Well she had a few admirers but they never stayed overnight or anything like that.

So there was no one who stepped in to become a father figure to you or anything?

No. It was a constant search for me after that. And it's not uncommon for young men to join the Army for precisely that reason although they don't realise it, and the Army itself becomes a sort of father figure. It certainly doesn't become a mother figure, but boys do volunteer to be disciplined and to be given some sort of purpose, and I was not alone. In fact I did my own little social survey when I joined up and found that there was only one boy in our intake platoon that had both parents in the same household. I always thought that was interesting because it's almost the same as the prison population.

You went to grammar school. Was that something that just happened naturally through school when they made everyone do the eleven-plus, or was it something that your mum or a well-meaning teacher pushed you into?

The school was in a working-class neighbourhood but it had a nice balance. That's to say our class, right the way through school — it was called Howard School, in Croydon — was very mixed in the classes. There were people that certainly had money. And there were the dirt poor as well. But we were all expected to pass the eleven-plus. And from about the age of nine I would say the course was developed to pass the eleven-plus. Now I was right in the middle. I wasn't the brightest kid, especially at maths, but I did all right at English and I was interested and I was quite well behaved, I wasn't a rebel or anything like that. And I enjoyed primary school in the main, and I think it was expected that I would do well at the eleven-plus and I certainly romped through the paperwork, I didn't have many problems with the papers I remember that.

But I wasn't prepared for the interview and it's really quite funny, because as I came in my mum had made me a new pair of trousers, because we didn't have any money for new clothes, mum used to make all our trousers out of old skirts and things that the lady upstairs would give us and that. So I had my new trousers on and I'd scrubbed my face rather too vigorously before I went and as I walked into this school hall for the interview a lady gave me a piece of card and said, "Read that!" and I sat down and just was like trembling and shaking I never looked at this card at all, and I had a quick look at it and then thought, "Why has she given me this?" and you know, it was like reading something the waiting room, you know, at the doctor's. Well I went up to the interview, they proceeded to ask me questions about what was written on the card and I didn't know what they were talking about. And when they realised I didn't know what they were talking about, they switched tact and asked me if I'd read any books lately . . .

Good for them.

Yes. I remember it so clearly. I'd read *Kidnapped* and they were very impressed he's read *Kidnapped* by Robert Louis Stevenson. What I hadn't told them was that it was on the back of *The Topper* comic at the time. And they said, "Well he's obviously a hero", and I thought hero in a sense like fantastic and gave the wrong name and — I can still remember my bloody interview — they asked me at one point what was a patron because it was a story about an otter on this card and he's the head of the family and I got everything wrong and I came away almost in tears thinking I've blown it. But though I actually didn't get into grammar school straightaway, what happened was a place became available and I passed what they used to call 'secondary selective'.

There was secondary modern, secondary selective and grammar school. And I got my first choice grammar school as a result and I can even remember my position in my first year: I came eleventh in the class, and I was promoted to what they called a university stream which meant we did our O-levels at fifteen rather than at sixteen and we were once again compressed, you know, where the pressure was really on us to do hours and hours of homework in the second year. I lived on a council estate and all I could hear was all my mates playing outside, it was torture. In the end it was shortly after I heard about my father that I just went to the headmaster and said, "I can't do this." And I got back out into an ordinary stream and went from top of the class to the bottom in two to three years because I just lost it. And that's when I joined the Army.

Apart from the Army and the working-class upbringing, I suspect I can relate to a little bit of that. I remember going from the top to the bottom as a result of family problems, and doing it a bit quicker than you did.

It's something to do with the battle with hormones isn't it? And I also became very aware of the other kids that had money, and mum was so poor but we still had to buy boots and jackets and all this stuff for the school uniform. I've actually done a search and there's a website of my old school, full of happy blokes with really great memories. But I just couldn't wait to get out!

What about music in terms of your family background? Was there any genetic material via your parents' backgrounds?

As far as we recall, my mum tells me that her grandmother and grandfather played accordions and were musicians. They played concertina and accordions, she said, not very well but there was definitely music there. And my grandfather made a one-string fiddle out of a cigar box and a broom handle which he gave me for Christmas one year. I got an old bow on it and I could get a tune out of anything.

But it was the harmonica, really, in the Fifties. You know, all the little boys had a harmonica and I was no exception, and my harmonica went everywhere with me. I could whistle in tune and play tunes. I also joined the choir at school. My mum is very musical in the sense that she used to sing and knows lots of words to songs and poems. She was a grammar school girl, she passed her scholarship as they called it, but she was sent off into service. I've asked her a lot about my dad. She said he used to whistle all the time and he was very fond of music. So just because he didn't actually play anything, I think there was music in the family but no instrumentalists that I'm aware of.

At school did you get things like Prokofiev's Peter and the Wolf or Britten's The Young Person's Guide to the Orchestra?

Sure. I didn't get it but they did do that. They did do *Peter and the Wolf*, yes — you've just reminded me of the first year of grammar school when we did that or maybe it was the last year at ordinary school.

So not really a defining moment. Was being in the choir such a moment?

I loved the choir. I still love the sound of a choir. I rationalise it like it's like socialist, isn't it? It's socialism, it's everyone striving for the greater good of the single corporate thing. I love the surrendering of ego within the choir and taking your place as part of a total sound. I felt it was very spiritually uplifting for me to sing in the choir. Unfortunately in our school choir I got bored because the music didn't touch me, but if I'd been in the absolutely brilliant choirs like those young fellows in the TV shows now, I think I'd have stayed in.

I did do a couple of performances in the choir at school, and I was dying to learn to play the piano, but not by notes because it was too mathematical. I got my mum to get me an old piano so we had one at home for quite a while until we moved to the council flat when I was about eleven. But we had a piano in the house before that — and my auntie had a piano. And as soon as I got married I got another piano. I still dabble and I'm playing this morning actually. But yeah I joined the church choir as well, but there was only two or three other boy tenors in the church choir and one of them was tone deaf, it was awful. I always had to stand next to him, so I found that didn't last.

What religion did you grow up in?

Well I had them all. I had them all covered except Catholic. I went to several churches on a Sunday when I was a little boy. I went to children's church in the morning, then left early to go and sing in the Church of England choir as a choirboy down at St Andrew's in Croydon. And then I'd go to Sunday school in the afternoon and sometimes read the lesson in the evening at the Mission in Croydon, the tin tabernacle behind the police station. But that all went belly up after I began to work things out. Religion happened slowly and it took a lot of courage.

But did that sort of music leave an impression on you, because it's pretty inspirational stuff?

Oh yeah. Church music is full of all the things that I love, it's thought-provoking, it's sombre, it's got these lovely harmonies, it makes musical sense with all the conventions in hymn music which you can trace right up to now. You hear it in ragtime music and marches and all sorts, proper melody and counterpoint and middle eights and descants.

Did you brother Bruce get caught up with the music at the same time when you were young?

My brother loves music but he's not musical at all. He can't even sing in tune. It's really weird. One of the most amusing memories that I've put in my book is about us going carol singing with me playing the harmonica to give us a slightly different sound. But my brother was one of the singers and his mate was just as tone deaf and it just sounded awful, you know, sort of bagpipey and vaguely Scottish sort of droning so it was a bit of failure that. But no, Bruce is not a musician at all. His two boys are musical, funnily enough!

My first musical experiences would really be from hearing my mum. I remember her singing Hoagy Carmichael hits in the early Fifties. But the songs that affected me would be what I heard on the radio and they all seemed appropriate to my mum's situation, you know, 'I Wonder Who's Kissing Her Now' *[lyrics by Will M Hough & Frank R Adams, music by Joseph E Howard, from the 1909 musical The Prince of Tonight]*, and things like that. And I wondered often if she knew the irony of it, even though I didn't know what the word irony was. But there she was, singing away in the kitchen about . . . well, was she singing about my dad not being there, love songs about parting or drifting about which were all wartime favourites?

My sensibilities were very sharpened by things like 'We'll Meet Again' *[1939 song made famous by Vera Lynn, written by Ross Parker and Hughie Charles, who also wrote 'There'll Always Be an England']*. That song touched me deeply as a little boy: God this is a song about someone going off who may never come home again. Or they're saying we'll meet again but *will* they? We're not told. I really got lyrics straightaway, the message that was in the lyric. And so those songs meant an awful lot to me and mum gave them the seal of approval by singing them. She tended to go for really good melodies, she liked Bing Crosby, Frank Sinatra and all that sort of thing.

As someone who continues to set the standard, is it easy to keep interested in what other singwriters are doing?

I've never stopped being interested in what my contemporaries are doing. I always easily want to hear what Bob Dylan's got to say for himself. I want to hear what *[the late]* Bert Jansch's latest album is like. I haven't always managed to stay on the roundabout with all my contemporaries but I'm interested in them. The other thing is when these young musicians say, "I'm really heavily influenced by, let's say, Led Zeppelin" — and that's their only starting point. Without the blues it's partly right but it's not embedded properly, it's not from the roots up.

I listen to stuff. I was listening to some music that this young fellow was introducing me to and it was all very fine except the music was without the structure that I know and it didn't rhyme. The sentiments and the expressions were all very good and arty and breaking young girl's hearts as they're supposed to do and making boys envious of their guitar-playing techniques, such as it was. But it didn't actually grab me much. I'm more traditional in that respect. I like proper songs in proper formats, I still love Randy Newman as a songwriter, I like Mark Knopfler as a songwriter, I like our Bob because he's Bob. And I tend to move towards more the conventional structures in songwriting because I can evaluate them better and appreciate them because they tick all the boxes that I feel are as important in my own life.

There's also what you've said about the blues and starting points, where people haven't done their homework and gone back to the roots of all this. We've seen whole generations of songwriters, guitarists, singers who may have been terribly flashy and very deservedly have millions of fans but there was something always missing in their work, lacking that bedrock.

That's exactly right and I feel it very strongly. You can nearly always tell now where there's someone that's got all the notes but in reality it's like BB King said about the blues. It's not the notes you play, it's the ones that you *don't* play, it's the spaces between that give music its maturity and its time to create the suspense and the waiting for a resolve, and then the next cluster you play are full out and excite you again. That's what great playing is like. You can apply that to the construction of all good tunes. You create a little tension and then you resolve it, the last chord always resolves the tune, or nearly always does unless you want it to not do so.

A lot of songs did break away from the rigid 32-bar structure, somewhere in the Seventies, post-Beatles. The Beatles were part of it, but probably David Bowie and his like did more in that respect to break up the format of popular songwriting, while producers like Tony Visconti understood it intuitively and made it all sound right. Joan Armatrading and other people have taken that sort of road on. But a lot of that music just doesn't touch me, doesn't reach me, and I'm still fairly conventional in my approach, I have to admit. I'm sorry about that but I am.

And yet you've explained in a minute what a lot of songwriters nowadays are still struggling to work out.

I really did enjoy talking to that young fellow the other day because I'd just shown him a couple of pieces on the guitar. I said, "You know this is 12-bars, right? See what's going on here, listen to the bassline." It wasn't a tutorial, it was just saying, "Look, open it up, you don't impress because you play fast, it's got to be grounded in something because we synthesised the music, because we've taken it from all sources and evolved it, and you probably have to do that too."

Our generation did acknowledge that blues influence, from the Rolling Stones, the Beatles and early rock'n'roll. You just can't come into it from listening to one jam twenty years back and expect to get it all right, which is how so much of the music is so bloody vacuous. I watch Jools Holland *[Later... with Jools Holland, BBC TV]* each week in hope for one act, just one act per week will do, that's got something I understand. And fortunately there nearly always is, but quite often I just despair. I think blokes my age, we've all become grumpy old men. It's very hard sometimes though . . . Anyway, enough!

But then if you were a young fellow now . . . well you've already told us the advice you've been giving because you've told us about the bloke you were talking to on Friday. But to put it into its broader perspective: if you were a singer-songwriter starting off today would you feel discouraged by it all, or do you think that if you do your homework there's still a lot that can be done, there's still new furrows to be ploughed?

There's a massive canvas out there. It's great to be young, you know everything don't you? Or at least some people do. It's a wonderful time because of your emotions, the way you feel about love, the way you feel about relationships, it's so incredibly intense and so important that it should inspire great work. So often our poets have written their most passionate and most wonderful work when they're young, and that goes for musicians too. And of course, they can then burn themselves out later and become clichéd and repeat themselves to get out of dead-ends and all that.

But I don't see music as a constant means of experimentation. We've all got to start somewhere. Punk arrived because of the music around that was so pompous and up its own jacksie in terms of the bands producing it. We won't mention any names, but it all got to become pomp rock, pompous great big titles and swinging symphonic stuff. Now people want to make music when they're young and you've got to go back to roots, so in a way punk reduced a three-chord trick to one chord whatever, and made it very loud. Well that's fine, and out of that some good songs emerged and good writers emerged. Few of them touched me deeply but I have to acknowledge they were a far more important movement. But in terms of which songs will last, if that's important, I suggest that the Sixties songs will outlast a lot of other songs, and in 2063 they'll still be playing the Beatles and, I wouldn't be a bit surprised, a lot of other writers from that time.

A highly personal question, can I ask you about your voice?

Yes. I don't know . . . I have to put my hand up and say I never wanted or expected to be known as a singer. I never practised, I sing out of tune and my phrasing is probably quite good and I can emote without trying, although if I do try it doesn't sound right! But I can create an effect, although I never thought of myself as a singer and I only started singing in order to . . . well at first to sing these lovely songs that I loved — about, you know, the Appalachian mountain tunes from America and Cripple Creek and then Woody Guthrie and these message songs.

But over the years I've always been sort of annoyed when I see 'Singer Ralph McTell'. I'm a guitar player who happens to sing that'll sing his own tunes, but I never thought of myself as a singer never, Nick, never. And here I am known as a singer. Amazing, you know. I don't understand it!

Your register at first listen appears all low and gravelly, earthy, but you also soar upwards at subtle points. You say that you don't emote, but you do have an extremely deceptively fluid range in that respect. Does that sound like a description that you recognise?

I'd love it if it was true! I mean I'm really not sure if it is. I've never been comfortable above a certain range, a tenor is about as much as I can manage without it hurting. I once did a song with a male choir down here in Cornwall, and they put me with the tenors and I thought, "Do I say anything?!" I mean, the choirmaster must know that I'm actually a baritone leaning towards a bass baritone. I think I can hit the lower A on the piano with clarity, although not with power.

So I tend to think of myself as a microphone singer. The ones I really admire are people like Bob Dylan who soars effortlessly like a cantor in a synagogue, he can soar without a crack in his voice. My voice does have the upper regions that are left behind although they're there quite clearly on my early records where it was fashionable to sing higher than you actually should. And I remember *[producer]* Gus Dudgeon saying to me when we did 'Morning Dew' *[Eight Frames a Second, 1968]*, "I didn't know you could sing that low" and I thought, "Well, I've always been able to sing that low, but it's not what you do is it?" You sing à la Nick Drake, à la John Martyn, and so on.

But I'm much more comfortable in the bass register, it's not baritone really. And I find that when I sing softly I get more . . . well this is something that's been pointed out to me by my engineers, I get more resonance from the lower end, singing softly, than when I sing high and loud. It's as if it gets compressed so I tend not to sing loud if I can avoid it. If I do sing loud, I also tend to go a bit sharp — and wearing headphones when you're overdubbing is notoriously bad for pushing you sharp.

Onstage I now use in-ear monitoring and I can say I think my vocals have got a little bit more accurate. But my wife Nanna said to me that since I've had these in-ear monitors I certainly sound more confident, but somehow there is a sort of fragility there when you were younger that seems to have gone. I suppose it's because I can hear myself a bit better and I'm trying, I'm being a bit braver at letting the vocal cords go. I sit at home here — and Nanna will tell you — and I play every day, but I never sing, I only play. I only sing when I'm writing to make sure the thing stands.

I toured with Steeleye Span and I hadn't realised before how Maddy Pryor goes through all her singing exercises. I do try to remember to do a bit of singing before I go onstage but mostly I just clear my throat with a little cough and wander out there and hope for the best. So I suppose I'm bewildered but flattered by your analysis . . .

I suppose applying a bit of back logic, it also helps explain why a full band is not appropriate to you. As you say, you don't have a Dylan voice that cuts straight through, you know your voice would just be lost, wouldn't it?

That's exactly right. And that's exactly what happens, I end up shouting when I'm with a band. I never learnt to cut through. Admittedly they can amplify Mark Knopfler's voice above a band and he's not got a loud voice, he's a talker really when it comes to it. If you think of his best songs, they are practically talked through. It is possible to mic up someone so you can hear them but I've never learnt to do that. You see, when I first started playing there were no mics in the clubs, so you played your acoustic guitar and you balanced yourself like that. The Cousins was the first place I had a mic and that was only running through *[club owner]* Andy *[Matheou]*'s hi-fi system with one speaker on a shelf. So I loved it as soon as I had a microphone. I found I could get a little closer to the mic and get lower, you know, a nicer warmer sound. But I have learnt to play in a rather muscular way considering I play fingerstyle. I'm blessed with very strong fingernails and I thumbpick so my bass end on the guitar is always quite strong. And I've got a few chops when it comes to fingerstyle. So I can balance myself without mics, and I still play much louder than most modern guitar players and singers because they're used to microphones. I have learnt and I have adapted but I think those early days when there were no mics in the clubs that sort of forged my style.

That's interesting! Apart from the occasional times you play piano, can you sing without a guitar? Personally, I can't sing without a guitar — I don't have to play it but it still has to be sitting in front of me.

Oh yeah, I'm pretty much like that. I don't know what to do with my hands. When we're overdubbing I find my hands are on my earphones or I'm holding on to something. But you know it's an unforced thing, your guitar and voice, they're a symbiosis — if that's the right word — you don't do one without the other. And do to it unnaturally, you can get a vocal that will please an engineer but you listen back to it and it sounds like it's not you.

I sing and play live, that's what I do. And I've been trying to do that on my most recent albums in terms of recording. Gus Dudgeon was a fantastic producer but he wanted everything to have sparkling clean underwear. It didn't matter what you did, it had to be clean. So your guitar had to be clean and then your voice had to be clean, everything was with no drift of anything playing down the wrong microphone. So Gus had total control over the final mix, and God knows he'd made some brilliant records. But I don't think his Ralph McTell productions were amongst his finest work because in effect he lost the essential thing that was working, which is one bloke and a guitar. That's what worked, so why should we change it when we're in the studio? I mean, Bob Dylan learned it early on, he just gets up there, they get a chord chart and he just shouts "one, two, three!" and off you go, and they all have to tag along and he does it all live. I don't think he ever does any vocals separately and never has done, I don't think.

How did Gus Dudgeon compare with someone like Tony Visconti, who's a bit more let's-throw-it-up-in-the-air-and-see-what-comes-down?

Well you've nailed it. That's exactly what Tony was, and he would say, "Well if that's the way you want it, then that's what we'll do." We did *Not Till Tomorrow [1972]*, he found this little condenser mic for 16 quid and he said, "Can we try this at my house?" I said, "If you want." So I went round to his house and we recorded all the vocals and a lot of the guitar on this particular cheap microphone. Then we took it to a studio — I think it was the one in Chelsea, Sound Techniques Studio — to do some overdubs and Tony played the organ and things. He was just so great, so easy to work with. And he'd really gee you up and get you to do things you wouldn't think of doing. I didn't think it was right him doing backing vocals on 'Zimmerman Blues', but people love that album.

In many ways I thought it was how my first album *[Eight Frames a Second, 1968]* should have sounded. The brief that poor old Gus got was to try and make me a crossover pop hit. He was previously a sound engineer at Decca and he was married to *[founder of Transatlantic Records]* Nat Joseph's secretary Sheila. It was Sheila who put Gus's name up when I arrived at the Transatlantic offices and that's how Gus and I started working. And we've had huge fun together and lots of laughs. But by the third album *[My Side of Your Window, 1969]* I did it on my own and then the fourth album we had Gus back to do the big symphonic productions on *You Well-Meaning Brought Me Here [1971]*. Incidentally Robert Kirby *[arranger of Strawbs and Nick Drake amongst many others]* did all those lovely string arrangements.

Who sadly is no longer with us.

Desperately sad. Bless his heart. I hadn't seen him for about thirty years and then he turned up to my box set launch and he looked robust and rather large. He's one of those real English gents. I loved Robert and I'm very sorry he's gone.

I wish I had more to say about Nick Drake myself because I did know him and in fact Nick did his very last gig with me. His final concert was with me over at a teacher's training college in Esher or Epsom or somewhere. I often drive past there and when I do, I always think of Nick. I saw him a few times in London too. At one particular gig, I thought well I'm going to go and sit in the audience, so I sat in the audience and listened to him. To be honest with you, I never quite got the lyrics side of things, but he was a very gentle, nice man. Ironically John Martyn probably knew him best of all. He was very fond of Nick and they evolved in a similar way, they had this similar vocal sound. Anyway that's another story.

So back to your formative years, we're at school and you're just hitting fifteen and pop's just blasted into your life . . .

Well, like everybody else, music was something that grown-ups had that turned out on the radio . . . and I'm really trying to tell which came first. I think it was Elvis Presely. My friend's mum asked me one day, "Have you heard of Elvis and his 'guerter'?" I didn't know what she was talking about. And of course it was Elvis and his *guitar*. I think I was ten or eleven when I first heard 'Heartbreak Hotel' *[1956, initially placed by a disapproving BBC on its 'restricted play' list]*. My cousin had it on her Dansette. It was incredible, it was instant communication, I thought it was the most wonderful exciting piece of music I'd ever heard. And I loved the B-side *['I Was the One']* too. I can't think of anything more exciting. Because it was dark and mysterious and there was something else besides the music that was being transmitted to me.

I loved Lonnie Donegan, and when I was about twelve at grammar school, we had a ukulele skiffle group. We'd have been all the rage now! We did all Lonnie's hits on ukuleles with the tea-chest bass and played at the school concerts and did one gig. I already had the taste by then and I suppose the Donegan thing made me aware of the sound of the acoustic guitar albeit in a mush. There was also a programme on the radio called *Guitar Club [BBC, hosted by jazz guitarist Ken Sykora]* that I listened to. I'd never liked Latin music and flamenco and stuff like that, but every now and then you'd hear a steel-strung guitar and I responded to that. And of course Elvis played it or beat hell out of an acoustic guitar. And that didn't matter to me, it was probably the stirrings of the awareness of sexuality through music that Elvis conveyed to me and I found it absolutely wonderful.

And Donegan gave you the structure.

And Donegan gave me the kind of the rhythmic swing and an introduction to this wonderful world of American folk music which he largely purloined and changed a word or two. But I didn't know at the time, because I was listening to Woody Guthrie and Lead Belly, through 'Bring a Little Water, Sylvie', 'Grand Coulee Dam' and all those things. So when I heard the real stuff it was much more authentic to me but probably didn't swing as much as Lonnie because Lonnie's energy is fantastic. I bought a record the other day to remind myself and the bloody thing is . . . it *steams* through! I met him a few times before he died and he was a bit of an old rascal but loveable all the same. When he passed away, I was part of the tribute at the Albert Hall in 2004 — I went on and did a bit which is great.

And then your first guitar, did that come before or after the Army?

My first guitar . . . I must have obtained a guitar around fourteen because I bought a picture of me holding this dreadful thing and I know it was before I went in the Army because of my hairstyle and the jacket I'm wearing, I remember buying the jacket, it was three guineas from Blake Brothers. An Italian striped jacket which I loved. But somewhere along the line I bought a guitar for £5 from a department store in Croydon. It was absolutely unplayable, made of plywood. I thought it would be just a jump off the ukulele and onto this thing even though it had two extra strings. I learnt to play a few chords but it was just so user-unfriendly that it stayed dormant until I went to college and I heard I think it was Jackie Elliott *[Ramblin' Jack Elliott]* playing Jessie Fuller's version of . . . well Jessie Fuller's song 'San Francisco Bay Blues' *[recorded 1954 by Fuller, 1957 by Elliott].* So I went home and got this beast out from the cupboard and worked out how to play the song, which told me my ear was quite good because I worked it out from the record.

It was then only a matter of months before I realised I could get something that I could keep in tune and that would actually play. My second guitar was my first tuneable, playable guitar, made by a German company called Hopf. Of course I wanted a jumbo-sized instrument. I knew the sound I wanted but I'd never seen the guitar that could do it because they just weren't coming to the country, but they did shortly afterwards and then I was like the kid at the cake shop window. Finally it took me two years working at college and working on weekends to save up and get my first proper American guitar, a Harmony Sovereign.

You ended up in college even though you left school at fifteen to go into the Army.

Secondary modern schoolboys could leave at fifteen, especially if they were going to do an apprenticeship. Because I was going into the Army, it was suggested it was an educational thing so I was okay leaving at fifteen. But I believe it had gone up to sixteen officially. But I was only in the Army for about six months before I managed to persuade my mum to borrow the money to get me out, because I got 'discharged by purchase' which was a legal loophole. And then the condition was if she borrowed the money that I would go back and try and get some O-levels and that was what I did. The only problem with that arrangement was that, of course, college was full of girls — and music!

So the hormones took over there

I struggled to be honest, and I underachieved spectacularly. I can even tell you now how I got English, History, English Literature and Art and that was it.

Well they're all the artistic ones.

I suppose they are. Maths, I wasn't even allowed to sit the exam, I was so bad. I actually went to my head of department and said, "Look I know I only got eight per cent in my mock exam but I did get *something* right and I'm just wondering if there was time . . . ?" And he said, "Mr May" — calling me by my real name — "you got *nothing* right but I'd never award a zero in the exam paper and you did spell your *name* correctly and get the *date* right, so I've given you eight per cent!" So that was that.

Well it was all hopeless. I got such bad marks for my GCEs *[O-levels/ GCSEs]* that I barely scraped two of them and got grade three for Literature, grade six for English and History, and Art I got six. But I decided to stay on another year to try and improve and the second year I failed them all so it was a waste of time. But by that time music and girls had completely taken over my young life, and there was the first of the blues packages arriving *[from the USA: The American Folk Blues Festival, 1963-66]*. They played next door to our college at the Fairfield Halls, and by that time I knew that I must get on the road with a guitar.

It sounds so stupid doesn't it and naive? But there were lads who were already doing it what I would call the first wave of the European travelling musicians — Wizz Jones and Alex Campbell, and lots of people that remained unknown but did the same thing. You'd strap your guitar on your back, learnt a handful of songs and went off to be Woody Guthries across the Channel and off to the South of France and to what else I've never been sure. I've written a song about it recently called 'Walking to the Morning' *[2006]*, which tries to look at why I went because I had no direction, I had no plan, I just had to do it.

So by that time I had already heard Memphis Slim, Big Joe Williams and Muddy Waters, Sonny Terry & Brownie McGhee, the Reverend Gary Davis. They all played in Croydon, they all came to Croydon and played for me and filled my head. I sent a couple of fan letters to Woody Guthrie and learnt a few tunes and went and did it. Off I went. And then it was all over really!

I've written about this extensively as far as my memory's allowed me to in my books. I know I had a kind of a set of rules established by my leftward leanings, my love of the guitar, and music and songs. And I could travel and play my guitar and live the life of the road, or so I thought. I didn't take a sleeping bag or any money because I knew . . . well, first I didn't have any money — I do mean I had none — and not having any meant that I didn't take any money! The second or third time I did take a ten shilling note which I brought back with me untouched. I had it folded up in my little Levi's jeans pocket, the one on the right-hand side. It was in there for emergencies — ten bob and that was it. I got as far as Istanbul and played in Italy and Yugoslavia and Spain and so on and eked out a living, not in a robust sort of "ee-oo!" market-stall shouting but my quiet introspective singing — and strumming because you couldn't fingerpick on the street. I made my way across Europe in a bewildered state not knowing why I was going or where I was going or what I was doing, but it was part of what I had to do.

So you launched yourself off into the Continent when you must have been about just turned seventeen? If you're born in December . . .

That's right, yes. Seventeen. And the first time I went away was with my mate Max, who was a great big lump of a bloke. His mum was a bit overbearing but you know it was hilarious the idea of us trying to hitchhike together. We nearly starved to death in Munich but we made it back to Paris and then he wouldn't go without me and I'd run out of impetus and I was ill and I had a gum disease and styes and all kinds of horrible things that you get when you're undernourished and on the road.

I went away with my girlfriend the next time, which was much more successful until she was practically carted off several times. And then I went off on my own, she went to America for various reasons, and that's it. Well I was never away for very long because once I'd got it out of my system I'd generally come home and pick up jobs, you know like the Woody Guthrie ethic: take a pride in whatever job you do. I can't say I took a pride in every job, but I was happy doing menial jobs and letting my mind wander free. I had jobs as warehouseman, Hoffman presser *[for clothing]*, builder's labourer, sheet metal work. I did all kinds of menial jobs, there was plenty of work around. So I did that and played music and drank cider and loved my girlfriend and dreamed the dream.

I never ever got to thinking, I have to admit, that it would ever be any more than what it was, and not really caring very much until circumstances meant that I might have to consider other responsibilities. Because I then fell in love with this girl and wanted to get married and all that stuff — I was only nineteen — a sort of working-class thing, and everything went a bit strange then. But I continued on the road and I went to Paris in 1965, and that's where I met my wife Nanna. I played over there and had some pretty good adventures. Then I came back and Wizz Jones asked me to come down to Cornwall with him, where I got discovered by someone who worked in an old publishing house and sent me up to London with my songs and gradually a record contract emerged.

There's that generational thing again. It's as if school didn't matter, nor college or university, which appears strange from the outside. You came from a working-class background without much to rub together, and yet it was an educated background. In going to grammar school, the idea of going on to college and getting qualified must have been everywhere — out of aspiration rather than the pressure of family/society. This was when they were opening up art colleges, technical colleges, vocational colleges left, right and centre. But your generation added to the freedom offered by all that choice by adding the option of dropping out. The early Seventies generation that followed went to college then then duly dropped out, and by the time you get to the Eighties you probably had to finish your degree in whatever. Today it's like you have to go to university to get your degree in guitar, vocals or even songwriting. Do you think there's a certain innocence that's been lost in all this achievement, or is it still possible to launch off as a creative person in the way that you did straight out of school?

It's a very complicated question actually.

My apologies.

No, no, it's a good question. It's one that I've not really thought of before because, like you say, it's as if the education didn't matter in some sense because it didn't. Unless you're fascinated by what you're being taught you're not going to take it in anyway. I had no objective. No one in my family had ever been to university that I know about, no one. So that wasn't an aspiration of mine. Having played at every university in the country during the Sixties and Seventies, I realised I could have been very happy at college and probably would have enjoyed it. In fact when I left grammar school, one of my teachers said, "What do you think you'll gain in the Army? You're capable of eight O-levels." No one had ever said that to me before and I was quite shocked and thought, "Oh blimey, perhaps I should have stayed on . . ." But it was too late then, because I'd already signed up. But if education didn't really change matters then and you had a set idea or something that you had to do, I suppose inevitably you get the corners knocked off you if you do it younger. If you're older you're probably going to have more baggage and more stuff to actually unload before you get back to probably where you would have been had you not. I think it depends on the individual.

That raises the irony of you saying that you didn't go to university but in the Sixties and Seventies you went to every single one of them.

People do ask, "Did you ever did you go to college?" and I say, "Yeah all of them!" It doesn't disturb me but I do think how lucky these bastards are. It's a difficult thing to know how I would have coped with going to college. My mum had no money to help out but of course I would have got a grant like everyone else at the time. I actually thought that college was for middle-class kids particularly, for them to find out what the world was like: you had to feed yourself, how much drink you could take, your first girlfriends . . . And of course it was exploited by a lot of the n'er-do-wells and layabouts and they wrecked the system for other people and now you have to pay to go, don't you? It was all free once upon a time.

You did find your own way of learning though, setting up all the building blocks of your craft that would put you in such good stead.

A lot of people say, "Oh I bet you learnt a lot on the road." I don't think the road changed me any way at all, except that one of my friends who was there before I went and also there after I came back said that my *playing* had improved and that I was perhaps more robust in my attack on stage or more slightly more confident. I don't know . . . But being on the road confirmed what I already suspected: it was the thing that I've always sought ever since I was a little boy and experienced the freedom of running around in the open air.

I had it again the day I left the Army at fifteen and hitchhiked on a lorry back to Oswestry station in Shropshire, where I took the train back to London with my mate who also got discharged. I experienced that same sense of freedom on the road, when the horizon is anywhere you care to make it — you know, I'm starving hungry, I've got my fags, I've got my guitar and I'm free. It's the most fantastic feeling and I do every now and then grab it. I'm trying to think of when it's happened recently . . . it was probably in the last year that I got it too.

Part of it is definitely being on the road when you're touring. It's a sense of freedom. You leave something behind and walk into something new on a daily basis. It can become a grind but it is going to be different if you want it to be different. Your life as a musician like that is wonderful, and I say to my young tour manager at times, "Listen, you've had a bad gig. Well sometimes you get them, but we're out of here tomorrow, we're gone, it's sorted out and it's gone." Sometimes you wish you never had to do it again because it was a *great* night! But it's gone, and tomorrow we're on to someone, somewhere else, where it's another roadside, another day, another adventure. I must say I feel that's one of the greatest things I've felt in my life. It's to be cherished and you have to be vigilant about trying to live it as often as you can.

*

Al Stewart

5

Al Stewart

'Once I heard Bob Dylan
I couldn't go back'

Al Stewart was born in Glasgow on September 5, 1945. He grew up in Bourne-mouth where he was part of the area's wave of pioneering British musicians, rubbing shoulders with Robert Fripp, Tony Blackburn and Andy Summers, from whom he bought his first guitar. After cutting his teeth playing R&B and pop standards with pub bands, Stewart went acoustic and made the move to London in 1965 when he was offered a weekly slot at Bunjies Coffee House in Soho, and later compered at Les Cousins' folk club. He played alongside the likes of Bert Jansch, Ralph McTell, Roy Harper, Van Morrison and Cat Stevens. A key figure in British music, he appears throughout the musical folklore of the revivalist era. He played at the first-ever Glastonbury Festival in 1970. His first album *Bed Sitter Images* was released in 1967, while the later *Love Chronicles* [1969] was notable for its 18-minute title track which made it the first mainstream record release to include the word 'fucking'. An accomplished guitarist himself, Stewart has consistently worked with other guitarists such as Jimmy Page, Richard Thompson, Tim Renwick, Peter White, Dave Nachmanoff and Laurence Juber. His critical success translated into international commercial stardom with a brace of albums: 1976's *Year of the Cat*, which spawned the mega hit single of the same name, and 1978's *Time Passages*, both produced by Alan Parsons. The focus of songwriting on his subsequent work has noticeably expanded on the deep 'chronicle' themes that always featured in his songs, often historical, such as wine, World War One, poet Edward Lear, the history of British popular music. He is based in the USA.

We could start at the very beginning . . . you were born in Scotland, in Greenock?

Apparently so. I was actually quite small so I don't remember it very well but if you tell me yes. September 5th, 1945. I was born in Glasgow and then I think that we lived for the first three years of my life in Greenock, or two-and-a-half or something like that. My father was a RAF officer — Bomber Command, Lancasters to be exact. He was killed right before I was born so I never knew him. My mother was a Red Cross nurse during the war.

Is that how they met?

You know I have no idea how they met, I really don't know! *[laughs]* But it's amazing — they were young, it was wartime, they met, they got married, and in World War Two I get the impression that everyone's lives were speeded up considerably. There really wasn't time to sit and think about this stuff. So they got married and my mother got pregnant with me and then my father got shot down in March of 1945.

So your mum ended up moving down to the South Coast of England with you, which must have been quite a change for her.

Yes. She was living in Scotland with my father's father, hence my grandfather, and I think he was a bit of a martinet from what I can tell and I think she had enough at some point and moved south. We moved a number of times while I was growing up, we continued south and went via the Midlands. I think we went south until we couldn't go south any more. I don't know why we kept moving. We moved at one point to Stratford-upon-Avon, but why we went there I haven't any idea.

Like you said, life was fast in the war, and it was a similar story for your own generation as that mobility icontinued at the same rate post-war with work opportunities and the promise of prosperity springing up across the country.

Yes, I think so. People didn't really move around very much in the Twenties and Thirties. People would grow up in a village and they would live there, much as they did in the nineteenth century, but the war discombobulated everybody and moved everybody around, or maybe people got more into the habit of moving. After the war's end, they just kept on doing it.

Eventually my mother remarried when I was nine to somebody who was involved in catering, so they had hotels and tea shops and all kinds of things — they were forever making cups of tea for people, as I recall. But by then I'd been sent off to boarding school and I didn't have much to do with all that any more. I went to Wycliffe College, in Gloucestershire. I was there from when I was nine to when I was seventeen — so I went through prep school, junior school and senior school. In fact I got basically thrown out of there at seventeen because by then I'd stopped doing any work and was just playing the guitar all the time. They wanted me to do all kinds of things and have all kinds of careers but that didn't interest me in the least. I said, "I want to play rock'n'roll!" — and they said, "Well you can't possibly do that because it'll all be over in six months."

I guess I sort of believed them, so I was in a real hurry to get thrown out of school because I thought well if it's all going to be over in six months, I'm going to miss it unless I get out of here. One of the funny things that's happened over the years is that all the companies that they wanted me to go and work for — because those were jobs that I would have for a lifetime, like *[vehicle manufacturer]* British Leyland — have all gone out of business. The one thing that hasn't gone out of business is rock'n'roll and the music industry. Well, rock'n'roll at least.

When you went home for the school holidays you were still going back to the South Coast which must have been an incredibly bustling place musically — at least in the summer months.

Bournemouth is a seaside town and it did bustle in its own sweet way. It wasn't like Blackpool though. Bournemouth was a lot more . . . oh I don't know, *genteel*, at least back in those days. There was an amazing number of hotels and boarding houses.

I left school in the middle of the Beatles boom, late 1962/early '63 when it was all getting going, and Bournemouth had at one point about eighty beat groups. I'm not sure if that's more than the average or not, but there was an amazing number of bands like that playing there all the time. Some of the people who I grew up with became quite famous. Obviously Andy Summers joined the Police and did pretty well, Robert Fripp formed King Crimson, Greg Lake of course went into Emerson Lake & Palmer, Lee Kerslake went into Uriah Heep, and Tony Blackburn went from singing to become a *[BBC Radio eventually]* disc jockey. I used to play in Tony's band on lead guitar for a while. All of these people knew each other and we all grew up with each other, so the Bournemouth scene was thriving in that way. In fact my first gig was playing with Tony at the Bournemouth Pavilion, right down near the pier. Zoot Money was the headliner every Tuesday on Big Beat Night and Tony Blackburn & the Sabres were the opening band — and I was a Sabre.

Don Strike was your guitar teacher wasn't he?

I took some guitar lessons from Don Strike. And although I never quite understood what he was trying to teach me, I did take about ten lessons from Bob Fripp, and I had a whole course of lessons from Don. I fortunately remember that they were always trying to teach me exotic jazz chords, which I will admit is a very good thing as a musician to know, but I've never used any of them in my whole career. I can't even remember one of those chords now. Bob tells a very good story about me, that of all his students I was the only one who made it and I did it by ignoring everything he tried to tell me.

Did you have a similar experience with Don as well, or did you get your knuckles rapped with a ruler instead?

Well . . . because Don had played in all the old jazz bands and orchestras, he was trying to teach us things that people would have played in the Thirties and Forties but by the Sixties we didn't want to do that. I wanted to be Hank B Marvin, I didn't want to be some old jazz guitar player.

Did you join the 'Crafty League of Bournemouth Guitarists' because you went to Don's classes or did he come recommended because you knew the other guitarists?

How it was, was if you played the guitar in those days then Don Strike's guitar shop was where everybody went, especially on Saturdays. Virtually every member of every band was in there on Saturday afternoon. They used to come in and pretend to try out guitars and amplifiers, but it was really just so that they could see the other kids, see how good or bad or whatever they were. I actually worked for Don for a while selling guitars and amplifiers. I wasn't very good at that either but I spent a lot of time there hanging out, so you'd just run into all these people.

Bands were pretty much interchangeable during that little two-year period before I moved up to London. I was in about six different bands, everybody just knew everybody. And when you weren't playing you went and watched the other bands playing, that's what we did. So I spent a couple of years just watching all these bands from Bournemouth, trying to work out what they were doing, and trying to understand what the ones who played better than me were doing and just trying to learn it. Eventually what happened was that after a couple of years of playing Chuck Berry, early Beatles and Shadows songs — I can play all the Shadows' catalogue or at least I could then — and Duane Eddy and all the people I liked . . . what happened is that some time around 1963 I heard Bob Dylan and he basically ruined my life.

Up until then I had a passing interest in literature but I wasn't paying any attention to lyrics or songs because nobody else was — it was all about sound. But once I heard Bob Dylan I couldn't go back. I realised that you could use words, not only with one syllable and occasionally two, but you could even use three or four-syllable words in songs, which just didn't happen since up until then it was all pretty much "ooh-aah, ooh-aah".

So I got totally seduced by this whole thing and learnt every single song on *The Times They Are a-Changin'* [1964] and a whole chunk of *The Freewheelin' Bob Dylan* [1963], and I used to sing them in between sets when I was still playing with a band in Bournemouth. The band would go the pub halfway through — they'd play a set and then they'd have a break and come back, play another set and have a break. But instead of going to the pub, because I didn't drink, I didn't care and I would get out my acoustic guitar and play Dylan songs while everyone else was in the pub.

Of course no one in Bournemouth had heard of Bob Dylan apart from me, and I got a remarkable response because people there had never seen anything like it. And whereas they didn't ever applaud when we were playing 'Twist and Shout' three times a night and 'Wipe Out' *[The Surfaris, 1963]* and all the other things I was playing, I sang 'Masters of War' *[The Freewheelin' Bob Dylan]* and everybody clapped. I thought, "Something's happening here. You don't know what it is, do you, Mr Al?" It reached the point where the Dylan songs were going down better than the band. And I thought, well, maybe I should investigate this. So I left Bournemouth and went up to London and plopped into a job at Bunjies *['Coffee House & Folk Cellar']* playing every Friday and Saturday, and somehow or other making just about enough money to get by. So at nineteen I became a folk singer.

It's funny, after reading the Pete Frame book *The Restless Generation [subtitled: How Rock Music Changed the Face of 1950s Britain, 2007]*, everything I've just said not only describes me but describes my first hero, Lonnie Donegan, because that's exactly what happened to him too. He was a banjo player with *[jazz bandleader and trombonist]* Chris Barber's band and when the band went off to the pub, Lonnie used to get out an acoustic guitar and sing songs. Although they didn't have a word for what he was doing, eventually they decided to call it skiffle. It all reached a point where the band would come back and Lonnie Donegan would be getting on course and everybody would be going crazy and he was actually going down better than Chris Barber.

Pretty much the same thing happened to me by singing these Dylan songs during the break, where I ended up, like Lonnie Donegan, doing my own gigs and playing in a lot of the same places mentioned in Pete Frame's book that existed in the Fifties. Although I got to London in the mid-Sixties, some of these places like the Troubadour were still going and I ended up playing in a lot of the places where people had ended up playing during the skiffle boom. Amazing!

It's interesting that audiences were also hungry for more thoughtful music. I mean, thinking about it, you were playing places where you were doing upbeat, near-dance music, but the same audience was responding to lyrics that you had to sit up and listen to, and to stop tapping their feet . . . well, not quite that, but their feet would have been tapping differently.

I think they were two different audiences when I was playing. In fact I didn't do that many of these interval things but whenever I did, people certainly liked it. And when I got up to London, there were always two different sides. Even during the Fifties all these art students, beatniks and what have you were the ones that hung around in the coffee bars and listened to skiffle music, and all that naturally morphed into the folk scene. By the time I got there, it was ten years after they'd been listening to, oh I don't know, Ewan MacColl or whatever, and now they were listening to Bert Jansch, but it was the same kind of audience in many of the same clubs.

Whereas the rock'n'roll audience never, either in the Fifties or Sixties, really listened to all that. Instead they were listening to Gene Vincent and then moved on to the Yardbirds. But there was always that folk-jazz audience, it was there for skiffle and traditional jazz in the Fifties and it evolved by the mid-Fifties towards folk singing, which was pretty much people like Bert, John Renbourn and Davey Graham. You can absolutely see the direct continuation there. So in 1965, when I got off that train at nineteen, there was an absolute distinct choice facing me — and I realised it too, because I was already standing in between two worlds.

Electric in one hand, acoustic in the other.

Exactly. Unlike a lot of people on the folk scene who had come out of that folk-blues and acoustic music, I had actually played in a rock'n'roll band and I knew how to do that. And, because I didn't have enough money, I remember taking this big decision. I could only afford one good guitar and I had a Gibson electric guitar, and when I auditioned for Bunjies and actually got the gig, I traded in the electric for an acoustic guitar.

And never looked back . . . You're not a heavy metal guitarist or a cardiologist, but do you feel that you're a singer-songwriter in the sense that the rest of us perceive you as?

It's what I do for a living yeah, so yes if people ask, "What do you do?" then I guess I would say, "I'm a singer-songwriter."

There does seem to be a certain mystique that goes with that designation, it's a bit more different for example if you say, "Well I'm a musician" or "I'm a drummer; I'm a jazz saxophonist" there's quite a mystique that goes with that, especially in view of the historical nature of a lot of your songs and the delving into the past and the way that you craft what you do. It certainly feels, certainly for those of us who don't do what you do, there is that sort of mystique that goes with it, a little bit more than with other people who work in music. Do you feel that you're doing something quite special by crafting these images you're not just creating sounds, you're doing a lot more than that?

Well it's theatre. It's theatre of the mind because it's all taking place in your mind but it's out there nonetheless, and you're telling stories but it's all laid out in a sort of theatrical way, you see characters develop and they do different things, they go to different places in the world and in different time zones and then everyone goes home. Basically I'm writing movies, little miniature movies. If you listen to almost any one of my historical songs, there you are in the scene, it's a movie, just as much a movie as Brad Pitt doing it really except it's playing out in my mind rather than playing out on a screen. It should play out in the mind of the listener. Most singer-songwriters are storytellers and they're making miniature movies. In my case, I'm making miniature historical documentaries half the time!

And in terms of your craft, one assumes therefore it's the lyrics that come first?

No, it's always the lyrics that come last oddly enough. One of the things that I think a lot of people don't know is that during the period probably starting around *Past, Present and Future [1973]* and encompassing the whole of *Modern Times [1975]* and *Year of the Cat [1976]* and *Time Passages [1978]* and probably *24 Carrots [1980]*, what we did was go in and record all the backing tracks before I wrote the lyrics. That really is walking on a highwire because you've spent the money at that point.

But what it enabled me to do was something really quite unique that the studio lets you do. I'll tell you what happens . . . The guitar player comes in and you've got a solo: "Okay, so play twelve bars of lead guitar." Then what they normally do is they'll take six or eight or ten or twelve cracks at it and you'll pick the best one: "Okay, take seven was good, take nine was really good." Sometimes you even glue the two bits together. But for the guitar player it's improvising, trying different ideas against the backing track. And I thought why not work in that way with the lyrics? In other words I take the backing track, say 'Flying Sorcery' *[Year of the Cat]* or whatever, and I take it home and I think okay I've got this piece of music that I can write for. Back in those days, I would write two, three, even four different types of lyrics on completely different subjects to those backing tracks. So then I could do what the guitar player does — pick the best one! As a result, a lot of these songs, especially from that period when we were selling lots of records, have multiple outtakes of different sets of lyrics, completely different sets or lyrics.

The box set possibilities would be endless.

We probably erased all the vocals but I'll just take one example: 'Year of the Cat' was originally called 'Foot of the Stage' and the lyrics were about *[British comedian]* Tony Hancock. The chorus went something like "And his tears fell down like rain at the foot of the stage bum-bah-dah-dah". It was about a show which Tony Hancock did in my hometown Bournemouth right before he went to Australia and committed suicide *[in 1968]*. He was standing onstage and he was saying, "I feel dreadful, I don't want to be here, I don't like my life, I don't like myself, I don't like you, I don't like anything about it." And of course the audience were all laughing, thinking he was joking. God knows if anyone else got it, but I realised instantly that he was completely serious and so I wrote this song at the time called 'Foot of the Stage'.

I played it to the representative for my American record company and he said, "This was absolutely fine, I love the backing track but no one in America has ever heard of Tony Hancock." So I went back and rewrote it as 'Year of the Cat'. But this is typical. Even looking at that record I remember one stage before it had originally been a totally different song — "Where the casual tweet of birds as they veer through the rain" — I like the idea of those birds veering through the rain to infinity. Then that got written into a song about reincarnation.

And it goes on and on and on. 'Antarctica' was originally called 'Doubting Thomas' — "Which you see, which you'd be Doubting Thomas da-da-da." Some of these versions are around, they surface occasionally as bonus tracks on albums, for example. A lot of the stuff we did in *[long-time guitarist collaborator]* Peter White's garage is still around, but a lot has been lost forever. Even on the last album I did *[Sparks of Ancient Light, 2008]*, there are four different sets of lyrics to what became 'Elvis at the Wheel', all on completely different subjects. So I'm still doing this, just the act of making a backing track, taking the music home, then I say to myself, "Wake up in the morning, just play the backing track and clear your mind completely, what does this suggest to you?" And it's as likely to suggest to me a bridge in Kazakhstan or a jam doughnut. I like to think at this at this stage of my life that I can write a song on any subject you gave me. It's basically having these backing tracks and doing it this way allows me to take numerous different shots at it lyrically. All

I'm doing is the same as that guitar player, who might give you four completely different solos, one acoustic, one heavy metal, one Hank B Marvin style or one classical style. Why can't I give you four completely different sets of lyrics?

Sometimes we would even do it the other way round and record different backing tracks in different styles. 'Broadway Hotel' *[Year of the Cat]* for example, we recorded the way you hear it on the record, and then there's another version of it which is floating around somewhere, where it starts as a reggae tune. To me it's another way of being able to improvise with my instrument being the flow of lyrics and the choice of different subject material. To me, doing the backing track first was my way of being able to use improvisation and then sit back and ask myself, "Do I really want this song to be about penguins or do I want it to be about tobogganing?"

You also encountered pressure as a songwriter in any case from the record companies and the rest of the business. That must have really weighed down on you, particularly after Year of the Cat. I've heard you even had to 'adjust' a song for one of your more recent albums that was originally much much longer, was it 'Elvis at the Wheel'?

No it was 'Class of 58', off *A Beach Full of Shells [2005]*, which coincidently is one of my favourite albums that I ever made — one of my top three or four. There is a long version. You don't have it but I've got it here, the original version which ran in excess of thirteen minutes and was basically all about the development of the British rock'n'roll scene from 1958 to '68.

I'd love to hear it in its full version.

Well it's floating around, probably available somewhere on the internet. It was issued as its own little CD with only that on it because it's such a long thing. You see, *A Beach Full of Shells* was one of the only records I've made where I like everything on it, but the people at EMI who I was dealing with — I don't think they'd ever made a comment about anything I've done, they just take the record and put it out — but this time they said, and they probably were right about this, "That 'Class of 58' is so long it dominates the whole record, and it skews things away from all the other songs." So they said, "Take it off and write some more songs." Which was actually a good idea because I went off and wrote 'Katherine of Oregon' which wasn't on the original tape I sent the record company. So I wrote a couple of new songs and then I found a way of editing 'Class of 58' so that it kept the flavour and the feel but ended up a lot shorter.

Well as you said, it wasn't a taste thing, it was simply a question of balance that they were talking about.

I don't think they did like it very much. Basically the guys at EMI like my historical taste, they liked 'Trains' and they liked 'The Coldest Winter in Memory' *[both on Famous Last Words, 1993]* and they liked 'Roads to Moscow' *[Past, Present and Future, 1973]* and they thought all this wittering about this thing about rock'n'roll was a little beneath my dignity. But I tried to point out to them that 'Class of 58' was another historical song. It had some wonderful lines that I don't think they got. With 'Class of 58' all they thought was, "Oh this is fooling around."

But the research in that song was quite formidable. For example, it sounds like a throwaway line when the band make their first single and it isn't a huge success, and the line I use is: "The song came out on Oriole and it did not make the charts." Now inherent in this to me is the entire history of Oriole Records. Just to make you understand, Oriole Records were the people who signed Ringo Starr's ex-band *[Rory Storm & the Hurricanes]* after Ringo had left. It's wonderful how Oriole signed about twenty or thirty different Liverpool bands but they signed all the wrong ones — and that was humorous for me. I became very sympathetic towards Oriole because EMI would sign all the top bands, and then the ones that somehow escaped their notice would sign to Pye or Philips, and then way down the bottom of the panel the ones who couldn't get the deal with anyone else could probably always get a deal with Oriole.

I was thinking of all of this when I wrote that deadpan, dry line about the song coming out on Oriole, I'm thinking of the whole history of the record company when I'm writing the song. But if you don't know the history of Oriole then the line just goes by and it doesn't mean anything. And then it had this wonderful line "I may not know much, but I do know I'm partial / To an E-major chord through a stack of Marshalls" — that line completely floored me, I thought that was wonderful. I'm not convinced the song completely worked but it was interesting on a lot of different levels because it had a lot of quite subtle stuff in there. When I'm talking about Johnny & the Hurricanes you can hear a little bit of a Johnny & the Hurricanes tune in the background and so on and so forth.

So sonically it makes sense as well.

Sure it makes sense.

So back to you at nineteen. You've come to London and you're about to tell me about how you really became a folk singer — and also about a guitar.

Okay so I'm nineteen, right? Well, when I came to London I had in mind to join a band because in Bournemouth, as I said, I was in about five different bands. And that was what I thought I was going to do: I was going to play electric guitar in a rock'n'roll band because that was what everyone else was doing. It was January 1965 and the Beatles ruled the world and the Kinks, the Who, the Animals, the Zombies, the Rolling Stones . . . I mean basically it was a time when every nineteen-year-old kid was in a band so I thought that's what I'll do. And I came up to London, I auditioned for four different bands. Two of them accepted me and two of them turned me down.

Unfortunately the two that accepted me were off to play American military bases in Germany, which is what a lot of bands did at the time. For not much money and the thought was just not appealing. Of the other two, one was a band called the Outlaws and I'd bought actually a whole bunch of their records. They were an instrumental band produced by Joe Meek. The lead guitar player was Richard Blackmore, who of course would go on to fame and fortune with Deep Purple but at the time no one knew it. I think Ritchie was leaving and they were looking for a guitar player. Ritchie was light years better than I would ever have been so they took one look at me and said, "I don't think so."

The other band was the Paramounts and my belief is that they turned into Procol Harum somewhere along the line so that would have been an interesting band to aim for. I played 'Memphis, Tennessee' by Chuck Berry *[1959]* but started it in the wrong key, so the audition was very short because I was making these strangled squawks because I couldn't reach any of the notes. Obviously I had begun the thing in the wrong key and that was the end of that. Long story short, I didn't get either of the bands that I wanted, I didn't become a Paramount or an Outlaw.

Now, in Bournemouth when I'd been in bands, as I told you, I'd been listening to Bob Dylan — and playing his songs. So now I was in London having already learnt those couple of Bob Dylan albums and I had already gone down to Bunjies coffee bar very very early on, probably in the first two weeks after I arrived. I had an acoustic guitar and, as luck would have it — because everything is luck — the owner was there and he saw me with the guitar case and he said, "Are you a folk singer?" And I smelled a gig. I most definitely wasn't a folk singer but I just thought, "There's a gig at the end of this if I say the right thing." So I said yes.

And he said, "Well, we run this coffee bar every night, we have a different singer every night. The guy who did Friday has just left, do you want to come along on Friday and if people clap then you've got the job." I said, "Fine!" So

I had an acoustic guitar and I went along. It was an old F-hole guitar, it wasn't a folk guitar at all.

Horrible things.

Yeah, I turned up with and I sang like a whole bunch of different Bob Dylan songs, 'The Times They Are a-Changin' ', 'Masters of War' and all of these things because it was pretty much all I knew at the time and the comment was, "Well you sing an awful lot of Bob Dylan songs . . ." But I obviously was doing them well enough and of course Bob Dylan was becoming quite well known in London. No one else was doing that, so they said, "Okay you got the job." I held that job for two and half years — February, I think, of 1965, all the way up to the fall of 1967, and then my first album came out.

So I was at Bunjies every Friday and then I discovered there was a club that had just opened right across Cambridge Circus a few hundred yards away, and this was the famous Les Cousins as everyone called it — *Les Cousins ['The Cousins']* of course in French, but a lot of people couldn't speak French. People were forever coming down and asking, "Where's Les?" And so I went over there, to . . . well I'd got one gig, I'll try and get another one. I walked over there and again, as luck would have it, they needed someone. They didn't want a singer because they'd book well-known acts — it was bigger club than Bunjies — and so they were booking people that people had heard of, but what they did want was someone to run the place. They wanted sort of an MC, a compere because it ran from midnight to six o'clock in the morning on Fridays and midnight to seven o'clock in the morning on Saturdays, and they were offering three pounds for each night, which is actually what Bunjies were paying me, *and* halfway through I could have a cup of coffee and a cheese & tomato sandwich, so I said, "Yes, I'll take it!"

So now I was doing seven to ten at Bunjies and then I took a break and then did twelve till six at Les Cousins, and then went back the next day and did twelve till seven. All of which was paying me £9 a week, which is actually more than my previous job at WH Smith had paid me. So I thought that this was a huge improvement. These basic three gigs allowed me during the rest of the week to just go round all the other folk clubs in London like The Troubadour and The Hanging Lamp in Richmond, all these sorts of places and I also did auditions. This went on for about two and a half years until I finally ran into *[folk singer & impresario]* Roy Guest and he talked CBS Records into letting me make an album. So yeah, I'm sure there's a lot more to it, but that basically covers that two and a half years!

A lot of things happened in 1965. There are at least four major things that happened but if I'd have gone to London in '64, I probably would have joined a band. The folk scene wasn't big enough, Cousins wasn't open, and I do think if I'd have gone in '64 none of this would have happened, and if I'd have gone in '66 it would have been too late. So the timing . . . it's all about timing. I mean here are the things that happened in '65: I got into Bunjies which gave me regular money, and I got into the Cousins which gave me regular money. The first person I saw at Les Cousins was Bert Jansch. I went down there and I watched him play the guitar and I thought, "This folk business is going to be a lot trickier than I thought." Because I'd never seen anyone play the guitar like that before and I figured I'm not going to be able to do that, this is beyond my abilities — and yet obviously it was a lot more interesting than I thought it was going to be. I thought it was just like you strum three chords like Woody Guthrie and you sang a few lyrics and that was it. But no. So Bert changed my entire way of thinking about acoustic guitars.

And then right after that in, I think, April or May — but you can always look it up — Bob Dylan came and played the Albert Hall for the first time. This is the acoustic one, this wasn't the electric one I think — or *maybe* it was the electric one, I'm not sure. Anyway . . . no it was the electric one I think, or was it? I think he did half and half, I don't know. Anyway I went there and I saw Bob Dylan and this moved the goalposts again because I'd watched the Beatles in Bournemouth and they played for 25 minutes and there were four other acts, Billy J Kramer & the Dakotas, and Tommy Quickly was on that show, a bunch of different bands. But headliners used to play 25 minutes. It was package tour and that was it. Bob Dylan came on with an acoustic guitar with no support acts and played for two hours, and I'd never . . . I didn't know that was possible. I didn't know that what Bert Jansch was doing on a guitar was possible. I didn't know that there were folk clubs. I didn't know that making a living as a folk singer was possible. And I didn't know that an acoustic guitarist could play for two hours at the Royal Albert Hall. I mean all of this was completely new to me.

And then of course, the other thing that happened to me, and again this is complete madness, it just happened. I moved into this flat in the East End of London and who should move in the room next to me than Paul Simon. So I'm sitting in my room, I'm listening to him writing songs through the wall. And so he finishes them and he comes out and there's no one there apart from me, so he has to play them to me. And I'm just a stupid nineteen-year-old kid, I don't know anything. But I'd got an opinion, and not always the one he wanted to hear.

And so in quick succession and just in the first month of 1965, I get a job in a folk club, two folk clubs, I see Bert Jansch, I see Bob Dylan, and I start living with Paul Simon. Now this is crazy stuff. Like I said, this wouldn't have happened in '64 and it wouldn't have happened in '66, but by the end of 1965

I was so immersed in all of this that I'd sold my electric guitar and in doing so I'd committed myself to being a folk singer.

And the guitar? Tell me about the Andy Summers connection.

Yeah, I did that, I bought a guitar off Andy in Bournemouth. But that's not the one I actually sold. I eventually traded the Gibson 175 which I bought off Andy, I traded it for a dark blue Fender Stratocaster, and then I traded that for, I think it was a Gibson Les Paul, and that's what I sold. At one point in 1965 I couldn't afford to buy the folk guitar I needed so what I did was I traded in the Gibson and I got an Epiphone Texan folk guitar. Of course once I got the proper folk guitar, people paid more attention because me playing the jazz guitar in folk clubs people thought was a little strange. But I had to make that decision. I had to say, "Am I going to play electric guitar? Or am I going to be a folk singer?"

And . . . ?

Really it was seeing Clapton and Page and people like that. I was going and watching bands and thinking, "I'm never going to be able to do that. It's like I can't do it." The ultimate was when I saw Hendrix and that was the end right there. I couldn't. So it was "I'm not playing electric guitar any more." Certainly by '65 I'd worked out that I really wasn't good enough. But this was '65 it was the height of rock band mania, every kid wanted to be a Beatle or a Rolling Stone, and there must have been 35,000 different kids in England in bands playing electric guitar and trying to be famous. As I say, I'd probably, if I'd really worked hard, might have been the 1,397th best, which as I always say would qualify me to play rhythm guitar in Uriah Heep. Basically that was it. No disrespect to Uriah Heep but that's probably how good I would have been if I'd have gone with it.

But I looked around and there were maybe ten people in the whole of the British Isles who were writing lyrics on a serious level. No competition at all, I mean the field was ours. So there was Roy Harper, there was Ralph McTell, there was myself and a handful of others and that was it. And I thought, "Well look, I can go and fight the good fight with a Les Paul and a Marshall stack, or I can just get an exercise book and a ballpoint pen and write." And that's what I did, and remarkably all the people — because we all knew each other — who were lyric writers back in that day, all did well. They all made records and they all became successful. Whereas probably of the 35,000 or so electric guitar players, 34,500 didn't — and I would have been one of those.

But in a lot of ways if you're going to have a career it's all about having the vision to see where you're going. After I saw Bob Dylan, I thought, "I may chuck that," but I also thought, "You can do this, you can make a career, you can make a life out of writing lyrics." But I didn't know that until I saw Dylan do this two hour concert, and I thought, "Well you know what, I can't be Eric Clapton, I can't be Jimmy Page but I might be able to be an English lyric writer." And, as it worked out fifty years later, that's exactly what I became.

Indeed. Now, you used the word 'English' there.

Yeah.

As opposed to 'American'.

Yeah, well, because I think the way that I write is very English. It just seems to me that it is. I wouldn't do what Dylan was doing. I mean Dylan has no respect for the English language whatsoever. You know, genius — but he leaves the Ts off, like 'fightin'' or 'runnin''. Dylan writes like a Mid-Western farmer's son. He doesn't pay attention to detail. When I was growing up in school I would definitely get beaten if I was ungrammatical, so I pay a lot of attention. I mean, I have made mistakes in songs over the years and of course everybody does, but I was definitely paying attention to making these things rhyme and trying not to end sentences with a pronoun or whatever. Whereas Dylan couldn't care less about any of that.

Two of the individuals you've mentioned as inspirations are Paul Simon, who was very British-inspired obviously so he might not count, and Bob Dylan, who is anything but British. And while they helped open you up to the possibilities of being a songwriter, you saw no temptation in taking onboard their own subject matter. You're certainly not going to talk about riding the freight train or doing Route 66.

No . . . I mean, I can't. I hadn't done any of that. You can't write about that. I could write about Admiral Lord Fisher because he's English and I kind of have an affinity of the scene but riding freight trains is . . . I can't write about that. So it's yeah, definitely not.

Now, talking about Paul Simon, there's a neatness element there. I mean Paul is a very neat writer. He will look for the prefect word. Dylan sits down at a typewriter, twenty minutes later he's written 'Desolation Row' *[Highway 61 Revisited, 1965]*. It freaks me out. There's a famous conversation that happened apparently between Dylan and Leonard Cohen, who is again a very assiduous and neat writer. Cohen had been working on 'Hallelujah' *[Various*

Positions, 1984]. It's something he'd worked on for two to three years, which apparently he used to do. And he ran into Bob Dylan, who had just written 'I and I' *[Infidels, 1983]*. And Leonard Cohen says to Bob Dylan, "How long did it take you to write that?" and Dylan in his usual way said, "Twenty or thirty minutes I think." And Cohen had played him 'Hallelujah' and Dylan said, "Well how long did it take you to write that." And Cohen said he was embarrassed that he took three years that he just couldn't answer.

I see that. These are very different ways of writing. Some people just bung it all down and they never revise, and some people revise forever. Leonard Cohen was revising songs from twenty or thrity years earlier. Looking for the perfect line.

Where do you fall?

I fall somewhere in the middle. I do write songs very fast. Usually if I haven't got it inside an hour then it's not going to work. But, having said that I do go back the next day and take out half a dozen lines probably and replace them with half a dozen, so I do do my revision.

And we need to also pitch in all that research you do.

Oh yeah, I mean 'Roads to Moscow' took three years of research and I think I read between forty and fifty history books just to get that one song right, so yeah—

Blimey.

—research is a very big part of it. I mean it helps that I read history books all the time. Sometimes they percolate for ten or twenty years before a song emerges, but you've got to do the research. Now that doesn't stop me from occasionally getting it wrong. I've made at least two major mistakes just because I was lazy, my mind was distracted. But I do know the difference between Henry Plantagenet and Henry Tudor for example. That's the biggest mistake I ever made. And you know why I wrote Plantagenet into that song? It was because of the sound of the word and I needed the syllables, I wanted four syllables and Tudor just didn't cut it and I think my mind just blanked. Of course in French it's different, but pronouncing it the English way, 'Plantagenet', it really fills the mouth. A lot of being a writer is the sound, the shape of words in your mouth, the way they come out the way they feel, and I was so enamoured by the word that I screwed up the song. But I don't do that often. In my defence, because I'm pretty clued in to all the other writers of my generation, they all make mistakes so I'm not going to beat myself up about it.

So you went through your rites of passage in that couple of years playing live and watching other people playing live, which led to recording your first album, Bed Sitter Images. Did you put songs on there that you'd been gigging around, or did you go straight in and write new ones?

Oh no. I mean, some of those sounds had been around forever: 'Bedsitter Images' and particularly 'Swiss Cottage Manoeuvres', which was a song that everybody seemed to love so it was probably my earliest — "Oh, he's got to play that song." It's always nice to have a "you've got to play that song". So certainly those two were around for a while and probably most of the others when I think about it. The only one I can remember writing right up towards the end of the record was 'Beleeka Doodle Day', which is also the last track. That's the most Dylanesque song on the record.

But we didn't know what we were doing. I always say that if that record had been made a year earlier it would have been an acoustic folk record and if it had been made a year later it would have been with an electric band. The only reason it ended up being made with an orchestra was actually Judy Collins' fault, because she'd made this wonderful album, *In My Life [1966]* with an orchestra. She did a few with an orchestra, and the combination of her voice and that was great and the arrangements were great — Joshua Rifkin did them. So of course she knew what she was doing because she'd made records before and I hadn't. But the record company thought, "Oh yeah a folk singer with an orchestra, Judy Collins, yeah that works, that's great." So I ended up in the studio with a thirty-five-piece symphony orchestra. It was a complete mess. We had no idea what we were doing and especially not me.

I did eventually throw that format out, and of course when I did the second album *[Love Chronicles]* it was with Fairport Convention/Jimmy Page, so we went back to folk rock, which is what it should have been on *Bed Sitter Images* but it wasn't. So I think at the beginning you do tend to experiment. In fact I think the time itself was so experimental that people would say, "Well, let's try this" and you would try it. Look at *Love Chronicles* — the title song is eighteen minutes long and it's in five or six different movements. I mean this is crazy stuff. This had nothing to do with pop. You wouldn't have got away with that in '64, you would have written 'Blowin' in the Wind' *[Bob Dylan, released 1963]* or something. And it would have been three minutes and boom. You wouldn't get away with it today, but back when I started recording it in 1968, I said, "I'm going to write an eighteen-minute song," and the record company said, "Fine, go ahead."

Was that developed live or in the studio?

Oh no, I played it live. I finished it in 1968 and thought, "This is going to blow people away." And the day I finished it I went to two different folk clubs in the West End of London and played it live in both places and it was immediately, "Oh my God, what's that?!" I didn't know what I had, but obviously people immediately warmed to it. I played it for the next four or five years, and then I expired every night and began to regret the length of it.

Of course that one has gone down in the history of popular music as as reputedly being the first recorded song to use the word 'fucking'.

It might very well be the first one, but I always temper that assessment by saying I used the present participle and I use in the true sense of the meaning of the word. I'm not using it as a swear word. And I don't really know how to say that line in any other way: "It grew to be less like fucking / And more like making love." How do you say it without using that word?

Well with that sort of context, it solves all argument doesn't it?

Well it should do, but it still got me banned from the Manchester Free Trade Hall. I opened for *[folk singer]* Julie Felix when the record first came out and the manager there accosted me on the stairs and said he was going to make it his job to see that I never worked there again. And I didn't . . . until 1973. So four years later I was actually booked there again and I thought, "Well I wonder how this is possible?" and I said, "Where's this manager who told me I was never going to work here again?" And they said, "Oh they fired him."

So let's have Al Stewart back . . .

There you go. What comes around, goes around. I didn't think I was saying a 'naughty' word, I thought I was saying what I wanted to say in the only way that I could have said it.

As you've said, you were very much riding a wave from '65 onwards, but you moved in directions that people wouldn't necessarily expect of an acoustic 'folk' singer-songwriter. You can see it in your work, absorbing everything that was happening around you to forge and maintain a body of work that has taken on an active evolving sense of identity through chapters, which a lot of people didn't always do — and still don't do. A lot of people didn't progress beyond 1970, '71,

'72, but you just kept on following your nose. But to anyone who bridged that beginning of the Seventies moment when the Beatles left the scene and their global benchmark disappeared, it meant there was now an open path to even more experimentation, which you certainly pursued.

Well, if you're looking at the Seventies, there were three different distinct phases of what I was doing as I became bored with the previous one and moved on. From *Love Chronicles [1969]* through to *Orange [1972]* I'm writing personal relationship songs — absolutely that's what I'm doing. It was the time of the confessional singer-songwriter like Joni Mitchell, people like that. It was if you have a love affair then you sit down and write a song about it. Most of Joni's songs are about that. And so I thought, "Well I'll have a piece of that." And I wrote *Love Chronicles*.

That was successful — it was the *Melody Maker* folk album of the year — but by the time I got to *Orange* I just couldn't write another love song. I'd had a disastrous love affair and I was terribly depressed, and I thought, "I just can't do this." It should work as therapy but it wasn't doing that, it was reinforcing the pain every night. So I looked around and thought, "What else am I interested in?" And the only other thing I was absolutely obsessed with was history, and I thought, "What would happen if I made an entire album of historical songs?" And then I thought, "Well it's probably not going to work because no one's done that."

I couldn't imagine that there was anyone else out there who thinks the same way as I do about it. Are they really going to care about Jacky Fisher *[Royal Navy admiral Sir John Fisher from World War I, 'Old Admirals', Past, Present and Future, 1973]*, are they really going to care about the Night of the Long Knives *['The Last Day of June 1934']* or the German invasion of Russia *['Roads to Moscow']*? I mean, probably not. I was obsessed with it but at that point I just didn't care and all I was thinking was: "I just can't write any more love songs." So we went in the studio and we made *Past, Present and Future [1973]* in exactly the way that I planned it as: an entire album of historical songs. The thing comes out and it sells more copies than the first four albums I'd made put together.

That shocked me, I mean absolutely shocked me. All of sudden I'd meet people who've 'met' Nostradamus or *[USA president]* Warren Harding, people are clamouring, banging down the door: "You've got to be doing these songs every night!" Basically it took me out of folk clubs and into concert halls. I started getting paid large amounts of money, by my standards. Not much to the pop stars of the day but it was a lot more than you would get playing at the Cousins, you know? All of a sudden I was playing the Royal Festival Hall, people want me, people want the songs of *Past, Present and Future*, and I was just thrilled by this because I'd reached a point where I just didn't want to play 'Love Chronicles' anymore. I'd had five years of it and how many times can you play that thing. But the problem was that up to that point 'Love Chronicles' was my most popular song and people asked for it every night, but as soon as *Past, Present and Future* came out it all stopped.

People wanted 'Roads to Moscow', they wanted 'Nostradamus' particularly, and all the other things off it, and so it just moved me into a completely different place. But two years after that, again, I'd reached the point where it needed to change again. These songs are long — 'Nostradamus', you can break so many fingernails playing that every night — it was all beginning to wear on me. Also the production on *PP & F* was better than on *Bed Sitter Images* but it still wasn't exactly right so we moved into yet another dimension, which was "I've got to get a great producer, a great guitar player, some great musicians!" because what I wanted was . . . You see, to me even with *Past, Present and Future* I hadn't reached a point where the record sounded great. I thought the lyrics had got there but I didn't think the overall sound of the record had got there. So I also thought "I've got to get a new manager" because I wanted to go to America, where I had always wanted to go and play. So it's: "I've got to get a manager who understands America, I've got to get a producer who understands sound and I've got to get a guitar player who can play in this melodic Hank Marvin style" which very very few English guitar players could play in.

So for the next stage, I went out looking. I found Luke O'Reilly who was a disc jockey in the States. English actually originally, but he was on the radio in Philadelphia *[WMMR, 93.3 FM]* and he knew exactly what to do in terms of getting a record out there. And I went out and I found Alan Parsons who obviously knew everything there is to know about producing records in that period, and we went out and we found Tim Renwick, who was in the Sutherland Brothers & Quiver. He was my favourite melodic guitar player, he played it exactly the way that I would play if I could play the guitar. And I put all of those elements together and then it was "let's be sneaky, let's have some thinly veiled love songs back in there, and then let's have a few historical songs but let's not make the whole album full of them". And the result of putting all these elements together finally came to *Year of the Cat*, and that changed my life yet again.

Briefly, in seven years I'd gone from being the confessional eighteen-minute love song writer to the historical bard, and then all of sudden, lo and behold I had a record in the Top Ten in America, which is what I'd been trying to do in the first place. So that was a highly interesting ride and, as you say, I'd been probably three completely different people in that short period of time.

Does that not take its toll on you? A lot of people in that position would be thinking, "No, no, no, I'll lose my inner voice, I won't find the muse in so many different directions." But that was water off your back, it seems.

Well, I don't know. You follow your instincts to a large degree. But it was also it was probably an inability on my part to do, oh I don't know, to go any further with what I had at the time. I just couldn't do the love song thing anymore and the historical thing was something that I adored but wild. There probably is some sort of a gut feeling for historical folk rock songs and I probably reached it with *Past, Present and Future*. So I thought, "I can't do this any better. That record is about as well as I can write historical songs." I'd got to go somewhere else and that somewhere else turned out to be folk rock, almost *pure* folk rock: the record, the middle record, the one that connects *PP & F* with *Year of the Cat* is of course *Modern Times*. It's not an American folk rock record, it's an English folk rock record. That's what it is. It's lots of lead guitar solos and a band chugging away at the background.

I had the long wordy historical songs with acoustic guitars on *PP & F* and the twangy folk rock on *Modern Times* and *Year of the Cat* is basically a combination of those two elements because they were pretty much the only thing I felt competent to do. I mean, I was changing but I would wake up in the morning and compose things like reggae songs. I liked so many different styles of music but I did stop myself from attempting to be Bob Marley because that way lies madness! It's not just a question of knowing what you can do, you also have to know what you can't do, and I was very aware of my shortcomings in a lot of areas so I tried to stay away from them.

it sounds as if you didn't have that self-indulgent phase, which you can argue a lot of people need to pass through in order to get the space to focus on what they originally set out to do and what they've learned along the way. Like all of your contemporaries, there's a lot more to you than just the recordings. You can see that you're pushing the direction of material on every album as part of a wider creative 'struggle' that makes it hard to find anyone else who sets out to write songs in quite the same way as you do. You seem to be either coming from a different direction or going in a different direction. I'm never quite sure which.

To me it comes from influences. For example, I've read so many books that I don't mind archaic phrases. A lot of writers will write in the style of the age that they're in. So if you look at 1967, you're going to have a lot of grooviness going on. A lot of "hey baby!" and "yo, where it's at!", phrases that only exist in a very very tight timeframe. Lots of words that go into popular songs have this peculiar half life — you come back two years later and no one is saying any of these words or these phrases, they've gone completely. All those hippy things from '67, they're just not there anymore.

No one is speaking that sort of language now, whereas if you look at my songs there's a lot of almost Victoriana in there. I would be happy to write something almost Dickensian, to add that level of language. I don't mind using words that maybe have been not used for centuries and I've been known to throw Shakespearean words in songs because it works for me. If it's a good word I'll put it in and that alone is worth the search, lifting up the stones and looking underneath. I like old words, I like old language. When I wrote the Fisher song *['Old Admirals']* I didn't read a contemporary biography, I went back and read the 1921 edition of his biography. Because it was written in exactly the stye of language that I wanted. So that process would pretty much make anything I write sound different because I'm not a contemporary writer. To me there is no present. I can spend a whole day in 1648 and then spend the next day in another year and find all sorts of things there that are going on in the world right now. I don't know how people live in this thing they call the present. And for that reason I don't write as if I live in this thing called the present.

And of course, there's the thing that those words bring cadences that affect the melodic content of the songs, I suppose.

They probably do, yeah. For example, I spent quite a lot of time listening to John Dowland *[sixteenth/seventeenth-century singer-songwriter & lutenist]* when I was growing up, and I like the way he wrote. I'm not even talking musically — although I loved that — but he has very interesting cadences in the way he writes. I wouldn't have thought that John Dowland would be an influence on many contemporary writers but he was on me. As were Gilbert & Sullivan, and I'm as much influenced by that sort of stuff as I am by Jerry Lee Lewis or Eddie Cochran who I'm equally influenced by. All of that is in there, it's not just the contemporary elements. I'm a very uncontemporary writer, that's the answer!

But very British as well in that sense. There's not going to be that many Americans who can put Eddie Cochran next door to Gilbert & Sullivan or Dowland, for example, and why should they?

Well no they wouldn't, because it's much more relaxed in a way in America, like all these writers in Laurel County. I can't imagine they're doing the same thing! There's actually a song I wrote about Los Angeles before I even got to Los Angeles called 'Electric Los Angeles Sunset' *[Zero She Flies,*

1970]. I drove myself completely mad because of a line in that song, "Movie queues *turn* into a Cinerama haze . . ." It wasn't right. "Movie queues *strayed* into a Cinerama haze . . ." No that's not right either. I knew, I absolutely felt in my soul, that there was a word out there that was the perfect word. And so all I did for forty-eight hours was just write down hundreds and hundreds and hundreds and hundreds of different words looking for that one. And the word is 'diffuse'. Now look at the line, "Movie queues *diffuse* into a Cinerama haze." Now that is a line, but it took me two days to find that one word. And I can tell you this because I've met lots of songwriters and there's not many outside of Leonard Cohen who would have done that. They would have gone "Movie queues strayed into a Cinerama haze"? That's fine, move on.

Of course it makes it different if you can find that one word. I can't say what it's like for the listener, but for me when I sing the song that's the only word I hear because I know how hard it was find it. It's like trying to find a gold nugget.

To come back to that inner voice. It's something I tend not to bring up because I feel it's an idea imposed by the audience or by the critics and academics on the creator to talk about their inner voice, their muse, to feel pressure to reveal it, which really only serves to establish a set of rules to judge that creator by. But in your particular case the inner voice seems to be a highly visible goad that gives you the confidence to launch out and not fall. The journey you made out from that fleeting folk background saw you emerge from its expectations into those of the commercial American AOR world, shaking all that away to settle in the States, and yet you've grown closer rather than further from what other people would perceive as your roots, off which you're clearly thriving.

Oh yeah, I remember sitting in a hotel room in West Hollywood writing the lyrics to 'Merlin's Time' *[24 Carrots, 1980].* It's about this character that Robin Williamson of the Incredible String Band turned me on to: it's not the Arthurian Merlin, it's a Merlin who was a Scottish warrior poet who lived about a thousand years BC. Nothing could be further than Sunset Strip and 'Merlin's Time', and I'm sitting in a hotel and I'm writing the song so it's totally internalised at this point. I could be anywhere in the world and I could be writing a song about this, that or the other in history. When I'm doing it, I'm in that time period, I'm constantly in other time periods. Jacky Fisher, for example, was such an incredible story to me, the whole thing of bringing the Dreadnoughts into service and then what happened to him after the Dardanelles campaign. I could be in Hong Kong writing that song, it wouldn't make any difference to me because it's all internalised.

But you don't appear to be nostalgic, at least in your songs.

I don't know. My nostalgia? Everyone goes somewhere I would think. I'm not writing about me so no nostalgia appears there. I did write about me when I was young and discovered that it just made my head hurt, so I just stopped writing about me and became happy.

That's a good show-closer quote.

Well I like it too, but it's true. If you look at, oh I don't know, any of the more recent things I've done, like how on *Sparks of Ancient Light* [2008] I was writing about Hanno the Navigator. I was never around in 500 BC and I wouldn't have wanted to be a navigator.

You're visibly enjoying yourself on that album, which reflects the evident enjoyment you have in your music to the extent that you will happily step back and let some other guitarist take your place and let rip.

Well yeah.

There's usually not much space on the singer-songwriter stage to encourage that sort of thing, so you're sort of blessed in that.

If they do it better than me why not? I think you need to, if you're making a record, the person who's listening to the record couldn't care less who played what. They just want to hear something that sounds good to them. I have no sort of ego that says, "Okay I'm going to play that solo." If I have Tim Renwick sitting in the studio then yes he's going to play it.

The one area where I don't let anyone into the box is the lyrics, because I take it I can do that. Everything else, if you're talking about production, or who plays what or arrangements, all the rest of it, it's up for grabs. The best person should do the best thing. In a way this comes from politics — I spent an undue amount of time following American politics. Because of this I became interested in the difference in managerial style between John F Kennedy and Richard Nixon. The Kennedy approach is to find the best minds possible and listen to them: you don't have to agree with them, but you find the people who are the best advisors and then you let them have it and make up your mind based on all the facts. The Nixon approach is exactly the opposite: what you do is find a room full of people who agree with you and then you tell them what you want them to do. It seemed obvious to me which of the two was the better way to go about things, and when it came to making records I just adopted the Kennedy approach and found the best producers, guitar players and arrangers and all the rest of it and let them at it. And that comes from looking at American politics!

From a structural point of view it's interesting so see that solos are an important part of your songcraft, at least the way they must be crafted in the studio for the recorded version.

Yeah totally. The guitar solo's very very, very important to me. 'Modern Times' has most of my favourite guitar solos *[by Tim Renwick]*.

Agreed.

And now that comes about because I had two prime influences when I was very young, we're talking thirteen, fourteen years old. On the one hand, like everyone else in Britain, I was listening to Lonnie Donegan, everybody did. I mean he basically is the Source of the Nile for British rock music. And for him, a song like 'Grand Coulee Dam' *[1958]* and "the misty crystal glitter / Of the wild and windward spray", the metaphor of "the pounding waters". It's a Woody Guthrie song *[recorded in 1941]* and it's really well written lyrically and I learnt a lot from that. I used to sing the song probably eight times a day when I was that age, singing it over and over and over again.

So that's the lyrical side. But at the same time I was listening to Hank Marvin and Duane Eddy and especially Hank's extremely melodic style of guitar playing. It takes you to another place. Just go back now listen to 'Apache' *[1960]* or 'Wonderful Land' *[1962]* or 'Man of Mystery' *[1960]*, just wonderful stuff. So at some point along the line I must have thought to myself, "Okay these are the things that you loved when you were growing up, what happens if you put them together? What happens if you put great guitar solos on top of complex lyrics." And the answer is you get *Modern Times*.

So what you're really saying is when you swapped your electric guitar for an acoustic, the rock never actually left you.

Oh no, of course not, *of course not!* I still love Eddie Cochran — a great lyricist incidentally. And don't get me started on Jerry Leiber. To me, he and Chuck Berry are responsible for modern lyric writing. Between them, they're just incredibly wonderful stuff. Anyone who could write a line like, "You're gonna need an ocean like calamine lotion" *['Poison Ivy', written by Jerry Leiber & Mike Stoller, 1959]* or Chuck Berry's first ever line in 'Maybellene' *[1955]*: "As I was a-motorvatin' over the hill / I saw Maybellene in a coupe de ville."

Motorvatin'! Now not only is it brilliant, not only does it work, but it's a pun on top of all of that because he's driving a car. Maybe that one line is the line that changed contemporary lyric writing. So yeah, I still have all the rock'n'roll things but I like 'Desolation Row' and 'Famous Blue Raincoat' *[Leonard Cohen, Songs of Love & Hate, 1971]* and all the other things as well.

How did that double way of thinking work out after the mega success of Year of the Cat?

After *Year of the Cat* and *Time Passages* what happened was that we signed to Arista and they gave us money because they wanted *Time Passages 2* and 'Year of the Cat 2', which is essentially what the song 'Time Passages' is — it was a million seller so I suppose it worked. But my problem was having these hits with saxophones on them. I write folk rock and there are no saxophones in folk rock since it's a jazz instrument, so by putting them on songs I was way out of step with what I actually like in music. Of course I know that record buyers and audiences love this thing, but to me it sounded like a cow being tortured. To me it wasn't a folk rock sound. I don't like the sound of rock instruments in general and all of a sudden I was having to put one on every album.

But we did do that for a while. We put the obligatory saxophone track on the record to get airplay but increasingly these were the songs that I didn't care about at all. It meant that we went through a period in the Eighties where we were trying to cater somewhat to American radio stations because that's what made it work in the first place. And instead of having them chase us, we were chasing whatever we thought they were playing.

That didn't work at all and I ended up making a series of albums that I didn't really like, and which eventually that led me to throwing the rulebook out the window and going back to playing the songs I do like, while working with a sympathetic producer. That's *[guitarist]* Laurence Juber. All four of the Laurence Juber records *[Between the Wars (1995), Down in the Cellar (2000), A Beach Full of Shells (2005), Sparks of Ancient Light (2008)]*, especially the last two, have got right back to what I thought I should be doing. In the Eighties records, I had done a lot of co-writing, especially with *[guitarist]* Peter White, and Peter is into the groove sort of music where he would suddenly come up these musical pieces that I would write the lyrics to, and I don't think that the combination was really working any more.

Now on *A Beach Full of Shells*, oddly enough that's like *Past, Present and Future* where every single song on the record is written exclusively by me, and in many ways I see the album as the follow-up to *Past, Present and Future*. And then the next one *Sparks of Ancient Light* is the follow-up to that. So in a way, if you're looking for a sort of summary of what I do, for better or for worse, you could take this whole middle section of saxophones and grooves and hits and all the rest of it and you could say, "Well that was done for a reason at the time and it was fun to be a pop star for five minutes." But you can easily excise that from my catalogue and go directly from *Past, Present and Future* to the last Juber record without any of this middle stuff because in a way that was all a blind alley for me. *Past, Present and Future*, *A Beach Full of Shells* and *Sparks of Ancient Light*, if you looked at those three albums you'd say, "Okay this is the essence, the soul of Al Stewart." Unfortunately, fans, because they bought the records, would say it would be *Modern Times [1975]*, *Year of the Cat* and *Time Passages*.

That's the reality of the business that you somehow have to balance in your head, isn't it? And respect your audience's tastes too.

True. Those three albums are actually not me at all, it's the other three which are me. So it's a little confusing, even to me, because the records that I particularly like are not the ones that everyone else likes, but what can you do?

Well A Beach Full of Shells and Sparks of Ancient Light are timeless for a start and there's a unity to all the songs yet every one is totally different. You don't see many albums like that these days. There's very few artists who are fortunate to have access to the platform to produce complete albums these days in any case. It's interesting to see how you view the trajectory of your own recent works.

Unfortunately they're not the ones that were the big sellers, but you can't have everything. I'm actually quite pleased how they went, because people nowadays aren't really buying records, mine or anybody else's, especially not records by sixty-year-old English folk singers, I could very easily have not made those last two records, there was no commercial reason for me to do them. It's just that I thought that in a way it was annoying to me that, apart from *Past, Present and Future*, I'd made so many records that were not really an expression of what I wanted to do. So I thought it would be tremendous to get all of this on with first one album, and then, as an afterthought, the second one. They are actually expressions of what I wanted to do and, oddly enough, that's exactly how they came out so I'm happy to have them. You know they won't be the ones that people will remember, but I'm happy to have them out there.

Something which we haven't touched on is the fact that you ultimately moved to America. Did you do that in one go, or did you find yourself spending more and more time over there, gradually transferring by osmosis, or was there a moment when you thought, "I have to stay here"?

Oh no, it was much simpler than that. When *Year of the Cat* came out, we came over for a tour and it was like a six-week tour we had booked, which made total sense because we'd done a lot of towns, we'd done all the groundwork and we wanted to promote the record. Records usually go up and down the charts very quickly, but for this one we'd done all the work on the East and West Coasts but it took a long time to crack the middle of the country.

So after six weeks the record was probably in the Top 50 somewhere, which was all very nice but it was still going up and we'd finished the tour and the record company said, "You can't possibly go home now, we're exactly at the point where you have to keep going." So we booked another six weeks and that took us up to Christmas 1976 when the band and I were playing at the University of Southern California. We were at the edge of the stage waiting to go on. The lights came up, and the band went on stage. At the same time our manager come running down the hall toward me. As he got within earshot, he panted, "We got RKO!" At that time, RKO was a national network of AM/FM radio stations that played Top Ten hits over and over. 'Year of the Cat' would go into the Top Ten. I ran onstage knowing this wonderful secret, which neither the band nor the audience had heard yet.

That was actually supposed to be the end of the tour but of course two weeks later the record, both the single and the album, were in the Top Ten and of course you can't go home. There's no possibility that you can end the tour just as you get there, so we booked yet another leg and we played all the way through January, February and March. But the record was still hanging around, it seemed to hang around forever! And they wanted to release another single which turned out to be 'On the Border', so I think I was still on this never-ending tour as late as April of 1977. Every time I finished one leg of the tour, they booked another leg because the record kept selling, so it just went on and on and on.

Now in the meantime, what happened was that in order to be convinced not to go back to England, I rented an apartment right in the middle of Sunset Strip. It was empty when I moved in: a refrigerator, table, a chair and a bed, that was about it. And every time the record went up another ten, twenty places in the charts the record company gave me some other small item just to make my life like a little bit more comfortable. I got a couch when we hit the Top 50. Then they took me out down to a record store and they said, "Just buy some albums, here's some money buy some albums." So I came back with a stereo and some albums. And then I got a few more chairs and eventually we hit the Top 20 and they got me a television set and somehow I also had a bookcase. It was just one of these things where every time we sold some more records, the record company would furnish my apartment.

So by the time we'd done with this by mid 1977, I'd been over in the States for about seven months and I actually had my own furnished apartment. At that point I looked over to see what was going on in England, and somehow *Year of the Cat* was a hit in almost every country in the world where they had record charts — places like Hong Kong, Peru and El Salvador. We sold 26,000 copies of the record in El Salvador. By contrast the only country in the world where it wasn't a hit was England.

And I'm sitting there, I've just had a Top Ten record, I've got this really nice apartment on Sunset Strip, and I'm looking over at England and, you know, "Sorry, no hit for you over here" — with the whole country freezing cold and on strike. And I thought there could be no reason, no conceivable reason to go back. It's obviously not going to be a career thing: why would I go back to England which is the only country which isn't buying my records, and why would I go back and live in a freezing cold country that is ignoring me when I'm sitting here in bright sunshine in a country that just gave me a hit where everybody seems to be happy, including me?

I owned a little mews house in Belsize Park at the time, so I just hopped on a plane, went back, sold it, came back to America, and that was it. If I'd been shown a little more love by English record-buyers at the time, I'd have come back! But, you know, I have no idea why it wasn't a hit in England. Possibly it came out at exactly the time when the Sex Pistols broke out and it was simply the wrong record at the wrong time.

Although, as I recall at the time, it got a respectable amount of airplay. But airplay didn't always translate into sales in Britain.

I think that's true everywhere else in the world but Britain. It's one of these weird things because the song got to No. 31. Now *[BBC chart show] Top of the Pops* was a star-making machine in the sense that everybody in the country watched it. So if you played on the show in those days you'd play to ten million people in one go. You couldn't possibly do that now. And the policy on *Top of the Pops* was: "We will play your record if it makes No. 30." My record made No. 31. It isn't possible to come any closer than that. In retrospect, all *[record company]* RCA had to do was to go out and buy another dozen copies at *[high street record retailer]* HMV and we'd be at No. 30. And of course, with the benefit of hindsight, that's exactly what they should have done, but they were so confident this record was going to make it. It was already in the Top Ten in Germany, Holland and everywhere else, and they said, "No, no, it's a hit. We don't need to do that." And so the record missed an appearance *Top of the Pops* by one place.

My feeling about it now is that if we'd done *Top of the Pops* the song probably would have been a smash in the UK too. But in a way, because it wasn't, all these years later I am able to be in the UK what I can't be anywhere else, which is a folk singer, because I never actually did become a pop star in the UK. I did in places like Spain where the single was No. 1 and 'On the Border' was a hit there too as it was in Holland, while 'Sand in Your Shoes' was a hit in South Africa. So we had all these crazy things all over the place at that time, but not England, which enabled me to continually go back and still be the folky that I've always been.

When you moved to Los Angeles, that must have been an interesting time because there was still a bustling colony of American singer-songwriters out there. Did you get the chance to hang out or cross-fertilise with anyone or had they already started to disperse?

Not exactly. There was a few years, from about 1970 through to about 1978, when FM radio was playing all the people you think it would play: the likes of Joni Mitchell, Simon & Garfunkel, Dylan, the Byrds, Jackson Browne obviously, James Taylor, all the people you would think of as singer-songwriters. And then what happened in round about 1978 is that there was a complete revolution in American radio and it all became much harder. It was as if there was much more rock'n'roll and all the existing singer-songwriters vanished seemingly overnight. Where you would have heard Joni Mitchell now you heard Loverboy. We all fell off the airwaves of the FM stations.

At this time, funnily enough, the same thing happened in England, just a little earlier with the Sex Pistols, but *Year of the Cat* in America just got in under the wire. *Time Passages* was caught in the middle of it, it got played on AM but it really wasn't rocky enough for FM. And halfway through that record we then didn't get as much airplay as we had on the previous one. But then of course you couldn't get on the radio at all by then, it just totally changed. But in terms of hanging out with singer-songwriters, well everybody meets everybody. It's not a very big business, at least for the singer-songwriter side of it isn't, and it's hard for me to think of anyone I haven't met.

So are there people whose work grabs you? You must have a good perspective on the singer-songwriting tradition on both sides of the Atlantic. Do you sense a major difference between British and American attitudes to creating popular music?

There might be a difference in approach in the sense that American music is almost entirely blues-based. It's all around the blues scale and the backbeat. I can't imagine American popular music not being that way, everything from early jazz onwards has all been that and all of rock'n'roll. Whereas in England there are other subtle influences that worked their way in — everything from Gilbert & Sullivan onwards. For better or worse, you can see the hand of G&S in the work of, for example, the Beatles, even in their singing. 'Maxwell's Silver Hammer' *[Abbey Road, 1969]* isn't everyone's favourite Beatles song, but you're hearing something very different because it's a song performed on the on-beat not on the off-beat, there's ne'er a hint of the blues scale anywhere in the whole song. The whole thing could have come from a Gilbert & Sullivan musical.

There were other songs too where especially Paul McCartney does this, like on 'Mother Nature's Child' *[The Beatles/The White Album, 1968]*, or "Blackbird singing in the dead of night" *['Blackbird', White Album]*. There is absolutely no blues involved in that at all, that's a very English thing. If any of these songs had been performed by, oh I don't know — what would be the equivalent in America, Bill Monroe? — it would just all be blue scales and a savage backbeat all the way through. So there's a sensibility in England where you are able to incorporate everything from the work of say John Barnard *[17th century]*, through Gilbert & Sullivan *[19th century]*, through a lot of other composers whose work doesn't involve those American elements.

So English music is very diversified. It also makes it incomprehensible on some levels if you play that kind of music to Americans who've grown up on the backbeat and blues scale. They don't really understand what's going on, it sounds alien to them. An example is off *Sparks of Ancient Light [2008]*, 'Lord Salisbury' *[last British Prime Minister of the 19th century and the first of the 20th century]*, which has nothing to do with anything that happened in the last hundred years of American music. That absolutely doesn't mean I don't like American structures, it just means that I'm putting influences of not only English history but English musical styles into songs.

Religon also has quite a different cultural and artistic influence on both sides of the Atlantic. Has religion had much influence on what you've done?

Well I'm not religious, although I have an hour of prayers every single day of my life. I was brought up a Methodist as I recall.

Was that your family?

No, it was just the school. They had a Methodist chapel and we had an hour of prayers every morning before breakfast, don't ask me why. The short answer is that this had a significant effect on me in the sense that I sang all those hymns so many times that I've sort of internalised all the chord structures and I still sometimes borrow chordal ideas from hymns. I mean I must have sung 'Hills of the North Rejoice' — hymn number 815 from memory *[words by Charles E Oakley, 1870; music by John Darwall, 1770]* — I must have sung that a hundred times. And I borrowed some of the chords for 'Optical Illusion' *[24 Carrots]* from it, so yeah I guess it had an effect, but not lyrically.

A lot of the Methodist hymns of the nineteenth century were written by two particular composers: Isaac Watts and Charles Wesley. But Watts was a truly appalling lyric-writer, he was in the sort of William McGonagall class, and he was savagely satirised by Lewis Carroll. I hadn't realised this that until I read *The Annotated Alice [by Martin Gardner incorporating Lewis Carroll's texts, 1960]*, all these wonderful poems that Carroll wrote are in fact parodies of Watts' hymns. Watts wrote just horrible stuff, it's really Victorian and plodding and dementedly stupid. But he did write this piece called 'The Sluggard' *[Divine Songs Attempted in Easy Language for the Use of Children, 1715]*, if you please, who spends all day in his bed and does not rise to do the work of God — and this must truly be said, it's a terrible poem and a terrible hymn which starts: " 'Tis the voice of the sluggard; I heard him complain . . .", and of course Lewis Carroll in his immaculately wonderful way turned it into ' 'Tis the Voice of the Lobster' *[Alice's Adventures in Wonderland, 1865]*. Carroll's whole poem is a parody of an Isaac Watts' hymn and it helps greatly when you realise things like this.

The music industry has changed so much now and everyone's saying that music has been basically dead since the Eighties and the music industry hasn't helped it one bit. But then there's the fact that you can do things like, seemingly at the drop of a hat, suddenly produce a brace of albums like A Beach Full of Shells and Sparks of Ancient Light, which your audience loves — and you do too. We play them and think, "Gosh where did that come from?" So clearly music is not moribund as we think, but simply reaching us in different ways.

I disagree completely. I think it's just because you don't listen to the music that's being produced. I'm constantly listening to new stuff. One of the nice things is that I make people send me compilations all the time of music that I might not otherwise hear, like Gabby Young & Other Animals, who's just twenty-five *[at the time of speaking]* and is clued into all of it. In the UK, Elbow aren't new, they've been around for a long time, and that album of theirs *The Seldom Seen Kid [2008]* is beautifully written. The first line on the record is "How dare the premier ignore my invitations / He'll have to go" — I would buy a record based on that line alone. And then you have writers like Laura Marling who may or may not turn into something special, but they are definitely different, definitely intelligent.

And then you've got Joanna Gibson, who's a harp player of all things. She's been travelling around America selling out 5,000-seater halls with songs that have never been played on any radio station anywhere. They can't because her songs range from eight minutes long to sixteen minutes, plus they're played on a classical harp. But people absolutely adore her, she's got the kind of following now that Dylan had right before he broke through with his first hit single. And I could mention more . . . There are as many significantly interesting lyric writers floating around now as there ever were. It's just that they're invisible to older people for the simple reason that older people don't keep up with them.

I suppose I could always ask you that old chestnut of your advice for a young aspiring singer songwriter starting off today, or an old aspiring one for that matter. Do you think it's more difficult today for people to start off doing something like that today than when you started off?

I think it's more difficult in the sense that the record industry has become totally vulcanised obviously so the new model is probably . . . well, you put all the stuff up on the internet and hope that somebody salutes it.

I know young singer-songwriters who come to my shows. I just did the London Palladium and there were a couple of them there who asked me exactly the same thing. I think it would be very tough now precisely because you can't do it in the way that we did it, which was you go to a club and there are thirty people and then you go back again, like at Bunjies or the Cousins — in fact when I first started playing there the room was empty. After a couple of years people are coming to see you, then you get a record company to come and see you and they see there's a room full people and they say, "Oh, mm." And maybe they let you make a record and then you make, in my case, six more records before you actually become commercially successful.

That model is just not there, because it disappeared a long time ago. At CBS Records they allowed me to keep making records even though nobody really bought the early ones. *Year of the Cat* was my seventh album and it had taken ten years to get to having a hit anywhere in the world. Record companies, even if they existed now in the way they used to, probably are not going to give you that sort of support — like you making seven albums before they get their money back. So it is a much tougher thing and the scene is so vulcanised, people don't make it the way they deserve. Oh, in the Sixties when the Beatles came out and everybody listened to the Beatles, and if they didn't? Well you had this thing where this was a universal youth movement and they were all listening to the same music. Now it's country people listen to country, rap people to rap, heavy metal people to heavy metal, dance music people to dance. What they don't do is listen to much of anything else. You don't have the phenomenon of FM radio playing all of these genres and then twenty-eight other genres as well.

Radio stations have their own audiences so the audience listens to what they listen to and they don't even socialise with people who listen to a different kind of music. The same thing has happened to politics internationally. In the States it's interesting how Republicans don't talk to Democrats anymore and the whole thing has sort of gone out the window. We are now like Scottish clans used to be in the sense that we are highly suspicious of each other and we don't talk to each other and every now and then we have a war. But of course. in the Sixties everyone followed the Beatles and if *Rubber Soul* or *Sergeant Pepper* came out then everybody listened to it. It should be like that today!

*

Richard Thompson

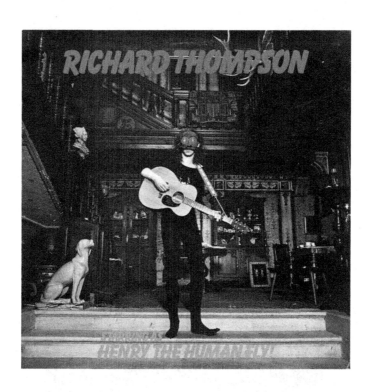

6

Richard Thompson

'My grandmother used to sing in Gaelic'

Born on April 3rd, 1949, in Ladbroke Gove, West London, Richard Thompson was raised in Highgate, North London, and started playing guitar in bands from early teenagehood. At 18 he become a founder member of Fairport Convention in 1967. After their first five albums, including the landmark *Liege & Lief* [1969], he left the band in 1971 to concentrate on his songwriting while becoming increasingly in demand as a session player. He released his first solo album *Henry the Human Fly* in 1972 after which he formed a partnership with his future wife Linda Peters. As Richard & Linda Thompson they released a string of critically praised albums including *I Want to See the Bright Lights Tonight* [1974]. By 1981 Thompson had emerged as a solo artist touring the USA regularly playing both solo and with a band, recording throughout the decade with producers Joe Boyd (who had first signed up Fairport Convention) and Mitchell Froom. Guest sessions and side projects, including numberous collaborations with members of Fairport Convention and their Copredy Festival, have added to his profile and his 1991 album *Rumor and Sigh* was nominated for a Grammy. He has toured *1000 Years of Popular Music*, songs from the elevnth century to the present, and 2010 he curated the Meltdown Festival at London's Southbank Centre. *Family* [2014] featured musical contributions from his extended family, including Linda and their children Teddy and Kamila. Now based in California and London, Thompson was awarded an OBE (Order of the British Empire) in 2011 for services to music.

This isn't a sex and drugs and rock'n'roll book.

Okay.

But if you want to tell us, you can . . .

Just Japanese salesmen's jackets.

And you are taller than you look on the album covers.

Well the album covers are usually a few inches, so I've got to be taller than that really.

That must help with the guitar because, since you spend so much time in the company of one, it always helps to be proportional so the instrument doesn't dominate you.

KT Tunstall has to be about 4 foot 6 inches. The guitar's huge on her. So it's always worth the buying guitars which are scaled up or down.

And so to start at the beginning . . .

Born in London, in Ladbroke Grove. Born at home and I spent the first five years in Ladbroke Grove. Then we moved to Highgate which was a bit beefier.

Very few of your generation came from Central London, they were more raised in the suburbs or towns within the London orbit. For that reason you have a fairly unusual provenance, apart from Cat Stevens, who was raised instead in Soho and a bit of Sweden.

But Highgate isn't that much further in to the centre of London than, say, Muswell Hill where Ray Davies was.

But it's not Pinner or the South Coast, for example.

It's not Pinner no. Now . . . who's from Highgate, who's from [nearby] Tufnell Park? [Drummer] Roger Powell who used to play with the Action, he's from Tufnell Park.

True. Then there's all the East End lot like the Small Faces, who were actually much closer to the centre of London but mentally definitely not.

Yeah, mentally the East End's in another century! It's interesting because the musicians I first played with weren't necessarily all from the same area. When I was at school of course they were right there, but then with Fairport Convention, two of the band lived in Muswell Hill and that became our centre, a little bit further out. And other people I knew increasingly came from across the North London suburbs.

Do you think that's why the Fairport movement didn't see its genesis in the Soho or Kensington clubs?

That seemed to be for grown-ups. There was sort of the 'original' people like the Stones, Yardbirds and Eric Clapton.

The great music shops, at least the shops where the ideas came from, were not all in the centre, but in places like West and South London, like Marshall.

Wembley, I think. Where was Jennings?

In the centre, Charing Cross Road, it became Macari's. Watkins was in Balham, South London. Of course, as the UK music industry mushroomed, a lot of the music shops had already moved into the centre like Jennings did or worked with dealerships in the centre of London. But in any case, the music centre of London increasingly became Tin Pan Alley and the West End, as music turned into a direct industry response to the baby boomers.

Well I was born just after the war, 1949, so I'm not exactly a baby boomer. That actually started during the war, people born from about 1943 onwards. You pretty much had to be a teenage by the late Fifties or something like that. And it was lucky that my family ended up in the capital. My father was a policeman, from Scotland, Kirkcudbright — John Martyn's father came from the next town. So my dad started out as a joiner, which is like a house carpenter. Then he got bored with his prospects and, since they recruited a lot of police for London from the Scottish Borders, he ended up a policeman.

He was a music fan and played a bit of guitar. He'd take the train up to Glasgow to see Louis Armstrong or Django Reinhardt playing at Green's Playhouse in the Thirties. He came down to London probably in 1937 and was in the police at the beginning of the War, went into the Army and missed going to Burma, which was lucky because he was transferred just before the ship sailed, good move. Then he was a rifle instructor for a couple of years and did something in military intelligence for the invasion of Germany. He stayed on after the war in the service in Antwerp for a couple of years.

After the War, Dad was plainclothes in the Metropolitan Police. He was in the Flying Squad, murder squad, vice squad, drug squad, all the Soho ones. They didn't keep you in any one place for too long to stop you from getting corrupted. God knows what he really got up to, but he was handy because he knew all the guys in the music shops. He was in the Army with a guy who ran a guitar shop called Lew Davis *[on Charing Cross Road]*. So as a young guitar player I could guarantee that I could go in and get an electric guitar for half price, get an amp for half price, so that was wonderful. And when the band *[Fairport Convention]* was starting up, we'd get things like a PA system. So useful to have contacts!

All these music shops where the kids hung out and played the latest riffs every Saturday morning were classic melting pots for British musicians. It must have been an incredibly interesting time to be launching out as a guitar player.

I particularly remember a guitar player called Dave Burrluck. Now he did live in Soho. I was in a school band with him, although he was at a different school. We used to go round his house sometimes because it's kind of exotic to know someone who lives in Soho. In fact Soho was full of exotic people then, like Maltese and Italians. I remember the 2i's coffee bar in Old Compton Street — the club was still going into the Sixties and it was where people like Tommy Steele were discovered.

In those days, a single year could churn out an entire musical generation via Central London.

Indeed. My sister worked at the 2i's and, being five years older, she had a different perspective on the music. She was into rock'n'roll then trad jazz, and then she got into the Beatles and the Stones. She even wanted to play guitar. But at home in London, when I was very young, my dad didn't have a guitar. After ten years, he finally brought one home for him to play. My sister picked it up and decided she was going to play, then she didn't and then I did, so I was sort of the third-choice guitar player in the family.

And was that the point of no return?

Oh yes!

And presumably you'd have got a guitar of quality coming home if your dad was sourcing it?

No it wasn't. It was a piece of crap.

It was a piece of crap because your dad cocked up or because there just weren't good guitars to have at the time?

Well it was a Spanish guitar and it was a sort of a £10 Spanish guitar. And it was broken. It had been smashed and they were going to throw it away and my dad said, "Oh I'll fix that up." So, having been a carpenter, he glued it up and brought it home. When I picked it up, I had three very strange chords to play on it that I got from his playing. They weren't C, F and G, just funny sort of jazz chords, sort of Django chords. So that's how the guitar came into the house and I moved straight on to playing the Shadows.

Did you have a piano in the front room like a lot of families did, or did your mum play records in the afternoon?

My mum just sang unaccompanied. She's a really good singer, sounds a lot like Vera Lynn, also looked like Vera Lynn. She could have substituted for Vera on some of those Far Eastern tours! She was musical and a musical fan, didn't know anything about music, she just sang all day, sang around the house. And my dad had records. Had some crap Teddy Johnson sort of stuff and Perry Como. But he also had Sinatra, Duke Ellington, Django Reinhardt and Les Paul. So that was cool. And early Louis Armstrong. That's a good place to start. Plus he had all the Scottish dance stuff too.

Interesting discoveries for a folkie, which you aren't. But people started to stick labels on people like you . . .

If you say I'm not, I am. If you say I am, I'm not.

Okay!

And then there were my sister's records, which were Elvis and a lot of Buddy Holly, a bit of Jerry Lee, a bit of Gene Vincent, you know, that kind of stuff.

Was there a record for you that did it, or a song or musical moment that made you go "wow!" Did you have a Hank Marvin moment, for example?

I had a Hank Marvin decade, pretty much! Well, that's what we played in groups until we figured out someone had to sing something. I started playing with my friend Malcolm round the corner when we were about ten and we just played the Shadows and that's all we did. And then there was the school band, which probably started when we were about thirteen — we were trying to play R&B. And then we were trying to be like the Who for a while. But it was mostly R&B covers, blues covers, R&B covers! And then with Fairport it became something else . . .

How old were you when you left school?

Eighteen.

Did you get A-levels or did you leave just before taking them?

I completed two out of three.

Already you were being pulled out of the system.

Yes. I really lost interest in school. I got two A's: in English and Art.

But you didn't turn up for the third subject?

I didn't turn up for the French exam because I figured I'd rather do the gig in Bradford than sit and do the French exam. I would have failed it anyway. I did no work in French for the last year because I figured I could only really study two subjects and be on the road at the same time.

That was very calculating of you.

Yeah, it was, very, yeah!

You time-managed that at a time when the word probably hadn't even been invented. British music-makers like you who were born in the Forties and very early Fifties period were canny teenagers evidently. Many of your generation were already working semi-professionally in music by the time they were fourteen/fifteen. Mind you, there's a maturity that must come from being in a system where they had only just raised the school leaving age from fourteen to fifteen, and you could still be indentured as an apprentice at that age.

Well I was going to be indentured actually.

To rock'n'roll?

No. When I was at school I was a stained glass apprentice. Although it wasn't something where you signed a piece of paper. But I was in the glass painters' guild, you know, all that kind of stuff, and I was figuring it was just a year before I went to art school or something. So that was fun. But again it was difficult to be on the road and do that as well if we were playing out of town.

It's near impossible nowadays to just go off and be a pick-up band in a bar round the corner, certainly at that age.

Yeah, because I'd say from the age of thirteen/fourteen I was working, getting gigs with the school band, mostly parties, a lot of parties, and a few other things like gigs on boats and weird stuff. And then with Fairport, we were working when we were sixteen, three days a week. When we were seventeen/eighteen we were working flat out.

Inconceivable in Britain today . . .

I know.

From talking to the prog rockers who started off around the same time as you, I realised that so many of them came from the South Coast. It was easy for you to get into London by rail then hop back on the 11pm from Waterloo and arrive home just in time for a hiding from your dad, but you'd be off again the next Friday night. And because there were still bustling holiday resorts along the whole South Coast, they were cutting their teeth through a steady stream of gigs in the pubs, hotels and end-of-pier venues.

I was talking to Dave Pegg from Fairport, who grew up in Birmingham. He said he left school at sixteen and took an insurance job, but he was working every single night of the week because every pub in Birmingham had live music. It makes such a difference. And then the musicians' union rule came in when they said you can't have more than two performers in a pub playing live at the same time.

Which killed off the live circuit pretty quickly in the UK. And then health & safety got in on the act . . .

Killed it. That came over here in the Eighties and it was a disaster. Just think of Kansas City in the Thirties where the mayor's corrupt and everybody's breaking prohibition laws, and there's streets of these nightclubs where the cops are all taking backhanders. But that's the foundation of the Kansas City jazz scene from which Count Basie and Charlie Parker came. So sometimes, the do-gooders, the health & safety people and the unions inadvertently kill off what they're trying to preserve.

Going back to your formative years, what sort of schooling did you have in London?

I went to the very local primary school then went to a slightly-less-local-but-I-could-still-walk-to-it secondary school, William Ellis School. It's by Parliament Hill Fields *[Hampstead Heath]* and has always been a really good school. But totally wasted on me. It's amazing how many Latin verbs I managed to retain through looking out the window. But it's the only time in your life when you memorise poetry and I can still remember all the poetry I learnt there. I remember so much of my Latin vocab it's ridiculous. But still . . . I was just looking out the window and I was a terrible rebel.

Where did that come from?

It was a generational thing. Having a father as a policeman just makes you want to . . . He was really tough. He was tougher on my sister. She bore the brunt of it and they'd kind of given up by the time it got to me, they'd just run out of energy. Because my sister was so wilful and independent and single-minded, bless her, she took a lot of the heat away, but it was still a very Calvinistic kind of environment.

I was going to ask about religion, so we're talking about . . .

Presbyterianism. My mother was raised Catholic but we all went to Presbyterian church before my father kind of fessed up and stopped going and said, "I don't believe in anything." Then we didn't go to church anymore. But my mother towards the end of her life went back to the church. She actually didn't go back to Catholicism, which was unusual, but went to the Church of England, I think Unitarian. She was a bit Scottish but mostly English.

That religious/cultural background or whatever your family ethic was must have affected your creative worldview.

I think it affected me later rather than at the time, because at the time I didn't particularly believe in anything as a child.

Do you think it's important to have some sort of belief values put into us?

I think everybody has belief values whatever they may be. "I don't believe in anything" — that's a belief value. But I think when I was about sixteen I started to cast around. I remember a book called *Zen Flesh, Zen Bones [subtitled A Collection of Zen and Pre-Zen Writings, 1957]* which is like short zen stories and a wonderful kind of what you'd perhaps call lateral thinking today, the sort of thing that makes us think, "Whoah, how do I figure this out? The only way I can figure this out is by not thinking about it!" So I thought wow this is tremendous. So a real interest in Zen. And then I got interested in Zen Buddhism. And this is all while I'm sixteen and I'm still at school.

The foundations for the mystical side that you've always manifested.

Absolutely. And then I discover right next to Travis & Emery Music Bookshop is Watkins Books in Cecil Court [Covent Garden, London] which is a sort of spiritual bookshop *[billed as "London's Esoteric Bookshop since 1893"].* So I worked my way through 'A for Anthroposophy' to 'Z for Zen'. I went through every shelf and actually ended up thinking the [mystics] are actually the ones who knew what was going on.

And in no way did this affect your appreciation of Hank Marvin?

No. Music is a spiritual thing. You listen to a Shadows record when you're twelve years old and it takes you somewhere else. It's been said often, but music is the most spiritual of the arts, it takes you closer to being out of your body, closer to the sound of your soul. Some songs you listen to and you just think this is almost the music of the angels. When I'm dreaming and I hear celestial choirs, this is pretty damn close to what I hear in my dream. So John Coltrane, messed up junkie whatever, creates spiritual music. Charles Mingus . . .

So to jump ahead then . . . You're an unusual person certainly for any time.

Trying to be.

Certainly in the music world you have a reputation for being a ferocious thinker which gives the impression that you could have done well in anything that you'd chosen to tackle.

Like drop-out loser.

Well, it was that generation.

It's just an observation of how many of the people I knew at William Ellis School who dropped out, tons of people, smart people destined for glittering academic careers, whatever, who just said, "Ah to hell with it, I'm not going to do that. I'm going to go off and live in a commune in Denmark", or, "I'm just going to sell drugs." Very strange.

For my generation, staying in education as long as possible during the Eighties seemed to be our lifeline — those of us who didn't become yuppies, that is.

The thing is, in the late Sixties there were jobs. It was easier to say, "I'm not going to do that. If I need money I can get hired on anywhere." You could really do that in the Sixties. And that's the reason that shaped that generation more than anything else.

Which contrasts with the Eighties and Nineties onwards where there were loads of jobs but in increasingly specific areas at the expense of everything else, where it all evolved into a job market that offered very little outside of those areas to those who wanted to make a living from their creativity. I came to a moment of my own when I thought well actually if I stay at home and just do the washing up without complaining I'd made a spiritual and even artistic statement, although no one's likely to experience it. And I thought okay that's a Zen thing isn't it?

Yeah.

Not much money doing the washing up though.

Washing up is under-appreciated by society.

Okay, so you were hailed from the outset as a guitarist of innovation and influence. You were also a singer-songwriter which you've defined as not by folky standards but by what they're not. You haven't trod the Path of the Guitar God in the Jimmy Page manner, but on the other hand you're not a singer-songwriter the way that say Robert Plant is, since the pair worked, at least for a period, as partners in a band. And yet you've always collaborated, you've got a band most times, and some of your band collaborations are quintessential line-ups.

Yeah.

Where does the spiritual journey come into all of that? Do you think the singer-songwriter thing is putting yourself in a place where you can actively channel the music to serve the message, to have most control over the shape of the music because of the words, melody and instrumentation . . . and you get to choose your producer and . . . ?

I think everything fits inside it somehow. What I really like is songs and I like song structures and I like to bring the singing and the guitar playing into the song structure.

You're not a guitarist who says I'm going to blow for the next five minutes and I don't care who's listening.

I hate that. *Fifteen* minutes should be the absolute minimum! But really, I hate playing instrumentals like that. I'm not an instrumentalist, I don't think. But I love taking solos within a song where you can just continue the narrative.

Your solos are definitely lyrical in a very trademark way. On your recordings I for one find myself going back in for repeat listens: what was that he did that I know I missed? That back and forth of lyrical expression between voice to guitar is subtle stuff. In terms of that continued narrative, when you're in the studio do you record your voice by yourself or do you always have to have a guitar in front of you, resonating against you?

Interesting. Well not always, but sometimes . . .

But it helps?

If I'm doing a vocal overdub, I strap a guitar on just so it feels right.

So the playing and the singings do go together then.

Otherwise I don't know what to do with my hands. Where do I put my hands?

Do a Whitney Houston and . . .

That's what I end up doing actually. I end up doing this thing in front of the microphone. Hopefully there's no cameras. Yeah, interesting observation.

Either way, that double voice must gives you an interesting level of control over where you can take a song.

It's nice to control the format. Whatever spirituality is in the song is something you put in the lyrics and you put into the general feel of the thing, the tuning of the thing, the way it fits together. And that becomes a vehicle of expression upon which you can lay a guitar part.

How then do you feel about doing other people's material?

Other people's material? Well fine. If I'm playing someone else's material it means that I kind of approve of it, if you like. So if I'm doing a cover version in a show of mine then I find something in the song that works for me. Plus you do what you do with producing or playing on someone else's records, and that can be a rewarding experience. Or not. Or else at least another hour to invoice.

Think of the 'washing-up'. I'm sure you don't descend into invoice-watching.

I hope I don't! I really don't usually. In the early Seventies, when I was doing a lot of session work, that's basically what I did for a year. But then, you know, you're always going to find yourself in sessions where you are thinking about the invoice rather than the record.

You didn't start off as a session player but you got into it in a period of change when the big orchestras or teams of session players weren't being used anymore, Archer Street had vanished, Denmark Street was on its last legs, people were starting to move to America because there they had studio set-ups where you had all that session stuff around them.

But when I was doing it it seemed pretty busy like 1971/72 when I did a lot of session work and I was *busy*!

Was it not slightly soul-destroying, did you lose a bit of your soul back there?

Absolutely. How could anyone do that for ten or twenty years? What did I get out of it was that you learn how to get a sound in a studio, you learn versatility, you learn to leave your ego at home. Because what you think is great might not be appropriate at the end of the day. You don't necessarily know the whole picture of what someone's playing. They might have the string section going on and you're going to stomp all over it unless you listen to it and take direction. And, yeah, I did seem to be busy and I did keep seeing the same musicians in the studio every day, which was interesting. There'd be like three bass players, four drummers, two keyboard players and you'd walk in in the morning and go, "Oh hello, it's you again!" There was kind of a folk-rockie little clique. We did the girl singer-songwriters and probably the softer stuff. Someone else was doing T. Rex and there were the real pros doing the Tom Jones gigs.

When you left school you found yourself gravitating towards the music scene that was emanating from Muswell Hill up the road in North London. Aside from that gig when you didn't turn up for your French A-level, that summer you must have found yourself suddenly doing music full time with people who were aspiring to a shared sense of excellence?

Yeah exactly.

Had things like Fairport Convention started to coagulate by then?

Coagulate disgustingly, yes, like a tin of Fray Bentos! The first gig as Fairport — officially Fairport — was May of 1967 *[in Golders Green, North London]* and that's where *[drummer]* Martin Lamble joined and then Judy Dyble. And that's actually the beginning of the band. We were working really quick — by the time it's July we were playing the Speakeasy Club *[Central London]* twice a week, and Blazes, and starting to play places out of town like Mother's Club, Birmingham.

By that winter we were really all over the country, we were playing Leeds, Manchester, Sheffield, Newcastle, Plymouth, Southampton, Isle of Wight, Wolverhampton, Birmingham. There were a lot of gigs and once we signed on to the Bryan Morrison Agency, all his acts would end up on the same bill with us. You'd see eight Bryan Morrison bands playing at Manchester University all night, you'd see thirteen bands all blockbooked at a Leeds University or Cambridge University all-night rave. So you kept on seeing Crazy World of Arthur Brown, Blossom Toes, Social Deviants, whoever else was on the circuit. It was a very supportive scene, where everyone was very friendly.

Everyone must also have been learning off each other. This was a unique window of opportunity to come up with a unique musical template. You must have been happy to be working and learning off each other because it was such a time of great discovery for everyone of revelation — and swapping new chords of course.

There was a bit of acid and a bit of sauce but peace, love, I love you man with all that as well, which is good. But when Linda and I were doing the folk scene in 1972 I couldn't believe how bitchy it was, comparing all that backstabbing and bitching to the rock scene of '67.

So the spirit of '69 never translated over to the Seventies.

I think it was more frustration on the folk scene, more people thinking along the lines of "Jasper Carrott's successful, he left the folk scene, he's successful, I'm really jealous of that". Every time a comedian managed to escape the circuit then it didn't go down too well which is surprising because the scene was filled with lovely people — but they did have a bit of a fishwife side.

Possibly attitudes were already becoming quite entrenched by then right across the UK's music. The Beatles split up and suddenly everyone jumped to claim a genre after that, I think. Something in the turn of the Seventies gave the music industry carte-blanche to identify some stuff and ignore other stuff.

That's always a warning sign. When the music industry figures out what's going on, that's always the bad moment.

Has your professional life always been defined by the battle against the industry side of music?

It's always been a mystery how they're going to market what I do, because basically it's a certain kind of music for an audience that doesn't really exist. It's about fifteen people that I write for. But it's not white R&B and it's not white blues. If I wanted to be popular we would have played an American style of music.

But you did move to America.

Physically, not mentally.

That rings true, there's still no twang in the guitar or in the voice.

No. I don't do twang.

How did you manage that? Or is it simply you are who you are and it doesn't matter where you are — Barcelona, Shanghai, Lagos — you'd still be doing the same thing. Obviously getting stimulus from what's around you . . .

The music's so good around. If I was in Seville I'd probably take it onboard, although I still think I would stay a bit more British than that. I might have become a New Orleans musician if I lived in New Orleans. As it is I'm quite influenced by Louisiana music ever since I listened to a Louis Armstrong record when I was three years old. I took Spanish guitar lessons when I was eleven so there's enough of the Spanish influence, so I don't need to live in Seville to absorb flamenco. If I live in Los Angeles, which has a bland culture, the only danger is I'm going to absorb rap, and I'm not going to do that. So in Los Angeles you can be whoever you want to be. You can be Korean, you can be Vietnamese, you can be English and nothing impinges on your culture. I married a Los Angeles person, an 'Angelean' union but I never actually said "I'm moving to Los Angeles."

So you're still rooted in your spiritual base in Blighty.

It depends. I think it's all up here *[taps head]*. You know, what's my internal landscape? Is it sort of Exmoor, a windswept moor, or something else, where's Heathcliff over there? It's certainly not sunny California internally. I can lie on a beach in Hawaii and write really bleak songs. James Joyce could sit in Paris and write with more intensity about Dublin than anyone else has ever written.

And there was Samuel Beckett writing about Irish music hall in Paris too — and in French! So often you hear people moaning about losing inspiration or identity or not being able to keep up their standards when they move. It's rare that you hear someone say of course you can do it, it's not a problem.

I also think sometimes as an exile you become a little bit more . . . Well, my father was a classic exiled Scot. He was more of a Scotsman than anybody in Scotland. He never missed Burns Night, always played Scottish music, it was just all that stuff like Walter Scott. And these days, that sort of thing is even more evident. So now you open your laptop and there's *The Guardian* as your home page. You hit a button you're listening to *[BBC]* Radio 4 while you're working. Driving in the car and the satellite radio's playing the BBC World Service. If you wanted to be a real nerd, to be someone I would hate, I could go to any of five British pubs in Santa Monica or any one of three British tea-rooms there, and play darts and eat fish and chips, I mean really!, and have afternoon tea.

Well the point is, would you necessarily do any of that in England?

No I wouldn't. But if I wanted to be a real exile nerd, I could.

To ask a bit more about your thoughts on inspiration: is there a template set up when you were 16, 17, 18 that you've been working off ever since? Or do you have something that is organically changing? Joyce took inspiration from a formative period of his past and went back to it again and again. That search for the spiritual meant that it wasn't obsessive or stopped him from developing as a human being. On the other hand there are people who find something new with every week, year, decade although they still do it according to the rules of that internal landscape. Which sort of do you fit into . . . ?

Both.

I can just leave your answer there, if you like.

Well, as far as I can see, for some songs if that you keep mining the same area, you keep digging away, and occasionally you find a seam that's promising. Other songs come very quickly from out there somewhere, but what happens is that you put them into your own language. So something happens to you in one place, you're walking down the street in Malibu and an incident occurs and you put it in Soho or somewhere else because that's what you know about, and that's what you know how to write about. And that fits the way you think of yourself as a writer, if you like. That's the area that interests you.

As a songwriter, I've always felt uneasy at the fact that I'm happy just wanting to write about the streets of Soho in the dead of night. But you're telling me that actually this is a good thing to do.

It's good! Because what you're writing about is a human condition. You see examples of the human condition all over the place and then you think well, you have to put this into a story, it has to become a story that interests you and would interest people listening. And when you do write a story it's still the streets of Soho at two in the morning.

Are you a spiritual teacher through your songs or are you a poet or are you a storyteller or, as I'm sure you're going to tell me, all three? Do you see yourself as actively any of those things or is it just that you don't need to analyse it?

I only analyse it when somebody asks me that question. Well that's not true, I mean sometimes I sit down and ask what am I doing, what is it that I do, why am I still doing this, is this where I fit, where should I change? You know, that's a sort of regular question every, whatever, six months, a year.

And does the direction of that question change or is it always the same question and you get a different answer?

No, it's not always the same question. It changes slightly sometimes. It's a funny sort of bundle of stuff, you know. I could say I write because I enjoy it and what I end up doing is tell stories without really meaning to. But I think I enjoy that process of "here's a character". Maybe it's just in the first person that you only know this character through what happens around the song, but it's fun to see what's going to happen to this character — you know, what's the situation that's going to develop? And it doesn't have to be a ballad to be a story, for example some songs are quite abstract with a million loose endings, and they can be quite effective songs. It's a kind of cinematic style of writing. Where there's no introductory verse and there's no last verse.

And it crossfades all the way through.

It's all kind of cinematic POV: you jump into the room and then . . . Sometimes with Dylan songs there's no connection between the verses, so he's doing that. The verses are all disjointed, they all come in at different times and different places and from this kind of strange sort of palette comes a story but it's a very modern story. It's twentieth-century modern technique. For example, I can think of something like seven hundred musicals where the songs are disconnected and have nothing to do with the plot. Or the plot winds its way torturously from one song to another regardless of what the plot actually is.

There's that Sixties documentary with Dylan and his typewriter. And David Bowie made it an active part of his craft, chopping lines up and rearranging them or lining them up seemingly randomly. People often forget about songwriters that they are wordsmiths as well as composers. The typewriter/laptop is as much a part of their ammunition as a guitar. It's very educational to see Dylan as writer with Joan Baez in the background probably dictating the words to him and he's doing it. It looks like he was actually writing a particular song but was pulling sheet after sheet — and out of that he would have picked out about four or five things and stuck them together.

I think it's someone who overwrites and then edits it down to something of a manageable length. Like a film script. That's the thing: some songs you work at for years.

And you're editing them rather than writing them past a certain point presumably? That's all part of the graft.

Well I don't know. I think of it as some songs are almost . . . I'm not sure how to put it, they're songs that lead to other songs. So you have a difficult song and you keep picking up this difficult song and you're thinking if only I could get a bridge for this song. Or if only I could figure out how to get from this key back to this other key, and every day for a week you pick up this song and you work at it. And while you're trying to write this song you've actually written three other songs without quite realising it.

Anyy examples you might admit to?

Well I could tell you the title of *the* difficult song — but it has never been finished.

A bit of a scoop here...

It's a song called 'Easy There, Steady Now' which came out a few records ago *[Mirror Blue, 1994]*. I'm trying to write this song and I'm thinking oh yeah, yeah, okay, yeah, yeah, yeah — it's fine. But I still can't quite get this from G to F, you know, but yeah that's fine, yeah, okay. But if only I could just get this sorted because this is important, this song's really important! So that's the important song you never finish, *The* Important Song You Never Finish — although TISYNF hardly makes a good acronym. But this song can be created in a whole different way, as in: you're trying to finish it, it gets your mind thinking along the right lines, and it gets your mind into the way of a passive state in which stuff starts to come through you. And almost unconsciously you can write new stuff while you're over here.

So there is a progression that you feel linking the creation of your songs?

Yes. Of course each song is different. But if you do that process with your own song you're actually . . .

. . . cannibalising?

Yeah I like that. Although it's a bit more subtle. It's more saying that it's more knowing what you miss with that song. It's why you can keep writing the same song your whole life because you never quite get it right. So, you know, I wrote this song and I was trying to do this and I got it three quarters right but there's a bit missing. But if I took it and started again, if I changed that there, this here and that there, I'd have a better song. And I could achieve what I tried to achieve the first time.

You can hear that in classic songwriting teams like Burt Bacharach & Hal David. There's just so much going on in there that if you join up the dots this way you've got their song, but if you join up the dots another way you've got something totally different. In fact they probably were doing that with their own songs really.

Of course you would.

And then there's Beethoven's opening chords at the beginning of the Fifth Symphony which are an inversion of a Mozart piece. Dean Friedman ended up reversing the chord progression of Paul McCartney's 'Blackbird' to come up with 'Company' [eponymous first album, 1977]. That's not playing around, that's hearing an inspiring direction to go in.

And that's okay. That's the way all these songwriters and composers need to do it. You borrow from Haydn and Bach and whoever, and you do your own variation, or you just change it a little bit and then it's kind of your song.

How do you pay your dues in terms of the music that went in that actually fuels what you do? You're not doing Louis Armstrong songs . . . or are you? Are you striving for the spirituality that Coltrane offered you?

In spirit I am doing Louis Armstrong and Coltrane, even though I play guitar, a wholly different instrument. That's also the building blocks of style. If you play any kind of solo in popular music, there'll be Louis Armstrong or the school of Louis Armstrong or something similar in it. For example, Armstrong's kind of choppier and more rhythmic and Coltrane is kind of smoother and sort of smooth melodic, beautiful melodic conversions and stuff. So when you're good enough to play a solo, you can play this kind of legato thing, this sort of rolling thing, or you're going to do this kind of choppy short thing. In a way, you can argue that everything in popular music comes from sources like these. Of course I know it doesn't, but it does seem to me that often those are the 'schools' on which you base everything.

How does a solo fit into a song? Or even, why do you need solos?

Because you're a guitar player and you've got to show off! If you don't do a few, then the crowds will complain that you didn't do any solos. I don't think you *have* to. You can have a perfectly good song, just a singer singing a song, and it doesn't need an instrumental interlude for the most part. But if you're a pianist and you write a song, then you've got to put a piano solo in it somewhere. And probably a trumpet solo and a sax solo as well. If you're Hoagy Carmichael you're probably going to put in that piano solo. If you're Fats Waller you're definitely going to put in a piano solo. It's just what you do. And as a piano player you're also actively looking for pieces of music in which you can play piano. As a guitar player you're looking for pieces of music in which you can play guitar. If your favourite thing is playing guitar in songs then you're looking for songs in which to play guitar — and a solo will probably follow!

Presumably when you first started off you were playing as a guitarist playing other people's songs and hopefully rising to the stage where you could play the songs that you wanted to play rather than the crowd favourites. So as Fairport coagulated, something original started to come out of that. Did the band come together because of a desire to do your own original material or it was just like-minded people who wanted to play?

We just enjoyed playing music. And the music we enjoyed playing was songs with good lyrics. The folk thing came from Fairport playing in folk clubs — Fairport would want to play live. This is pre-Fairport as well, when we were looking for gigs. If we played acoustic we could go and play at the Starting Gate at Wood Green or we could go and play at the Black Bull folk club at Whetstone and even get paid like ten quid. Wow, fantastic! If we were a blues band we could play in the blues club so it was just a way to get gigs. And the folk thing comes from what we all grew up listening — we all knew what folk music was. At school we got the kind of Victorian cleaned-up versions of folk music, but that was how it was very deliberately taught in British schools, the Percy Grainger folk collections.

Were you taught that in any greater depth at William Ellis School?

No, I think that was standard national curriculum. But we got all the folk as well from my family. My grandmother used to sing in Gaelic. She was from the Isle of Skye. I'm very happy to do a song that she would sing when I was five years old or something. So you sort of pick up bits of it, and being in folk clubs you'd always hear people sing an occasional traditional song so we got a bit of it there too. But Fairport, we were a bunch of white intellectual suburban kids who worried about what our music was. We had to have a theory. We couldn't just be another blues band, we couldn't just be another R&B band doing covers. We had to be different and we had to have a reason.

So we'd sit around and figure out what kind of band we should be, what music we should be playing. Anyway, we enjoyed bands like the Byrds who were doing Dylan covers. And we enjoyed Phil Ochs. Intellectually we said, "Well, let's put the emphasis here but we'll still do the odd blues song and we'll do the odd R&B song but no one else in London is doing songs by the Byrds and no one is doing a Phil Ochs cover, no one's doing a Richard Fariña song that's for sure!" So that was our way of being different.

It's interesting how you all took an outsider's point of view and yet, a couple of generations down the line, you still came up with something that was absolutely quintessentially English — and yet it seems a lot of the stimulus came from contemporary America. Or was this simply that it was America's turn to be in the UK during that Sixties transatlantic cultural pingpong and so they momentarily held the torch of fusion?

We did a Bert Jansch song, 'The Needle of Death' *[eponymous first album, 1965]* and we'd no doubt do a Ewan MacColl song. It didn't matter where the songwriting came from. If it was from America, there were just more singer-songwriters to pick from. When Dylan went electric, that kind of legitimised serious lyrics in popular music, so that was a big clarion call for us, and we definitely wanted to pursue that kind of area. And by 1967 we were saying, "This is us, reflecting and thinking and worrying about what kind of band we should be." So we said, "Right, we're going to start writing our own material we can't just be a covers band, even if we're doing these really clever arcane covers that nobody else has heard of we've really got to start writing, we've got to become writers." So we taught ourselves to be writers. And then the stage after that was, "We need to go further, what we need to do is play a style of music from where we come from."

Amazing to have that depth of vision.

Absolutely! Well, we were just thinking and worrying and . . . So the next thing was "We have to play music that's true to our roots, music that will mean something to the audience because it's true to their roots as well, it's where they come from. So somebody's going to come and invent a style of music that fits our time and place. And the time is the rock'n'roll era but the place is Britain. And we're English, Irish, Scottish, mixed, whatever, so this is what we have to do. So we've got to take these old ballads but blend them, fuse them, with rock'n'roll and create this music that will mean a lot to us and hopefully mean a lot to the audience." I think it never meant as much to the audience as we thought it was going to.

The fifteen people, you mean.

The fifteen people have been very loyal and have been very moved by the music. But we actually thought it was going to be a sort of pandemic, that it was actually going to blow the lid off in Britain. But there was always a cult there!

But what you opened up didn't burn itself out to become just another isolated period noted in the annals of British music. The tentacles spread far and wide, and they're still here today. After the Seventies, which was all about having only the one forward gear so it looked as it a lot of music was left behind, the Fairports oversaw a massive affirmation of that living legacy. I found that funny at the time since that was the decade we weren't allowed to like bands like Abba or Led Zeppelin. The fusion you created found its space and it's been going ever since, and the audiences are there of all generations.

The last few years it's been pretty healthy and I think the least that we wanted to happen was that folk music would move closer to the mainstream. Or the mainstream would move closer to folk music. So it's just another section.

If Tom Jones can play Glastonbury anything's up for grabs now. Indeed, when Jay-Z played Glastonbury last year [2008], everyone was up in arms as if it was Mary Whitehouse in 1971.

And he should be playing the Cambridge Folk Festival. In a sense, yeah.

Except he's too big to do it, but why shouldn't he? I regret not going to the Cambridge Folk Festival in something like 1982 when it was the first year David Cousins stepped out post-Strawbs and said, "Okay, this is what I do stripped down," and he took out his banjo and just played. The idea of that was as punk as punk rock. So too was what the Fairports were breaking open: "We're going to do it and we don't care and we don't need any justification for what we're doing." And you did it. That acoustic side to you is important, because what's also meant is, "We can do it here and now with nothing but a light bulb and an audience, one man and his dog in the audience. We don't need amps, we don't need a structure, we don't need whatever." There's an inbuilt flexibility there too with an ability to respond on the spot to the audience. Perhaps that's why you all became such consummate session players — just look at the way guitarist Simon Nicol and drummer Dave Mattacks led the team who turned around the debut album by Beverly Craven [Beverley Craven, 1990] who wasn't happy with the overly slick version her record company had got her to record in LA. But it wasn't only the instruments in Fairport Convention — the songwriting began to be carved out amongst you. Was that problematic, or was it whoever comes up with something gets it put into the pot?

It was whoever came up with something. There wasn't any carving out, it was just whoever had a song, then we'd look at it. But that created a kind of schism in the band. Ashley *[Hutchings, bassist]* wanted to keep playing traditional music. Having made *Liege & Lief [1969]* he wanted to add more people to the band, make the band like an eight-piece and just play traditional music. I knew Sandy *[Denny, vocalist]* and I thought we'd rather be writing. That logical step for Fairport was okay, the traditional music statement, now we needed to write songs in this kind of trad/rock style — which is what we did anyway, and what I still do really. So we wrote songs that were influenced by the British traditional as well as rock'n'roll. And that was a breaking point for the band.

Very much like the Monty Pythons, everyone free to contribute but if it wasn't up to scratch you had to come back with something better the next day. Was there that sort of pressure?

I think so, yeah. At that point the band was a six-piece, the same as Monty Python, and you had little kind of pairings-off of things. Often it was project by project, so Ashley would be working with Swarb *[Dave Swarbrick, violinist/guitarist]* on something and then Swarb and Sandy would be working on something and then I'd work with Ashley on something, and then Swarb and I worked together. So for different material, differnet pairings.

But your natural pairing ended up with Sandy Denny?

Only in the sense that we were both songwriters, and I think that we had some respect for each other, that was important. And we did work with each other later. My natural pairing was actually probably with *[guitarist]* Simon Nicol. I was probably closest to Simon as a human being.

But he wasn't as prolific a songwriter, was he?

He didn't *persevere* as a songwriter. I think he could be a fine songwriter, but maybe he doesn't have the confidence or maybe he just doesn't have the drive. You have to be kind of driven.

Yours is what?

I don't know. I'm afraid to find out. I'm sure if I went for therapy I could actually lose all impulse to write!

Well you probably have natural immunity, since you went to Los Angeles and somehow didn't do the therapy.

I can't say how many people in America say to me, "Here's my card!" and "I've listened to your music, if you need any help just let me know."

Maybe there's a double album in there about the sapping of the creative process by therapy. Anyway, it came as no surprise that it was you who made the break with Fairport Convention.

It was Ashley first of all. He left because he wanted to do his traditional thing and we said no thank you. Simon said recently that he thinks a lot of that breaking up of the band was from the road accident that we had in 1969 where [drummer] Martin Lamble was killed. He thought that we're all still in shock, which is quite possible. We were unable to settle, in a state where you can't concentrate on anything.

So the band was, understandably, in an unsettled state in any case?

Maybe, maybe, who knows? But Ashley went off to form Steeleye Span which was a great band. We got Peggy [bassist Dave Pegg] in and then Sandy left because . . . well I think really because she hated flying, she couldn't fly. She was going out with [guitarist] Trevor Lucas who was in another band, he was in Eclection [and later Fairport Convention], and they never saw each other because they'd be doing their bands all the time. So it was a real strain on her, I think she couldn't see how to get through it.

Is that how you ended up doing sessions, while you were twiddling your thumbs working out what to do next?

While I was still in the band I did do a few sessions as well. But after Fairport Convention, that's fair enough, yes. Yeah, a master plan. Through twiddling my thumbs I built a master plan! But I don't remember ever consciously planning to do more sessions, I just rolled into it. I suppose word went out that I wasn't busy, so work came in, and that was fine.

How did you find the energy and focus to start writing songs again? Although obviously I'm jumping to the conclusion that you just concentrated on the guitar work in hand and let the creativity lie fallow a while.

No, I was working on songs all through that period. While I was still in Fairport I started writing *Henry the Human Fly [1972]* and I thought these songs just don't fit, don't fit this band. So I figured at that time I needed to get away and do some thinking and just find myself, I suppose.

With The Human Fly you're putting in songs there which are not necessarily what you are but simply what Fairport Convention wasn't. So in order to sort of have a master plan — well at least a direction to start off in — you needed some sort of voice. I hate to use that word but . . .

Well I've never had a plan year to year. At age twenty-one, my direction was "what's happening in the next three months?" I didn't know what I was going to do in six months, didn't have a clue. But it seemed like I could remain employed in the music business because I could get hired by Sandy Denny or Iain Matthews as a guitar player, go on tour and get paid for that, that was nice. Get paid as a session guitar player. Then when I hooked with Linda *[Thompson, singer]* we thought, "Well, what are we going to do? You know, I'm working with Sandy, you've got this sort of pop career, and we're going to end up not seeing each other, so let's be a duo." *[Husband and wife at the time, they performed and recorded as Richard & Linda Thompson.]*

Sounds logical enough.

"Yeah! We'll get some bookings in the folk clubs to get started." We thought, "Well it's a living. I haven't got a driving licence but you've got half a driving licence, so you can drive for now. And we'll get an agent — Jean Davenport's very good, so we'll just get Jean Davenport to book us some gigs." And in comparative terms we probably earned more money than we've ever earned since. Like £100 per folk club.

Evidently a lot of money in those days.

From £40 a week with Fairport! Petrol was really cheap, hotels were cheap, or you'd stay on the promoter's floor. Rent was £12 a week. We were comparatively rich just by folk clubs. So that's why we kept doing it for a year or whatever it was, a year and a half. And there was some point where we thought, well, we need a manager — fatal words — because you can't do this forever. You've got to get up to the next level, you've got to start doing theatres, concerts, something. So we hired *[producer & founder of Hannibal Records]* Joe Boyd, who did take us to the next level, etc, etc.

So how do you get from there . . . ?

Well I go in eras anyway. There's the Purple Era, Fairport Era, Duet Era with Linda, and then Solo Era onwards. Which are kind of distinctive for me. The last one's very long and the others are really quite short, but people are far more interested in the early ones than they are the late ones. On which I have less perspective . . .

Even in, say, the days when you had less profile but were just as busy, you were always sort of around. For me, one of the most evocative of all the great album covers from that period is the one with you and Linda with the Sufi-style headgear on [Pour Down Like Silver, by Richard & Linda Thompson, 1975]. For me it was stunning to see and hear . . . that whole album was a statement that was pure stick-your-finger-up attitude to me. I don't know what you were thinking of, but it did make an impression.

I wasn't thinking very much.

We can run with that.

Publish and be damned I say!

So what was growing up in London like in the Fifties? Do you remember things like your first orange or you were too old for that?

Yeah. It was great. Because you were a kid. Whenever you're a kid it's going to be great. Fantastic fogs, pea-soupers. So I couldn't actually find my way to school sometimes. How great is that? You couldn't see!

Just like Sherlock Holmes.

Worse. At least you could sort of see Sherlock Holmes. Just like a foot away visibility. But it was kind of grey. And I just about remember some things still being rationed when I was a kid. Right into the Fifties. It was a little austere, there wasn't a lot of money about. And neighbours sort of tinkering with their motorbikes, tinkering with their Norton Commandos and stuff. You'd go camping on holiday because it was cheap, that kind of thing.

Do you think that sort of thing stays with you, because it made everyone working-class regardless of your background in a way, didn't it?

It would be practical habits that came out of World War II, people could tinker with stuff. They could rebuild a radio and they could fix things. They'd still got all those shops. Right to the Sixties all those shops down Charing Cross Road selling transistors and valves. You know, "Have you got an F9623?" "No, we've got an F9624, we've got an F9623b, but we don't have the

F962a." But it was kind of bleak and it was like sort of an episode of *[Fifties/Sixties BBC radio/TV comedy]* *Hancock's Half Hour*, it was always raining outside and everything was a bit dour. My dad was a bit like Tony Hancock, you know, "Oh, bloody hell, what's… oh, *what's* going on?!" Really sort of dour and slightly miserable and complaining about everything. But he also had a sense of humour sometimes, but you seemed to have to dig into it to get it out. And I think the radio was an incredible outlet for kids anyway.

Did you build a radio? A 'cat's whisker' set?

No I didn't. I knew lots of people who did. But the content of radio definitely was a saviour sometimes. *The Goon Show* was pure anarchy. When you're a kid it's like discovering someone who understands kids, that was *[show writer & performer]* Spike Milligan, through being a surreal adult who went almost into a child's state of mind. When you're a kid, you think, "I get it. I get the Goons totally."

Do you think the spirit of all that comedy had an influence? It's certainly something which writers and actors acknowledge, which you can see in their work, but it's harder to spot in music even though that Golden Age of radio and early TV was absolutely pivotal in opening up a very British sense of rebellion for anyone who was listening, if that's the right way to put it.

Anarchy. Anarchy. Absolutely. In the Fifties we grew up in what was still Victorian Britain, or certainly Edwardian Britain. It hadn't been dismantled. We didn't make fun of judges or the police or the queen, any of that stuff. The Establishment was still the Establishment. And the ghost of Queen Victoria still reigned over everything, and the landscape was dominated by Victorian buildings that kept everything in order and the Empire was still just about functioning under the guise of the Commonwealth. You know, the Old Order . . . everyone pretended it was still there.

And then the Suez Crisis came along *[1956]*, and then *[BBC Radio comedy]* *Round the Horne*. Monty Python was kind of the last nail in the coffin, the final mockery of the Royal Family, where judges can be perverts and the rest of it. And Pete and Dud *[Peter Cook & Dudley Moore's various TV series]* of course. I thought they were the greatest. And *Beyond the Fringe* was unbelievable, 1960. I got the CD recently, and I looked at it and said, "1960?" I mean, that was staggering! That blew a door off, right there.

The Goons preached anarchy to kids and adults alike, definitely, on so many levels, Pete and Dud too. Do you remember when they became more rock'n'roll than rock'n'roll when they did the Derek and Clive tapes [1976-79]?

Yes, but Derek and Clive was a kind of a dilution of their spirit though. Peter Cook might have been the greatest comic genius. Inadvertent comic genius maybe. Because in a sense he's not a comedian, he's kind of a monologuist if he's anything. It's his ideas and his world, it's so extraordinary. And in Dudley Moore he had just the most talented foil you could possibly have. He was an incredible musician *and* a comedian.

Yet terribly Establishment at the same time.

Oh, totally, yeah. But the surviving Pete and Dud stuff, it just kills me.

These things are important because Britain during the Sixties really was quite drab, because the Swinging Sixties only happened in a couple of streets in London really, didn't they?

Actually it was one street!

Even as late as the Eighties I remember seeing houses with outside loos in London's Mile End, for example, and reading shocking statistics then that there were still something like 20 per cent of buildings in Britain that didn't have things like running water or electricity. And they weren't just talking about the remote areas.

We had an outside loo in the Fifties, but that was par for the course. We got a fridge in about 1963. But we did have a TV. One of those ones with a lens in front that was about that big *[indicates with hands]*. We watched *[BBC/ITV Forties/Fifties kids puppet show] Muffin the Mule* — it was hardly worth the effort. I always thought, the radio was . . . you know, *Journey into Space* on the radio, it was far far better than anything on TV. *[BBC Radio, 1953-85, it was the last UK radio programme to attract a bigger evening audience than TV.]*

And cinema must have been highly influential.

Oh that was fantastic. Certainly what I saw. I didn't do Saturday morning pictures or anything like that. I went once and got beaten up so I didn't go back. It was just like a madhouse, there were kids screaming and hitting each other. When I went, some big bully just whacked me and I thought well I'm not coming back here next week. If this is Saturday morning pictures, no thank you. I think one's sense of being British was reinforced, certainly, by the stuff that we saw like *The Cockleshell Heroes*, *A Town Like Alice*, a bit later *Mutiny on the Bounty*, *Zulu*.

Revolutionary films, all fighting against authority, all the little things you've mentioned.

I suppose authority, but also the Brits prevailing in World War II, that was the big hangover. And for us that was great because that went with our model Spitfires and Wellington bombers. And getting the lighter fuel on a Messerschmitt and throwing it out the window. We used to run a wire from my friend's bedroom down to the garden. We attached some of our Airfix models that were losing propellers and were getting a bit tacky to the wire, and then set fire to them and divebomb down to the garden. It was fantastic, what fun!

That's a very British cultural melting pot, which gives a great sense of curiosity which must have put you in good stead as a musician and songwriter. Possibly anyone who does what you do has to have a musicologist side to them, otherwise they can't fully practise the craft. You've always got to be finding out more, not only the stuff that interests you but listening to other songwriters, or at least the more traditional ones, always tapping into the motherlode.

If you grow up right in the middle of a tradition you don't have to do that. If you've grown up in Scotland and you're surrounded by traditional musicians, there's pipers and fiddlers, and maybe there's even songwriters, maybe your family were singers or writers. You don't really think about it. If you live in Louisiana, you're a Cajun musician, you're surrounded by Cajun music, you don't even think about it — like Marc and Ann Savoy's kids Joel and Wilson who grew up playing music, very natural, and now they're professional musicians, they write songs, they play, they don't have to think about it. But from Fairport onwards, the Fairport theory of music — that you put traditional together with rock'n'roll — is an artificial construct.

So you've got to keep working at it to keep that construct together?

In a sense yes, or . . . the construct has become second nature.

So you've created your own tradition.

Your own genre. Because that's the way you came into it. You also have to keep working on the construct, you have to keep finetuning the construct and asking, how is it? Does it need a little more salt? Does it need a little more chilli powder?

Are there other singer-songwriters who . . . no, obviously in your generation you all respect each other, so it's pretty pointless to ask who likes who and who doesn't.

I hate all of them.

Well the rest of us will always lump you together so you're stuck with them. But are there other singer-songwriters who you rate when looking to the future of music?

No, the future of music is right now. There's lots of good writers around. I might not be a good judge, though, because I don't really know what they've gone through to be writers.

Is that sort of experience important?

If you're talking about what makes people do what they do, and how the world has changed, then yes. I don't know how difficult it is for them at this point because I don't really know what the music scene is. I've got a daughter, Kami Thompson, who's a singer-songwriter and struggles to get her music out there. It's tough for her. I think she's really talented, great singer. *[His son Teddy Thompson is also a singer-songwriter.]* Twenty years ago she'd have been snapped up by a record company, but that doesn't happen anymore.

And she's resolute about what she does?

That's what she wants to do. She's a really talented girl, she can do a lot of things. She started on a degree in classics and she's also a good actress. But she wants to be in music, and that's her choice. I'm not quite sure what to say to her. I think what I say is, "This year is a bad year, keep your head down, start writing the next album, at least you can always write. Even if you do a gig a month or something, you're still honing your art to the point where they can't refuse you. You'll be such a force because you look great, you've got a great voice, you just refine your writing and your songs to the point where you're a tsunami, you're irresistible." And I think that's about all you can do.

How's the balance between record sales and live work looking nowaways in the general trend of things?

Oh, it's changed. I mean everything's live now. It was explained to me, or I think I heard it on the radio yesterday, that people like Madonna don't mind free downloads, they're quite happy about them because it means more bums on seats, it means more people come to a concert, where she makes a lot of money.

Prince giving away his latest albums on the front of the national Sunday newspapers.

That doesn't help people like me.

On the other hand you've always had the live work whereas a lot of these people don't even get a sniff at it. Madonna or Britney can't exactly do the clubs, they can't get up in the morning and think I need to make some money, I know what, I'll book the hall down the road and see who turns up.

It's not about making money though, I don't think.

No?

No. If you're Madonna, it's not about making money. She doesn't need it.

True. But for most other musicians there's always that pressure, to bring in the readies in order to justify what you're doing, if not for yourself then for others.

On the whole, that's a good thing. I mean it's a good thing in that you have to work. That keeps your feet on the ground, keeps you realistic and stops you spending two years on that incredible concept album that's going to end up probably pretentious and stupid. I wouldn't mind some more time off to write. If I think about the amount of time I've worked over the last ten or fifteen years, twenty years, if I'd worked a bit less I could have written a bit more, because the one does deduct from the other, there's no question. And as a writer/performer you have to allow yourself time to write.

But that goes with the job.

Yes, if you're a writer, you're a writer, that's what you do, that's all you do. You sit at home and write, you sit in Nashville, you write songs, that's all you do. But if you're just a writer you're also frustrated probably that you're not a performer.

You must have had points when you felt like giving up.

I took a couple of years off in the Seventies when I didn't do much at all.

But was that consciously taking the time off, or was it dropping out with the intention maybe of going somewhere else?

It was kind of getting more interested in "oh we're famous?" for a while. Also not seeing where I could be useful in a sense. And I think when punk came along that kind of solved the problem. I thought, okay, music's re-energised now, and I should be re-energised and the scene should be re-energised. You know, the Seventies sort of punk rock. The Seventies I thought were very directionless musically, it was almost like easy listening in a sense. There was some good stuff but a lot of filler, a lot of crap. Still, I thought punk was a real shot in the arm and I did think, "I can see myself existing in this music scene, or at least holding onto its coat tails."

You were in good company in the UK. There were so many amazing musicians who came in at the same time and aligned themselves with that energy — and not necessarily the movement. But not everyone had the vision to realise just how far-reaching that energy would go. Certainly not most of the actual punks themselves.

It was that lot of people who were slightly younger, people like Elvis Costello, the Pretenders and Joe Jackson, none of whom were really punk.

Exactly, a whole new generation of singer-songwriters who come out of it. They were not necessarily everyone's cup of tea but there was a sort of late Seventies generation that broke through. In any case, like I said, what the Fairports were doing was very very punk. You could hear it in your guitar playing if only that.

Well we were very loud certainly, we were a really loud band at the time. Not acoustic, but when Fairport played electric it was loud!

Talking about performance then, looking at the comedians, when you don't have a band around you, just solo, do you sense a similarity between what you so and a stand-up comedian, particularly those who have a message? Builing on Pete and Dud, the sort of comedy of Richard Pryor and Bill Hicks became very rock'n'roll and then very lyrical as well in the post rock'n'roll period of the Eighties and Nineties.

I think there's a similarity there. You have to be insane to do either. You've got to be insane to get up on a stage on your own.

Do you feel totally exposed, the way a stand-up often does?

Yes. It's ridiculous to do it. But it's almost like saying, "Prove to me that you're a musician!" You know, get up on stage and play something, just you, no props. It's what I want to say to Britney, Spears, or Madonna, and say "You're a musician? Okay, just sing to us now, here's the room of dinner guests, just sing to us now." Which is something I force myself to do sometimes if I'm at a party, someone says, "Do you want to do a song?" and my reaction is "No way." And then I think "No, I should."

And you do?

I'm the musician, give me the guitar, yes, I'll play something. Because it's my job.

It's not a politeness-to-your-host thing, a bowing to the audience's wishes?

No. It's my job and it's proving to myself that I'm a musician, because I can get up and play, pick up a guitar I've never played before and get something out of it. Just like I'd expect a classical musician to turn up at a party and open a piano and play something and not be precious about it, just say, "Okay!" Or if I hadn't got a guitar, then stand up at a wedding and *sing* a traditional song. You should be able to do that!

*   *

*

Appendices

Web links

David Cousins

www.strawbsweb.co.uk

Arlo Guthrie

www.arloguthrie.com

Iain Matthews

iainmatthews.nl

www.facebook.com/Iain.matthews.77

soundcloud.com/iain-matthews-352985544

Ralph McTell

www.ralphmctell.co.uk

Al Stewart

www.alstewart.com

Richard Thompson

www.richardthompson-music.com

Selected memoirs & books of lyrics

David Cousins

Secrets, Stories & Songs (annotated lyrics with bonus CD), by David Cousins, 2010.

Exorcising Ghosts: Strawbs and Other Lives, by David Cousins, 2014.

Arlo Guthrie

This Is the Arlo Guthrie Book, by Herbert Wise & Arlo Guthrie, 1969.

Arlo, Alice & Anglicans: The Lives of a New England Church, by Laura Lee, 2000.

Arlo Guthrie: The Warner/Reprise Years (American Folk Music and Musicians Series), by Hank Reineke, 2012.

Iain Matthews

Thro' My Eyes: A Memoir, by Iain Matthews & Ian Clayton, 2018.

Al Stewart

Al Stewart: Lights, Camera, Folk Rock: A Life in Pictures, by Neville Judd, 2001.

Al Stewart: True Life Adventures of a Folk Troubadour, by Neville Judd, 2006.

Ralph McTell

Time's Poems: The Song Lyrics of Ralph McTell, by Ralph McTell, 2005.

As Far as I Can Tell: A Post-war Childhood in South London (single-volume set of *Angel Laughter/Summer Lightning*), by Ralph McTell, 2008.

Richard Thompson

Richard Thompson: The Biography, by Patrick Humphries, 1997.

The Great Valerio: A Study of the Songs of Richard Thompson, by Dave Smith, 2004.

Discography/Timeline

This is a somewhat cursory and, indeed, disgracefully subjective list of events in post-war popular music. But it represents a serious attempt to put the albums of David Cousins, Arlo Guthrie, Iain Matthews, Ralph McTell, Al Stewart and Richard Thompson into a wider context beyond folk & blues in the UK & USA (a field that reflects the interplay between the two sides yet is a limited definition of their actual music). The events listed here are intended to be the spur for discovery beyond them rather than debate, selected as examples of shifts, 'next moves' and 'transmitting the message' that have had a lasting effect on music and society. The works included here by the subjects of this book are studio albums plus selected key live works and collaborations.

1936

Gibson launches the 'Electric Spanish' guitar.

1939

Start of World War Two.
The BBC combines the National and Regional Programmes to form the single Home Service radio programme.

1940

Woody Guthrie – *Dust Bowl Ballads*.
BBC Forces Programme starts on radio, precursor of the post-war Light Programme.

1945

End of World War Two.
Second British Folk Revival, 1945–69.
The BBC starts the Light Programme on radio.
Benjamin Britten's English-language opera *Peter Grimes*.

1948

Columbia Records introduces the 33 1/3 rpm record – the LP.

1949

RCA Victor introduces the 45 rpm record – the single.

1950

Alan Lomax arrives in the UK, fleeing McCarthyism in the USA.

1951

Festival of Britain.
The English programmes of Radio Luxembourg move from long wave to the medium wave frequency of 208m.
Ike Turner – 'Rocket 88', hailed as the first rock'n'roll song.

1952

Peter Kennedy & Seamus Ennisfrom start BBC Radio folk show *As I Roved Out*.
Official UK singles chart launched.

1953

Ewan MacColl opens the Ballads & Blues Club.

1954

Fender launches the Stratocaster guitar.
Elvis Presley's debut single – 'That's All Right'.

1955

Lonnie Donegan – 'Rock Island Line' kickstarts British skiffle.
Alan Lomax's ballad opera *Big Rock Candy Mountain* premieres at Joan Littlewood's Theatre Workshop, featuring Ramblin' Jack Elliott.
Little Richard – 'Tutti-Frutti'.
Bill Haley & His Comets – 'Rock Around the Clock'.

1956

The first Eurovision Song Contest held in Lugano, Switzerland.
Ewan MacColl & A L Lloyd – *The English and Scottish Popular Ballads (The Child Ballads) Vols 1-5*.
Woody Guthrie – *Bound for Glory*.
Ella Fitzgerald – *Ella Fitzgerald Sings the Cole Porter Songbook*.

1958

Cliff Richard & the Drifters – 'Move It', the UK's first rock'n'roll hit.

1959

Berry Gordy Jr founds Motown Records.
Miles Davis – *Kind of Blue*.
Rodgers and Hammerstein – *The Sound of Music*.

1960

The Shadows – 'Apache'.
Joan Baez – *Joan Baez*.

1961

The Beatles play their first gig.
Frank Sinatra forms his own record label, Reprise Records.

1962

The Dubliners form.
The Beatles – 'Love Me Do'.
Bob Dylan – *Bob Dylan*.

1963

Philips launches first cassette tapes.
Topic Records release *The Iron Muse (A Panorama of Industrial Folk Song)*.
Odetta – *Odetta Sings Folk Songs*.
Bob Dylan – *The Freewheelin' Bob Dylan*.

1964

Sam Cooke dies.
The Beatles appear on *The Ed Sullivan Show*.
British Invasion begins of America.
Radio Caroline starts, the first of the offshore pirate stations.
Davy Graham & Shirley Collins, *Folk Roots, New Routes*.
Bob Dylan – *The Times They Are a-Changin'*.
The Beach Boys – 'I Get Around'.
Simon & Garfunkel – *Wednesday Morning, 3 A.M.*

1965

Bob Dylan goes electric with *Bringing It All Back Home*, 'Like a Rollin' Stone', being booed at the Newport Folk Festival, and *Highway 61 Revisited*.
Bert Jansch – *Bert Jansch*.
The Beatles – *Rubber Soul*.

1966

        Dylan heckled as 'Judas' for his electric set in Manchester.

        Joe Boyd & John Hopkins open the UFO Club.

        Ewan MacColl & Peggy Seeger start the London Critics Group.

        A L Lloyd – *The Bird in the Bush*.

        The Beach Boys, *Pet Sounds*.

1967

Arlo Guthrie – *Alice's Restaurant*.

Al Stewart – *Bed Sitter Images*.

        Woody Guthrie, John Coltrane and Otis Redding die.

        The BBC launch BBC Radio 1, and BBC Radio Leicster, the first of its local radio network of stations.

        The Light Programme is rebranded as BBC Radio 2.

        John Peel starts at Radio 1, first with the Top Gear music programme.

        Monterey Pop Festival.

        The Beatles – *Sgt Pepper's Lonely Hearts Club Band*.

        Moody Blues – *Days of Future Passed*.

        The Jimi Hendrix Experience – *Are You Experienced*.

        Aretha Franklin – 'Respect'.

        Judy Collins – *Wildflowers*.

        The Velvet Underground & Nico – *The Velvet Underground*.

        Bob Dylan – *John Wesley Harding*.

1968

Iain Matthews: Fairport Convention – *Fairport Convention*.

Ralph McTell – *Eight Frames a Second*.

Richard Thompson: Fairport Convention – *Fairport Convention*.

        Van Morrison – *Astral Weeks*.

        The Small Faces – *Ogdens' Nut Gone Flake*.

        The Kinks – *The Kinks Are the Village Green Preservation Society*.

        The Beatles – *The Beatles (The White Album)*.

        The Rolling Stones – *Beggars Banquet*.

        The Jimi Hendrix Experience – *Electric Ladyland*.

        Johnny Cash – *At Folsom Prison*.

        The Band – *Music from Big Pink*.

1969

David Cousins: Strawbs – *Strawbs*.

Arlo Guthrie – *Alice's Restaurant Soundtrack*.

Arlo Guthrie – *Running Down the Road.*

Iain Matthews: Fairport Convention – *What We Did on Our Holidays.*

Iain Matthews: Matthews Southern Comfort – *Matthews' Southern Comfort.*

Iain Matthews: Matthews Southern Comfort – *Second Spring.*

Ralph McTell – *My Side of Your Window.*

Ralph McTell – *Spiral Staircase.*

Al Stewart – *Love Chronicles.*

Richard Thompson: Fairport Convention – *Liege & Lief.*

Richard Thompson: Fairport Convention – *Unhalfbricking.*

Richard Thompson: Fairport Convention – *What We Did on Our Holidays.*

> Judy Garland dies.
>
> Woodstock music festival.
>
> Nick Drake – *Five Leaves Left.*
>
> Rod Stewart – *An Old Raincoat Won't Ever Let You Down.*
>
> The Beatles – *Abbey Road.*
>
> King Crimson – *In the Court of the Crimson King.*
>
> The Who – *Tommy.*

1970

David Cousins: Strawbs – *Dragonfly.*

Arlo Guthrie – *Washington County.*

Iain Matthews: Matthews Southern Comfort – *Later That Same Year.*

Al Stewart – *Zero She Flies.*

Richard Thompson: Fairport Convention – *Full House.*

> Jimi Hendrix dies.
>
> Beatles break up.
>
> John Lennon – *John Lennon/Plastic Ono Band.*
>
> George Harrison – *All Things Must Pass.*
>
> Black Sabbath – *Black Sabbath.*
>
> Tim Rice & Andrew Lloyd Webber – *Jesus Christ Superstar.*
>
> Crosby, Stills, Nash & Young – *Déjà Vu.*

1971

David Cousins: Strawbs – *From The Witchwood.*

Iain Matthews – *If You Saw Thro' My Eyes.*

Ralph McTell – *You Well-Meaning Brought Me Here Famous.*

> Led Zeppelin – *Led Zeppelin (IV).*
>
> David Bowie – *Hunky Dory.*
>
> Joni Mitchell – *Blue.*
>
> Carole King – *Tapestry.*
>
> Funkadelic – *Maggot Brain.*

Marvin Gaye – *What's Going On*.
Isaac Hayes – *Shaft*.

1972

David Cousins: Strawbs – *Grave New World*.
David Cousins – *Two Weeks Last Summer*.
Arlo Guthrie – *Hobo's Lullaby*.
Iain Matthews – *Tigers Will Survive*.
Iain Matthews: Plainsong – *In Search of Amelia Earhart*.
Ralph McTell – *Not Till Tomorrow*.
Al Stewart – *Orange*.
Richard Thompson – *Henry the Human Fly*.
Richard Thompson: Morris On – *Morris On*.
Richard Thompson: The Bunch – *Rock On*.
    Horslips – *Happy to Meet – Sorry to Part*.
    Slade – 'Cum on Feel the Noize'.
    David Bowie – *The Rise & Fall of Ziggy Stardust & the Spiders from Mars*.
    Yes – *Close to the Edge*.
    Deep Purple – *Machine Head*.
    The Rolling Stones – *Exile on Main St*.
    Steely Dan – *Can't Buy a Thrill*.

1973

David Cousins: Strawbs – *Bursting At The Seams*.
David Cousins: Sandy Denny & the Strawbs – *All Our Own Work [1967]*.
Arlo Guthrie – *Last of the Brooklyn Cowboys*.
Iain Matthews – *Valley Hi*.
Al Stewart – *Past, Present and Future*.
    John Martyn – *Solid Air*.
    Elton John – *Goodbye Yellow Brick Road*.
    Pink Floyd – *The Dark Side of the Moon*.
    Hawkwind – *The Space Ritual Alive in Liverpool and London*.
    Roberta Flack – 'Killing Me Softly With His Song'.

1974

David Cousins: Strawbs – *Hero And Heroine*.
Arlo Guthrie – *Arlo Guthrie (live)*.
Iain Matthews – *Journeys from Gospel Oak*.
Iain Matthews – *Some Days You Eat the Bear... Some Days the Bear Eats You*.
Ralph McTell – *Easy*.
Richard & Linda Thompson – *Hokey Pokey*.

Richard & Linda Thompson – *I Want to See the Bright Lights Tonight.*

Nick Drake dies.

Fairport Convention start the Copredy Festival (later, Fairport's Cropredy Convention).

ABBA win the Eurovision Song Contest with 'Waterloo'.

Mott the Hoople – *The Hoople.*

1975

David Cousins: Strawbs – *Ghosts.*

David Cousins: Strawbs – *Nomadness.*

Arlo Guthrie & Pete Seeger – *Together In Concert (live).*

Ralph McTell – *Streets.*

Al Stewart – *Modern Times.*

Richard & Linda Thompson – *Pour Down Like Silver.*

Queen – *A Night at the Opera.*

Bob Dylan – *Blood on the Tracks*, and begins the Rolling Thunder Revue.

Patti Smith – *Horses.*

Bruce Springsteen – *Born to Run.*

1976

David Cousins: Strawbs – *Deep Cuts.*

Arlo Guthrie – *Amigo.*

Iain Matthews – *Go For Broke.*

Ralph McTell – *Right Side Up.*

Al Stewart – *Year of the Cat.*

Paul Robeson dies.

The Band's final concert, *The Last Waltz.*

Joan Armatrading – *Joan Armatrading.*

Stevie Wonder – *Songs in the Key of Life.*

The Eagles – *Hotel California.*

The Ramones – *The Ramones.*

1977

David Cousins: Strawbs – *Burning For You.*

Iain Matthews – *Hit and Run.*

Mark Bolan dies.

Sex Pistols – *Never Mind the Bollocks, Here's the Sex Pistols.*

Bob Marley & the Wailers – *Exodus.*

Ian Dury – *New Boots and Panties!!*

Bee Gees – *Saturday Night Fever.*

The Jam – *In the City.*

Motörhead – *Motörhead.*

Jethro Tull – *Songs from the Wood.*
David Bowie – *"Heroes".*
Fleetwood Mac – *Rumours.*

1978

David Cousins: Strawbs – *Deadlines.*
Arlo Guthrie – *One Night.*
Iain Matthews – *Stealin' Home.*
Al Stewart – *Time Passages.*
Richard Thompson: The Albion Band – *Rise Up Like the Sun.*
Richard & Linda Thompson – *First Light.*
> Keith Moon dies.
> Siouxsie & the Banshees – *The Dream.*
> Steel Pulse – *Handsworth Revolution.*
> Dire Straits – *Dire Straits.*
> Gloria Gaynor – 'I Will Survive'.
> Blondie – *Parallel Lines.*

1979

Arlo Guthrie – *Outlasting the Blues.*
Iain Matthews – *Discreet Repeat.*
Iain Matthews – *Siamese Friends.*
Ralph McTell – *Slide Away the Screen.*
Richard & Linda Thompson – *Sunnyvista.*
> Sandy Denny & Sid Vicious die.
> Sony launches the Walkman.
> The Clash – *London Calling.*
> Pink Floyd – *The Wall.*
> Sister Sledge – 'We Are Family'.
> Sugarhill Gang's 'Rapper's Delight'.
> Rickie Lee Jones – *Rickie Lee Jones.*
> Michael Jackson – *Off the Wall.*

1980

David Cousins & Brian Willoughby – *Old School Songs.*
Iain Matthews – *Spot of Interference.*
Al Stewart & Shot in the Dark – *24 Carrots.*
> John Lennon, Ian Curtis & Bon Scott die.
> Magazine – *The Correct Use of Soap.*
> AC/DC – *Back in Black.*
> Talking Heads – *Remain in Light.*

1981

Arlo Guthrie – *Power of Love*.
      Bob Marley dies.
      MTV launches.
      The Specials – 'Ghost Town'.
      UB40 – 'One in Ten'.
      Phil Collins – *Face Value*.
      Rush – *Moving Pictures*.

1982

Arlo Guthrie & Pete Seeger – *Precious Friend (live)*.
Iain Matthews: Hi-Fi – *Demonstration Record*.
Iain Matthews: Hi-Fi – *Moods for Mallards*.
Ralph McTell – *Water of Dreams*.
Richard & Linda Thompson – *Shoot Out the Lights*.
      Sony & Philips launch the compact disc.
      Iron Maiden – *The Number of the Beast*.
      Joe Jackson – *Night and Day*.
      Asia – *Asia*.
      Michael Jackson – *Thriller*.

1983

Ralph McTell – *Songs From Alphabet Zoo*.
Richard Thompson – *Hand of Kindness*.
      Muddy Waters dies.
      Now That's What I Call Music! launches.
      New Order – 'Blue Monday'.
      Wham! – *Fantastic*.
      The Police – *Synchronicity*.
      David Bowie – *Let's Dance*.

1984

Iain Matthews – *Shook (1984)*.
Al Stewart – *Russians & Americans*.
      Marvin Gaye dies.
      The Levellers play to 300,000 at the Glastonbury Festival.
      The Special AKA – 'Nelson Mandela'.
      Band Aid – 'Do They Know It's Christmas?'.
      The Smiths – *The Smiths*.
      Prince – *Purple Rain*.

1985

Ralph McTell – *At the End of a Perfect Day Telstar.*
Richard Thompson – *Across a Crowded Room.*
        Live Aid & Farm Aid.
        The Pogues – *Rum Sodomy & the Lash.*
        Tears for Fears – *Songs from the Big Chair.*
        Suzanne Vega – *Suzanne Vega.*
        Tom Waits – *Rain Dogs.*

1986

Arlo Guthrie – *Someday.*
Ralph McTell – *Bridge of Sighs.*
Ralph McTell – *The Best of Tickle on the Tum.*
Richard Thompson – *Daring Adventures.*
        Metallica – *Master of Puppets.*
        Madonna – *True Blue.*
        Paul Simon – *Graceland.*

1987

David Cousins: Strawbs – *Don't Say Goodbye.*
Richard Thompson – *The Marksman (music for BBC TV series).*
Richard Thompson: French Frith Kaiser Thompson – *Live, Love, Larf & Loaf.*
        U2 – *The Joshua Tree.*
        Whitney Houston – *Whitney.*
        Michael Jackson – *Bad.*
        Guns N' Roses – *Appetite for Destruction.*

1988

Iain Matthews – *Walking a Changing Line.*
Ralph McTell – *Blue Skies Black Heroes.*
Al Stewart – *Last Days of the Century.*
Richard Thompson – *Amnesia.*
        The Traveling Wilburys.
        Enya – *Watermark.*
        Tracy Chapman – *Tracy Chapman.*
        N.W.A – *Straight Outta Compton.*
        The Pixies – *Surfer Rosa.*

1989

Richard Thompson – *Hard Cash (music for BBC TV documentary).*
        Kate Bush – *The Sensual World.*
        The Stone Roses – *The Stone Roses.*

Janet Jackson – *Rhythm Nation.*

1990

Iain Matthews – *Pure and Crooked.*

Ralph McTell – *Stealin' Back Castle.*

Richard Thompson: French Frith Kaiser Thompson – *Invisible Means.*
> The Three Tenors.
> Ice Cube – *AmeriKKKa's Most Wanted.*
> A Tribe Called Quest – *People's Instinctive Travels and the Paths of Rhythm.*

1991

David Cousins: Strawbs – *Preserves Uncanned.*

David Cousins: Strawbs – *Ringing Down The Years.*

David Cousins: Strawbs – *Sandy Denny & The Strawbs.*

Richard Thompson – *Rumor and Sigh.*

Richard Thompson – *Sweet Talker (film soundtrack).*
> Miles Davis & Freddie Mercury die.
> Nirvana – *Nevermind.*
> Cypress Hill – *Cypress Hill.*

1992

Arlo Guthrie – *2 Songs.*

Arlo Guthrie – *Son of the Wind.*

Iain Matthews – *Skeleton Keys.*

Ralph McTell – *The Boy* with *a Note.*

Ralph McTell: The GP's – *Saturday Rolling Around (live).*

Al Stewart & Peter White – *Rhymes in Rooms (live).*

Richard Thompson & David Byrne – *An Acoustic Evening (live).*
> John Cage dies.
> R.E.M. – *Automatic for the People.*
> *The Bodyguard* soundtrack.

1993

Al Stewart – *Famous Last Words.*
> Frank Zappa dies.
> Maria Carey – *Music Box.*

1994

David Cousins & Brian Willoughby – *The Bridge.*

Arlo Guthrie & Pete Seeger – *More Together Again (live).*

Iain Matthews – *The Dark Ride*.
Iain Matthews: Plainsong – *Voices Electric*.
Richard Thompson – *Mirror Blue*.
>Kurt Cobain dies.
>Oasis – *Definitely Maybe*.
>Blur – *Parklife*.
>Nine Inch Nails – *The Downward Spiral*.

1995

David Cousins: Strawbs – *Heartbreak Hill [1978]*.
Ralph McTell – *Sand in Your Shoes*.
Ralph McTell & Billy Connolly – *Musical Tour of Scotland*.
Al Stewart & Laurence Juber – *Between the Wars*.
>The BBC begins regular Digital Audio Broadcasting.
>Coolio feat. L.V. – 'Gangsta's Paradise'.
>Robert Miles – 'Children'.
>Los del Río – 'Macarena'.

1996

Arlo Guthrie – *Alice's Restaurant (The Massacree Revisited) (live)*.
Arlo Guthrie – *Mystic Journey*.
Iain Matthews – *God Looked Down*.
Al Stewart – *Seemed Like a Good Idea At The Time (B-sides & rarities)*.
Richard Thompson – *You? Me? Us?*.
>Ella Fitzgerald & Tupac Shakur die.
>Spice Girls – 'Wannabe'.

1997

Arlo Guthrie – *This Land Is Your Land: An All American Children's Folk Classic*.
Richard Thompson & Danny Thompson – *Industry*.
>Jeff Buckley dies.
>Radiohead – *OK Computer*.
>Celine Dion – 'My Heart Will Go On'.

1998

Iain Matthews – *Excerpts from Swine Lake*.
Richard Thompson: Mr Philip Pickett with Mr Richard Thompson & the Fairport Rhythm Section – *The Bones of All Men*.
>Frank Sinatra dies.
>Eliza CVarthy – *Red Rice*.
>Robbie Williams – *I've Been Expecting You*.

Lauryn Hill – *The Miseducation of Lauryn Hill.*

1999
Iain Matthews: Plainsong – *New Place Now.*
Richard Thompson – *Mock Tudor.*
> Napster launched.
> Fatboy Slim – *You've Come a Long Way, Baby.*
> Ricky Martin – 'Livin' la Vida Loca'.
> Blink-182 – *Enema of the State.*

2000
Iain Matthews: No Grey Faith – *Secrets All Told: The Songs of Sandy Denny.*
Ralph McTell – *Red Sky.*
Al Stewart – *Down in the Cellar.*
> Coldplay – *Parachutes.*
> Craig David – *Born to Do It.*
> Britney Spears – 'Oops!... I Did It Again'.
> Eminem – *The Marshall Mathers LP.*

2001
David Cousins: Strawbs – *Baroque & Roll.*
David Cousins: Strawbs – *Strawberry Sampler Number 1 [1969].*
> Apple launches the iPod.
> George Harrison & John Lee Hooker die.
> Gorillaz – *Gorillaz.*

2002
David Cousins & Rick Wakeman – *Hummingbird.*
Arlo Guthrie – *Banjoman: A Tribute to Derroll Adams.*
Ralph McTell – *National Treasure.*
> Lonnie Donegan & Joe Strummer die.
> Launch of BBC (Radio) 6 Music.
> Kelly Clarkson wins the first *American Idol (The Search for a Superstar).*

2003
David Cousins: Strawbs – *Blue Angel.*
Iain Matthews: Plainsong – *Pangolins.*
Richard Thompson – *1000 Years of Popular Music.*
Richard Thompson – *The Old Kit Bag.*
> Nina Simone, Celia Cruz, June Carter Cash & Johnny Cash die.
> Myspace launched.

2004

David Cousins: Strawbs – *Full Bloom.*

David Cousins: Strawbs – *Déjà Fou.*

     Green Day – *American Idiot.*

     Kanye West – *The College Dropout.*

2005

David Cousins: Strawbs – *Painted Sky.*

David Cousins & Conny Conrad – *High Seas.*

Iain Matthews – *Zumbach's Coat.*

Al Stewart – *A Beach Full of Shells.*

Richard Thompson – *Front Parlour Ballads.*

Richard Thompson – *Grizzly Man (film soundtrack).*

     Live 8.

2006

Ralph McTell – *Gates of Eden.*

     Syd Barrett dies.

     Taylor Swift – *Taylor Swift.*

2007

David Cousins & The Blue Angel Orchestra – *The Boy In The Sailor Suit.*

Arlo Guthrie – *In Times Like These (live).*

Ralph McTell – *As Far As I Can Tell (audiobook).*

Richard Thompson – *Sweet Warrior.*

     Oscar Peterson, Karlheinz Stockhausen & Don Arden die.

     Live Earth.

     Radiohead sell *In Rainbows* online.

     Amy Winehouse – *Back to Black.*

2008

David Cousins – *Secret Paths.*

David Cousins: Strawbs – *Broken Hearted Bride.*

David Cousins & Ian Cutler – *Duochrome (live).*

Arlo Guthrie – *32¢ Postage Due.*

Iain Matthews & Egbert Derix & the Searing Quartet: *Joy Mining.*

Al Stewart – *Sparks of Ancient Light.*

     Isaac Hayes, Miriam Makeba & Odetta die.

     Adele – *19.*

     Lady Gaga – *The Fame/The Fame Monster.*

2009

David Cousins: Strawbs – *Dancing To The Devil's Beat*.
Arlo Guthrie – *Tales of '69*.
      Susan Boyle – *I Dreamed a Dream*.
      Michael Bublé – *Crazy Love*.

2010

Arlo Guthrie & Wenzel – *Every 100 Years - Live auf der Wartburg (live)*.
Iain Matthews – *Matthews Southern Comfort – Kind of New*.
Iain Matthews & Ad van der Veen – *Ride the times*.
Iain Matthews & Egbert Derix – *Afterwords*.
Ralph McTell – *Somewhere Down the Road*.
Al Stewart & Dave Nachmanoff – *Uncorked (live)*.
Richard Thompson – *Dream Attic*.
      Drake – *Thank Me Later*.

2011

Ralph McTell – *Don't Think Twice It's Alright*.
      Amy Winehouse, Bert Jansch Gerry Rafferty & Gil Scott-Heron die.

2012

Iain Matthews & Egbert Derix – *In the Now*.
Ralph McTell – *Sofa Noodling (instrumental)*.
Richard Thompson – *Cabaret of Souls*.
      Whitney Houston & Etta James die.
      Psy – 'Gangnam Style'.

2013

David Cousins: Strawbs – *Of A Time*.
Iain Matthews – *The Art of Obscurity*.
Richard Thompson – *Electric*.

2014

Ralph McTell – *The Unknown Soldier (EP)*.
Richard Thompson – *Acoustic Classics*.
Richard Thompson: Thompson – *Family*.
      Phil Everly & Pete Seeger die.
      Sia – *1000 Forms of Fear*.
      Slipknot –*.5: The Gray Chapter*.

2015

David Cousins: Strawbs – *Prognostic*.
Iain Matthews: Plainsong – *Reinventing Richard – The Songs of Richard Farina*.
Richard Thompson – *Still*.

Lemmy, Rod McKuen & B.B. King die.
Twenty One Pilots – *Blurryface*.
Lin-Manuel Miranda – *Hamilton*.

2016

Ralph McTell & Wizz Jones – *About Time*.

David Bowie, George Martin, Leonard Cohen & George Michael die.
David Bowie – *Blackstar*.
Leonard Cohen – *You Want It Darker*.
Beyoncé – *Lemonade*.
Rihanna – *Anti*.
Childish Gambino – *'Awaken, My Love!'*.

2017

David Cousins: Strawbs – *The Ferryman's Curse*.
Iain Matthews – *A Baker's Dozen*.
Iain Matthews: Matthews Southern Comfort – *Like a Radio*.
Ralph McTell & Wizz Jones – *About Time Too*.
Richard Thompson – *Acoustic Classics II*.
Richard Thompson – *Acoustic Rarities*

Stormzy – *Gang Signs & Prayer*.
Ed Sheeran – ÷.
The Greatest Showman soundtrack.
Luis Fonsi feat. Daddy Yankee – 'Despacito'.

2018

Richard Thompson – *13 Rivers*.

Aretha Franklin dies.

To be continued . . .

*   *

*

Index

Printed by Printforce, United Kingdom